PENGUIN BOOKS

The Midnight Hour

By the same author

Black Rabbit Hall
The Vanishing of Audrey Wilde
The Glass House
The Birdcage

The Midnight Hour

EVE CHASE

PENGUIN BOOKS

PENGUIN BOOKS

UK | USA | Canada | Ireland | Australia
India | New Zealand | South Africa

Penguin Books, Penguin Random House UK,
One Embassy Gardens, 8 Viaduct Gardens, London SW11 7BW

penguin.co.uk
global.penguinrandomhouse.com

Penguin
Random House
UK

First published by Penguin Michael Joseph 2024
Published in Penguin Books 2024
004

Typeset by Jouve (UK), Milton Keynes
Printed and bound in Great Britain by Clays Ltd, Elcograf S.p.A.

The authorized representative in the EEA is Penguin Random House Ireland,
Morrison Chambers, 32 Nassau Street, Dublin D02 YH68

A CIP catalogue record for this book is available from the British Library

ISBN: 978-1-405-95616-1

www.greenpenguin.co.uk

For my family

'I am out with lanterns, looking for myself'

— Emily Dickinson

I

Maggie

Paris, 22 May 2019

Any danger has surely passed. Cycling into the unfolding Paris morning, Maggie can breathe easily again.
She'd been dreading yesterday's anniversary. But here
she is on the other side. Weirdly fine. Maggie knows,
as people who have survived things do, that fine is
everything. A quiet triumph. She takes nothing for
granted. Not the sun glitter on the Seine. The rhyth-
mic brush of a horse-chestnut leaf, stuck in her front
bicycle wheel. The waft of coffee. Paris. *Life*.

Rising from the saddle, Maggie stands on the pedals
and cycles faster, her blouse sleeves swelling with
air, the river's truffle tang. Her oversize sunglasses –
Le Bon Marché sale, a rare present to herself – slip
down her nose and she thumbs them up. The bicycle
wobbles.

Although capricious, with iffy brakes, Maggie's
second-hand *vélo* is the perfect red of a Parisian's lipstick so she loves it. Bouncing inside its front basket is

an unravelling straw tote, flopping open to reveal a baguette, a honking Camembert, and a stuffed bag of peaches, perilously perched and seeping in the early-summer heat. Reaching to nudge them back in, Maggie's fingertips touch their downy skin, and she starts.

Peaches. Something inside Maggie snags, like a chain unexpectedly shifting from one gear to the next. She'd buy her mother peaches at the market. Carry them home in a brown paper bag that would disintegrate in the London drizzle. For a vivid moment, she sees her mother holding a peach in her long, elegant fingers. Her small smile of anticipation.

Thrown by this – how can the past arrive in a bag of peaches? – Maggie swerves to the left, just missing an overtaking cyclist. Over his rattle of fast-fire French, her phone rings. Voicemail nips the call. A second later, it goes again. Since Maggie is incapable of leaving a phone unanswered – a neurosis baked into her two decades earlier – she brakes abruptly by the bank, where the young and beautiful smoke and loll, and fishes inside her bag. No caller ID. 'Hello?'

'It's me.'

You. That voice – husky, London – reaches deep inside, steals the air from her lungs. 'Hey,' she manages, after a beat, as if they'd last spoken a week ago, not years before.

He's changed his number since: she's tried it, more

2

than once, just to see. Maggie is glad she's never changed hers. So many questions. Is he married? Kids? Would he still fit the lumberjack shirt she keeps hidden at the back of her drawer? All she's got. No photos: they didn't back then. She wonders if he dreams like her, bucking out of sleep, that dark bloom of fear and longing.

'How's things?' he asks, guarded, soft. She can hear a city – oh, God, which city? – churning in the background, another life, impossibly running in parallel to her own.

Midway through nervously rushing an answer – a book deal, a divorce, a move to Paris! – Maggie stops, shocked by the sun-damage freckles on the thirty-eight-year-old hand clasping the bike's handlebar. How on earth did she get to this age without him?

'Some news, Maggie.' It never was going to be a social call. His voice lowers, hesitates. 'About your mother's old house in Notting Hill.'

A bolt of heat rolls over Maggie. Legs jellied, she clambers off the bike, which crashes down, much like the woman she'd been moments before. The peaches leap from the basket.

'Some new owner is renovating.'

'Right.' Maggie must fight to stay in her hard-won grown-up life. Stop it rupturing.

'In January a basement planning application went in. Maggie, I didn't contact you because I honestly didn't think they'd get permission. But . . .' he swallows hard '. . . they got it.'

She could hang up now, un-hear this. Focus on the boats frilling the silver-green water. The lovers embracing on Pont Neuf.

'There will be digging,' he adds, in case she hasn't grasped the implications.

Maggie feels light-headed. Slightly unreal, slightly sick. Despite knowing this day could come, as the years have passed, she's allowed herself to believe it wouldn't.

'Still there?'

Maggie whispers, 'Yes, yes.' But parts of her are already sheering, flying over the Seine and the kitten-grey rooftops, drawn back to London, as if trying to recover something. The group of young Parisians glance over with amused curiosity – what's with that woman, surrounded by peaches? – and, for the first time in weeks, she feels inescapably, lumpingly English.

'Soon as I find out more, I can let you know.' A moment passes. 'If you'd like me to?'

Yes, she'd like that very much. They hover on the line, connected by their silence, their quickening breath, their appalling secret, neither wanting to be the first to hang up. Then, with a click, he's gone again.

2

Maggie

Notting Hill, London
21 May 1998

That Thursday evening began like any other. The
London sky was turning a pretty polluted orange.
Still warm. The bedroom window was wide open,
and I perched on the sill, fiddling with one of Mum's
lipsticks, rolling it up and down in its shiny gold case,
as she expertly swished blush across her cheekbones,
barely needing to glance in the mirror. I knew what
came next. The crunch of an eyelash curler. Flicks of
whiskery mascara. Lip gloss, lightly pat-pat-patted
with a fingertip. After decades' modelling, my mother
applied make-up fast and efficiently, like a chef sliced
an onion. Grabbing a pashmina from the drawer, she
held it against her face. 'Yea or nay, Maggie, my
darling?'

I shook my head. My mother's smile faltered, and
she tossed the cashmere shawl onto the chair. I felt a
little bit of power, a little bit of shame. Of course the

beige pashmina (she described the colour as 'camel': in her world, everything was called something else) looked beautiful on my mother, catching the sunlit bronze of her eyes. But I didn't want her to look beautiful. Or be gawped at by strangers. I wanted her to stay in, wearing her old dressing-gown that smelt of buttered toast.

Known simply as Dee Dee – big in the eighties – Mum was forty-one, so nearly extinct modelling-wise. But she'd been forging an unlikely comeback, her approachable glamour proving a hit on daytime TV sofas, sharing confessional tips on fashion and, fist-gnawingly, motherhood. There were talks about a high-street childrenswear line and a parenting column in a newspaper magazine. A feeling she was on the edge of something exciting. Adored by the camera and the TV viewers, she was drawing back the curtain on our life. Except none of it felt true.

Her fame rekindled, she'd started to wear bigger, darker sunglasses. Even on the greyest days. Sometimes a baseball cap pulled low. A lot of black. That evening, a satiny black slip dress with spaghetti straps. Mouthing along to Fleetwood Mac's 'Gold Dust Woman' – she'd been playing that song all day, like some sort of anthem – she flashed me a loving, distracted smile, tipped her head to one side, and shook her fingers through her blonde hair, now tumbling down her back. Dad had been gone for at least six cuts.

Leaning against the flaking window frame, I tipped back slightly, so Mum would look up and say, 'Oh, be careful, Maggie.' She didn't, her mind elsewhere, turned inwards.

Smells wafted up from the street – car exhaust, cigarettes, crab-apple blossom, weed – and mixed with Mum's perfume, in a fancy glass bottle on her dressing table labelled Comme des Garçons (didn't smell like any boy I'd ever met). Spilling from the terrace of tall white stucco houses, a roar of laughter, arguing, singing, a dog barking, the fading *douff-douff* of music thumping out of an open car window. In the distance, traffic rumbling on the Westway. It was never silent. In a few hours, stalls would clank together, and the street market start to rage down nearby Portobello Road like a high fever.

Nine months after moving, London didn't sound like home. It didn't feel like home. More like I'd gone on a school trip to the capital and the coach had driven off, accidentally leaving me behind.

'Don't stay stuck in Surrey, sweetheart,' Mum would plead. But my heart was stuck. I missed the dull Home Counties, desperately, uncoolly. I missed my dad. And I didn't want to start again when, at seventeen, I'd barely begun.

As the sunset washed over the bedroom walls, Mum turned side on to the gilt-framed mirror and eyed her figure combatively, smoothing the dress over her hips.

She'd lost weight again. I tried not to mind but I was three dress sizes bigger than my mother. With a thatch of ungovernable hair and glasses, my provincial plainness made me feel both invisible and exposed in Notting Hill. 'You are gorgeous,' Mum insisted. But I'd started to wonder if she introduced me as 'Maggie, my daughter' to clear up any doubt.

'I'm all fingers and thumbs. Could you, sweetie?' Mum lowered, so her necklace clasp was accessible, her skin surprisingly hot against my fingertips, as if something was burning inside. She took one last glance in the mirror, a longer, private look, a reminder that she wasn't just my mother: she pre-existed me and flowed beyond my edges.

'*To infinity* . . .' My brother threw back the door and pinballed into the room wearing a muscle-padded Buzz Lightyear top and dragging a metal Slinky toy, chased by Nico on her stumpy French pug legs. Noisy, irrational, stop-in-the-street pretty, Kit had a sparky energy, always in motion. Blond curls coiled so tight you could stick in your fingers and wear them, like Hula Hoops. At six years old he could already read a dress like a room, so he stopped abruptly, and his eyebrows drew together. 'Why are you going out, Mummy?'

Kit's question – in hindsight, a good one – momentarily threw my mother. 'Your big sister is in charge tonight,' she answered. 'Don't look like that.' She crowned his forehead with a kiss. 'You'll have fun.'

Kit's olive-green eyes rolled up to meet mine. Neither of us was convinced by this.

Mum silenced Stevie Nicks and pulled down the window, leaving it ajar. 'Be a good boy for Maggie, Kit.'

'Yeah, don't be a moron,' I translated for my little brother, who could be what most people called 'a bit of a handful' and Mum's Notting Hill friends called 'a free spirit'.

'Maggie,' warned Mum, head on one side, fiddling with the butterfly back of her earring. 'Pop to Blockbusters and get a video? But watch it together. Don't just stick it on and vanish back into that black hole of your bedroom. Please. And make sure he does his teeth. He's got a wobbler.'

I was still bristling that she'd lined up Kit as my date for the night and presumed, correctly, that I had no social plans for the evening. Or ever. By that May, my world had shrunk to my bedroom. Folding myself up smaller and smaller, I knew every inch of it – each loose floorboard, each heating pipe, foil-wrapped, warm as baked potatoes under my bare feet – but not the streets beyond my window.

'Night night, sweetpea.' Mum tried to hug Kit, but he pulled away. Little boys are a bit like dogs. They hate it when you leave. They sense things.

Kit ran off, chased by Nico, and Mum's face fell.

Hand over her mouth, she stared at the space where he'd just been standing.

'Just go, Mum.' I stood up, untangled myself from the gauzy curtains, and tossed the lipstick onto her dressing table. 'Seriously. It'll be easier.' Words that would later haunt me.

'You're right, Maggie.' Mum grabbed a tailored jacket and a slouchy handbag then slid on her ballet pumps, quilted black with a white toe, like a half-moon, the flats she wore to walk locally, not heels, which required a taxi. She glanced at her watch. 'Argh, running late.' For what, it never occurred to me to ask. Mum was going out and she'd be back. Usually before midnight. I didn't overthink it.

'I love you, Maggie.' Mum held my face in her soft cream-scented hands. Worry passed over her features. 'You do know that, don't you?'

I nodded but started to feel a bit jangly. Like when you smell smoke but can't see a fire. But only for a second or two. Then it was gone.

After selecting a steamy bonkbuster from my bedroom – easy to read on the sofa while Kit watched a video – I drifted downstairs. To my surprise, the front door was still open, Mum stood in the porch, leaning back on one of the white columns, very still, her fingertips on her forehead, like an actor who'd forgotten her lines. My spirits lifted. Another of her headaches was coming on! She'd turn back inside, pop a painkiller, and we'd snuggle, my head on her lap, and watch a movie. *Bang.* The front door slammed shut. From the living room's tall windows, I watched as Mum walked – head back, hipbones first, that ingrained out-of-my-way model strut – in the direction of Portobello Road, the sunset ribboned in her hair. And she didn't look back. Not once.

3

Maggie

Paris, May 2019

Maggie paces the parquet, bracing for a gendarme's stubby finger to press the apartment building's intercom: 'Just a few questions, Madame . . .' Her lovely life to detonate. Obsessive fans to rewrite Dee Dee's Wikipedia page feverishly and bow-wrap it in a scandalously dark finale. It could happen next week. Next month. Never.

Craving fresh air, Maggie folds back the green shutters and steps onto the narrow, wrought-iron balcony that looks as though it might loosen from the old stonework and crash to the Saint-Germain street below. Six floors up, the noise of the city – and her anxiety – quietens, and Maggie starts to feel less like a pistol is pressed against the side of her skull. She must hold her nerve. Quit the hysteria. And finish her sodding book.

Back at her desk, Maggie takes a punishing gulp of cold black coffee – she hasn't earned a fresh one – and valiantly tries, once again, to write chapter thirty-four. To slip from the brute shock of the morning – that phone call, the terrorizing image of a digger – to her corset-laced romance, set in the gas-lit streets and grand villas of eighteenth-century Paris. But her work-in-progress has turned on her, refusing to behave. She scrubs sentences, starting again, making them worse. Her vocabulary has shrunk, words streaking past, then vanishing. She cannot concentrate, let alone plot. Every few seconds, Maggie's eyes are sucked to her mobile phone, her thoughts orbiting its last caller, a house in Notting Hill – and the one story she'll never write. Or tell.

Call back, call back.

A bad idea. Terrible! Even if he's using a burner phone, as Maggie suspects, he's always insisted any contact could be incriminating down the line. But she hungers to hear his voice again. Leaning back in her chair, she presses the heels of her hands hard into her eyes so the inside of the lids pulses purple. Overriding the smell of frying garlic from the next-door apartment, an olfactory memory twitches: WD-40, beeswax polish, the trace of boxing-glove leather. Then she hears that voice, close to her ear, 'Maggie Parker.'

With a small groan, she drops her forehead to the keyboard, and dozens of Ts fly across her manuscript. She is Margaret Foale, historical romantic novelist, not Maggie Parker any more, and she must hold on to that.

A second later, ignoring her own advice, she flips to the Eurostar website and scans the timetable, fighting the dark tidal suck back to London, the city holding all her secrets. And her brother's big soft heart. If something *is* discovered in the grounds of that Notting Hill house, Kit's world will turn upside down. How can she be here in Paris, three hundred miles away?

Caging her fingers over her mouth, her heart battering in her chest, Maggie tries to think strategically. Call Kit now? Warn him of what might happen, and admit everything? She bucks away from this, as she has always done. Jesus, how to begin? What to say? She doesn't even *know* what happened, not exactly, just a grim set of possibilities.

Maggie always vowed that one day she would find out. When she was ready. But life has come at a zillion miles an hour: the most she's been able to do is cling on. One moment she's seventeen, her bespectacled nose in a book, the next she's thirty-eight, struggling to write one. She's never felt ready. And now there's no time.

The past *is* another country, she tries to reassure herself. She's found peace in Paris. Freedom. Feeling a bit like Julie Delpy in *Before Sunset*, she's cut loose from the leaden English skies, her day job as a secondary-school

English teacher, the humiliation of a failed nine-month marriage, and the undignified tussle over the marital Tufnell Park flat. There's been liberation in admitting, finally, that *non*, that life was not meant for her and accepting that romantic endings will only ever belong in her novels. And why not? That's okay. She'll take it. Books have been her longest affair, her favourite lovers arranged alphabetically on her shelves, writing a deep solace, this little Saint-Germain apartment a revelation.

Here, Maggie answers to no one. She can hang her bras on the chunky iron radiators, leave coffee cups in the sink, write late into the night, the city a jewel box outside the window. She can wake late to the sweet chatter of the children next door, or the reassuring territorial clunk of Madame Nord's walking stick with its ivory handle, carved into a cat's head, on the communal landing. Rather than feeling lonely, Maggie's felt giddy with her aloneness, glorying in it, and a heroic amount of cheese. Far more cheese than sex, in fact. But in Paris there's always another day, another date. Possibility. Well, there was.

She snatches her mother's moth-nibbled pashmina off the back of her chair and presses it to her nose. But its musty smell brings no comfort today. Only a jolt of loss so intense it's muscular. She glances at the phone again, willing it to ring. Writing is out of the question.

If she stays still, she'll lose it. What to do? Something. Anything. A walk. *Se promener!* That'll sort out her head. Maggie can always walk in Paris, her favourite route taking in the city's grandest public clocks, the Conciergerie, the Musée d'Orsay. She'll think about the long-dead writers who once walked the same streets, wrestling with language and love and the tricky nature of existence, and, far more importantly, what to eat for supper and with whom. Perhaps she'll arrange to meet Halima, or Manon, her Parisian friends who know little of her life before. Wash down oysters with a spicy Margarita. Relish every hard-won joy. The relief of making this small decision releases a knot in her neck with an audible click. She downs a glass of water. Searches for her keys. Pulls on her trainers.

As Maggie steps into the metal birdcage lift, her mobile rings. Her stomach swoops, already free-falling. She knows it's him.

4

Maggie

Notting Hill, May 1998

It always took a second or two to hit. Then, no longer protected by sleep, I'd remember: Dad was dead, fifteen months dead. And my heart was crushed anew. I'd lie in bed seething that Mum had moved us away from the Surrey house he'd loved: growing up poor in an edgy bit of urban north London, he'd worked hard to bring up his family somewhere 'safe and green'. And I worried that if Dad, in whatever form, came back to find us, he'd not know where we'd gone.

'Oh, it got me at the pink door, Maggie!' Mum declared last August, barely six months after he'd died: the bad stuff moved at a whip in our family. I'd stared in bewilderment at the photo: a scruffy end-of-terrace townhouse – white stucco, three-storeys tall, six steps to a flaking columned porch – that a friend of Mum's friend Clemence wanted to hastily rent, cheap, with a possible view to selling later. Had my mother lost her mind? 'No, no,' she said. 'It's the solution, sweetheart.'

To a problem I hadn't known existed. 'We can't stay here. Not with this monster mortgage.' I hadn't known that either. 'I can't afford it, Maggie. Not on my own. I'm so sorry. We'll sell up, rent for a bit. Until we're back on our feet. You'll love London. You *will*, Maggie! And it'll be so much easier for me to get work.' I'd later realize it was far more than that. Some places get under your skin, leave identifying isotopes in your bones. Since Mum had lived in Notting Hill as a young model starting out, it was already in hers. I refused to let it into mine.

So, little point in getting out of bed. Only I was hungry. I was always hungry. I could eat and still be hungry: a gap I couldn't fill. Grabbing the closest knickers off the floor and a washed-out Nirvana T-shirt, stained from a hair-dyeing misadventure, I ventured forth in search of carbs.

Across the scratchy seagrass landing, Kit's bedroom door was open, a crash site of Lego. Mum's was shut. The house was promisingly quiet, raising hopes Mum had taken out Kit for breakfast, and I might have the place to myself, free to graze and roam without being watched, or judged, Mum's anxiety about my social isolation humming in every well-meaning word. 'Tiff on Ladbroke Grove has a daughter about your age, Maggie. Shall I get you guys together?' Words to strike horror into a teenage heart. She couldn't understand that I didn't want an 'in' to the fashionable neighbourhood. I wanted a way out, which I found in books, the places I could truly live, and the local library, hoovering my way through its shelves.

As I walked downstairs, yawning, the rag-rolled cobalt walls shook me fully awake. Unlike our Surrey house, which was all country creams, Dad not a fan of colour, the Notting Hill place was a party in a paint factory you couldn't leave.

The kitchen on the lower ground floor was the colour of dry earwax – 'Ochre, Maggie!' Mum would squeal – and ran the depth of the house, filled with our landlord's furniture: unravelling rattan seventies chairs and a leather sofa, cracked like a saddle, a set of dusty bongos and DJ decks. (Although the sale of our old house wasn't yet complete, and had been rumbling on for months, it included the furniture: 'I need to start afresh, Maggie.') Under a framed poster for the movie *Blow Up* – some photographer guy squatting over a prostrate model, I wanted to tell him to back right off – there was a big table, where Mum's London friends would congregate, hooting with laughter, gossiping, and picking at a bowl of salad leaves with their fingers, smoking and drinking bottles of white wine late into the night.

That morning it was just Kit, thankfully. Kit wearing Superman Y-fronts and eating cereal direct from the packet. He'd been busy: a neat line of cornflakes circled the stack of coffee-ringed fashion magazines and trooped to the fruit bowl, reigned over by a withered giant Bramley apple we'd nicknamed Ma'am because it resembled the face of the Queen. 'Is Mum up?'

'I'm playing cornflakes, Maggie,' Kit said, which I took as a no. He stuck another cornflake to the line.

Drinking water straight from the tap, I noticed Mum's coffee pot lying in two unscrewed bits on the draining board. After a lemon slice in hot water, she'd always drink black coffee, taking it back to bed. I wiped my mouth, glanced up at the big station clock on the wall, which had a minute arm that trembled whenever it moved, as if it found punctuality stressful, as my mother had in recent weeks. Almost ten. A lie-in, then.

Unlocking the patio doors, I stepped outside and lifted my face to the sharp May sunshine. Our little stamp of terrace – 'garden' was pushing it – ran adjacent to the street, enclosed by tall brick walls, catwalked by foxes at night. Over the neighbour's boundary, honeysuckle tumbled in a tangled thicket, colliding with a rose, its budding flowers still tight as fists. Closer to the house, a mildewed white parasol, always open due to a jammed mechanism. Yellow metal chairs and a mosaic tile table with a citronella candle and a ceramic Moroccan ashtray, filled with soggy cigarette stubs.

And then there was what Mum called, That God-awful Hole. Three-foot wide, almost Kit's height deep, the crater in the patio was the unfinished work of a local builder known as Bucket – obviously Kit and I thought this hilarious – who'd dug down to fix a pipe problem and, rather than filling it in afterwards, had left for another job down the road. (Less funny. But normal for London, apparently.) Three weeks old, the rubbly pile of soil was already sprouting weeds. A builder's spade dozed against the wall.

Since our landlord was travelling abroad, any house issues fell to Clemence's friend Pippa, a warm, scatty local woman who seemed more preoccupied by finding homes for her cat's freakishly large litter of kittens. She hadn't yet pinned down Bucket, but she could offer us a free ginger kitten instead. A fair exchange, I thought. Mum disagreed. 'It's because I'm a woman on my own,' she said crossly. 'If your father was still around, it'd all be different.' Like I didn't know this. We were always moving around Dad's absence, a dense airless thing too big to be seen.

I turned back to Kit. 'You want some milk with that cereal?'

Kit shook his head solemnly. 'It smells like football socks.'

I bit into a bagel unearthed from the depths of the breadbin. Stale. I'd eat it anyway.

'Can I have sugar?'

'Ha. You'll be lucky.' Earlier in the week Mum had flushed the last packet of Tate & Lyle down the loo, like a baggie of drugs, saying it was making Kit hyper, but Kit was just Kit. He wasn't the one who'd changed. 'Let me have a look. Okay, what have we got?' The cupboard frowned back. 'Lentils, vitamins, SlimFast powder, tinned tuna, and dried figs. Mum is spoiling us.'

The house we'd left – home, as I still thought of it – had had a walk-in larder, everything organized in heavy glass jars with cork tops. Spices and chutneys and flour and sugar. Fairy-cake decorations for school bake sales. Mum, despite her preference for leafy salads, often roasted rosemary-speared hunks of glistening lamb because Dad was a meat man, who liked beef stew and shepherd's pie, homely dishes that reminded him of his late Irish nana. The story of our life was the story of our kitchen cupboards.

With no warning, Kit swept the line of cornflakes to the floor, watching in delight as Nico scoffed frenziedly. 'You've missed one!' Kit shouted. 'Over there, Nico, left, left! Maggie, she's so happy she just farted!'

Nico had a wind problem, and I had a brother problem. Kit was a baffling little human, who'd appeared six years before, already a few weeks old, with a full head of white-blond hair and a huge pair of lungs, less new kitten than asteroid.

Mum had miscarried many times – once leaving a drop of red jelly gunk on the bathroom floor that I could never unsee – before making peace with having only one child. But Dad hit forty and became fixated on adopting a son. I'd overhear my parents talking, Mum saying no way, the age gap, it was her time now, Dad pleading, buying her jewellery, promising to do all the night feeds himself, which, of course, he didn't. Other fathers had mid-life crises and bought sports cars or, in my school friend Amy's dad's case, climbed Everest and lost a big toe to frostbite. A little boy was a bigger mountain. And there was more to lose. I'm not sure my parents' marriage was ever quite the same.

'Whoa. Oh no you don't.' Before Kit could shake out the rest of the cereal packet, I carried him, upside down, giggling, to the 'play area' under the stairs. Baskets of crayons. Educational toys he ignored. Mum's childhood doll's house, with rubber dinosaurs peering out of its windows. Also living inside it, the story of how my aunt Cora, as a girl, had hurled the resident doll's-house family, my mother's pride and joy, into the river. Possibly still the doll-hurling type, my aunt lived in Paris. Mum didn't like to discuss her.

'Don't move, Kit. I'm getting Mum. No, don't even . . . No more mess.' I quickly made a mug of hot water with a shrivelled lemon slice, and sloshed it up the stairs, hoping it'd grease my case for cash to buy pastries at the market. Peaches too. Mum loved those. Said they tasted of childhood holidays in Antibes. They made her smile.

'Mum?' No answer. I knocked again. Nothing. A breeze ruffled under the gap in the door and over my bare feet. Cautiously, I stepped in, ready to bolt out again if she was wandering around naked; no inhibitions after years of stripping in studios full of strangers and, ironically, given how much Mum loved clothes, she loved being naked best.

The window was still ajar. The chandelier on, head-butted by a mustard-brown moth. It was like a set on a show, the show being Mum, after she'd walked off it. An electric bolt of fear passed through me, then quickly dissipated.

'Tune in for Dee Dee's stylish motherhood tips after the break,' I muttered darkly, sitting down on Mum's bed, waiting for her whereabouts to present themselves. I couldn't call. The Nokia her agent had finally persuaded her to carry lay lifeless on her bedside table, having slipped into one of her oceanic bubble baths. Mum wasn't bothered. It took up too much room in her handbag and was a fad – 'I've been around the block enough times to know.' Anyway, who wanted to be contactable all the time?

I scanned the room for clues. A pair of black heels with scarlet soles, one on its side, as if it'd been shot. A lanyard – 'Dee Dee Parker, Guest' – looped on the back of a chair. A vase stuffed with pink peonies, an end-of-day freebie from the flat-capped bloke at a florist market stall – 'Dee Dee, your favourites! On the house.' That sort of thing happened to her all the time. Painkillers. Sunglasses. Water glass with a lip-gloss smudge on its rim. A silent conspiracy of things.

On the walls, mostly framed photographs. A terrible picture of me – even my mother agreed I was 'tricky' to photograph – and an arty, beautiful one of Kit, who'd sometimes gamely model children's clothes on breakfast TV, appearing alongside Mum.

Above the fireplace, a hazy 1970s photo of the Old Rectory in the countryside, where Mum and Aunt Cora had grown up and a stroke had felled Granny in April. Above it, a wedding portrait: Mum in filmy Chanel with a garland of flowers in her hair, like a fairy queen, Dad alive. Leaning on the mantelpiece, Mum and Dad, photographed ten years later, an unframed print that had been badly ripped. Mum blamed Nico. But there were no bite marks, and Nico was quite fussy about what she chewed. I'd carefully Sellotaped it back together.

On the far wall, favourite fashion photos. Wearing a flesh-pink ballgown, Mum riding an elephant. Windswept in tartan and pirate boots in the Highlands. Very young and very nude, sun-crusted and tanned, draped over a boulder. That one hadn't been up in our last house. Dad had been funny and old-fashioned about the nudes: Mum would tell him it was daft to be jealous of a camera lens. Those images weren't really her, though. As a little girl, I'd gone on shoots, plonked on some assistant's knee, and seen how in the shutter-snap of a lens, Mum became someone else.

Where *was* she? I checked every room. When I got back downstairs, Kit was curled up on the sofa with Nico. 'Where's Mummy?'

'At work,' I replied, after a pause, not wanting him to worry, reasoning that Mum was unlikely to have gone far. Her car sulked, flat-battery-dead, further down the street. 'Looks like you're stuck with me this morning.'

He warily assessed my pants and T-shirt ensemble. 'Are you taking me to school?'

'What? Oh, no! It's Friday not Saturday?' I winced. My days mashed into each other. 'Sorry.'

Kit brightened. 'I can stay at home.'

'Er, no.'

'But you don't go to school.'

'That's different.' Moving in a rush last September, Mum couldn't get us into the good local state schools so enrolled Kit in an arty prep and me into a sixth-form college, where everyone had made-up problems and I felt like the loneliest teenager in the world. Having been a grade-A student at my old grammar, in London I'd fallen behind so far, so fast – reaching a semi-glorious terminal velocity in my plummet to the-bottom – that six weeks ago it'd been politely agreed I'd do the year again starting afresh in September. At a different college.

'Mason can look after me?' Kit suggested hopefully.

'Mason doesn't work for us any more.' A twenty-something, six-foot, long-haired Kiwi who could walk on his hands, Mum had hired him to help with childcare last autumn. But things had become odd between them and there'd been some sort of argument. I didn't like to think of it.

'I'll be so, so good, Maggie,' he pleaded.

I hesitated. Kit was seriously late. One day off school wouldn't affect his life chances, would it? And if it did it was Mum's fault. 'Fine.'

I was about to suggest a trip to the library when Kit sprang off the sofa. 'Skatepark!'

'No way.' The skatepark under the Westway flyover involved people in chunky trainers moving very fast, very noisily. But Kit looked so crushed, I heard myself say, 'Skateboarding on the street instead?'

Sunshine sprayed over the pavement. No sign of the movie crew, with the big boom mics and cameras on wheels, that had been filming on the street earlier that week, watched by bemused neighbours concerned about the residents' parking. Just a steady crowd of people filtering down our terrace towards Friday's Portobello Market. I saw Mum everywhere – tall, blonde-ish women with leggy strides – and I'd stop and stare, forgetting not to step on the pavement cracks. But it was never her.

On the emptier backstreets, Kit skated faster, curls flattened, shimmering, made of light. I struggled to keep up, running, panting, the fastest I'd moved for months. Past the dolly-mixture-coloured houses and, finally, turning into Powis Square where Nico's lead got looped on her leg. I bent down to free her: only one distracted second, but Fate wriggled inside it. When I looked up, Kit was airborne, the skateboard flying off the kerb. A parked white van starting to reverse. 'Kit!' I screamed. 'No!' A flash of red, a body roughly shouldering past, an arm reaching for Kit, and everything hurtling forward, already unstoppable, with its own ball-bearing spin.

5

Maggie

The Old Rectory, The Chilterns, May 2019

Oh, God, Cora's been rescuing again. Five dogs – no, six – rush out of the Old Rectory's porch, yapping, springing up in a frenzy of tails, paws and gravel dust as Maggie drags her wonky wheelie suitcase up the drive, a geriatric milk-eyed collie nudging the back of her knees. The canine excitement is at stark odds with the Old Rectory itself, a biscuit tin of a house, symmetrical, crumbly red-brick, with a sweep of uneven roof – home to protected bats, the occasional barn owl – meeting a sky the colour of cornflowers. Swept clean of clouds, the rural air is gauzy. A bee clumsily whirls past. It's been a while. Last time Maggie visited in February, her aunt had been shovelling a path through a bank of snow.

'*Inside!*' Cora bursts out of the porch, holding a fat brown chicken with one hand, and in the other, a gnarled wooden spoon that she points at the marauding dogs, which turn sheepishly and trot back into the house. '*Salut!* Apologies for the ambush. Two new dogs . . . I know, I know. I can't help myself. This is an unexpected pleasure, Maggie.'

Pulled into a tight, hard hug, Maggie gets a mouthful of Cora's hair, rock-grey and bristly, as if cut with a pair of rusty secateurs. 'You smell of Paris. Delicious. I must honk of *eau de chien.*'

'Undernote of horse,' Maggie says, and Cora grins, taking this as a compliment.

After the last few days' reeling dread, Maggie feels a relieving inner clunk, a landing sensation. Easy to forget how much she misses Cora until she's in her company again. There's a capability about her aunt, a refusal to conform, that she finds reassuring.

Today Cora's wearing her uniform of vest top and torn dungarees – her wardrobe restricted to what she doesn't mind being 'shat on or eaten' – that exposes the faded green-black mass of tattoos on her upper arms. Slightly incongruous now, they're a reminder of Cora's wilder, heavy-drinking years. Her complexion is tanned, wind-scrubbed, with broken spider veins mapping high cheekbones, as if she's been foraging berries for her supper. Entirely possible. In her early sixties, every hard life lesson etched on her skin, Cora looks years older, and couldn't give a damn.

'You all right?' Cora narrows her pale grey eyes. Even the chicken stares intently. 'You look shattered, Maggie. Pale. Are you ill?'

'I'm fine.' Maggie tries to brazen out the appearance of fine-ness. Alone in Paris these last few days, she's come scarily close to unspooling. Since the second phone call confirmed the basement dig was well under way, she's been unable to work or sleep or eat, her plan to wait it out proving hopeless. Her concentration shot, all she could think about was how quickly anything discovered in that Notting Hill house might be connected to their tenancy in the late nineties. The accuracy of radiocarbon dating and other forensics she daren't google for fear of the damning digital footprint. And, worst of all, the fallout for Kit.

Maggie realized she needed to do something, anything, to stay sane. To feel some control over the situation, however illusory. The goalkeeper's urge to leap in one direction or the other, when they'd be better off standing still. The British police could easily find her in Paris anyway, she rationalized. In England at least she's on the ground.

'You've been working too hard, then.' Cora taps Maggie's arm with the spoon.

'Not exactly. I've hit a wall with my writing.' Not a lie at least. 'The dreaded writer's block.'

'Really? That isn't like you,' says Cora, unsatisfied by this explanation, knowing Maggie's always been sceptical about such a thing.

'But I have my laptop. I thought I'd write here

for a bit? Might dislodge something.' Maggie tries to force a smile. 'And I can spend some time with Kit.'

'Well, selfishly, I'd love that. Stay as long as you like.' Cora frowns, suspecting something else is amiss. 'Hang on. Is anything up with Kit? That's not why you're back?'

'Oh, no. Kit's good.'

'You would tell me?'

'Of course.'

Cora's face softens again. 'Now, it is rather handy you're here because . . .'

Maggie can guess what's coming. Her aunt is always looking for a spare pair of hands.

'Monday morning I've got an absurdly early breakfast meeting in London about a bit of translation work, much needed to pay for the roof repairs. If you could dog-sit?'

Maggie nods, although she can barely see that far ahead.

'Well, that solves that problem!' Cora puts down the chicken, which flutters off to the safety of the hen-house, then turns her attention to Maggie's suitcase. 'No point even trying to wheel that thing on gravel. Give it to me.' Grabbing the overpacked suitcase, she swings it easily in one hand. Maggie has seen her carry armchairs, large dogs and, once, a butler's sink across a field.

They edge between the pair of old planters frothing with cow parsley at either side of the porch, and in the hall, muddy wellies, trowels, dog-chewed balls, an acoustic guitar in a battered case, and a saggy floral cushion, where an aged bold chicken likes to sit. When Maggie's late grandparents lived in the house, she wouldn't dare rest a glass of squash on a table without a coaster. Her meticulous military-moustached grandfather – much older than his wife, he'd looked like a Victorian – would use a ruler to gauge the height of the lawn.

'Right, you must be gasping for a cup of tea. Don't know about you, but I rarely drink a drop after the Gare du Nord. I've never been able to pee, wobbling about in a train.' Cora shoves the suitcase against the wall with her booted foot. 'Also, you're in luck. Yesterday I made a cheesecake to end all cheesecakes.'

Cora is A Feeder. Few visitors emerge from the Old Rectory without a couple of extra pounds. Whoever said that nothing tastes as good as skinny feels had not tried her aunt's wild bramble Pavlova. But it'll all be wasted on Maggie, who has lost her appetite, her stomach a knot.

'A coronary on a plate. I'm thinking of throwing a murderous garden party and hand-feeding some to my new neighbour. A monster. Moved into the Montgomerys' old place.'

Maggie's shaky hand ruffles the ear of Harold, the

golden retriever, who has lumbered over for love, shedding bales of hair.

'*Five* cars. I hold him personally responsible for climate change.' Her eyes flash with that slightly feral, mischievous Cora quality. '*Red* trousers.'

'Ah.' Maggie tries to smile. She'd normally laugh at this. Instead, unexpectedly, her eyes moisten with tears and she blinks very fast, trying to hide them from Cora.

'Now tell me why you're really back,' Cora says waspishly, filling a kettle entombed in limescale. Sunlight stipples through the ivy brushing the kitchen windows. 'Are you homesick?'

'No, no. Paris feels like home.' She stares at the age-pocked farmhouse table, feeling the searching heat of Cora's gaze. Her aunt misses nothing. 'But I've been thinking a lot about . . .' Maggie steels, anticipating resistance '. . . Mum.'

'O-*kay*,' says Cora, after a beat. The atmosphere in the beamed, low-ceilinged kitchen starts to spark slightly, like the crackle around a pylon.

'Actually, I thought I might visit Notting Hill,' Maggie says weakly, unable to explain the powerful draw back, the enormous pressure rising inside her, or the compulsion to see the house, the basement works, with her own eyes.

'*Notting Hill?*'

'I've not suggested a trip to Mars, Cora.'

'Might be preferable! I hear it's all bankers, Tory politicians and dressage-pony wives who treat the place like a theme park now.' Cora dunks teabags into the boiling mugs of water with her earth-tipped fingers, not shrinking from the heat.

A blueberry rolls off the cheesecake to the floor and is pounced upon by Vera, an ancient Jack Russell, Cora's – 'I don't have favourites' – favourite.

'Oh, God.' Cora whizzes around, her face flushed. 'Not you too?'

'I'm sorry?'

'The twenty-year anniversary of *Notting Hill*, the movie! All over my Sunday newspaper. Hugh Grant inescapable again. You've been reminded of it all.'

'Yes, yes, that's jogged things a bit.' Maggie seizes this excuse, even though she's never been able to watch the film. Her chair creaks as she shifts.

'Bloody movie,' mutters Cora, under her breath, splashing milk into the mugs. 'Here, tea.'

'Thanks.' Maggie strokes the collie, now lying on her feet. 'You don't happen to have contact details for Mum's old friends? The Notting Hill lot.'

'God, no.' Her aunt's shoulders stiffen. No doubt it stings that Dee Dee's close circle hasn't been in touch over the years. 'I imagine everyone has moved on by now anyway. Here, try this.' She swipes away a pile of seed packets and puts down a daunting slab of cheesecake. 'But why go back?'

'Well, I never have.'

'Perfectly sensible.' Cora's always discouraged it. She pulls out a shabby kitchen chair, its legs squeaking over the uneven flagstone floor, and sits down. 'I know you don't want to hear the Serenity Prayer. Accept the things you cannot change . . . I saw it! I saw that grimace, Maggie.' Cora smiles, impossible to offend. 'But it saves time. It really does. You can't return to the past.' She snaps her fingers. 'See? Already it's further away! Nor can you change it.' Her face darkens. 'Believe me, I know that better than anyone.'

Cora's words hover over the table, like the tiny black fruit flies.

'Isn't understanding a sort of change?' Maggie balances the tarnished dessert fork on her finger and watches it tip one way then the other. 'A change in me?'

'Oh, Maggie. I'd like to alter most human beings on this planet. A tweak here or there. A full personality transplant in others. But you? No. We need more Maggie Foales in the world.' She leans forward intently, her chin in her hands. 'Sounds like you might be better off working things through properly. Should I ask around my old Paris network? Shake the shrink tree and see what drops?'

'No, no, not that.' Maggie sips her tea. 'I don't want someone asking questions. I want . . .'

A muscle flickers under Cora's eye. 'What, Maggie?' she says, less patiently.

Maggie inhales to speak. It's always easier to accept the family line, the one that causes the minimum amount of hurt to those left behind, the illusion of 'closure'. But as a writer, she knows you can alter a story entirely by cutting out one strand – and that there *was* an undercurrent, something unspoken, bubbling through her mother's life, their family, always felt, never explained, and it had played a part in her mother's walking out that May evening. Therefore this, all that came after. 'You have to admit, some things still niggle, Cora.'

'No, not really,' Cora says, more briskly, pulling Vera onto her lap. 'Your mother is not a fictional character to be researched. You can't approach everything like a writer, Maggie.'

'Can't help it.' Maggie dutifully tastes the cheese-cake, which is perfectly sweet and tart, but tainted by the metallic flavour of her own anxiety. 'Delicious.'

Cora lifts Vera into the air, her paws paddling. 'My advice?'

It's coming whether Maggie wants it or not.

'Enjoy Paris, the life *you* have created for yourself,' Cora says, underplaying her own role in it, not least by offering Maggie the apartment at a peppercorn rent. 'Count your many blessings. Imagine. You could still be married alive in that dreary flat in north London!'

Maggie wishes Cora were a little kinder about

Tom. But that's the thing with Cora: you're either in or out. She'd fight to the death for the people she loves and not think twice about feeding an enemy to a hungry rescue dog.

'There's absolutely no need to return to Notting Hill now and upset yourself. And everyone else.'

Maggie blanches. 'What do you mean?'

Cora rests Vera over her shoulder and lightly pats her back as if burping a baby. 'I'm not sure it's helpful for you to stir up all this now, that's all. I mean, think of your brother.' Her voice pitches, as it always does around the charged subject of Kit, the only person on the planet able to affect Maggie's feisty aunt in this way. 'Can we not forget him in all this?'

'I've not forgotten Kit,' says Maggie, quietly, fighting a wave of tears again, and desperately wishing she was free to explain that Kit lies, unknowingly, at the dark heart of the story, that she's returned to it – and England – for him.

6

Kit

London, May 2019

Stepping into Highgate Cemetery in his treasured Tricker loafers, Kit flicks his phone to silent. Mark of respect and all that. The sky, pale grey, delicately veined, like the best Carrara marble, is soon hidden by a rustling roof of leaves. Moving through north London's gentle forest of the dead, carrying his bunch of peonies, Kit feels satyr-like and, compared to the surrounding company, exceptionally alive. At twenty-seven, the finality of deadness still blows his mind. Visiting once a year in May, ideally alone, he comes to rub against the past, like a tomcat against a dirty brick wall.

Shamefully, Kit almost forgot this year, swiping away yesterday's calendar reminder as a customer's Instagram message pinged in: *Thanks for table measurements. Sorry if this sounds like a strange question, but did you live in Notting Hill, late 90s? As a kid.* ☺ @treazurehunter.

Kit hasn't yet answered that message. But he's

reread it an unhealthy number of times, unable to stop his imagination taking flight, playing with the possibility that a person he has wondered about on and off for twenty-odd years – and has been unable to track down – might have found his way back to him. Kit knows it's silly. What are the chances? And yet.

15 January: @treazurehunter made his first contact with Kit's Instagram antiques store. He checked the dates last night. Since then, whenever he posts an item, or a chatty reel, @treazurehunter is the first person to like it, or comment. There have been a few direct messages too, leading to small purchases – a 1930s circus sign, a set of Edwardian crystal figurines, all sent out without issue, or complaints about an old thing looking old – as well as interest in more big-ticket items, and a bit of banter that has notably intensified in the last week. Nothing that seemed out of the ordinary. Not until last night's message. Who is this guy? Presuming it is a guy.

Last night, Kit scrolled far too late, lit by the underwater glow of his laptop, Red Bull and dodgy duty-free vodka, trying to discover @treazurehunter's real identity. He never posts and has no followers. Apart from Kit, he follows a handful of vintage and antiques accounts, and the Royal Borough of Kensington and Chelsea. But beyond that Kit has drawn a blank. It turns out not everyone is traceable. But, of course, Kit knew that already.

No profile photo either. Kit is always staggered that whole decades of the lives of pre-camera-phone natives, like Maggie, are undocumented. Little evidence they happened at all! In later years, they tend to photo-dump enthusiastically or, like his sister, rarely post anything. @treazurehunter is in the latter camp.

Kit's magpie mind darts to his phone again, warm, alive in his pocket. His fingers twitch. No, he won't check if another @treazurehunter message has dropped. Not until he's paid his respects.

Walking further into the cemetery, the air grows vaporous, mushroomy. Something about the way the tree roots writhe out of the earth and hug the gravestones of long-forgotten Londoners finger-taps at Kit's heart. At the path's edge, the ground is spongy under his shoes, suggesting what lies underneath: cavities, voids, and the terrifying, thrilling possibility that one could sink through the turf into a long-forgotten catacomb, a mattress of Victorian bones. Resisting a detour to the mawkish splendour of the Egyptian-style vaults, he crosses the narrow road into the East Cemetery, the more recent dead. His dead.

The faux-rural hush unnerves as it enthrals him. A reminder of why he moved back to London at the earliest opportunity, craving the city he'd doggedly refused to forget, and kept close, like a map hidden in a pocket. Unless he was riding a horse, he'd been a hopeless country boy, a dandyish misfit, who'd disliked the gluey mud and Gore-Tex. The double-takes in the village store. The way conversations stopped when he and Maggie walked past, the adults all smiling too hard. He's sure that's one of the reasons Maggie eventually reached for anonymity, taking Dee Dee's maiden name, Foale, delighting Cora. But Kit didn't want more change. Or the name Foale, frankly. He wanted to stay himself, Kit Parker, even if he isn't entirely sure who that is.

Thinking of Cora, Kit's conscience tweaks. He owes her a phone call or a visit. It's much harder for Cora to pop to London: she can't leave the animals unattended. But things always seem to come up: auctions, estate sales, parties, opening nights, or the sudden urge to buy a new pair of socks. And he cannot help but baulk like a teenager at that loaded question, 'What are you doing on Sunday, Kit?' knowing she'll snare him for a three-course lunch if he dares admit to being free. Even now, Cora will instantly respond to a text with a phone call, so he keeps texting to a minimum too, just in case it sets off a chain of live communicative events. Then he feels guilty, which makes him resent Cora, which adds more guilt, and so the wheel turns. It's complicated. Weeks can pass. But with a polite distance comes peace.

Over the years, there have been many eruptive arguments about his lifestyle, his scrapes, Cora, somewhat hypocritically, warning him not to end up like she did, this her nightmare scenario. Other things too. Kit has no desire to hurt Cora, but she's intense, always trying to make up for the years she wasn't in their lives, which pushes him away. You can't retouch the past. Or make memories years after the event.

Bumping Cora to the back of his mind – difficult, she's one of those people who keep elbowing to the front – Kit walks faster, all long limbs and bouncing curls, listening to the brushing sound of his skinny Dior trousers, a joyous King's Road charity-shop find, and skim-reading the gravestones, relishing the names such as Cornelia, Herbert and Elsie, the history flat-packed inside them.

Too bad that humans don't last as long as their things, Kit thinks, although he'd be out of work if they did. The flotsam of life, its curiosities, heirlooms, dusty personal treasures, buried in attics, sold by mercurial relatives, often ends up on a market stall or at an antiques fair, where someone like him – passionate, curious, hopelessly unsuited to any sort of desk job – will buy it cheap, restore it, if necessary, and sell it for a profit.

A few steps further on, Kit sucks in his breath. Still gets him every time. That lozenge of pale stone.

Kit squats beside the gravestone that refuses to age. He'd coat it with live yoghurt, a trick to give a bit of patina, but Maggie would do her nut. Holding back one peony, he arranges the others in an old French confit pot that somehow hasn't yet been nicked. There. Perfect. So retro! So nineties! 'You know the colour of cream left in a bowl after strawberries have been eaten?' he'd asked the bemused florist. He wanted them to be perfect for Dee Dee. That was all.

According to an old interview in *Good Housekeeping*, Dee Dee had adored pale pink peonies. Having trawled eBay for vintage magazines featuring her, he now has a collection that spans eighties pin-up – a sort of British Christie Brinkley, big hair, big smile, legs that go on for days – to sultry *Vogue*, to cheesy tabloid Sunday-newspaper-magazine features, to the obituary in *The Times*. '*She is survived by . . .*' Was there ever a crueller line?

After a solemn nod, Kit steps one plot along, kneels and lays the remaining peony on the gravestone of his adoptive father, Damian Parker – '*The very best of men*' – whom Kit recalls, very hazily, as a deep voice that vibrated against a bearlike ribcage. A bench of shoulders to ride upon. A scent like the inside of a new leather belt. Kit's glad that Damian, born a north Londoner, was laid to rest here. It feels right.

During the havoc of Kit's early twenties, he'd often emerge from a club at dawn, still wired, skin steaming in the cold air, eardrums pulsing, and wander through Soho to a once-glamorous office with tall glass doors, Damian's advertising-company workplace. He'd imagine Damian Parker, the accounts director *Wunderkind*, his success forged during the bullish Thatcher years, swaggering in and out of the atrium turnstiles in his baggy beige Armani suit. Wonder how his own life – and Maggie's – would have turned out if Damian had not gone for a drink after work that night but straight home to his wife and kids and his warm Surrey house, the domestic idyll displayed in that *Hello!* spread: 'Dee Dee shows us around her for-ever home.' A dream life. But short and breakable.

Standing by the Parker graves, Kit bows his head self-consciously, and waits for The Feelings. A rush of grief. The sting of tears. But he cannot summon them, or step inside that luminous candlelit house of sadness and nostalgia other people claim, rightfully, enviably, as their own. Instead, he has to arrange his fragmented memories like relics on a shelf, their edges smoothed, their surfaces tarnished by his endless handling. He does his best to piece together Dee Dee and Damian posthumously, slotting himself into their story, fighting the nagging feeling that he doesn't belong there. Anywhere, really. Sometimes he feels as if a structural part of him is missing, like a strut on an old chair; a weakness that only reveals itself under pressure.

When it comes to family, Kit thinks, you can only really claim what you remember. Mostly, that's his sister. Always Maggie. Which is probably why it's her voice he hears in his head when second-guessing himself. Not his mother's.

There's another voice too. The older Kit gets, the more he hears it, like a favourite song played over and over, its lyrics somehow relevant to every era of a life. His thoughts turn to @treazurehunter again and, as if Bluetoothed to his brain, his mobile vibrates with a notification. Kit grabs it, inevitably losing his resolve, and hungrily flicks to his inbox: *Just checking u got my last message?* Persistent, then. The hairs on Kit's arms needle under his poplin shirt, and he's struck by the novel sensation of no longer being the seeker, but the one sought.

He should probably be cautious. Dee Dee fans still lurk in corners of the internet. His family's dark glamour has long attracted a certain type of person who, drunk on the fumes of tragedy and notoriety, do not see *him*, twenty-seven-year-old Kit Parker, but a ringlet-haired boy in a car, caught in a bank of flashbulbs, a satellite of his famous mother. To his closest friends, though, the ones who rib him, love him, he's just Kit, curious, silly, spends more than he earns, worships his big sister, seventies funk, Spurs, sweatbox clubs in east London, flea markets, *Strictly*, a dirty martini, Heinz spaghetti hoops eaten cold from a tin, Sally Rooney and Oscar Wilde. His drunken late-night party trick? An ability to quote *Notting Hill* the movie, line-by-line.

Still. Maybe Maggie's got it right. Avoiding the loons by hiding behind an author pseudonym. She's always refused to do any social media, despite pressure from her publishers. 'Margaret Foale has wanted to be a writer since she was a little girl. She loves macaroons and cluttered bookshops and lives in Paris,' reads the author biography inside her book jackets. And that's it.

Kit is tempted to call her right now. But she's left a rambling, slightly nuts message and, since she's at the Old Rectory, is likely to relay any conversation to Cora. Also, given @treazurehunter has mentioned Notting Hill – an unexploded bomb of a subject – Maggie will be on her guard, and try to take control of the situation. Ever the protective Wendy to his Lost Boy. Ridiculous, really.

Anyway, he doesn't need to tell her everything. Maggie has her own secrets. He's pretty sure she's never told him the full story of what happened all those years ago. He's always felt things humming in the gaps. Hovering just out of shot. No, he won't call her right now, he decides. Why can't he have a tiny secret of his own for once?

So, Kit turns from the graves, the mulchy shadows, the Parkers, everything dead and finished, and strides towards life, the leonine roar of his beloved raucous city. The thrill of the chase. And he starts thumbing out a message, the burning question that's been bugging him: @treazurehunter *Are you Wolf?*

7

Maggie

Notting Hill, May 1998

'Wolf?' I repeated, dazed, thinking I'd misheard. Where the van had been a moment ago, a shimmering puddle of petrol. The air was close, electric sticky. It felt like a scene change in the theatre when the lights come on again after a brief blackout, and everything is rearranged.

'Yeah.' His smile was slow, hesitant, making up its mind about me.

What sort of name was that? I hadn't been prepared for his eyes either. Neon blue, overhung by unusually thick eyebrows, much darker than the chaotic wavy hair on his head and slightly alarming.

'Thank you for saving my idiot brother.' It'd happened so quickly, Wolf lunging forward, grabbing Kit off the road, swinging him to safety. Now the skateboard lay in the gutter, upended, a back wheel bent inwards. Sacrificed in Kit's place. Proof that I should have kept my liability of a little brother safely penned indoors until Mum's return.

Kit sat on the kerb, dazed, inspecting the blood beading on his gashed knee, his red Kickers turned inwards, laces forlornly undone. I rested my hand in his nest of sweaty curls and my thoughts flew to my dad, dead in his crumpled car. The solemn police-women in our Surrey kitchen. My mother saying, 'Oh, no, Damian is just late home. He phoned to say he was having a drink after work – he'll be back any minute.' Then I slammed down to earth on the gum-spattered pavement, the sound of kids yelling in the square's playground. Wolf.

He didn't look like a Notting Hill kid, certainly not one of the boho poshos from the villas, or the pea-cocking guys with their designer underwear peeking above low-slung trousers. Or one of the baseball-cap-and-trainer-clad film crew who'd been hanging around. Wolf looked like he'd walked out of a dirty garage or just broken in a horse in a dusty corral. A small chip on his front tooth. Nose smashed to the left at some point. Pale and lightly freckled skin, like the relatives on Dad's Irish side. Greasy streaks across the knees of jeans, the dodgy acid-wash sort. A red lumberjack shirt. Scuffed Timberland boots. And a certain woody quality, like you could sniff his neck and it'd smell of a freshly sawn plank.

'What's your name, mate?' Wolf asked, squatting next to Kit.

His voice belonged to the market, I realized, trying to place him. It had a huskiness, as if he'd been shouting over a crowd of heads and wouldn't waste his breath for no reason.

'Kit,' my brother whimpered, trying to be brave.

'Say thank you, Kit,' I said.

'Can you howl?' Kit asked instead.

Nonplussed, Wolf lifted his face to the London sky. 'Ow-ow-ow.' A proper howl, without any self-consciousness. 'Do I pass?' he asked, a playful sort of cockiness about him.

Kit sniffed back tears, too impressed to speak. He was drawn to older boys and young men. Like our nanny guy, Mason. I guess it was a Dad-shaped hole sort of a thing. Either way, a sister didn't cut it.

'Hey,' Wolf said softly, nodding at Kit's knee. 'You'll get a blinder of a scab from that. A perfect specimen. Like a tiny pizza.'

'I'll put it in my matchbox.' Kit wiped the blood, licked his finger. 'I have a scab collection,' he said, with cautious pride.

'Then you are a very cool kid.'

Kit lost his battle with tears then, fiercely wiping them away on the back of his arm. I'm not sure he was even crying about his knee. Big hurts sneakily hitched a lift on smaller ones. Not for the first time I felt bad that, out of all the families who could have adopted Kit, he'd wound up with ours.

'Since you're a collector too . . .' Wolf shoved a hand into the back pocket of his jeans, pulled out a toy car, no bigger than a finger, the paint flaked, ketchup-red. '. . . Mustang. 1953. Yours if you want it.'

Kit snatched it, spun the rubber tyres with his fingertip, the big bad universe shrunk to the simple joy of that little car.

'My uncle's shop just got a load in,' Wolf explained to me, reading my reservations about the sort of guy who gives out toys to random kids. 'Antiques. Golborne Road. I work for him.' He paused. 'For now, anyway.'

'Oh, right,' I said, as if this all meant something. All I knew was that my mother bought *nata* tarts, like soft yellow suns, from a Portuguese bakery on Golborne Road – 'I never could find these in Surrey, Maggie' – and ate them with her eyes half closed. My mother. She'd be back at the house by now, wondering where we were. 'Come on, Kit. Let's get you home.'

As soon as Kit stood up, he was freaking out at the blood pansies dripping to the pavement. 'I'm bleeding to death!'

'Kit, you're really not.' Nico was now grossly licking up the blood. I tightened the lead, brought her to heel.

'I am! I can't walk!'

It was a piggy-back or a melodrama. If Kit said he couldn't walk, he wouldn't. He wasn't naturally compliant, which I usually found quite funny, and Mum didn't.

When it came to Kit, Dad had been such a soft touch, unable to say no, treasuring Kit like a foundling prince: this probably hadn't helped. After fathering a quiet un-sporty girl who hid under tables to read, he'd revelled in having a son who kicked balls, swung cricket bats, climbed trees, and fell out of them – on first-name terms with the local paediatric A and E – and would dangle his socks over the fire just to see what happened. Behaviour Mum found exhausting, and Dad had encouraged.

In Kit's company, the pressures of work seemed to slough away. Dad would gallop across the garden with Kit on his back. Toss him upside down in the air. He built a ramshackle tree-house that rocked in the wind, a citadel of boyhood, and they'd sit on its perilous platform, kicking their legs, laughing. My mother would watch from the kitchen window, her arms crossed, smiling but sad somehow, like she was cut out of it.

'On you get, Kit.' I bent down, helped him up. His hands throttled my neck. 'Bye then,' I said to Wolf. This felt kind of inadequate. 'And, really, thank you.'

'Watch out for white vans, eh? Just assume they're all driven by myopic maniacs, and you'll live another day.' He smiled. 'Only the paranoid survive.'

I bit back a laugh and started walking away, Kit like a stone-filled rucksack on my back.

'The skateboard,' Wolf called after us.

I stopped, turned, wishing he hadn't mentioned it.

'It's broken, Maggie,' Kit wailed.

'Maggie?' Wolf said softly, and I nodded, surprised by how different my name sounded when spoken by him. His gaze zigzagged curiously over my face. Then he turned back to Kit. 'Few things are broken that can't be fixed.'

Not true. But I liked hearing it all the same.

Wolf bent over to pick up the board, his shirt tightening over the muscles of his back as they moved and slid, like tectonic plates. He took a penknife from a leather sheath on his belt, flicked open an attachment, and tried to do something fiddly and impressive to the back wheel. It didn't work.

'Don't worry about it,' I said, embarrassed to have drawn this guy into our messed-up morning. Also, a bit wary of the knife.

Wolf put the skateboard into Kit's outstretched hand. Again, I started walking, Kit twisting, watching Wolf, slamming the skateboard against my back, Nico snapping forward on her lead. A few paces on, the skateboard slipped from Kit's grip and crashed theatrically to the pavement. In the yelling and scrabbling, Nico shot off. I stumbled on a pavement crack: more bad luck. I should never have left my bedroom.

Further up the street, Wolf hesitated then sauntered back from wherever he was going – the life he'd
otherwise have lived – and picked up that stupid
skateboard then reached for Nico's trailing lead.

'I'll carry it for you, no problem,' he said, not even
asking how far we were going. As we walked, his gaze
slid sideways to me, away, back again. I smiled shyly.
We chatted a bit, but it was the silences I'd remember
after, their rich easiness. And the funny way our footsteps synchronized, feet landing on the pavement at
the same time. Too soon, our terrace. The crab-apple
tree. The pink door. 'This is us,' I said, and he smiled,
as if he knew. Something in the warm air cracked.
Over the rooftops, lightning. Thunder. *Ba-boom, ba-
boom, ba-boom*, like a restarted heart.

8

Maggie

London, May 2019

Maggie's heartbeat thrashes in her ears. Her neck. Her wrists. She can hardly believe she's dared to return. Rooted to the Notting Hill pavement, stunned by her own recklessness, she blinks up at the smart house, her body trembling. Over the years, what once happened here has shrunk to a fractal, a tiny replica of itself. There has even been the odd day she's not thought of it at all. But the house confronts her with its solidity, its persistence. The secrets she has kept – not just to protect Wolf, but also Kit – and is powerless against a digger clawing open.

Smart black basement-company boarding jackets the ground floor, leaving a dinner-shirt gap for the pale stone steps. The front door is now that ubiquitous matt charcoal grey. Maggie feels stupidly affronted by this: her mother had loved their blistered pink-painted door. An ornate porch lantern hangs where there used to be a flickering plastic light, a hammock for bugs. The stucco is now pristine.

Maggie's stomach churns. In a slightly self-defeating attempt to avoid attention, she wears a wide-brimmed straw sunhat, swiped from the Old Rectory's boot room, and her Parisian sunglasses. Still, she can't help glancing over her shoulder.

For two decades it's been easier to pretend that the neighbourhood as she knew it ceased to exist when they left. But the crab-apple tree on the pavement outside the house, twenty-one summers older, is still in bloom, just as it was that May. The familiar mundanity of the lamp post opposite her mother's bedroom gives her a small jolt: likely last January a copy of the planning application was taped to it, alerting residents to the proposal. She fights an internal voice urging her to walk away, very fast. Wolf would be horrified that she's here. But Wolf has not called again, not since Paris, and as he withheld his number, she cannot contact him to discuss it, even if she was minded to. She doesn't have a clue where to find him either. This deliberate distance deeply upsets her – as it's always done. If Wolf is not in her life, she thinks defensively, he doesn't get a say in it.

Taking a shaky breath, Maggie wonders who might live here now. An ageing pop star maybe. A pin-thin American in yoga gear, on her third husband perhaps, drawn to the area by the eponymous movie. A crypto wizard, barely out of college. The world of the one per cent. Her mother's old circle was quaint – and skint – in comparison. Rather than overweight, bespectacled teenage girls in faded Nirvana T-shirts, charging back from the market with fruit and veg, there are Ocado and organic veg delivery vans. Dog-walkers with six leads. Nannies.

Despite this, nostalgia plucks at Maggie's sleeve. Smells. Sounds. A feeling. The soul of the place. There were always dozens of different Notting Hills, she realizes, each a self-contained world yet criss-crossing the others, lacing the neighbourhood under the surface, holding it in place. For a short while, her family had been a tiny part of that, their story one of many here: infamously thuggish landlords, *Windrush*, race riots, rock and roll, artists, antiques and Carnival, as well as hundreds of quiet unrecorded stories, lives and ... loves.

Mauled by a flood of memories, Maggie almost cries out, covers her mouth with her hand. She wants the house's history to be erased, of course, and yet, contradictorily, hopes it still contains something of its past residents' lives, all the different eras co-existing, sealed and enfolded within, invisible to the human eye (and impervious to a basement digger's scoop). Because then her mother might still be glimpsed in the first-floor bedroom, blow-drying her hair, mouthing along to Stevie Nicks. Nothing lost.

Aware of a curious look from a neighbour emerging from a house further down the street, Maggie knows she can't linger. Time is ticking on. She's still got to shop for lunch stuff to take to Kit's flat. Thinking of her brother, her pulse quickens.

Despite agitating about it for days and nights, Maggie is still unsure what to tell Kit, given there *is* a chance nothing will be found on site. Or that it will remain another unsolved London mystery. Pre-empt it, revealing the truth of what happened here one day in May years ago, she risks shattering his world unnecessarily.

Checking left and right, Maggie wipes her damp palms on her yellow dress, and steps closer to the house. Pegging forward, she peeks through the gap in the boarding. Through the lower-ground-floor windows, a glimpse of industrial yellow, some sort of building equipment. Fear fizzes into her fingertips, and she steps back. Maybe she should have listened to Cora after all.

'You don't need to put yourself through this, Maggie,' Cora had shouted earlier, over the diesel rattle of her knackered Land Rover Defender, Vera dozing in her lap. The lift to the station used to dissuade – 'We can turn back, just give me the word!' – and probe, leaving Maggie circling around the truth and, as ever, hating herself for lying. The folly of her madcap return to England grates against the instinctive feeling that she must be here for Kit. At least until the excavation part of the basement build is finished.

Unsteadily, she steps away from the boarding, intending to walk down the side street, somehow peer over the garden wall – part of it appears to have been removed for vehicle access, a piece of hinged boarding acting as a gate – and assess where they're digging in the garden. But movement snags her eye. The front door starts to open.

Maggie freezes. For an irrational moment, she's quite sure it will be her mother, hiding here all this time, her death a magician's trick.

It's a man. A big bloke, wearing a baseball cap, pulled low over his face, a dark navy jacket, sharply cut over brick-block shoulders. Silver trainers. Not a corporate, then, she thinks, grimly fascinated, unable to look away. She feels sorry for him, this unsuspecting man, wealthy and silly enough to throw money at a basement he almost certainly doesn't need, digging down, oblivious to what might lie beneath.

Maggie knows she cannot gawp in this sort of street, at this sort of man, like a crazed stalker. But her feet seem screwed to the pavement. She cannot move a muscle, only take little sips of air. Because there's something registering, hazily tuning. A thick gold ring, worn on a thumb. The cap taken off, a plate-sized palm run over a bald head. And the nineties come roaring back.

9

Maggie

Notting Hill, May 1998

A mother's job, not mine. Cleaning Kit's gashed knee with wet loo roll, I switched back and forth between concern and crossness. It was time for Mum to come home, apologizing, sheepishly blaming a last-minute job, or a girlfriend having a drama. I wouldn't necessarily believe her. Kit would show off the toy car from Wolf – who kept sliding into my mind: those mineral-blue eyes, something about him – and I'd hammer home that if it weren't for a stranger, Kit would have been under the wheels of a van, and the guilt would be hers not mine, and she'd take us all out for lunch, which would be nice since there was so little food in the house. I was hungry, pissed off, and quickly discovering wet loo roll just turned into useless rags. But when the doorbell rang, I rushed to answer it, like a toddler who'd lost their mother in a supermarket, ready to fall into her arms.

'Hey, Maggie.' A colossus on the doorstep. The

whiff of hairspray. My heart sank. Not Mum at all. She'd use her key anyway, of course.

'Marco!' Kit ran up, waggling his car.

'Ah, my favourite house, my favourite people. You look great, Maggie.' Marco was skilled in flattery, bordering on deception, a hairdresser thing. His hazel-green eyes, bright against his olive skin, settled on Kit. 'Women would pay me seriously good money for curls like yours, little man.' That was probably true.

Marco's own dark hair was so closely shaven you could see the gleam of his scalp underneath. The same sort of contrariness that made fashion people wear black, I guessed. Those outsize shoes you see in shops, and think, Oh, my God, who the hell would fit *them*? Marco did. He lived not far away in the soaring concrete Trellick Tower, like a gentle giant at the top of a beanstalk. An urge to confide in him flew up inside me, like the way your stomach lifts when you go down a hill in a car.

Mum didn't come home last night. Those words jammed.

I didn't want to mention it with Kit there. Or make it real by saying it aloud. Not yet. By telling an outsider – even an insider outsider – I might as well have announced it on the front step with a megaphone.

Mum's friends loved a gossip. I knew this because I'd heard them enough times at our kitchen table. Marco would surely tell Clemence, and Clemence would tell Suki, and then, like a hank of hair released from

Marco's hot wand curler, things would quickly spiral.
And, God, Mum would hate that.

As the TV work had taken off, Mum had got more
private. Publicly chatting about her life seemed to
make her feel vulnerable when the cameras stopped
rolling. Always friendly when strangers recognized
her in the street or asked for an autograph – she rolled
her eyes at famous people who thought they were
above it – she'd started walking with her head down,
trying to avoid attention. Mum missed the relative
anonymity of modelling. But she was the sole earner.
A single mother. Needs must.

Marco glanced up at Mum's bedroom window. 'Can
you give your ma a shout?'

'She's not in right now.' The weight of admitting
she hadn't come home pressed in my throat again.
'Haven't seen her, have you?'

'No, darling.' Marco swivelled the ring on his thumb,
a thick stack of gold, coiled like a serpent, with pin-
prick ruby eyes. 'Hang on, come to think of it, wasn't
she working today? Some knitwear shoot?'

Mum hadn't mentioned it. On the other hand, it
was entirely possible she had, and I hadn't been listening. 'Oh, yeah, maybe.' I felt a bit better.

'Bah. Me and the ladies . . .' Marco glanced over his
shoulder at a battered yellow Mini, parked haphazardly in the road. Emerging, the tiny figure of Suki, a
jumble of leopard print and peroxide-blonde hair,

TESCO

Port Glasgow Extra
Any questions please visit
www.tesco.com/store-locator
VAT Number: GB 220 4302 31

1	The Midnight Hour Eve Chase	£6.00
1	Coca-cola Original Taste 500ml	£1.95
1	Players Bright 20 Pack	£13.55

TOTAL:	**£21.50**
Card	£21.50

Clubcard points earned: 7
Clubcard points balance: 171

Visa Debit
AID: A0000000031010
Number: ****0435************
Pan sequence no: 0
Authorisation code: 012504
Merchant: ****4805

║║║║║║║║║║║║║║║║║║║║║║║║║
PHPH-103X-T03Z-MWNV

12/12/2024 14:33 Store: 5441 Checkout: 092

Every little helps

Tesco Stores Ltd.,
Tesco House, Shire Park, Kestrel Way
Welwyn Garden City
Hertfordshire, AL7 1GA, U.K.
www.tesco.com
© Tesco 2018
Company Number 519500

Thank you for using Pay at Pump.

MIX
Paper from
responsible sources
FSC® C018525

TESCO

Pay at Pump

Every little helps

Tesco Stores Ltd.,
Tesco House, Shire Park, Kestrel Way
Welwyn Garden City
Hertfordshire, AL7 1GA, U.K.
www.tesco.com
© Tesco 2018
Company Number 519500

Thank you for using Pay at Pump.

MIX
Paper from
responsible sources
FSC® C018525

then, unfolding from the passenger seat, one long, bare leg, another, Clemence, her black hair coiled over her shoulders, a strappy lime-green dress billowing in the breeze, almost neon against her dark brown skin.

'Hi, darlin'. We're escaping for a cheeky impromptu lunch. My niece is on the stall.' Suki, who sold vintage clothes in Portobello Green, gesticulated with her packet of Marlboro Lights. 'Haven't long.'

Busy energetic people, Mum's friends either seemed to be talking at a million miles an hour, glass of wine in hand, or working round the clock, little in-between.

'Vital to check out the competition, right?' smiled Clemence, whose buzzy, cosy café drew a community crowd. 'Can we kidnap your mother, Maggie?'

'Dee Dee's got a gig,' said Marco, filling in the blanks. I didn't contradict him.

'Oh, shame. Tell your mum I've put aside an Ossie Clark crêpe jumpsuit that's going to look a million dollars,' said Suki, distractedly, scanning the street behind and muttering something about a traffic warden.

Clemence's gaze dropped to Kit's cut knee. I prayed she wouldn't ask about it since I'd left the cursed skateboard by the bins at the front and didn't want Kit freaking out again. He was an out-of-sight out-of-mind kind of kid, and Mum would buy him a new one when she got back. She smiled quizzically at Kit. 'Not at school today, honey?'

'He's under the weather.' Answering for him,

I discreetly jabbed Kit with my finger, code for 'keep your trap shut'. Kit, looking robustly healthy, beamed up at Clemence.

'Are *you* okay, Miss Parker?' Marco tilted his head to one side and examined me, with kind concern, as he might a bad haircut he'd come to rescue.

'Fine, thanks.' Habitual defensive answer. Was I? I had to be. Kit didn't have anyone else. For the first time in weeks, it struck me that my Friday had a vague sense of purpose. A reason to leave my bedroom. Also, I hated any sort of pity. Since Dad died, I held my feelings possessively close. Talking about them didn't help. No one else could possibly understand, least of all the three people standing on the doorstep.

Marco, Clemence and Suki had been Mum's flatmates in a Portobello Road 1980s flat-share – pre-marriage, the golden era, otherwise known as Back In The Day – when they were all young and hustling, trying to get a break. Since then, life had often kept them apart – work schedules, travel, divorces, children, the occasional falling-out – but they 'would always have each other's backs,' Mum said.

But the trio hadn't been regular Surrey visitors. I'm not sure how well they got on with Dad. Mum had always met up with them in London: 'girls' nights', she called those evenings, despite Marco's presence. But in Notting Hill they were the home crowd. And Mum rarely saw her old married Surrey friends: 'I can't be the widow at the dinner party who might steal a husband any longer.'

'Don't nick me! I'm coming,' yelled Suki, as a traffic warden hovered beside her car, notebook poised. Tugging Clemence's hand, Suki sprang away. 'Feel better soon, Kit,' Clemence called, over her shoulder.

'You look after your big sister, Kit,' Marco said, ruffling his hair, not falling for the sickness schtick.

I watched the Mini accelerating down the street, my chance to say anything gone. Nico sat by my feet forlornly, as if also recognizing the missed opportunity.

'Maggie?'

'Yes, Kit.' I braced for one of his unanswerable questions.

'I've decided I don't want to be older when I grow up.'

'Ha. Good luck with that.' Shutting the front door, doubt started to nudge. Maybe I should have told Mum's friends. No, I reasoned. I didn't know any of them well enough.

In the hallway, I stood by the phone, twisting my finger in its spiral cord, and ran through possibilities of someone I could call.

One of my old Surrey friends? I missed them, their bookish earnestness. But moving had created all sorts of distances: I'd deserted them for a supposedly shiny metropolitan life – this put them on the small-town defensive – with my famous-again mother. Worse, I'd discouraged any visits since the London life described in my long, largely fictional letters bore no relation to the reality. Also, I knew they'd tell their mothers, who'd freak and contact *Crimewatch*. So, no. Not an option.

Mum's agent Lucinda? Mum would say I'd made her look unprofessional. Also, I had no personal relationship with Lucinda, who was extremely glamorous, forthright and quite terrifying.

If Granny hadn't been in an urn in the Old Rectory's boot room, awaiting dispersal, she'd have known exactly what to do. Sharp, wry, with eyes the colour of cold milky tea, a rope of pearls at her throat, Granny had been highly practical. 'A plan is needed,' she'd always say, irrespective of whether she'd run out of parsley or a friend had tumbled catastrophically down the stairs.

Chewing the inside of my cheek, a bad habit – Mum said I'd chomp clean through it one day – I scanned the cork board above the telephone. Coloured pins, a scrappy collage of Mum's life: a faxed call sheet for a shoot, a receipt from the restaurant 192, a Polaroid of Mum, an overdue unpaid parking ticket, a birthday-party invitation for Kit, a yoga timetable and, at the bottom, swinging at an angle from one pin, my aunt's telephone number, the French dialling codes in brackets.

I lifted the phone, my fingers hovering over the round dial, the beeps loud in the hush.

Aunt Cora existed in brackets too. I'd barely seen her in the last few years, far more when I was younger. Although I was unable to date them, the earlier memories were sharp. A petite redhead with tattooed arms, spectacularly drunk and acerbic at family weddings. A Christmas, long ago: in the driveway of the Old Rectory, shouting at my grandparents, 'Fuck your fucked-up Christmas! The hypocritical lot of you!' – it was the rudest language I'd ever heard, I was mesmerized – then storming away without a coat. Dad gallantly ran off to find her in the dark and carried her back, muddy and frozen.

As my aunt's behaviour had got worse, the sightings and intel grew sketchier. A bad influence, I guess Mum kept her away from us. But I'd overheard mutterings about drunken blackouts and bad company and a clinic that 'cost far more than the Ritz', Granny saying that setting up Cora in Paris was 'the best solution for everyone'. The last time I'd asked after my aunt, a subject generally avoided, Mum had said, in a controlled, neutral manner, that Cora was working as a freelance translator – my half-French grandmother had succeeded in moulding one bilingual daughter – and everyone wished her well.

Death had brought back my aunt, first to Dad's funeral, a brief appearance at the rear of the church: under her netted black hat, delicate features, skin pale as the church's roses. She didn't come to the wake.

Last month she'd attended Granny's cremation, then tea at the Old Rectory. Over the sea of grey hair, the hushed reminiscing, my aunt cut a lonely figure in a neat navy dress – Granny's friends side-eyed her disapprovingly – but she shot me a small tentative smile, like a question, and started to make her way over. Before we could chat, Mum steered me into a car to be whizzed back to London and pick up Kit from school. I complained about this at the time. Although she never came to family events, my aunt always sent me and Kit, whom she'd barely met, books, good ones too. Couldn't I stay for a bit longer?

No. She and Cora had complicated practical grown-up things to discuss, Mum had explained – The Old Rectory's future, where to scatter Granny's ashes – but admitted afterwards they hadn't resolved anything. I wasn't sure if that was because my aunt had got explosively drunk again. Or if it was something else. Either way, a bad idea to call, I decided, and hung up the phone.

10

Kit

London, May 2019

Knocked out of his stoned screen-slip of an after-noon, Kit buzzes open the Bloomsbury flat's front door. Maggie runs up the narrow, dark communal stairs, wearing a limoncello-yellow dress and a mis-shapen straw sunhat, as if she's come straight from one of Cora's mad garden parties.

'Hey, sister,' he says, a bit flustered. They hug, tangled in Maggie's laden grocery bags. She feels hot, as if she's been sprinting through the city. The sunglasses are new, Kit notes, but don't quite fit. He knows she'll have bought them in a sale, and wouldn't have done other-wise, and suddenly loves his sister just for this. 'Very glam sunnies. Excuse my pyjamas,' he says, scrambling to look more together. 'And the mess. You're early?'

'Kit, I'm horribly late. It's almost teatime.' She flips up her shades. Her brown eyes have an anxiously ani-mated glint, something he can't read, bruise-dark shadows beneath.

Kit wonders why Maggie's back in London, and radiating a fractious energy that's chopping up the still air of the flat, like the blades of a fan. Hang on. It's *May*. Maggie usually goes a bit manic in May. And you can't have a childhood like theirs and not have bad days. Like a clever mend in a damaged ceramic, the uneducated eye might not see it, but if you tap it, the sound is different. He knows that sound because it's his too. 'Here, let me take those . . . Oof. You've done a Cora. So much food.' Walking past the plaster heads on plinths towards the kitchen, he calls over his shoulder, 'So, where have you been?'

'Notting Hill.'

Kit stills, then turns. Normally, his sister breaks into a cold sweat if she's forced to venture further west than Paddington. 'You are joking?'

She shakes her head, clearly rattled.

Kit tries to adjust to yet another hard unexpected shove back into the nineties. The last one from @treazurehunter, who disappointingly claims not to be Wolf: 'Ha, no! I'm Roy. Boring old Roy Smith. Although I did know of a bloke called Wolf once. Antiques? I used to dabble in dealing them a bit myself.' And that'd been it. Another tailspin. Another delicious head-squeeze. More hours lost on the internet. 'Weird one.'

Her gaze slips to the floor. 'Yeah, it is.'

Kit becomes aware of a mistuning. He may have

had a bit of a smoke, but he's pretty sure the vibe isn't coming from him. Normally, however long he and Maggie have been apart, they snap back together instantly. He visited Paris only last month, and on his arrival at the Gare du Nord they'd reverted to excitable kids, charging from flea market to gallery to wine bar. But there's little sign of carefree Paris Maggie today.

Outside, a lorry thunders past, shaking the building. 'Let's get this bounty into the kitchen,' he says, shooting his sister a puzzled look.

Maggie is so preoccupied she doesn't even notice the kitchen doors' new red and mustard stripes – inspired by a Galliano dress Dee Dee modelled, spring–summer 1993, a detail he's not going to risk mentioning. Maggie grieves, he reassembles. 'Hello? I repainted! You like it?' Still. He can't help wanting her approval.

She glances around. 'Yes! Shouldn't work but totally does, Kit.'

'Like me.'

Finally, she smiles properly.

Kit's home is everything. Coming into a Parker inheritance aged twenty-one had felt like gold falling from the sky. He'd thrown all of it at this little flat, resting on the narrow shoulders of the old map shop downstairs. Possibly the only wise thing he's ever done. Every year his filigree roots thread deeper into this street behind the Foundling Museum. The shallow Georgian foundations. Further down, medieval plague pits, a trough of Roman sewers and, not far away, the subterranean river Fleet, a dark cold rush of history, spilling towards the Thames at Blackfriars.

Kit could never do what Maggie's done, pack a life into a suitcase and start again, once he'd convinced her – and himself, almost – that he really could survive without a big sister a cab ride away. If you love someone, set them free and all that. He's long suspected she hung around London for years to be there for him, keep an eye.

Sometimes Kit fears Maggie married Tom, a fellow teacher – maths, nice, handsome, dry as a stub of chalk – out of an unconscious desire to create a stable family for him again. He detests that idea. Before the brief marriage collapsed – what took it so long? – Tom confided in Kit that Maggie occasionally called out for wolves in her sleep, and how bizarre was that? Kit loyally quipped he'd heard far weirder things in bed. But Maggie not telling Tom about Wolf seemed a fatal omission of intimacy. So, he's glad she broke free, left that gruelling job and her marriage and committed to her writing and Paris. Maggie's always had a thing for Paris and has been so happy there this last year. Only she doesn't look too chipper now, which troubles Kit as he unpacks the deli boxes.

The food feels like a wholesome corrective to his last couple of days. But Maggie still seems distant. Normally, she'd be inspecting his fridge by now, tutting, pulling out the bag of decomposing watercress, suspiciously sniffing the milk, and interrogating him about his chaotic love life. 'What is it, Maggie?'

Maggie leans back against the work top, arms crossed. 'I passed our old house, Kit.'

Surprised, he looks up from the grocery bag. 'Oh, yeah?'

'The oddest thing.' She takes a breath. 'I recognized the guy coming out of the front door.'

'Celeb?' He brightens shamelessly.

'A friend of Mum's.'

'Plot twist!' Kit sniffs a tomato. He loves their red smell.

'Mum had a hairdresser friend. Big guy.'

Kit frowns, hazily raking backwards. 'Marco?'

'That's him. But it can't be, can it?'

'Not if he's still a hairdresser. I mean, have you seen the house prices?' Kit twists off some sourdough, jaws on the crust. 'Maybe he was doing a bouff for a private client.'

'Oh, yes! I hadn't thought of that.' Maggie palms her cheek and looks relieved.

'You said hello to him, right?'

'I . . . I couldn't, Kit.' For an awful moment he thinks his sister might cry. 'All I wanted to do was get out of there. And . . .' Maggie opens her mouth as if to say something else then closes it. Eventually she says, 'I lost my nerve.'

He frowns. 'Hang on. Why are you in London, Maggie? Grand as it is to see you, obviously. Aren't you meant to be finishing your new book?' He breaks off more bread. 'I thought you had a June deadline.'

'Yes, yes. And I . . . I'm about to blow it.' She runs her fingertips over her mouth, her eyes panicked. 'I'm screwing up big-time, Kit.'

'You? No way, Maggie.' His sister never misses a deadline. She'll sit up working all night if she must, and produced two novels while working full time as a teacher at a rough inner-city comp, sacrificing weekends and holidays, possibly her marriage. 'Last month you were writing before breakfast, like a woman possessed. You were on fire!'

Maggie flinches at the reminder, then starts rambling about writer's block, the need to return to England and piece together their lives in London.

'And that will unblock you?' he asks sceptically. 'But you don't even like *talking* about that time. Not with me anyway.' Kit almost mentions Wolf. How she jerks whenever he mentions his name. If he asks how he might get in contact, or why Wolf's impossible to track down, her answer is always a tight 'I don't know,' the subject shut.

When Kit was a kid, even, embarrassingly, quite a

big kid, he'd sneakily tap for more information by asking for a bedtime story. Pretending to be half-asleep, he'd murmur, 'Tell me about Wolf and the little antiques shop.' Maggie would try to say nothing – he would see her lips twitching – but wouldn't be able to help herself because she loved telling stories, and Maggie loved Wolf, and it'd just slip out in the soft lamplight, and Kit would secretly squirrel away every detail. When she'd gone, he'd lie in the dark, replaying, obsessing, Wolf colonizing his brain.

'I'm sorry, Kit,' she says, after a beat. 'We will talk. We will have that conversation.' She closes her eyes and seems to be breathing very fast. 'Just not . . . yet.'

Confused, he's torn between demanding to have 'that conversation' right now, and not wanting to upset her further. 'Glass of vino?' he asks helplessly.

She shakes her head, the weight of the world pressing down on her shoulders.

'Come and see my booty from last week's auction.' Desperate to lift her mood, he leads her into the malachite-green sitting room, where small curios are laid on newspaper sheets, awaiting cleaning or fixing. One of the many things that Kit loves about antiques is that, if broken, they can be mended, lost parts re-assembled, made whole again. And he'd have finished the job if he hadn't slipped into an is-it-Wolf? vortex.

Seeing his notebook lying open on the sofa, Kit leaps towards it, slaps it shut and moves it to the side table. He really doesn't want Maggie to see his stoned, scrawled jottings on his internet searches for @treazurehunter.

'Do you need more stock, Kit? It appears to be breeding.'

'Don't even . . .' Crammed on a rack of industrial metal shelves: automatons, wooden artists' figures with articulated joints and an eighteenth-century elephant's foot. A Boucheret clock. All delights that sweep in and out of his possession on the currents of fairs and auctions, the buying and selling that goes on between dealers and clients. Unlike the Italian fifties rattan furniture and Swedish paintings, which sell fast, often direct to interior designers before they go online, the curiosities attract a rarer customer. 'Slow. Tough market.'

Kit's too proud to admit he's not made a big-ticket sale for a while. Sometimes the right dealer and the right customer must meet, that's all. Then beautiful things can happen. His attention swings back to Roy – @treazurehunter – who has requested further photos and condition reports on a couple of spendy items. Kit feels a nudge of excitement. If he plays his cards right, this Roy chap could turn out to be a very lucrative client indeed.

Hurriedly showered and dressed, emerging from his bedroom, Kit finds Maggie's piled the table in the living room with food. The salad is in a delicate antique Wedgwood bowl, too precious to use; he won't say anything. She has also tidied up. As she spoons food onto his plate, he's struck by a déjà vu so strong he can taste it. Maggie playing Mum all those years ago. Ice-cream for breakfast. Heaven.

'You know you've got to go back, don't you?' he says, biting into a feta pastry, which is excellent but not as good as Cora's.

Maggie, who's barely eating, pulls a face. 'Oh, I don't know if it's such a good idea, Kit.'

'Don't overthink it. You've come this far. And you obviously returned for a reason.' One he still doesn't really understand.

A moment passes. She studies him, tussling with something. 'Kit?' she says softly.

'Sister?' He starts hungrily to pile up his plate again.

'We're good, aren't we? You and me.'

'Depends,' he teases, a little unsettled she should ask. Also, on the adjacent chair, he's just spotted Dee Dee's old pashmina falling out of his sister's hand-bag. Uh-oh. Showing up at critical life moments – Dee Dee's funeral, Maggie's wedding, the day Maggie moved to Paris – it's the cashmere canary in the coal mine. And here it is.

'Whatever life throws at us next, Kit.' Maggie leans forward, her eyes pleading. 'Whatever happens.'

11

Maggie

Notting Hill, May 1998

Mum wasn't missing. We just didn't know where she was yet, I told myself. When my mind flew to bad places, kite-like, I snapped it back, and thought about my brother, his maddening aliveness, reasoning no one that small and that unfinished loses their mother and father and a granny in the space of two years. No one's that unlucky. Even if they deliberately walked on paving cracks, arms outstretched, as Kit often did, just to wind me up.

Still, as the second night swept in, Mum not back, a new sort of fear hung like heat, that first clammy sweat of summer. I switched on all the main lights so the house would glow like a lantern in the dark, drawing her back. When Nico crept upstairs, refusing to settle in her basket in the kitchen where she was meant to sleep, I didn't send her down again. She burrowed under Kit's Spider-Man duvet, unable to believe her luck.

After reading Kit a story and trying to answer his questions – not one about Mum, conspicuous by its absence, he demanded I sit there until he fell asleep. Even after he'd dropped off, I remained, listening to Nico snuffling, and watching the way Kit's breath lifted one curl on his forehead, making it unfurl slightly, like a fern frond. I'd never done that before. Watched Kit sleeping. Truly noticed him. I allowed myself to wonder about his birth-parents, just for a moment, and how they didn't know what they were missing. Then, unsettled by this, I returned to my own room.

Time now surprisingly relevant, I wound up my redundant alarm clock, shook it into life. Watched over by its luminous face, the insistent creep of its hands, I skated across the surface of sleep, listening for the front door, the turn of Mum's key in the lock. She often used to say, 'I'll be back by midnight,' so I was primed for her to return. But she didn't come back by midnight. And the hour between midnight and one a.m. crawled, like it might never end. I dropped off, woke again at two and went into her room to see if she was back. She wasn't. Hands on the cool glass, I peered out of the lit window, which had thrown two yellow canvases on the street outside. Moving across them, a bloke in a hat, walking almost on his toes, like one of the London foxes. The orange dot of a cigarette. Catching me by surprise, he stopped and looked up – I couldn't make out his face, just the shape of his hat, his loping slim frame – and I quickly stepped away and turned off the bedroom lights, so he couldn't peer into Mum's room, as if it were a glass display cabinet.

The next morning, a hard kick on the shin woke me: Kit had crept into my room in the night. Nico too. All of us were squashed into my single bed. The lights in the hallway were still blazing, apart from the bulb on the landing that had burned out, fried moths stuck to it like brooches.

In Mum's room, her bed was unslept in. This was bad. But I couldn't work out exactly how bad, or what kind of bad on the scale of badness that ran the gamut from walk of shame to dead in an alley. If we'd been living in Surrey, where mothers didn't fail to come home unless they'd run off with their tennis coach or had an accident, it'd have been a crisis. In anything-goes Notting Hill, with the steady compass of Dad gone, Mum in such a funny mood lately, it was still, I decided, a drama.

Easier to tackle the problem of breakfast. Kit had unearthed mint choc chip ice-cream at the back of the freezer, welded to a lump of pea-studded ice, and I couldn't see a good reason why not.

Considering what to do next, I stood by the patio doors, breathing mist islands on the glass, and staring at That Godawful Hole. At what point should I call the police? Day one or two or three? I didn't know the answer. Only that the police would make everything official, and likely public, and bring social services, who could pluck away my adopted little brother like one of those mechanical grabber hands in a box at fairs that picks up small defenceless toys. And then there was the press. Mum would be hung out to dry too. Lose the motherhood column. The TV gigs. All her earnings. No, I should definitely say nothing and brazen it out for her sake, I reasoned. And Kit's.

'Maggie.' Kit ducked under my arm and stood on my feet, his bare ones folding over mine, like hot monkey paws. He'd loved to do that ever since he could walk. Normally, I shrugged him off. I didn't that morning.

'I'm hungry.'

'Ice-cream for breakfast not hitting the spot?' Feeding Kit was turning out to be frustratingly circular.

'It's too cold.'

'Right.'

'I'm never allowed doughnuts.'

I thought how my mother would hate this idea – doughnuts for breakfast, all that hyper sugar! – and how she'd not bothered coming home or told me where she was, and fear flipped to mutiny. 'You deserve a doughnut. And Nico needs a walk.' Without Mum, dog care was also proving repetitive.

Kit beamed. It struck me that if you went along with him, rather than tried to impose the rules, things were a whole lot smoother. 'We need money, Kit. You do the sofa cracks. I'll search the dresser . . .'

Kit had already leaped off my feet and sprinted away, Nico following, kicking over her metal food bowl with a clatter.

The old pine dresser in the upstairs sitting room acted as a depository for all sorts of things and was where Mum tossed spare change if her purse was too heavy. I poked around. One small drawer still harboured our landlord's gubbins: airline-branded cutlery, cufflinks, a flyer for a rave, a handful of American cents. Another was stuffed with Mum's lidless lipsticks, painkiller packets, stamps, taxi receipts and, happily, a couple of ten-pence pieces. Not enough, though.

The drawer under the *Yellow Pages* was stiff. I gave it a hard yank, and it grumbled open.

Our passports. I exhaled a breath I didn't know I was holding. Mum wasn't abroad at least. But any relief was quickly lost among a stack of unpaid bills: Kit's school, BT, interest on a loan, 'Urgent' stamped in shouty red at the top. This wasn't like my mother, who was smart and would splurge on beautiful 'forever' things, but always 'cut her cloth', as she put it. Beneath the bills was a stack of letters and forms about the not-yet-complete sale of our old house –

one sale seemed already to have fallen through – and worrying ones from lawyers and accountants about Dad's estate. I read, shocked, understanding just enough: cliff-drop losses on his investments, loans, inaccessible accounts, and complications from Dad dying intestate, which limited how much money Mum could easily access. She'd never mentioned any of this, confirming my long-held sense that much of my parents' marriage was private and hidden from me. An adult conversation that occurred only when I was in bed. And I'd been just fine with that. Suspended in a state of childish ignorance, neither their happiness nor fortune my responsibility. Suddenly, I wished I'd paid more attention.

No wonder my mother had been behaving oddly recently. No wonder she'd been distracted. Or had peered out of the living-room window with a frown, nibbling her lower lip, as if she was worried about who might be walking to the door, like the postman. All those things. Although I was glad to have worked it out, the explanation was crushing.

Nico appeared, her round eyes worried, and pressed needily against my legs, sensing my disquiet. I had the odd sensation of growing older suddenly, very fast, like a speeded-up time-lapse film. 'It'll all be fine, Nico,' I mumbled, bending down to reassure her. And with this change of perspective, a slither of silvery blue and green. Right at the back of the drawer. I straightened again, shoved my hand right to the back and drew out an unsealed envelope. Fat with cash.

Holding my breath, I flicked through the notes. New-smelling, crisp. Mum had debts, but she had money too? This threw me. Perhaps she'd been paid for a job in cash. Or it was next month's rent to give to Pippa. Whatever, I slipped a couple of tenners into my back pocket and shouted to Kit, 'Doughnuts are go!'

We were rushing out, Kit in anticipatory sugar frenzy, Nico catching it, yapping, when Kit grabbed my arm and gasped, 'It's *him*.'

Sauntering towards us, a skateboard tucked under his arm. Wolf.

Something inside me quickened. Kit stared, open-mouthed, as if Buzz Lightyear had just landed.

Wolf had smartened up since the previous day, a clean shirt (lumberjack again, blue not red). But his dark hair still splayed over his crumpled collar, sticky-uppy, like disarrayed feathers, the sort you couldn't gel down. 'Morning.' He smiled, revealing the chipped front tooth I hadn't forgotten. 'Nicked the board from your bin store yesterday,' he said, like this was a perfectly normal thing to do. He handed it to Kit. 'Fixed it up a bit. Hope you don't mind.'

Kit flipped over the skateboard, revealing the mended back wheel. Wolf watched, surveying his work with quiet pride. Mum always said the difference between a great model and the rest was the nuance of the eyes: 'Like in a silent movie, they have to tell a story.' And Wolf's eyes did. Also, I'd never met a guy my age who could fix anything beyond a slipped bike chain.

'You made it better again,' Kit whispered in awe, spinning its wheel with his finger.

'I am the king of random spare parts.' Wolf shrugged. 'If you've ever got a missing bit, however rare, however small, Kit, come to me. I'll sort you out.'

Kit listened solemnly. 'Can you fix *anything*?'

'I'll give it my best shot.' Wolf stuck his hands deep into his jeans pockets. 'But, you know, sometimes you just have to accept the thing's broken, and love it in a different way. You don't need to throw it.' He glanced at me, and I coloured. 'I mean, you could have hung that skateboard on your bedroom wall, like a fancy bit of art.'

Kit considered this. 'I could start a collection of broken things?'

'Do it,' Wolf said, then shot me a smile on the verge of a laugh and muttered, 'Sorry.'

To busy myself, I stroked Nico, waiting for Wolf to leave. But, for a Londoner, oddly, he didn't seem in a rush, or to have anywhere else he needed to be, or in any hurry to fill the silence. I was wondering how to politely extricate us when Kit, in that random, literal way of his, blurted, 'Mum's not come home for two sleeps.'

Blood rushed to my face. I wanted to say it wasn't how it sounded. But, of course, it was.

'So, Maggie's taking me for doughnuts,' added Kit, cheerful at the trade-off.

I saw Wolf's reappraisal zip across his eyes. Feeling exposed, I tried to hide my fluster by taking the skateboard off Kit, and rolling it into the hallway, not in the mood to risk my brother on it again. 'You all right?' Wolf asked, directly, gently.

I nodded.

He didn't press for more. Instead, he studied me, head tilted, as if mentally taking me apart. The air felt charged, busy. As though dozens of dot-to-dots were being connected all at once in the faintest, quickest pencil lines. It also felt as if an unknown part of myself had just pitched up: the strangest feeling, not one I'd ever experienced, and wouldn't ever again. Wolf's off features, broken, mended at the wrong angles. The smudge of oil on the edge of his jaw. None of that helped either.

'There's this bakery stall at the market,' he said, after a while. 'Sheila's. Perfection.' He leaned back against the porch column, where the house number had been scrawled on by hand. 'Love a doughnut. The way it looks like a boring old bun . . .' His low story-around-a-campfire voice drew Kit closer. 'But it hides a secret in the middle. Makes you work for it. There you are, wondering if you've been cheated of jam when . . .'

'Splat!' yelled Kit, delighted. Wolf high-fived Kit.

I held back my laugh like a cough in the throat, their silliness infectious.

'You come with us,' Kit told Wolf.

'Kit,' I warned, not about to humiliate myself. It wasn't a good look, seeing a big girl eating doughnuts. A breeze blew the tree blossom, and a few petals drifted down to the pavement.

'But he fixed my skateboard, Maggie.' And, when this didn't work, 'He saved my *life*.'

Hard to argue. 'Come if you want,' I said to Wolf, shyness making me gruff.

'Sweet,' Wolf said, and we started moving away from the house, the unpaid bills, the envelope of cash and the lonely midnight hours. Kit curled his hand into Wolf's – he looked surprised but didn't seem to mind – then fired off a rattle of questions. Which football team? Spurs. Where did Wolf live? In a rented room off Edgware Road. No, nothing like Kit's house. Who was his best friend? Tyrone. From school. How old was he? Nineteen. Was his dad dead too? No, in prison. There was a hiccup of surprise before Kit continued. If Wolf could be anyone, who would he be? Himself in five years' time. He'll take a punt. Favourite colour? Indigo. Word? *Craquelure*. Meaning? The tiny cracks that form on the surface of a painted or varnished surface as it ages. And so they went on. Normally, I'd have told Kit to shut up, but there was a raplike rhythm to it, the questions, the answers, our footsteps, the scuffle of Nico's paws, our long shadows falling on sun-bleached pavements I'd walked before but which in Wolf's company felt completely different.

12

Maggie

London, May 2019

Maggie ropes her gaze to Marco. Luckily, he's one of the taller people in the crowd surging down Portobello Road, a roiling river of black braids, pink hair, tonged blonde waves, piercings, prams, dogs, toddlers on shoulders, and clouds of weed and vape.

Kit was right. She's come this far. Don't overthink it. But she's still desperately clinging to the hope that Marco is a visitor to their old house, rather than its owner. Even though she'd just spotted him in the living-room window. Even though, a couple of minutes after that he appeared, double-locked the front door, and stepped out in silver Air Maxes, like the nineties had never ended. It's one thing imagining a stranger living in that house, unaware of its history, far worse to have a familiar face. Memories of a deep rumbling laugh. But it also gives her a glimmer of hope, a minuscule chance.

So, she's followed Marco from the house to Portobello Road, steeling herself to make an introduction, waiting for him to get off the phone clamped to his ear. Walking a few steps behind him, Maggie takes in the antiques arcades, the rickety stalls selling silver, old glassware, vintage clothes, vinyl records and leather bags. It's not so different here, not on market day, from what it was. The street-food stalls have multiplied – paella bubbling gold in huge pans, jerk chicken, tapas, falafel – and it feels less antique-y, more touristy. But much is the same, that mash of people, voices and life, and it tugs at her heart.

Because part of her is here too, Maggie realizes. And her mother. Wolf. Kit.

Thankfully, Kit wasn't free this afternoon, or he'd have insisted on coming too. Some meeting with a customer in Piccadilly, he said. She'd persuaded him not to cancel it, so she wouldn't have to explain why walking past their old house makes her tremble and sweat, or her new-found interest in the construction process of basements. But she misses Kit's company, his wry, gossipy commentary, and his dealer's eye that always sees the mischievous wink in stale old things. Kit's Notting Hill is different from hers. That's the problem with secrets: corrosively leaking over time, they sit between you and the people you love.

At first, Kit had been far too young to tell. As he grew older, this sensitive, brave boy who'd already been through so much, Maggie found she just . . . couldn't. (Or Cora. Or her ex-husband. Definitely not her ex-husband.) And there's never been a point in the last twenty-one years when she's thought, Yeah, Kit will be able to cope with this one.

Earlier that morning, having stayed over on Kit's sofa, watching Kit spoon granola, Maggie didn't see a hip young antiques dealer but a boy in scuffed red Kickers, a graze on his knee, eating cornflakes. His eyes were tired, shot pink, the normally well-kept flat in disarray. As for the notebook he'd whipped off the sofa in such a hurried way, it instantly made her wonder what he was trying to hide. A quick peek revealed the last few pages were full of doodles of Wolf's name, an obsession that worryingly refuses to fade, however much she discourages it, and the name Roy, circled by question marks. She hadn't liked that one bit.

Roy? Never heard of him. Maggie knows most of Kit's circle, his exes, his confidants, and adoring female friends, loyal and protective, aware of the vulnerability beneath the puppyish passion and catalysing charm. And how Kit lives as if death is always waiting, legs crossed, one foot wagging like that of an actor in a dressing room before the curtain lifts. Throws himself into things too hard. Falls in and out of love easily, with absolute conviction each time, his heart ablaze or broken. Whenever he introduces a new girlfriend – once a boyfriend – Maggie fights the urge to pull them close, and whisper in a mean-friendly *Goodfellas* voice, 'Take good care of him, or you'll have me to deal with, okay?'

Marco suddenly stops at a flower stall, and Maggie almost slams into him. Tenting his fingers, he peruses a staggered theatre of beautiful blooms in galvanized metal tubs. This is it. Now or never. She takes a breath. 'Excuse me,' she begins nervously. Too quietly.

The sun is swallowed by a cloud, and Maggie can smell rain. She steps forward. 'Marco?'

He turns slowly, puzzled at first, and flicks up his sunglasses.

'You may not remember me. I'm Maggie. Maggie Parker?' she stutters, her adolescent self-consciousness circling back.

'Oh, my goodness.' His face lights up. 'How could I not remember you? Dee Dee's girl!'

Suddenly, this is all she is. All she'll ever be. Just Dee Dee's girl standing on Portobello Road. Looking for her mother once more.

'I'm not often lost for words.' A disbelieving laugh. That same mellifluous voice. 'But you got me.'

'Have . . . have you a minute?' Maggie's heart is bouncing like a ball in her chest. And time is ripping again, hard, with a hot wax-strip sear and yank, and she's hurled back to her father's funeral, a scene she hasn't thought of for years. The mountain of Marco hugging her mother, who collapses like a rag doll in his arms. The funeral a blur of black dresses, black sunglasses and feathered black hats, as though it's been gatecrashed by mad crows. Dad's north London side of the family sobbing noisily. Kit kicking the dangling hassock and wriggling on the pew. One of Dad's colleagues, red-eyed, delivering a speech: 'Not only did Damian look like Richard Burton, damn him, he was an industry star, a loyal much-loved colleague and friend, but far and beyond all this, Damian was a family man, a devoted, loyal husband . . .'

'Am I happy to see you again,' Marco says quietly, marvelling. 'We have a bit of catching up to do!'

'Are you free now?' Maggie seizes her chance. 'Could we grab a coffee?'

Marco hesitates. Maggie fears she's come on too intensely. That all her secrets, all her shame, are inked across her face. She has the sensation of being sickeningly suspended between the past and her future, as if walking a trembling high wire between tall buildings.

He steals a discreet glance at his watch, one of those hi-tech chunky sports ones. 'Of course, darling.'

Maggie exhales. 'Clem's Café?' she asks tentatively. She could talk to Clemence too.

'Oh, Clem shut up shop donkey's years ago! Rent went bonkers.' Drops of rain start to polka the pavement. 'How about we head to mine? Two-minute walk.' A smile twitches. 'I want to show you something.' Maggie doesn't move. Marco shrugs an arm around her shoulders. 'Funnily enough, I believe you might just know the way.'

13

Kit

London, May 2019

Londoner-fickle, the weather has turned. Sunshine gone, rain starting to fall, hard and thin, like picture pins. Kit's loafers slap the water-skinned Piccadilly pavement, sending up a fine spray on his trouser hems as he cuts a line through central London towards the stranger waiting at Green Park's gate. A bloke who may lead him to Wolf – well, there's a splinter of a chance. Worst case, Kit will meet a new customer with a casket of cash to blow. Whatever the deal, a deal to be done. Win–win.

Adrenalin-tanked, Kit's legs move fast, his trench coat snapping, the small red flower in his lapel shedding petals. As he clears the Royal Academy's grand entrance, his thoughts slide back to his sister.

Over breakfast, he'd been tempted to ask if she remembered some bloke called Roy Smith from their Notting Hill days. Dabbled in antiques. But Kit didn't ask. He knew Maggie – annoyingly sharp, with all her sluicing 'gut feelings' – wouldn't buy his feigned nonchalance. He'd get the big-sister inquisition. Overly protective, she'd try to deep-mine Roy from the internet and vet him first. She wouldn't be able to help herself.

It's the author in her. She yearns to control every story. Small ones. Big ones. Take his biological relatives. If Kit wasn't so averse to going there, he's no doubt Maggie would wrestle them to the ground too: sieve those ancestry websites for DNA matches, do the detective work. But . . . no. The thought of curling a cotton tip inside his cheek, sending it off in the post to be digitally matched to strangers with whom he has nothing in common yet who might have some claim over him: horror. Kit would rather not know. And why should he? He's not an antique collectible, valued by a manufacturer's mark, or proof of provenance: this is the throwaway line he keeps in reserve for people who say, 'If it were me, I'd want to know': 'Not you, is it?' – and that suffocates the conversation pretty quickly. Given his inauspicious beginnings, Kit doesn't see why he can't write his own origin story, with a cast of his own choosing. Seek the person who did show up, changed his life for ever, and continues to inspire him, all without ever knowing it. Wolf.

But as Kit nears the Green Park gate, his confidence falters. If it hadn't been for Roy claiming to have known Wolf, would he have agreed an IRL meeting? Unlikely. An appreciation for a William Morris Sussex chair is not, unfortunately, a reliable test of good character. Kit also knows he's a sucker for the theatre of it – 'I'll wear a red flower in my lapel!' – and it could be a stitch-up. A meeting with a fraudster. A wackadoodle Dee Dee fan. Anything.

Worst of all, Kit's early. Not wanting to be the one standing like a lemon, unwittingly examined, he tries to slow down, but overriding his own fast factory setting proves impossible. He's soon past Fortnum & Mason's eau-de-Nil arched windows, the Wolseley's doorman, the Ritz's long, sheltered portico and, finally, the railings of Green Park, where he stops. To buy himself observation time, he removes the flower from his coat and stuffs it into his pocket. Peering through the turning cogs of umbrellas around the tube's entrance, he spots two men standing close to the iron gate's pillars. One is scruffy, unkempt, leaning back, his hands jammed into leather-jacket pockets. The other is affable-looking, in his sixties. Dapper in a navy tailored coat, silk paisley scarf, shoes polished to mirrors, he scans the crowds as they pass with a speculative smile. Yes, that's his man.

Nerves lifting, Kit approaches. Just as he's about to speak, a woman darts across the road, to protesting honks from the traffic, and they kiss. Not Roy, then.

Kit hangs around, suspecting he's been stood up and feeling like a bit of a twat. After five more minutes, annoyed, mostly with himself, he cuts his losses and is walking into the park, those lush drizzly greens, when someone taps his shoulder. 'Hiding that buttonhole flower in your pocket, are we, Kit Parker?'

14

Maggie

Notting Hill, May 1998

The shop had no obvious number or name. Not even a door. From under a rolled-up metal shutter, old furniture surged onto Golborne Road's pavement, like the disgorged contents of a country house: tall lamps with tattered silk shades, marble fireplaces, paintings and jowly armchairs. Sliding between a chest of drawers and a crumbly mirror, shedding gilt like skin, we followed Wolf inside.

'What is this, Maggie?' whispered Kit, his small hand, damp with skittery boy heat, curling into mine. Even Nico stayed close.

'A shop, Kit,' I replied, not entirely convinced. No till. No shopkeeper. No customers. But after devouring doughnuts from Sheila's market stall, Wolf had had to go back to work – and why didn't we come? He'd give us a tour. Since I wasn't exactly fighting off social invitations, and figuring the longer we stayed out of the house, the likelier it'd be that Mum would be back when we returned, I agreed.

Notably cooler than the street, it was autumnal inside. Spore-y. Brown. Smelling of beeswax polish, leather and dust. Muddy oil portraits on the walls. Dozens of clocks – gold clocks, carriage clocks, cuckoo clocks – hands pointing in different directions, ticking in the hush, arguing about the right time. The concrete floor seemed to slant slightly towards the back of the premises, the ceiling lowering as if the shop was tunnelling beneath the street.

Beside a startled-looking stuffed elk, Kit stalled, refusing to go any further. Unsure, suspended between two worlds, he glanced back at the street, then to the dimly lit rear of the shop. Nico sat down in solidarity.

Seeing Kit's hesitance, Wolf stopped. 'My uncle shares the premises with another dealer. A lot of this stuff is his. Better things north, I promise, Kit.' He shrugged. 'But your call entirely. What do you say?'

Was that the point of no return? If it was, I didn't know it.

At the back of the shop there was a worn-in trestle table, enclosed by stacks of crammed shelves. An ash-tray and, inside it, a roll-up cigarette stub smouldering. A packet of Rizlas. A pair of red boxing gloves. Tools, pens, gum, a chunky paper invoice book, and a grubby half-drunk mug of tea. Nico wanted to get her nose into everything.

Wolf pulled out a chair. 'Want to sit, little man?'

Kit eyed this chair, with its spindled back and woven-rush seat, and said firmly, politely, 'No, thank you very much. It's ghosty.'

'Probably,' said Wolf. 'A lot of people now very, very dead would have sat in that chair. You're bang on about that. But that's why it's a good chair, mate. Look.' Wolf picked it up, spun it upside down, lightly, on his fingertips. 'See that?' He pointed to a joint under the seat. 'Mortice and tenon joint. Hand sawn so that it fits just right. Snug as a bug. No nasty glue. No nails. Nothing like your landfill modern chairs.' He took Kit's index finger, ran it across the grain of the wood. 'Nice, isn't it? Oak. Tree would have been around a hundred and fifty years old when it was lopped, and this chair is a hundred years old. You do the maths.'

I could see Kit eating up Wolf's words as he'd devoured the doughnuts earlier, like a half-starved thing. He touched the chair again.

'And . . .' Wolf spun the chair the right way round and sat down in it, hard, releasing the smell of wood and something else, a male tang that hung in the air, fresh sweat maybe, which should have repelled me but didn't. '. . . still solid as . . .' He just stopped himself saying the F-word and stood up. 'So?'

Kit cautiously took Wolf's place, his fingers gripping the chair's edges, just in case.

Wolf prodded the dusty CD player – the Verve's 'Bitter Sweet Symphony' – then took a battered Quality Street tin off the table, offered it to Kit. 'Jammie Dodger?'

Kit took two biscuits. The song swelled. I stole glances at Wolf. His body was compact, muscular, and he moved with a deliberate light quickness, the sort you see in dancers and cats. I got the impression he was still sieving what Kit had told him earlier – Mum not coming back for two sleeps – and my startling, red-faced reaction.

'Here, Maggie.' Giving me no time to prepare for his touch, he turned me to face a long fairground mirror, its glass rippled, silvered, squashing us together. I laughed. Nothing to do with our reflection, just his proximity, Wolf saying, 'If this was the only type of mirror available in the history of mankind, do you reckon the world would be a better place?'

It struck me as one of the strangest questions I'd ever been asked. 'No one would be able to take themselves seriously.'

'Exactly what I've been thinking.' As if he spent his days considering such things.

'Where are the toys?' Kit piped up. Quickly Wolf removed his hands. There was a metallic tingle on my shoulders where he'd touched me and would be for hours afterwards.

'Toys! Reveal yourselves.' Wolf switched on a metal lamp, and a dim corner of the shop lit up. Deep shelves: an ornate doll's house; a wooden boy in a top hat; arm-sized dolls of grown women wearing a variety of dresses, smocked, luxuriously trimmed with brocade and fur. I stepped closer, fascinated.

'Pandoras,' Wolf said, answering the question I hadn't vocalized. '*Poupées de mode*. Not sure I pronounced that right. Probably not. French fashion houses would send them out to their best clients. Gave them a taste of what they were buying before they coughed up the full price. Nineteenth-century supermodels, really.'

'Mummy is a model,' Kit announced.

'Cool,' Wolf said, with an unimpressed nod. I tensed, waiting for signs he was threading this fact with her absence, and waited apprehensively for him to ask Mum's name, or if she was famous, as most people did, but Wolf didn't.

Relieved, I stroked a doll's soft locks. 'Feels so real.'

'Human hair,' said Wolf.

'Ew!' My hand leaped away, and he laughed.

Wolf had a good laugh. The crackly sort that seemed to run around inside his chest after the laugh had stopped.

'Here, Kit. Watch.' Wolf flicked the wooden boy's top hat and the whole head snapped back on a hinge with a clapping sound. 'Punters paid to throw a ball, knock off his head. Grisly, eh? This is my fave, though.' Wolf picked up a skeleton, about the size of a tennis racket, white bones, held together by strings, and he made it dance before its limbs flew from each other, dislocating mid-air then re-forming themselves.

'Again!' said Kit.

The skeleton dismembered itself once more.

'One more time,' begged Kit.

'Nineteenth-century Tiller-Clowes marionette. From old travelling shows. A rare example,' Wolf said, catching my eye.

I nodded, trying not to be swept away, like Kit, now poking around the doll's house. Unlike my mother's forlorn toy residence, it was fully furnished. A loo with a chain. A toy train track on the floor. A silver birdcage, a parrot inside, the size of an earwig.

'Careful,' I warned, although there was no need. I'd not seen Kit be so gentle with anything.

From the back of the shop, a clanging, the sound of something dropped, cursing. Wolf's expression changed, and he stepped towards a lacquered collaged screen and shouted, 'Gav? You out back?'

A grunt.

'Uncle,' he mouthed to me, and it sounded a bit like a warning.

'Gav, I've brought back some mates,' he called, as if trying to temper his uncle's reaction to our presence.

'Get on with your bloody work,' Gav Out Back yelled, his voice muffled. 'If you've got any hope of boxing later.'

Wolf rolled his eyes. 'On it.'

The boxing gloves on the table, not part of the stock after all. I'd never met anyone who boxed either.

'Just the local club,' Wolf said, following my sight-line. 'My head gym, really.' Since his biceps bulged under his shirt, like yams from the market, I wasn't sure I believed him.

Although I'd never gone to any sort of gym – sooner die, I'd tell Mum whenever she gently suggested it – boxing, at least, had a purpose, unlike aerobics. Picking up a glove, I was surprised by its heft.

'Here.' Wolf took my hand and slipped it into the glove, turned my arm over and laced the inside by the wrist, slowly, shyly, as if it was my dress, and I could feel my face burning, and a strange tightening sensation between my legs, my body all nerve-endings.

'Now you're a fighter,' he said, and there was something about the way he held my gaze that made the glove feel claustrophobic. Hours had surely passed since we'd left the house. Panicking, I pictured Mum returning, finding it empty.

'Kit, we'd better head back,' I said, flustered, tugging off the glove. Wolf helped, unlacing it. I couldn't meet his eye.

Kit ignored me anyway. Kneeling next to a metal crate on the floor, he pulled out a finger-sized boy peg doll in a sailor suit, with a mop of blond curls, not unlike his own, and examined it in the same way he did a beetle or a pigeon feather, right up close, his nose nearly touching.

'It's a little you, Kit,' said Wolf.

'Little me,' muttered Kit.

'No Tamagotchi. But have it if you want.'

'He's not really into dolls,' I said, when Kit didn't answer. I didn't know then that the little boy who'd leave the shop wouldn't be the same as the one who'd entered it, his neural pathways already fizzing, branching, lighting up a whole new postcode in his brain.

'But keep it under your hat, eh, Kit?' said Wolf, taking no notice of me.

'I'm not wearing a hat,' Kit pointed out.

'Fair point.'

Kit was stuffing the doll into his shorts pocket when a large, overweight man barrelled out from behind the screen, red-faced, bellicose, and armed with a screwdriver.

'This is my uncle Gav.' Wolf tensed. 'Gav, this is Maggie, Kit.'

In the multi-clock ticking silence, Gav inspected us crossly, small green eyes darting like fish in the fleshy bowl of his face. 'What is this? *Les Mis*?' he said, gruffly, ruffling Wolf's hair with such force that his neck snapped back, like the wooden fairground boy's. A moment passed, a rattle of tension. Wolf looked like he wanted to swipe back at Gav.

'I love your shop,' I said, trying to distract Gav from the incriminating sight of the doll in Kit's pocket. Nerves made me sound prissy.

'Love don't pay the rent,' he shot back churlishly. 'Feel free to buy something. Oh, what have we here, then?' His expression immediately softened, and he bent down to stroke Nico. 'You're a little sausage, aren't you?'

'Her name is Nico,' said Kit, proudly.

Gav's gravelly guffaw of laughter – like a lawn-mower starting up – revealed teeth with gold fillings. Upholstered in a brown leather apron, his large belly quivered. 'If I had a pound for every dog called Nico round here.' He straightened, and his eyes narrowed suspiciously. 'Local?'

'Sort of,' I answered, and mentioned our road. Gav wearily rolled his eyes, as if to say, 'Course, the likes of you would live on a street like that and have a dog called Nico.' Pulling out a crumpled packet of tobacco, he started making a roll-up, his fingers moving fast. 'Just had news of an estate sale next month. Private affair,' he said to Wolf, his unnerving tongue licking the edge of the Rizla. 'Way out in the country. Cotswolds. Could be good.'

'Granny lived in the country,' said Kit, who never knew when to zip it. 'In a big old house with owls. But she's in a pot.'

Gav's mouth twitched with a smile. 'A pot, eh?'

'Our grandmother died at Easter. He means an urn. She's waiting to be scattered,' I explained.

'Sorry to hear that.' Something in Gav's expression sharpened. 'This big old house. Need to be cleared by any chance? Or do you need anything valuing?'

Wolf shot me a wincing look.

'I don't know what's going on with it.' Until Mum and my aunt were talking again, it'd just sit there, presumably, unlived in and unsold, with the bats happy in the roof.

Gav dipped his hand into his apron pocket and slid out a business card from a slim red plastic holder. 'If you need any help.' He smiled, all charm.

'Thanks,' I said awkwardly. *Gav Jones, antiques and collectibles.* 'I'll give it to my mum. Come on, Kit.'

'Goodbye, little pudding,' said Gav, stroking Nico's head before eyeing me sternly. 'Don't lose that card, eh? You never know when you might need it.'

Outside, the street was bright and busy. The scent

of Moroccan mint tea. A moped backfiring. And at a pavement café table opposite, a man was smoking, staring right at us. Skinny black suit, sharp, chiselled features under the trilby hat. He held my gaze, casually puffing out smoke rings – O, O, O – and I thought of the person I'd seen from my mother's bedroom window during the night, with his stealth-slink walk and his cigarette, and I held my little brother's hand tighter, and hurried him on.

15

Maggie

London, May 2019

On the sixth step, Maggie's courage falters. Marco opens the charcoal-grey front door wider, as if a view of the elegant interior might be persuasive. But the huge blossom branch in a vase, the Scandi-white floor, and the towering fiddle-leaf fig with its joyful jazz hands do nothing to alleviate her trepidation. Beneath the polish, it is still their old house.

'I . . . I don't think I can do it.' Maggie's feet refuse to move over the coir doormat that might as well be a trap-door, ready to spring open, hurling her down two decades. 'I'm so sorry.'

'No, no, I'm sorry, Maggie. Of course I get it, I do, honey.' Marco eyes her kindly, curiously, a look of concern passing over his face. 'It's a builder's site downstairs anyway. Save yourself. The dust gets everywhere.'

Maggie steeples her hands over her mouth, her breathing fast and shallow. The shock of being at the threshold of this house – she'll *never* be able to set foot inside it: what on earth was she thinking? – shoots through her body in little pulses. Aware of Marco staring, she tries to utter something vaguely normal. 'I can't believe you're living here.'

'Oh, I regularly pinch myself. Of course, no co-incidence. I bought this place because of your mother. I like to think that a bit of her is still here, you see.' Marco smiles sadly. 'Always was my favour-ite house. Good bones.'

Maggie flinches at those last two words. 'So . . .'

'Long story short, after my salon company buy-out, for the first time in my life, I had money, so when this came up on the market, offensively expensive . . .' He sighs. 'But houses are like lovers. We pick them with our hearts not our heads.'

Maggie nods numbly, slowly realizing how hard he must have worked for each snowy slab of stucco. 'Well done on all your success, Marco.'

'Make it happen or die trying, no?' He smiles. 'You've not done too bad yourself, Margaret Foale.'

She starts, taken aback.

'Don't move.' Marco slips inside the house then taps at the living-room window, proudly waggling her first novel in his hand. He reappears. 'I'm your number-one fan.'

'Oh, Marco. I'm . . . stunned. Honestly, so touched.

Thank you.' Also, confused. Her pen name – and resistance to social media – was meant to hide the link with Maggie Parker, the part of her life she's tried to leave behind. 'But – but how did you know it was me?'

'Oh, hairdressers know everything,' he says breezily, locking the door. 'I have to say, you do a good line in hot heroes in breeches, Ms Foale.'

Her face blazes. Wolf, each one.

'So, what's the next book about?'

'I don't want to jinx it.' Maggie ducks the question, deadline panic balling in her belly. She's been unable to write a word since Wolf's call.

'Fair enough. Come on, caffeine.'

The café has glossy green-tiled walls, jungly houseplants, its air steamy with coffee machines and chat. Not a million miles away from Maggie's memories of Clem's Café. The waitress greets Marco warmly. At a nearby table, two stylish women blow him kisses. A pregnant actor Maggie vaguely recognizes walks to the door, her progress tracked in the café's bistro mirror, presumably the point of it. She also waves cheerfully at Marco, who seems to know everyone. A reminder of how fast any news will travel here. How small London can be. Maggie's relieved when they're finally seated and less conspicuous.

'So, Kit. I can't imagine him taller than . . .' Marco holds up his hand, a few feet off the ground.

'Six foot one. Otherwise breathtakingly himself.'

Marco's eyes crinkle with a smile. 'So, he's well?'

'He is.' For now. Her stomach starts to churn again.

'Am I happy to hear that,' Marco says, with obvious relief.

Maggie's cappuccino arrives, with a cantucci biscuit on the side that shatters as she bites it.

Marco watches her with a thoughtful smile, his chin resting on his hand. 'You know, Maggie, I see more of Dee Dee in you now.'

'Even while I'm making a total mess of this biscuit?' She swipes the crumbs off her front. 'But thank you, I'll take it.'

Maggie had inherited her father's strong features but in the last few years, laser-surgery-liberated from glasses, edging towards her mother's final age, more maternal genes have emerged. Maggie likes to think she and Dee Dee would have grown more alike as they got older, like two roads drawing together in the distance.

'So,' Marco says, after a beat. 'Are *you* well?' She catches his silver-quick glance at her bare ring finger. 'Settled?'

'I – I'm great, thanks,' Maggie lies badly, unable to bear going near the category-five mess of her marriage, how unknowable she and Tom had remained to one another.

Now the wreckage is no longer acridly smoking, she's started to wonder if she said yes to Tom when he proposed – publicly, at a party, watched by colleagues – because she couldn't bring herself to say no. Apart from having an audience that night, she and Tom had been dating for almost two years. He got on with Kit (non-negotiable as far as any partner was concerned). And she loved him. Even if it was a quiet sort of love, so quiet she sometimes couldn't hear it, and doubted her own judgement because, as Tom often pointed out, she'd had too much loss too young. So, split or marry? Twist or hold? She made the call and got it wrong. As Kit says, she's not the first to do so. And won't be the last.

Tom will keep fading, Maggie knows that. Unlike Wolf, who has been maddeningly impossible to shunt from her thoughts. It's powerful stuff, craving for something unfinished and untested, a fantasy fed on absence, what-ifs, and a wildfire relationship that, despite its brief and disastrous duration, still damned every one that followed to monochrome.

She shakes away these thoughts. 'I live in Paris now.'

'Paris!' Marco slaps a palm to his chest. 'Oh, Paris is everything.'

Maggie swallows hard. Paris – her fresh start, her writing life – feels further away than ever. 'In my aunt's Saint-Germain apartment. She moved back to England a while ago. Took over the Old Rectory, where she and Mum grew up.' She registers the momentary freeze in Marco's features. 'You remember Cora?'

'Vividly,' Marco says, with an unexpected catch in his voice. A message beeps on his phone. 'And that gorgeous old pile in the country. Excuse me one sec.' He rapidly thumbs a reply, looking irritated. 'Project manager for my basement works. Never stops. Currently shaving years off my life expectancy.'

Maggie sits upright, her breath held. Seize this moment, she tells herself. 'Do you really need a basement, Marco?' She doesn't mean for it to shoot out quite so forcefully.

'Need?' Marco looks surprised at having to justify it. 'Probably not. But I do desire a little cinema and a gym.' He sits back on his chair, eyeing her with bemusement. 'So I can watch movies while battling against my ever-expanding waistline.'

She leans towards him insistently. 'But, Marco, you mustn't.'

Marco stirs his coffee, the teaspoon chinking. He raises an eyebrow. 'Mustn't?'

'Sorry, I just mean, houses, they can collapse. Sink holes, these massive sink holes, open up. I've seen it on the news.' Maggie knows she's overdoing it. But she can't stop. Her heart is racing. 'And the clay soil in west London – I mean, I really, really wouldn't.'

'Don't worry, Maggie. Best people. Bankrupting me like you wouldn't believe.'

'How long have they been digging?' She sounds demented.

'Oh, they started three weeks ago. Dear God, it's noisy. Like they're boring a new tube line. But I'm assured this is the worst bit.'

Maggie's heart leaps to her throat. Three weeks is further on than she – or Wolf – realized. She should tell him, but she's got no bloody number. Her foamy coffee slops out of her cup and, with an unsteady hand, like an old lady, she jerkily clinks it to the saucer. 'Have they dug up the patio yet?' she asks, when she can trust her voice.

'Not completely. And not too far out. I want to keep as much of it as possible, given it's hardly Downton's rambling acres out there.' He sips his coffee. 'Resumes on Monday.'

'Monday,' Maggie repeats, under her breath, struggling to compose herself. The noise of the café grows louder, the lights brighter. Everything too much.

'Hey. Nothing stays the same,' he says gently, mistaking her alarm for something else. 'It can't, Maggie. But I am keeping the old rose. Dee Dee loved it. *And* we'll be planting a peony in the sunny corner, a blowsy pale pink one with flowers resembling a 1950s swimming cap, just as your mother adored.'

'Thank you,' mutters Maggie. It strikes her that if Marco's builders find something next week, dragging a decent man into her nightmare, this could be the last time he'll freely talk to her. And Marco is readying to leave, slipping his phone into his pocket, a tenner under the saucer. 'Do you have a couple more minutes? To chat about my mother?'

It must be her intensity that makes Marco's eyes flare black. He nods guardedly.

'It's just that, well, I'm not sure I knew Mum as a woman, rather than as a mum to a teenage girl. There's a gap, Marco. If I knew her now, at my age, I'd know her in a different way, right? We'd be having different sorts of conversations. But . . . I've been robbed of that knowledge. Those conversations. You see?'

Judging from Marco's frown, he doesn't. 'Your mother was a beautiful human being,' he says, after a pause. 'Inside and out.'

'But Mum was more than that. She was . . . three-dimensional.' Maggie's throat constricts. 'Marco, as her close friend, you had her ear . . .'

He clasps his hands together on the table, his big thumbs circuiting each other, the ruby eyes on his gold snake ring glinting.

'Back then it felt like something else was going on. Some sort of inner conflict that I didn't know about,' she says, articulating what she's always held – at a distance – as a possibility.

'Your mother was grieving for your father.' Marco spells out the obvious.

Maggie doesn't want the obvious. She wants what's stitched beneath it. 'But –'

'I can't add anything more,' Marco says quickly, perhaps too quickly. 'Only that she loved you and Kit with all her heart.' He stands up with a gracious but more distant smile. 'I'm afraid I do have to shoot. But it's been a joy, an absolute joy, seeing you.'

'Are you still in contact with Suki and Clemence?' asks Maggie, as they walk, slightly awkwardly, to the exit. She catches sight of herself in the bistro mirror. Even her hair looks frenzied.

'Indeed. They're not in Notting Hill any more, but they aren't far away.'

'Do you think they'd want to see me?' Maggie asks tentatively. 'I'm around all . . .' She remembers Cora's meeting. 'Actually, not Monday – I'm dog-sitting at the Old Rectory for Cora, but I could come –'

'I tell you what, give me your number,' Marco interrupts and he prods it into his phone.

After a brief hug, he turns to walk away, and she calls after him, 'Marco?'

'Yes, Maggie?' he says, with a wary sweetness.

'I know this sounds ridiculous. But I need to ask.' Maggie takes a breath. 'Did Mum die with secrets? Things she'd have told me in time maybe but never got the chance?'

Marco is silent for a moment. 'Okay,' he says reluctantly, with a heavy sigh. 'Here's the thing, Maggie. In my experience, wherever there are beautiful women, there are secrets. But if these women confide in their hairdresser – and who else can one trust in this big bad world of ours? – it's always on the understanding that they will be the very last person to give those secrets away.'

16

Kit

London, May 2019

Disaster. It's too late to pretend to be someone else. Any fantasies about who Roy Smith is – the suave antiques buyer, a cool ex-dealer friend of Wolf – unravels on the Piccadilly pavement and wraps around Kit's ankles like piano wire.

'Kit! At last.' Roy smiles and stabs out a hand to shake. The backdraught from a passing bus lifts his wispy grey hair, revealing his scalp.

'Hey. Good to meet you.' Roy's skin is cool and loose, his tendons stringy, but he has a surprisingly strong grip. Difficult to age – sixties? Maybe older. Worn-in hard. Not what Kit was expecting. That leather jacket. Those teeth. Stick legs but a protruding beer belly. No wonder there's no photo with his profile. Kit sternly reminds himself he's sold to millionaires in frayed jeans and holey hoodies. And he'd always rather sell to someone who truly loves a piece, even if they can't pay top dollar. 'How did you find my shop, Roy?'

'What took me so *long* to find your shop, I've been asking myself. Anyway, there I was, back in January, googling antiques, as you do, and – bing, the algorithms finally work. Up you pop. Kit Parker. Your name rang a bell. Thought, That's Fate! Here's my man. He'll sort me out. Bring a bit of soul into my new apartment. Fancy west London man-pad, you know.'

'I can certainly help you there.' Roy's Instagram post likes started in January: the alignment of dates reassures Kit. After the rain, the sun starts to blaze. Umbrellas shaken, snapped shut, are replaced by sunglasses, a new mood, the city summer-light on its toes again. 'What are you looking for?'

'I tell you what, let's grab a pint, talk shop. Lovely little boozer two minutes around the corner, seventeenth century.'

For some reason, Kit hesitates, his instincts whispering, *Leave*. But his instincts aren't always right: he's chalked up enough misadventures to prove it.

'There's a shorthand if you've been in the business, isn't there?' Roy says gently, picking up on Kit's wavering. 'Man, I miss it.'

Kit's guard inches down. He's comfortable with antiques people, grand or otherwise, whether he likes them on a personal level or not. The only place Kit's ever fitted in. 'Where did you . . .'

'Oh, I sold this and that to expats in Spain, then

ran a little wine bar instead. Easier life, frankly. But it doesn't leave you.'

That might explain why Roy is hard to categorize. Kit doesn't know the scene in Spain. 'So, you move back and forth?'

'Nope. Returned last year. Brexit. Health scare. I'll spare you the details. Anyway, back with our glorious NHS. Twenty years away, it feels good to be home.' He rubs his hands together, dry skin making a brushing sound. 'Come on, let's get a drink. My plantar fasciitis starts up if I stand too long.' He raises an eyebrow and smiles wryly. 'Don't make me buy off someone else, mate.'

So much of dealing is a dance, a poker game, a battle between heart and head and wallet. An item only ever worth what someone will pay for it. Even taking a potential lead to Wolf out of the equation, he could do with making a good sale. 'Just the one.'

Tucked down a narrow alleyway, the pub is painted soot black, its threshold stone smoothed and hollowed by centuries of feet. Inside, it's serene after the bustle of Piccadilly. Middle-aged women in office clothes talk intently in one corner, a couple of smart-suited Mayfair lone male drinkers in the other. The dim alley light fuzzes through leaded windows.

Not a beer man, Kit asks for a half-pint, lets Roy order, and observes him sidelong. Bellied against the bar. Fingers wheeling the cardboard beer mat. The bladed cheekbones beneath the haggard skin.

'Cheers.' Roy raises his glass, sits down on a bar stool. His gaze is quick, shrewd, and pats down Kit like a pickpocket's hands. He wipes froth off his upper lip.

Kit sips his beer, a moody London draught with a mineral tang. It's like sipping the Thames. They discuss the items that Roy's interested in.

A few minutes later, Roy has already downed his pint and is raising a finger, calling over the barmaid, and ordering two whisky shots. He shoves one towards Kit with the tip of a long fingernail.

Kit smiles, shakes his head. He hasn't finished his first drink. 'A bit early in the day for me.'

'I don't believe you,' Roy says, and Kit feels a bit too seen. 'Go on, chase it.'

The whisky scours Kit's throat but oils the inevitable question. 'So, you mentioned in your message that you knew Wolf?'

Roy's nostrils inflate slightly. Something tightens in the air between them. 'Yeah, yeah. Everyone knew everyone back then.' He seems to choose his words carefully. 'I'd been into that funny little antiques shop on Golborne Road a few times.'

Gav Out Back's shop shimmers in Kit's mind. The

fairground mirror that warped the shop's interior yet somehow reflected it exactly as it was. 'Wolf's uncle's shop. Gav Jones?'

Something in Roy's face closes. 'Yep.'

Kit goes straight in: 'Any idea where either of them is now?'

'Rather hoping you'd be giving me a lead on that, mate.' Roy unsticks the cardboard beer mat from his glass. 'Wolf owes people I know serious money.'

Kit starts. Wolf shirking on a debt doesn't tally with the Wolf he's mythologized. But people are rarely all good or all bad, he reasons. Like his eighteenth-century clock, which is wrong but it's right twice a day. 'I don't remember Wolf like that.'

'Well, you wouldn't, would you? He could be charm itself, I hear.'

Through the thickening whisky haze, Kit feels a wave of irritation.

'You had a good life, then?' Roy muses, circling a knobbly finger over the rim of his glass. 'All in all.'

'What? Me?' He shifts away his arm, instinctively wanting more distance. The guy is kind of intense. 'Big question! But so far, yeah. Er, why?'

'Oh, one gets nostalgic at my age. When the bones start to ache, you know. I often wonder what happened to everyone.'

Kit studies Roy more carefully, unsettled, something not stacking. 'But why would you wonder about me? How did you even remember my name? I was a kid.'

Stretching out the pause, Roy clinks down his empty whisky glass and raises a finger to order another before turning to Kit, an excitable light in his eyes. 'Knew your mother, didn't I?'

17

Maggie

Notting Hill, May 1998

'Is Dee Dee in?' The man in the trilby who seemed to be everywhere – our street at night, watching us from a pavement café table as we came out of Gav's shop – was now on our top step, standing so close to the door when I opened it that I flinched. One of his hands rested on the door frame and he leaned into it casually, but also like he could use it to propel himself into the house. I guess you don't notice things like personal space until they're breached.

Saturday, six thirty p.m., and another motherless midnight was gathering, our third. I was already dreading the slowest hour between midnight and one, the time at which Mum would normally have come home if she'd gone out. Kit and I had recently returned from searching for her – 'A dog walk,' I'd told him, smiling too hard – trailing from Clem's Café to the beauty salon to the little shops of Westbourne Grove in the stubborn hope she might be sipping a coffee or having her nails done.

'No, sorry, Mum's not in.' I held the door firmly, wanting to slam it shut.

His gaze searched over my shoulder, as if he didn't believe me. The *Captain Pugwash* theme tune blared from the next room. 'Could you say her old mate Cooper called?'

I nodded, although I didn't remember Mum mentioning a Cooper. He made me uneasy. The way he was standing so close. I imagined closing the door, and this scraggy, whip-slim man just standing there, ready for when I opened it again. Finally, he tipped his hat and left.

I was still watching him lope away, a guitar on a multi-coloured strap across his back, as Wolf approached on the same pavement. Cooper didn't step out of his way, instead seemed to shoulder him as he passed. Wolf whipped around and called, 'What's your problem, mate?' Cooper kept going.

'Hey.' As Wolf sprang up the steps to our house, the noises of the street faded and all I could hear was my wildly whacking heart. Standing near him set off some sort of embarrassing chemical reaction. I desperately hoped he couldn't see it.

'Missed my boxing session. Gav got me working.' A corona of evening sunlight fizzed in his dark hair.

And suddenly I wished I'd brushed my own. 'Fancy going to the pub instead?'

'Pub?' I blinked, surprised to be asked out anywhere, my thoughts still scattered. 'I . . . I can't leave Kit. And the dog doesn't like being left alone.'

'Your mum's not back, then?' asked Wolf. Kit's 'two sleeps' indiscretion clearly not forgotten.

I shook my head, trying to appear like it was no big deal. I'm not sure I pulled it off.

'Come on, let's get you out, Maggie.' If Wolf minded an eccentric six-year-old and a flatulent Frenchie joining us, he didn't show it.

The sky was starting to turn the colour of cocktails, those Bellinis Mum loved. Portobello Road buzzed with the high-jinks mania it caught after a day's sunshine and people walked with a slight bounce, as if the pavement was sprung like a dance floor. Reggae blasted out of a bar, mixed with the violinist busker's tune, the laughter and chat, the words jumping and diving so fast over the heads of the crowd that I couldn't catch them. Used to the silent glide of suburban Surrey streets, I'd often felt intimidated by this gutsy jostle. But not that evening. Walking next to Wolf. I shot him a smile, my gnawing fear about Mum coin-flipping into a confusing elation.

The pub crouched on the street corner, like a

grizzled English bulldog, soaking up the last of the sun. 'Not very glamorous,' Wolf apologized, misjudging my expectations: I'd have happily sat on a littered kerb and drunk a Snapple from the corner shop.

We stepped into a choke of cigarette smoke, a blast of Pulp's 'Common People', and over a man's leg encased in a white plaster cast, scrawled with graffiti, protruding from under a table. The skinny silver-grey lurcher guarding it eyed dumpy Nico with haughty disdain.

I tried to act cool, like going to a London pub was something I did all the time. My experience of pubs had mostly involved sipping lemonade in waspy country gardens with Dad, who had loved them, never happier than nursing a Sunday pint in the sunshine. Mum had never been a pub person. In the evenings, she preferred restaurants, or a stiff white VIP invite, preferably attached to a persuasive goodie bag.

The pub was busy, limbering up for the evening. Again, I looked around for my mother, knowing the chances were slim. No Mum. Instead, quite a lot of Cooper lookalikes, one apparently asleep, cradling a guitar, an unlit cigarette in his mouth, which made me wonder if I'd been actually spotting Cooper everywhere or variations on a theme. In one corner, a group of elderly men, drinking beer, were playing dominos. At the back of the pub, an animated redhead, wearing a sausage-tight gold lamé dress, was holding court, her small audience roaring with laughter.

Wolf nodded at a quieter table near the window, close to an old bloke in a tatty three-piece suit and a spotty cravat, playing cards on his own. Then he glanced at the crowded bar. 'What can I get you?'

Since my experience with alcohol ran the gamut of a few sips of my mother's Bollinger (awful) to a disastrous experiment with a Thunderbird cider mix, I decided to play safe. 'A Coke, please,' I said, refusing to order Diet Coke on a feminist principle that I'd forgotten.

Kit registered the same request by shooting up his hand, still clutching Little Me, the peg boy from Gav's shop he now treasured. 'And a . . . a . . .' he rifled through his mental larder of contraband luxuries '. . . a knickerbocker glory!'

'They won't do that,' Wolf said, trying not to laugh. He never laughed at Kit or talked down to him. 'But they totally should. I'll see what else they've got. Leave it with me.'

Self-consciously marooned at the table, I pulled Nico onto my knee and locked my eyes on Wolf at the bar, not wanting to lose sight of him. Occasionally, he'd look over his shoulder at me, and I felt a hooking, tautening sensation in my lower belly.

'You, young fellow!' the guy in the cravat on the

next table called, gesturing at the cards. His voice was so posh it was almost unintelligible.

Before I could stop him, Kit ran up to see what the game was about. The man pointed for him to sit on a stool and started pontificating on the principles of Clock Patience. Kit listened, fidgeting, desperate to get his hands on the cards.

Wolf returned, a bouquet of drinks at the end of his fingers, bags of crisps under his chin, and my heart flooded. Evening sunlight slipped behind his irises, revealing hidden flecks of aqua. He sat down, his knee just touching mine under the table and we watched Kit, who was already turning over cards with a flourish, as if born to do it. My Coke was sweet and cold, the best I'd tasted even though they were all meant to be the same.

Wolf tipped his beer bottle, held it against his mouth. 'Going to call the fuzz, then?'

'I'm sorry?'

'The police. About your mum.'

'Oh. No.' I didn't say that that afternoon I'd picked up the phone, stuck my finger in the 9, and started dialling, almost to see if I'd dare do it. On the third 9, I put down the receiver. 'Not yet. I mean, I hope I don't have to.'

I explained why I'd resisted so far: my fear of social workers taking Kit and getting Mum into trouble. I didn't mention the press, not wanting to sound show-offy, and I was unsure that he'd keep it secret if he knew Mum was famous. 'I want to give her a chance to come home first. Like, it could easily be work. Or a . . .' I stopped at the word 'lover', hating the word, and the idea, its treachery to Dad. 'She wouldn't want me to make a fuss and call the police.'

'Okay,' he said thoughtfully.

'And if she stays away for longer . . .' finally, I was going there '. . . I turn eighteen in ten days. I'm pretty sure they won't be able to take Kit away then. I mean, I could be his legal guardian. They can't just take him.'

Wolf didn't look entirely convinced.

'But Mum will be back before then, obviously. She'd never not be here for my birthday.'

Wolf turned his beer bottle slowly in his hands, studying me, like he was trying to see under the surface. It felt like a long time since anyone had done that. 'So, how are you finding it, playing mum?'

I thought of the messy house, the pizza slices and bowls of cereal eaten at odd times. Nico sleeping in Kit's bed. The startlingly rapid disintegration of his daily routine. 'More useless big sister making it up as she goes along.'

'Tsk.' Wolf shook his head. 'Never call yourself useless, Maggie.' He tapped his temple. 'Get the mind-set right. Think like a boxer.'

'A *boxer*?' I laughed, spluttering. 'Do they even think?'

'The fight is in the mind.'

My gaze dropped to his hands, his knuckles, their pleasing squareness. I couldn't imagine them hurting anyone.

'Keeping focus when you're right up against it and you're losing, and you just want to give up and slide to the floor, a pulped mess.' He shot me a sidelong glance. 'You know that feeling?'

'Maybe.' I did.

'That's when you have to dig deep. Believe you can win. Especially if you're losing.' Wolf paused, then added more gently, 'You have to believe that you matter, Maggie.'

I coughed so he wouldn't notice my eyes watering. He ripped open a bag of salt-and-vinegar with his teeth, and we shared it, our fingers brushing under the greasy wrapper.

'I always thought families like yours were perfect,' Wolf said simply, not like someone else would have said it.

'We were once.' I ran my fingers down my Coke glass, drew a smiley in the condensation. 'Then my dad died.'

The moment I'd said this, I knew I wasn't being entirely honest with myself or him. This was the version that was easiest to explain. And I didn't want to say out loud that Kit's arrival in our family had brought turbulence, a change in my parents – they'd barely rowed before – and in my mother, a palpable frustration, a loss of confidence. It was better to stick to the big plot points. And that was my dad.

'I'm sorry, Maggie. It must be so hard to have had it and lost it.'

Clearly Wolf had never had it and I didn't know what to say back.

He tapped his foot under the table, mulling things over. 'Was anything wrong before your mum left?'

'No, not at all.' I answered instinctively, having grown up in a place – and in a family – where dirty laundry was never aired in public. But I found I couldn't meet Wolf's gaze and lie to him again. It felt like lying to myself. So, I took a breath, and as Kit worked his way around the card clock face, I began to reveal what had been happening at home.

Mum's headaches and mood swings, the way her sentences had started trailing off. Her continued, barely explained refusal to speak to my aunt in Paris, even about the Old Rectory, empty since Easter, which needed sorting. Mum's impatience with Kit, worse without Dad as a kindly buffer. Last week, after a battle about bath time, she'd despairingly told me she wasn't the right fit for Kit, unlike Dad, who'd been so great with him. And I was genuinely scared she'd try to exchange him, like a pair of shoes.

But outside the house, Mum held it together, helped by call sheets, her agent, producers and friends. An

Addison Lee cab would pull up at dawn to collect her for the studio, and a couple of hours later there was Mum on the TV, caked in terracotta foundation, smiling like her life depended on it. And I'd think, Well, she's fine.

Wolf said little, just let it all pour out of me. He was one of those people who listened with his whole body, leaning forward, absolute attention. I mentioned the wad of cash I'd found in the drawer, and his eyes widened slightly. The unpaid bills. When I admitted my mother was Dee Dee and sort of famous, he didn't go fame-goofy, or look remotely impressed, just saw us as any other family with stuff going down.

'She isn't a bad mother,' I said, running out of steam, worried about the picture I'd painted, staring at the rubble of ice cubes in my glass. 'I don't want you to think that. She's lovely . . .' My voice wobbled. No way was I about to start crying in front of him. 'Tell me about your mum,' I muttered, closing the discussion of mine.

'Ma?' Wolf frowned at the table, then looked up with his chipped-tooth smile. 'Amazing. Best woman, tough life. Married the wrong man.' He went silent for a bit, then spoke more quietly. 'I was her boy. She'd have done anything for me, and she did. Died when I was fifteen.'

'Sorry, Wolf.' Not that I'd have wished it, but his loss made me feel less alone in mine. Like I'd been shouting, 'Anyone there?' into the empty echoing universe for months, and finally someone had called back.

'So, I went to live with Dad.' Wolf rolled his eyes. 'Hope over experience every time. Yeah, big surprise, he got into trouble.'

Prison. That was what he'd told Kit. And it'd been on my mind since. But it was so far out of my experience – I didn't know anyone who'd gone to prison – that I wasn't sure how to broach it. 'What . . . what did he do?' I asked awkwardly.

'This time? Stolen goods.' Wolf sipped his beer. 'GBH.'

It took me a second or two to work out this meant Grievous Bodily Harm, and I was shocked, then just sad for Wolf.

'I don't know why I'm telling you all this, Maggie. I don't normally advertise it. You have the weirdest effect on me.'

Neither of us said anything for a bit.

'Put you off me, does it?' he asked then, less sure of himself.

'No! You're not your dad.' Wolf wasn't like anyone else.

He eyed me sideways, muttered, 'Thanks, Maggie,' and sounded genuinely grateful. The lager had glossed his mouth, and the light caught on his bottom lip, its slick swell.

'Funny to think we're strangers, isn't it?' Wolf said, eyeing me curiously. 'I mean, it doesn't feel like that.'

'I don't even know your real name,' I said shyly, wanting more of him. 'Is Wolf your . . . your boxing name?'

He laughed. 'No, I wish. It was Mum's nickname for me from when I was a baby. Because of the eyes. It stuck. Better than William, right?'

'You don't look like a William.'

'I don't feel like a William.'

Wolf suited him. Wolf was perfect.

'I win!' At the other table, Kit leaped up, shaking his fists in the air.

'Tick tock!' said the old guy raising his glass. He grinned at me, nodded at Kit. 'The luck of the devil, this fellow.'

'Again,' Kit said, sitting back down, shuffling the cards.

A new crowd burst into the pub, dressed up, glittery, fresh for the night. Mum might be home by now. 'I should get Kit back.'

'Wait.' He touched my bare arm. 'I've got a theory. About your mum.'

I clipped Nico's lead to her collar. Wolf held up his beer bottle to the light to see if there was anything left in it. 'Could she have a whole other secret life going on?'

'I doubt it. She hasn't got enough time to live the

one she's got.' But it made me think. My mother had spent so much of her working life dissembling, with a model's chameleon ease, that the logical end to it might have been stepping out of herself entirely, as if it were her favourite Alaïa dress.

'Not everyone wants to stay in the life they've got stuck in. That's all I'm saying, Maggie.' Wolf drained his beer, not wasting the last drop. 'Don't plan to stay in mine. I've got big plans.' His eyes flashed, a thrill of blue, tinged glass-green by the bottle. That slow questioning smile again. 'What about you?'

18

Maggie

The Old Rectory, May 2019

Until a few days ago, Maggie's life had astonished her. The dream had been happening. Writing full time, earnings modest but covering her rent. Book sales up. Her ill-suited marriage over. Hitting a word count of almost two thousand a day, she'd been well on course to meet her deadline. High on her own talent and hard work, the future felt bright and expansive, a whirl of stars, anything possible. Since Wolf's call, it has shrunk to . . . a black dot. The more she stares at it, the smaller it gets.

Leaning back against the stable half-door, Maggie anxiously watches the fat country sun setting over the meadow. It'll sink twice more before the excavation of Marco's patio garden resumes on Monday, a calculation that brings another spike of fear.

'What's up?' Cora calls from inside the stable.

Maggie turns towards the scent of horse and hay. 'Just wondering if I'll ever be able to write again.' She attempts to make this sound like a joke, but the humour falls flat.

Cora looks up from brushing George's piebald flank. 'Don't be ridiculous, Maggie.'

'And I was musing on what Marco said. About beautiful women and secrets.'

Cora brushes more briskly. 'Sounds to me that this Marco is relishing his confidant status rather too much.' She's been out of sorts since she picked up Maggie from the station earlier in the evening and has little patience for any micro-analysis of the Notting Hill encounter. 'Anyway, most secrets are so banal, they should stay under wraps. Can you imagine the sort of confessionals a showbiz hairdresser like Marco has had to endure over the years? "I lost control and broke into the breadbasket." "I cut my fringe myself." Honestly.'

George pushes his marshmallow-soft nose towards Maggie. She pats him gingerly. 'Even when Dad was alive, I had a feeling Mum held certain cards close to her chest. Things that troubled her. Then he died and that was so . . . so huge it wiped out all those smaller questions.'

'*You* knew your mother, Maggie.' Cora rakes back her grey hair with her hand, depositing straw in it. 'Don't let Marco throw you.'

'But I keep trying to work backwards, to see the start of the fault line –' Maggie stops abruptly, worried she'll say too much.

'What fault line?' Cora's gaze sharpens. 'Is there something you're not telling me?'

'I just mean . . .' She pauses, trying to be careful. 'It's hard to know the precise moment one story stops, and another starts.'

'No idea what you're talking about, Maggie.' Cora turns to her beloved horse. 'Good night, old boy.' After tidying the grooming brushes, bolting the stable door, she starts to stride away, all energy and crackle. Cora doesn't like being kept in the dark.

Grasses whipping her legs, Maggie must half jog to keep up. 'Don't be pissed off.'

'I'm not!' Cora says crossly, walking faster. 'I just don't see the sense in rummaging around in the past like this. You should be writing your book.'

'I'm trying!' She had attempted to squeeze in a writing session when she returned from London, her fingers crouched on the keyboard like house spiders, ready to dart across it. But they refused to type. Instead, she'd stared at the screen wretchedly, grieving the author she'd been in Paris, those same fingers flying, tightening her plot, notch by notch.

'And you can do it, Maggie. If you don't get distracted – and look forward not back.'

Maggie wants to believe this too. But that May in Notting Hill runs through her, like the tiny honeycomb hollows in a bone. She has no idea who she'd be if it hadn't happened.

They walk in silence through the garden towards the silhouette of the house. The evening air is soft, sweet and starting to chill. The early summer greens almost fluorescent in the low light. Bats scratch at the sky.

'Sorry, Maggie. I don't mean to sound harsh,' says Cora, unexpectedly. They stop by a bed of tall, aubergine-dark tulips. 'The truth is, it's still very painful. Dee Dee was your mother, and you have a far bigger claim on her than me, I know that. But she was my sister too,' she adds quietly.

Realizing Cora feels cut out, she slips an arm inside her aunt's. 'We could talk about you two growing up here?' Over the years Maggie has had to collect these old stories herself, picking them up like bruised windfalls, never knowing when the next one will drop. 'But don't feel that you have –'

'Fine. If it'd help get all this out of your system,' Cora says crisply. 'But I'll need a stiff hot chocolate first.'

Night leaps in. The dogs circle the outdoor fire pit, guarding against the shadows in the fields beyond. Embers hop into a violet sky and the column of smoke swings in the wind, like a mad hand around a clock face, requiring endless shifting on the seating logs and sucking Maggie back into other summers, other smoky evenings warmed by fires and mugs of cocoa. Same tin mugs: enamelled white, chipped blue rims. Different dogs, which never live long enough.

'Beauty is a form of currency, Maggie. I realized that very early.' Cora blows on her drink, sending up a quiff of steam. 'Earlier than your mother, who wasn't the least vain by the way. But, like money or power, you notice what you don't have,' she adds, with a laugh.

'Oh, Cora.' Maggie has always thought her aunt one of those vital, interesting women whose beauty reveals itself slowly, and at unexpected angles, while never seeking to please.

'I was a tomboy,' Cora says, reading Maggie's mind. 'Mother hated that. Always sewing Dee Dee smocked, frilly dresses to compensate.'

'Ah, that old sewing-machine.' Maggie pictures the gold-painted maker's name, Singer, down its side. 'Don't you still have it?'

'Can't bring myself to throw it away. Silly, really.'

Holding one knee, Maggie cranes her head back to stare up at the star-freckled country sky. As the Plough looks alarmingly like a digger, she quickly looks down again, her heart beating faster.

'My parents allowed Dee Dee to start modelling aged fifteen, you know?' Cora pulls an old saddle blanket over her shoulders. 'Fifteen! But Mother loved crowing about it. When I voiced my doubts, she said I was envious. Oh, maybe I was.' She stuffs another log onto the fire, shoves it further in with her booted foot. 'Late teens, my parents were tearing their hair out about me – The Problem, the flame-haired terror, corrupting boys in the woods, bringing shame on the poor upstanding Foales! But they should have been worrying about Dee Dee, modelling in Paris and London, surrounded by predators. Honestly, some of the stories from back then, Maggie. Horrendous. I think that's part of the reason she settled young with your father. Security, you know.'

Maggie nods, recognizing truth in this. Her mother had apparently dated all sorts of starry men. But she married Damian Parker, the bloke who'd approached her on Wardour Street and earnestly declared her the most beautiful woman he'd ever seen, and could he please, please, buy her a drink: different times. Because he was cheeky and grounding and normal men rarely asked her out and her flaky fashiony friend had just cancelled, Mum said yes. By the end of that drink – it lasted until dawn – he teased that they'd be married by the new year, she barefoot and pregnant the next. And they were. And she was. Madly in love. Blissfully happy. At least in those early years.

'For the record, I don't think Dee Dee should have let Kit model as a kid either,' Cora remarks, tugging Maggie out of her thoughts.

'So, go back to you as kids.' Maggie flaps away the smoke and the stickier subject of Kit. It's rare to have Cora so frank and free-flowing and sitting still for once, rather than running around, feeding or fixing things.

'Right, yes, okay. Well . . . if Dee Dee was good at something – most things, apart from French and horse riding – I made sure I wasn't.' Cora smiles. 'Silly, really.'

'No, no, I get it.' Maggie never felt competitive with Kit, partly, she supposes, because of the age gap. But she remembers feeling side-lined by the way her dad relished his new son. She'd also resented Kit's draining effect on her mother. She pulls her attention back to Cora. 'But Granny and Grandpa must have still loved you, Cora.'

'In their own way, I suppose.' Cora stretches out her legs. 'So buttoned-up, for a long time I thought they were dead inside, which, of course, they weren't. It was all boiling away under the stiff collars and rows of pearls.'

Maggie smiles. Her memories of her long-dead grandfather feel uncertain, as though she might be recalling photographs rather than life. But her grandmother . . . the light floral scent of her French perfume, the carefully darned woollen cardigans, her upright posture, and fine-boned elderly beauty, yes, she remembers all that. Granny had been slightly aloof but loving, at least to Maggie.

'I rejected their small bourgeois life because I wanted to *feel*, Maggie. Of course, the irony being that the drink and drugs eventually numbed feeling.' The flames flick reflections across Cora's face, catching in her skin's weathered contours like a brass rubbing. 'I never felt their love was unconditional.'

'And Mum?'

'Oh, Dee Dee went along with it.' Cora is silent for a moment, then adds quietly, in a charged voice, 'She went along with everything.'

They sit in silence, listening to the hiss and pop of the logs. The sky has deepened to a dark, strange indigo, the sort of colour that always makes Maggie emotional. Wolf's favourite. The mood switches with the bonfire smoke.

'But she was golden of heart, your mother. Kind. Sweet. So easy to love. Even as a girl, I'd always be in some sort of trouble, drawn to the eye of the storm or whipping one up, and she'd be maternally grooming her doll's-house family.'

At the mention of this, Maggie sits up, alert. 'Cora, is that old story true? Did you *really* toss them into the river?'

'I'm ashamed still, Maggie.' The pause stretches. 'Funny what matters in the end, isn't it?'

Maggie stars her hands and toasts them closer to the fire. 'The little things?'

'*Are* the big things. Because the big things are always seeded in the little things. Oh, hello, Vera!' The little dog scrabbles onto Cora's lap. 'There, there. Cold paws. How on earth would you survive in the wild?'

She gently tucks Vera under the blanket. 'Although the house is trying to rewild itself, Maggie. The ivy's got inside the attic again. Another thing to be dealt with.'

'You love it, really.' Maggie wishes they'd done more of this. Talking. Fires. Honesty. Rather than waiting until now, time running down like sand in an hourglass. She leans over, picks a bit of straw out of Cora's hair.

'Oh, I do. To think that I was once a mayhem-in-the-city person. Couldn't abide it now. Even my sober Paris years seem like another life. I just wish Dee Dee were . . .'

'I know.' Her mother should be with them, sipping cocoa, coughing in the wood smoke.

'And Kit,' says Cora, with a sigh.

'I'll re-hassle him to come to Sunday lunch tomorrow, I promise.'

'He makes so many excuses not to come, Maggie. It hurts my tough old boot of a heart.'

'Kit is caught up with his friends. His business.' Maggie wishes she could somehow bring the two of them closer. 'Typical twenty-something behaviour, really.'

'There is nothing typical about Kit, as you very well know.' Cora reaches over Vera to hurl another log onto the fire, releasing a violent spray of sparks. 'I should just stick to dogs, shouldn't I? They'll forgive anything. So much simpler.'

19

Kit

London, May 2019

His sanctuary invaded, Kit is rapidly sobering up. The streetlamp glow outside the living-room window catches the animated flex in Roy's shaven cheek as he drags a finger along the spines of Kit's vintage-magazine collection: *Vogue*, *Marie-Claire* and *Elle*, and the others in which Dee Dee is immortalized, for ever beautiful, young, folded between the scent samples and 'Hello Boys!' ads.

The not-too-clever third whisky shot and Roy claiming to know Dee Dee did for Kit. Roy back-pedalled slightly: 'Oh, everyone knew of Dee Dee back then. That's all I'm saying. I mean, you couldn't miss her when she moved to Notting Hill. She had proper glamour. Star quality, Kit.' He rubbed his fingers together, suggesting banknotes.

As they'd left the pub off Piccadilly, Roy declared he was walking Bloomsbury way too – off to meet a mate – then outside Kit's front door asked if he could quickly use the toilet. That was thirty-five minutes ago. And it's now pouring, sheets of biblical rain, and Kit is wondering how he might inhospitably force out Roy into it. If rude, he risks losing business. Too nice, and Roy settles in for the evening. Kit's flat has this effect on people. Maggie says he needs a stricter door policy. He's taken in waifs and strays, offered his sofa, sent them off with his last tenner. But Roy isn't that. Roy is something else. Kit is just not sure what. And he feels outmanoeuvred.

'So sweet you've collected all these magazines,' Roy says, over his shoulder. 'Trying to fill the gap Dee Dee left?'

Kit finds this emotional insight disarming and slightly intrusive. He wishes Maggie were curled up on the sofa, deceptively docile, ready to rip the man to shreds should he prove to be a fruitcake. But she's messaged: she's back at the Old Rectory – helping Cora on Monday morning – but please, please, please, could she persuade him to come to the country for Sunday lunch tomorrow? Still in the pub at the time, habit made Kit rattle off an excuse. Now he feels a pang.

'Dee Dee must have earned a fortune over the years.' Roy whistles under his breath.

'Most models earn far less than people think.'

Roy moves to the shelves of antique curiosities and reaches for a little red toy car. 'How much for this?'

'Not for sale.' Kit strains to be polite. *Put it down.* 'But I can source you something similar.' *Put it down.* 'Would you mind putting that car back? Delicate, thanks.'

Roy shunts it back onto the shelf. 'Have to say, you've got a good eye, Kit Parker.'

Wolf's eye, Kit thinks.

'So, I'm going to ping over my wish list in the next few days. Screw it, blow the budget!' Roy glances around the living room, admiringly. 'I want what you've got, Kit. A flat like yours.'

Kit's not sure what to say.

Uninvited, Roy drops to the sofa, his legs stretched out, revealing the skinny lower calf above a thin grey sock, hairless and shiny skin. There's something pitiful about Roy's socks and legs, the vulnerability of them. Something irritating about the way he's spread his arms along the sofa back.

The rain throws itself harder at the windows. Kit doesn't offer a drink but still hasn't the heart to turf Roy into the squall. They chat for a bit about favourite boyhood antiques, the things that first sparked their interest. Roy talks about his grandfather's set of Edwardian tin soldiers, Kit a little Victorian peg doll, with a mop of blond hair, and a blue sailor suit. 'I called it Little Me,' he admits. Heartbroken when he lost it. But it suddenly feels too intimate to discuss, exposing, so he swiftly changes the subject to nineties

Notting Hill, the old shops that are no longer. It stirs a piquant nostalgia in Kit, who mentions he's got a lunch with an interior designer in that neck of the woods on Monday, and maybe he'll swing by Golborne Road afterwards, have a sniff around.

Hearing this, Roy straightens, his expression more alert. 'Good idea.' He picks up a conch shell from the side table, presses it to his large fleshy ear then puts it down again. 'You know what I hear in that shell? The rabble of a market.' He stretches out his hands, wriggling his long fingers, like someone coming to the end of a long stiff journey. 'Have to say, talking to you this evening brings back a bunch of stuff, Kit.'

'Really. Like what?' Curiosity overrides his impatience for Roy to leave.

'Well, something I've never forgotten . . .' Roy leans forward, elbows on his knees, and lowers his voice conspiratorially. 'Look, I'll only tell you, Kit, because you seem like a great guy and I think we have a connection, don't we? I'm not one to badmouth or gossip and I don't like spreading muck. But some things just stick in the old grey matter.' He stops, catches himself. 'No, probably shouldn't say.'

'You have to now.'

'Okay, okay. If you insist.' Roy sits back, taking his time, lacing his hands over his belly. 'One day, oh, late nineties, I went into Gav Jones's shop and there was your Wolf fellow. All pumped up he was, like a fighting dog, wild-eyed, threatening to kill his uncle. Clearly just had a punch-up. And I tell you, Gav, an old bull of a bloke, came off a lot worse.' His face darkens, perturbed. 'To this day I'm not sure what would have happened if I hadn't interrupted them.'

'That's not good.' Unsettled, Kit doesn't want another seed of doubt about Wolf, or any revision to how he remembers him. The unpaid debts Roy mentioned are one thing. Violence another. Kit hates violence. He's a dancer not a fighter.

'You didn't pick up on it?' Roy asks mildly. 'The atmosphere in that shop.'

'I can't really remember.' Kit frowns, trying to squeeze memories out of himself. But they are muddled with Maggie's bedtime stories about Wolf, a magical antiques shop: stories like a toy theatre in his head. Perhaps there was tension whenever Gav appeared. Yes, he does remember that, vaguely. But it's all so shaky, buffering, like a homemade movie. 'Gav was larger than life. Cantankerous?'

'Ha, yes. That's a polite way of putting it. See? You *do* remember, Kit. Everyone underestimates kids. But they're life's best witnesses. If you want the truth, ask a child, I say.'

The whisky repeating on him, Kit feels as if he's just unwittingly collaborated in something. And it sits uneasily since he's been imagining the reunion with Wolf again. The flung-open arms. The affectionate ruffle of the back of his head. The soundtrack: Bill Withers, Al Green and Elvis Costello. Like *Notting Hill* the movie.

'I'm banging on, aren't I?' Roy leaps up, apologizing. He grabs his leather jacket. 'Time to get out of your hair and into that tempest! And thank you. I feel very honoured to have been invited into your home.'

Kit isn't sure why he has goosebumps, as if something very big has flown over him, casting him into a shadow. 'You're welcome. Here, my umbrella. Take it, Roy.'

'You are too kind. Oh, nice brolly. I'll make sure to return it.'

Kit hovers on the landing, watching Roy walk slowly, reluctantly down the narrow communal stairs. As he opens the street door, a strong gust blows in, shuffling the residents' unopened post on the shelf. Roy hesitates as if tempted to inspect it before springing open the black umbrella. Eclipsed, he sinks into the brawling Bloomsbury night.

20

Maggie

The Old Rectory, May 2019

'Where's Dee Dee? Schedule change!' yells a scribble of a woman holding a clipboard. Maggie surfs in and out of sleep. She's a little girl again, an only child, backstage at her first fashion show because the nanny is sick, and it's London Fashion Week and Mummy is walking for a designer friend. Behind the screen that separates the photographers and rows of women in sunglasses from the chaos and sweat of backstage, it's a jungle, hot and humid with clothes steamers, roaring hairdryers and scalding hair tongs. Models prowling and jostling, some naked, all legs and elbows and thongs and cigarettes, as people zip and pin them into dresses, a dozen hands moving at once. Everything running late, on the verge of some undefined world-ending catastrophe.

Maggie is deeply worried by the sight of her mother. The kisser of grazes, the nit-comber of hair and reader of bedtime stories has been threaded into a jellyfish puff of black tulle, her pink mouse-nose nipples visible under the sheer fabric. Her mother's feet – when they share a bath, Maggie buries them in bubble foam and names the toes – are trapped in hard metallic heels, much, much higher than those in the wardrobe that Maggie likes to try on.

There's a line of models, necks like baby giraffes, waiting for their turn on the catwalk. Maggie worries for them too. The mouth of the catwalk is terrifying, ravenous, flashing with light and music so loud it hurts her ears, which she covers with her hands. And now her mother is at the front of that line. A woman is powdering her forehead, someone else frantically adjusting the dress. The music stops. There's a snatch of silence, a tug in the air, like ears popping on a plane. The tense woman with a clipboard nods. Music starts again – *douff!* – and her mother lifts her chin, her face blank, and she's walking away, hip-bones first. Maggie calls, 'Mummy!' But her mother doesn't look back.

Maggie's own shout wakes her up. What the . . . ? She's slicked in sweat, the marmalade light of late morning sliced through tear-wet lashes.

She sits up with a bolt: Monday. She's overslept. She's meant to be dog-sitting for Cora, who must now be at her London breakfast meeting. And Marco's builders will be *digging* again. Oh, God. Her thoughts start to cycle. If she can just get through this week . . .

if they don't find anything by the end of Tuesday, maybe Thursday, perhaps they won't. Marco did say he didn't want to lose too much garden. There's a chance.

In the kitchen, Maggie tries and fails to eat breakfast while reading emails and messages on her phone. Her Paris friend, Halima, suggesting coffee and asking where she is. A publicity request to read a fellow novelist's book proof: she can't read, she can't even think. Her editor checking in about the delivery date in June. Her pulse races. It feels surreal that the publishing schedule can continue while her life falls apart. Unsure what to do, Maggie leans back on the Aga, trying to take shuddery yoga breaths, while the dogs stare, perturbed, knowing something is up.

Maggie feels like a taut, mistuned string instrument. She feels quite mad. And she's not sure she can exist in this state for days or weeks, or however long this torturous basement excavation lasts. She could go back to Paris, but she'll take herself with her. She can stay here, and she's just as inescapable.

'Nothing will be found under the patio,' Maggie repeats to herself, like a mantra. She will not have to confess to Kit. She'll kick that can down the road to another day, a time when he can deal with it. Then her fictional worlds will light again, whirl back into life.

The sound of knocking interrupts Maggie's now

fully oxygenated galloping thoughts. She slugs down her coffee, shuts the dogs into the kitchen and rushes to the door.

She starts, blinks, less from the morning sunlight than the pair of incongruously stylish women standing among the earth-clagged boots and garden tools in the porch. She spots a white not-muddy car in the drive. City people.

A tall elegant Black woman, with an intelligent searching gaze, her hair worn in a natural silver crop. Dark jeans, a crisp white shirt. A smaller woman, very small, despite the platform heels, wearing severe horn-rimmed glasses, a full skirt, and a plaid jacket twisted and nipped at the waist, so it looks almost eighteenth century, a vintage butterfly brooch on its lapel that winks in the sunlight. With no warning Harold, having hidden in the sitting room, barrels forth, his wagging tail at full mast.

'Hi.' Maggie yanks him away, and wonders if the women are twelve-step friends of her aunt – all sorts have visited over the years, addiction being a broad church. She tries to smile, waits for them to speak. 'Cora's not here, I'm afraid,' she says, when they don't.

'Have we changed that much?' That voice. 'No, don't answer that, darlin'!'

It takes a second to register. Time buckles. Maggie gasps. '*Suki? Clemence?*'

The women beam and nod, and no one seems to know what to say or do next. If they should hug.

'But . . . how . . . why . . .' Maggie is astounded.

'Marco,' says Clemence.

'Said you'd be dog-sitting here alone this morning,' says Suki, her gaze shooting quizzically over Maggie's shoulder at the word 'alone', as if checking this was the case. 'He had this address from way back, so I called Clemence, said, "Let's just do it! We've waited long enough!"'

'I hope you don't mind, Maggie,' says Clemence, more hesitantly.

'No, no, of course not. I just wasn't expecting . . .' Maggie's head is still fuzzed, steeped in grinding mechanical machinery. 'I – I can't believe you're here.'

'Your aunt isn't?' Suki asks.

'No,' Maggie says, wondering why her aunt's absence is relevant. 'Would you . . . would you like to come in? The dogs are not nearly as rabid as they sound.'

'Shall we take off our shoes?' asks Clemence, stepping onto the slab of filthy rush mat.

'I wouldn't advise it,' says Maggie. Clemence laughs – funny how you can remember a laugh – and a little of the awkwardness dissipates.

The two women walk into the old house behind Maggie, the smell of log fires, damp dogs, and worn cloth. 'Your aunt has made a cosy home here,' says Suki, sounding surprised.

Maggie wonders how Suki imagined Cora might live. She wants to say Cora has been sober for decades.

'And, my goodness, just look at you, Maggie. So grown-up!' Clemence opens her arms. 'A hug?'

Clemence's hug is warm and blankety and is followed by a harder, brisker one from Suki who, to Maggie's amazement, appears to be welling up. She'd always thought of Suki as fierce. A memory surfaces: Suki sprinting, in her cowboy boots, after a man who'd nicked a jacket from her Portobello Green vintage-clothes stall, marching him back in a headlock, and making him pay double for the jacket in lieu of calling the police.

'You know, darlin', you're forever fixed in my mind sauntering down Portobello Road with little Kit and Will Derry, all golden in the light. Like an album cover.' Suki takes off her glasses, knuckles the tears from her eyes. 'And here you are, a proper woman.'

Maggie rakes over those words again. 'Suki, what did you just say? No, the name. You – you just said, Will . . . ?'

'Derry. Ah, sorry. You probably knew him as Wolf.' Suki runs a small bejewelled hand appreciatively over the velvet back of an old armchair, her beady vintage hunter's gaze starting to roam the room.

Her heart thumping, Maggie stands very still, clasping the surname she never knew. *Derry.* 'How do you know his name?'

'Oh, after we realized you were together, I did a character check, as you do. Asked around a few antiques and market people,' says Suki, shamelessly. 'Anyway, you'll be pleased to know no one had a bad word to say.' She arches one eyebrow. 'The uncle, however . . .'

Maggie nods, dazed, fighting an urge to race back to her laptop and start searching for Wolf.

'Maggie, sure you don't mind us descending on you like this?' Clemence asks, throwing Suki a worried look.

'No, not at all,' she says, trying to collect herself. Her mother's friends are here and she must not waste this opportunity to talk to them.

'You've never dropped from our thoughts. Or Kit. I want you to know that,' Clemence says, mistaking Maggie's overwhelm for coolness. But not entirely misinterpreting it either. Because they could have kept in contact over the years.

'You didn't need to wait this long, Maggie. You could have reached out to us at any time, you know, darlin',' Suki says. As if this makes it all okay. As if this gets them off the hook.

'I haven't heard from any of you since Mum's funeral.' Maggie has to say it.

A moment passes. From the kitchen, the sound of

dogs whining. Through the window, the smell of manure spread in a nearby farm. And it seems impossible that she's in the country with Suki and Clemence, while an hour or so's drive away in Notting Hill, a scoop bucket gouges into fleshy soil, and somewhere, God knows where, Wolf – *Will Derry!* – is carrying his dread alone. And in Bloomsbury Kit is unaware that she knows Wolf's real name. A headache starts to press at her temples.

'Didn't Cora pass on our messages?' Clemence asks eventually, exchanging another loaded look with Suki.

The flagstones seem to shift a little beneath Maggie's feet. 'What?'

'I knew it,' Suki growls, her cheeks flushing.

'We contacted your aunt,' explains Clemence, slowly, precisely, not wanting to be misunderstood. 'Many times. We told her that we were here for you and Kit, whenever you needed us.' Her dark eyes flash. 'Cora said . . .'

'. . . in no uncertain terms . . .' mutters Suki.

'. . . we weren't to get in contact, that you and Kit were too unsettled, and it'd only make things worse,' Clemence explains more softly. 'Honey, we had to respect that. I hope you understand.'

Maggie closes her palms over her nose and mouth, wondering how Cora could have got it so wrong. 'I didn't know,' she breathes.

'What a . . .' mutters Suki, and Clemence puts a quietening hand on Suki's arm.

'I'm sure Cora did what she thought was right, Maggie,' Clemence says, diplomatically, trying to smooth things over and shooting Suki a warning look. 'She had your best interests at heart.'

21

Maggie

Notting Hill, May 1998

On my stomach, in the dark, I held my alarm clock, watching its luminous face, Saturday become Sunday. And in that awful hour between midnight and one I tried to be brave, but ended up crying anyway, then threw the clock across the room in frustration. Later, Kit snuck into my bed, shaking me awake, whispering, 'Maggie, are you dead?' and when I groggily assured him that I wasn't, he said, 'I just wanted to check,' and fell back to sleep while I lay rigid, heart pounding, dread gnawing. As the sun started to rise, red and astonishing, I went into Mum's bedroom, with its discarded shoes waiting for her feet, the lipstick I'd wound up and down in its gold case while chatting, four days before, and I peered out of her window, hoping to spot her approach.

A bold fox, investigating the bins this time. Two women, dressed up, laughing, weaving down the pavement, their arms linked, one of them swinging a pair of high heels in her hand. And I could hear my heart-beat, like footsteps running, and I knew I couldn't keep it up, the hoping, the denial, the hyper-vigilance. I felt like I was standing at a dangerous, busy road, holding Kit's hand, unable to find a gap in the traffic, knowing we had to cross at some point and make a dash for it.

I had to call the police. Otherwise . . . what? We could still be here days later, just me and Kit, working our way through the cash in the envelope.

We could do it. We could survive. I was sure of that now. If I knew Mum was all right, I'd enjoy the freedom.

But I didn't know that. So I crawled into Mum's empty bed and curled up, clutching her pillow, feeling like a small child again.

Later that morning, I woke to Kit shrieking, 'I've lost Little Me!' The hammering of his feet around the house as he searched for the doll.

Sleepily trudging downstairs, I saw the front door open, the mop-haired back of Kit. A reedy male voice said, 'So what's going on, little fella?'

'I lost my boy doll,' Kit was explaining. 'He's called Little Me, and he's got my hair and a blue . . .'

I sprang to the door and pulled Kit inside. My skin crept.

Cooper again, lazily exhaling a scarf of cigarette smoke, casually leaning back on one of the columns, as if it was his house, not ours.

Refusing to be intimidated, I lifted my chin. 'What do you want?'

An amused smile, like he saw right through this. 'Is your ma back yet?'

'No.'

'Can you pass on a message? Tell her that I'm waiting to hear from her, will you? That I'm not going anywhere . . .'

I closed the door, sharpish, and leaned back against it, heart slamming, thoughts wheeling. Was he an ex-boyfriend? A lover? A fan? I dismissed the first two possibilities. Not her type. A fan was a possibility – Mum attracted a lot of unwanted male attention – but they tended to be overawed and sweet.

Hearing the snuffling sounds of Kit crying, I rushed into the living room, took him into my arms and promised we'd find Little Me.

But the place was a tip: I hadn't realized how much housekeeping Mum had done. How quickly the house – and any order – unpicked itself. Lego and dog toys everywhere. Nico's dinner bowl upturned, the smelly kibble scattered, which she kept returning to graze on. Human food in curious places. A flotilla of socks down the hall. Dirty washing-up stacked by the sink. A filmy puddle of Nico pee in the corner of the kitchen because I'd twice forgotten to take her out for her toilet, so she'd created her own. While I wasn't looking, or noticing, Kit had doodled felt-tip butterflies up the cobalt hall walls. Outside, the patio chairs were on their sides, now Kit's antiques shop, a builder's plank along the top displaying an artful arrangement of wares, a broken potato peeler, shells and foreign coins. The heap of soil next to That Godawful Hole had sprouted a dandelion. And, like Mum, Little Me seemed to be nowhere.

We were still in the garden, Nico giving herself a morning walk by whizzing around the perimeter dementedly, Kit blowing the dandelion clock, making wishes, when over the street-side wall, a shout: 'Kit? Maggie?'

A rocketing in my chest.

'Catch!' Something flew over the wall. Kit picked it up, a smile lighting up his face. A cardboard box containing three cinnamon buns.

'Have they survived?' he shouted. I told Wolf to come to the front door and ran upstairs to open it cautiously, in case Cooper was still lurking.

In the front porch, Kit hugged Wolf as if he was a long-lost relative. Wanting to talk to him alone, I suggested Kit eat his bun in front of the TV – Mum never let him eat in front of the TV – and he scampered off, thrilled by this small transgression, Nico in optimistic pursuit. Wolf and I sat on the front step in the crisp morning sunshine, and I told him about Cooper, the guy who'd shouldered him in the street. And that I was going to give Mum until midday, then call the police. I knew it was time.

'Sounds like a plan.' Wolf shot me a quizzical sidelong look. 'Until then, should I hang around? I mean, only if you'd like that, Maggie.'

'Stay,' I said quickly, hating the thought of him leaving.

We went inside, down the stairs to the lower ground. His footsteps were springy, almost soundless. Wolf moved differently from other people. Like he had a secret strength that buoyed him.

The patio doors were open. Warm air riffling. Wolf stepped into the garden, 'This is nice,' then saw That Godawful Hole and laughed. 'What the hell is *that*?'

I explained. Wolf rolled his eyes. Yeah, he knew Bucket the builder, everyone knew Bucket. Jack of all trades, master of none. They'd had him in to fix up the back of the shop, never again. Lovely guy but a stoner. Wolf promised he'd have a word.

'Would you?' I pictured my mother's smile on seeing the hole fixed – and knowing I'd made a local friend too, even if Wolf wasn't the sort she'd likely have picked. 'That would be amazing. Now all I need to do is tidy up the house.' I coloured, embarrassed by our squalor. 'Kitchen's a bit of a bombsite. Sorry.'

'Shocking, Maggie,' Wolf teased, grabbing Mum's leopard-print apron off a hook, and tying it around his waist.

'What are you *doing*?' I started to laugh, despite everything. I hadn't laughed since I'd seen Wolf last. Nothing was funny. But I had all this heightened energy, this nervous fizz, and it shot out when I was around him.

Wolf swiped a tea towel and pressed it into my hands. 'Drying duty.'

It felt unbearably intimate. The hot wet plate moving from Wolf's hand to mine, the small pause in the handover, our fingers almost touching. The washing-up bubble on the underside of his jaw. His shirt sleeves pushed up on his forearms, his boxer's hands rooting in the soapy water. The way our eyes kept catching, sparking, setting off little explosions under my skin.

'You don't need to do this, Wolf.' My father had rarely, if ever, washed up. 'Thanks, though.'

'My mum trained me well.' Almost done, he took a clutch of wooden spoons off the rack. 'Where do these go?'

I pointed to the utensil pot to the left of me. I could have taken those spoons. Or moved out of the way. And he didn't need to stretch over like that, so close I caught my breath, the lemony smell on his hands. Neither of us moved. We just stood there, faces inches apart, time slowing, and everything felt astonishing and inevitable, like watching the sun coming up.

'Maggie Parker,' he said quietly, rolling my name on his tongue, as if he couldn't leave it alone. 'What is this . . . this thing between us?'

I swallowed, scared to acknowledge it, not wanting to lose my new and only London friend.

'You feel it too?' he whispered.

'I think so.' I knew so.

Wolf tucked a hank of my steam-frizzing hair behind my ear. 'I've been wanting to do that for a while.'

'My hair is out of control.'

'I love your hair.'

I didn't know what to say, unsure if he was joking.

He smiled, tilted his head curiously, searching my face. 'So, what do we do about it? The thing.'

Worst timing. Mum was missing. Kit my priority. At midday, I'd call the police, unleashing God knew what. And, in my limited experience, boyfriends were precarious, likely to go cold if you liked them too much or dump you if a prettier girl came along, or if you forgot to act less smart than you were. 'We could pretend it's not happening?'

His mouth twitched with another smile. 'We could try that, Maggie Parker.'

My breath quickened. The pull wasn't just between our bodies, although it was that, really that. I'd known Wolf only a few days, but those days were not like normal ones: they had different dimensions, every minute condensed into a second, every hour a day. He felt so familiar, like I'd known him all along. Or maybe it was just that I felt more myself with Wolf than I had with anyone else.

'Or I could kiss you?' Wolf said, after a pause. When I didn't say no, he took off my glasses with care, as though they were parts of a precious clock he was to dismantle and put back together. 'If you want me to?'

I nodded. His warm, washing-up-damp hand slid into my hair, the nape of my neck. And the distance between our mouths started to shrink, and he was smiling, and I was smiling, and it was slow, and soft, the most natural thing in the world, yet a thrilling shock. I'd never been kissed like that before. He drew his body closer, pressing me up against the kitchen unit, his arms slipping down to my waist.

That was when Kit ran in.

Kit had a sugar-crystal moustache, and a plan. We'd show Wolf the roof terrace, high above the streets, and spot faces in the clouds.

'Roof terrace' was stretching it. The doorway was a window from the top-floor landing, the roof just a roof, a low ridge of crumbling brick delineating the drop. Mum always said it was too dodgy up there for a livewire like Kit. But that morning, I gauged the risks, the rules: *in loco parentis*. Also, I had Wolf, who wouldn't let anything bad happen. He was sitting against the chimney stack, legs extended, jeans, lumberjack shirt, the exact weft and weave and button dangling on its thread I'd remember decades later. Kit played with Wolf's boots, annoyingly tying the laces then unknotting them, unable to leave him alone. Wolf's crackly Walkman played Radiohead's 'No Surprises'. Below us, Notting Hill became a paper pop-up: the articulated spines of the crescents, the communal gardens, the snaking of Portobello Road, birds – swifts, I think – swooping and lunging around the church tower. A messed-up sort of heaven, I thought, surprising myself, forgetting to hate the place.

I lay back on the brick dust and broken slates, hands under my head, stared up, and the blue sky pressed down softly. Half closing my eyes, I was sure I could feel the slow turn of the earth. Wolf's fingertips circled my bare anklebone, and we talked about everything and nothing, and he asked questions and listened as if he was going to be tested on the answers. And I found myself telling Wolf stuff I'd never told anyone, embarrassing little things – *Anne of Green Gables*, the name of my first hamster – and big things: the randomness of how a stupid drink after work was enough to place Dad on a stretch of road, a slip junction, in the path of a lorry, and how I felt lost in London, so anonymous, so cocksure of itself, look, look at *the size* of it. I couldn't see its edges, I'd never belong.

Wolf insisted London wasn't big, not really, more like lots of little villages, and within those, hamlets, each with its own local history. Everyone who lived there, wherever they started off, they all belonged. 'Just by being here, you belong, Maggie.' He pointed across the rooftops, farmland once, then pig farms, and west, the old potteries, and those streets, formerly slums, and over there, a hub of the Black British civil-rights movement . . . A settlement here for a thousand years. London contains all the Londons that went before, Wolf said. Like nesting dolls.

Kit sat, riveted, pulling Wolf's words right into him. I got my first glimpse of the enormous expanse of what I didn't know, and had never been taught, or even considered, as a sheltered white girl from the Home Counties.

'How do you know all this stuff, Wolf?' I wanted to kiss him again.

He shrugged. 'I just pick up interesting things, I guess.'

'Like us.' Kit grinned.

'Exactly.' Wolf ruffled my brother's hair. I liked the way Wolf liked my brother.

Church bells rang out. I counted eleven chimes beneath my breath, and the mood tipped. The dreaminess gone. Mum had one hour left to get home. Wolf shot me a sympathetic look.

Come on, Mum, I pleaded silently, sitting up, wrapping

my arms around my legs, staring at a clump of leggy yellow wildflowers growing, improbably, in the mossy gunk of the open drainpipe and wondering if Kit and I would even be together tomorrow, or if social services would have removed him. We had to be like tough little flowers, I vowed, glancing at Kit, who was lying on his back, entertaining himself by making a viewing hole with his fingers and inspecting the clouds.

On the street, every woman could have been Mum approaching but wasn't. At the Portobello end, I wondered if I'd seen Cooper again, his loping gait, like his body had too many joints. Nothing was clear, everything a confusing melange of desire for Wolf and anxiety about my mother, calling the police and not calling them, each state heightening that of the others.

I remembered my grandmother telling me about the Blitz, how it'd made strangers fall in love, seize the day, and I thought about lovers clinging to one another as bombs rained down, the sky flashing with fire. We were just on a roof, under benign blue skies. But something felt the same.

A snore. Kit was now asleep, Wolf's leg his pillow. 'Get you. The Kit whisperer.'

'He's the boy in *Where The Wild Things Are*, isn't he? My favourite book as a kid.' He reached over and stroked the side of my face lightly with the back of his hand. 'You all right?'

I nodded. But I'd got The Fear again. What if I'd

already seen Mum for the last time? Heard her last words? The last words Dad and I had exchanged were something along the lines of who'd finished the milk and had anyone fed the dog? I loved my mother's voice. The way small laughs would bubble through it, like a Soda Stream. I missed it.

'Would you keep an eye on Kit for a minute?' I blinked back tears.

'Long as you like, Maggie.'

I sought Mum out in her bedroom. The sheets that smelt of her moisturizer. I buried my face, muffling my sobs for a few minutes before patting my eyes to counter the ugly puffiness, then went downstairs for a glass of water. And that's when I saw it. The wink of the answer-machine. Not daring to hope, I pressed the button.

Beep

'Dee Dee, it's Cora again. You never return my calls! We have to discuss the Old Rectory. The house can't just sit there empty, running up bills. Please, Dee Dee.'

Beep

'Dee Dee Parker, your agent here!' Lucinda's throaty, actressy voice. 'Remember me? Where the hell were you on Friday? I've grovelled, sent cupcakes, said you were having your appendix out. But you can't have the damn thing out twice. So, I've just had confirmation you're rebooked for Friday next week. Be there. I love you, darling. Just bloody be there, okay?'

Beep

'Maggie, it's me, Mum.' My gasp was hard, and I held it inside, straining to hear the faint and muffled words. 'I'm sorry . . .' Crackle. A pause. 'Sorry . . . I'll be back soon . . .' The message ended abruptly, the tape cut. I played it again, again, listening to my mother's voice, searching in vain for clues as to her whereabouts before sinking to the floor with relief, pressing my head against the warm dirty skin of my knees. She was okay. We were okay. And I had Wolf now. Everything was going to be fine.

22

Kit

London, May 2019

Kit wants to scrawl out the shop's name, its smart black lettering, and write, *Gav Out Back's Shop Actually*. Instead he lights a cigarette, the first after his lunch meeting, and stands on Golborne Road, inhaling too hard. Shielding his eyes from the sun's glare with his hand, he peers into the shop's polished plate-glass windows. The premises have been divided. No sign of the chaotic, endless dimly lit space of the nineties.

Kit hasn't been able to stop thinking about Gav's shop. The edgy atmosphere Roy mentioned the other evening. Roy witnessing Wolf threatening to kill his uncle. He doesn't want to believe that. But he has only half-glimpsed recollections, overexposed in some places, out of focus in others. Why has no one designed a way of retrieving and processing childhood memories, like a 3D printer, so you can hold one lightly between your fingers, and inspect it? Also, just as frustrating, there's now nothing left of the original spirit of Gav's shop. No antiques or vintage sold in this store, just expensive cabinetry and designer lamps, a thirtysomething couple self-consciously browsing on a Monday morning.

It's the way of things in London, Kit knows. Landlords hike rents. Fashions change. Independents boom, then fade, like dying stars. Shoppers and tourists don't realize they have to spend money in the antiques shops and at the market stalls – rather than just Instagram the hell out of them – or they will pack up and close, in this case taking an irretrievable part of Kit's childhood with them.

Kit is finishing his cigarette, about to walk away, when he hears it. Quiet, at first, then louder, and louder still, an internal orchestra of ticking clocks. *Tick tock*. The memory cogs starting to turn. Superimposed on his own reflection, he can almost see Wolf picking up a chair, swinging it upside down weightlessly on his fingertips, revealing its dovetail joints. Yes, that happened. Kit *is* certain of that. And he is grateful.

During Kit's lost years, late teens to mid-twenties – art school dropout, club boy, barman, barista, carpenter's assistant, Chelsea's Lots Road auctions gofer, sometimes all at once – he was the wrong shape for the world. Couldn't see a place within it, certainly not in the beige centre, where normal, functional people lived. Instead, he was drawn to the edges, the twilight corners. Apart from his sister, what and who was there to lose? Why not push things? He'd rock his life like a small boat until it capsized, and he'd sink in a blaze of glory!

He almost managed it.

One afternoon, Maggie took him aside, firmly, furiously, and said that you entered the world through one door, and never knew when you'd be ushered out of the other. He needed to sort out his shit. Did he want to wind up dead? Or in rehab, like Cora? He'd hated Maggie for saying that. He'd also needed to hear it. So he ditched the coke, the ket, cleaned up his act and his flat. Gave himself permission to follow his broken-boy heart, a different path, a new life – Wolf's life, the quiet joy of a dovetail joint. And here he is.

Funny how things turn out.

A jolt of clarity. Kit's life has been one long attempt to re-experience the thrill of Gav Out Back's shop, hasn't it? The discovery of random, quirky treasures that felt like missing pieces of himself. Maggie by his side.

Kit wishes his big sister were here now. Why hasn't she called him back? He's already sent one message. He leaves a voice note. 'Little brother here. Now outside Gav's place on the Golborne Road. You should be here with me. Has your muse returned? And when do you go back to Paris? Call!'

Kit is puzzled. Maggie always takes his calls. He's been known to phone in the early hours, drunk as a lord, demanding she listen to a fucking genius *song* – 'Not another fucking genius song, Kit,' she'll say, with a yawn – or simply because he cannot sleep and his brain is hopping, and the Bloomsbury dawn is ravishing, the colour of wild hyacinths. Whatever his nonsense, however weary Maggie's reply, she'll always take the next call too, even if it's at four a.m.

Kit may be a mess, 'magnificently damaged', an ex used to say, which, confusingly, turned him on, but he's still the best version of himself given everything. He puts this down to Maggie. If he were prime minister, he'd hoist a monumental bronze on the fourth plinth in Trafalgar Square, a normal girl in jeans, a hoodie and terrible glasses, and call it *Big Sister*. It's the unsung who save you.

To Kit's relief, his mobile vibrates with a message: *Suki & Clemence, Mum's old friends, rocked up at the Old Rectory! Will call bk soon & explain all x*

This narks a bit. Fine for Maggie to revisit the fenced-off late nineties, yet his own attempts to search for Wolf over the years have always hit a Maggie-like wall. Also, she won't 'explain all', will she? Never does.

Like that time in Notting Hill, just before they left. Kit recalls clinging to Maggie as she carried him up the stairs, the urgency of her footsteps, the butterflies he'd drawn on the bright blue wall whipping past, and this feeling in his belly, a new knowledge, like darkness had entered the house. Also that pure monsters-under-the-bed terror, particular to childhood when you're too little to control anything. Which is why he wonders if he's repressed other memories. Whenever he's asked Maggie about that day, something in her wide, open face closes, and she'll say softly, 'I'm so sorry but I can't really remember, Kit.' He's pretty sure she can. One day, it'll all come out. Maybe he'll wish it hadn't.

Another text from Maggie buzzes in: *Btw, Suki says Wolf's name is WILL DERRY!!! What?* His heart leaps. Kit is feverishly typing the name into Google when there's a jerky tap on his shoulder.

'Morning.'

In the daylight Roy looks rougher, skin chapped, flaking red and grey.

'You following me?' Kit jokes, with an edge.

'You mentioned you were heading up here after your lunch,' Roy says, breezy. 'I was down the road and thought I might find you outside this shop. More importantly, your brolly, sir.' He hands it over.

Alarm twangs. Pity softens it. Just a lonely boomer blurring the dealer–client boundaries, mistaking it for friendship. This has happened before. But Kit hasn't time for it. Not today. He wants to get home to a decent Wi-Fi connection so he can start hunting for Will Derry. 'Thanks. Don't forget to send over that wish list, and I'll get sourcing for you.'

Roy nods but doesn't move.

'See that store?' Kit points at an established dealer

further down the street. 'They don't have any bad stock. Have a browse in there. Expensive. But great for inspiration. I can probably source you similar, a little cheaper,' he adds cheekily.

But Roy is not looking at the store. Roy is staring as if the only stock he's interested in is Kit himself. 'I owe you an apology.'

'Sorry?' Kit says distractedly. *Will Derry*. This could change everything. No wonder previous searches for William Jones, based on a guess that Wolf shares his uncle's surname, have come to nothing.

'I feel like I overstepped the mark. At your flat.'

Kit hesitates. Feels like an insect stuck on fly-paper, Roy the glue. 'What do you mean?'

'You looked so upset when I told you about Wolf and Gav. The threats. The fights, all that,' Roy says, contrite. 'I didn't mean to dredge back bad memories for you, Kit. I was just being honest. Too honest. I should have kept the old trap shut. I'm sorry, mate.'

'We remember Wolf differently,' Kit says tightly, but he feels disoriented again. He'd been an imaginative kid, easily impressed. Perhaps he projected remarkable qualities onto someone unremarkable. And why wouldn't he have done? His dad had died. Mason, his adored manny, had left. His mother had vanished. If Wolf hadn't appeared, he'd have had to invent him.

'I get it.' Roy shakes his head sympathetically. 'Probably easier to tell yourself that, Kit.'

Irritated now, Kit starts to walk past a deli, the smell of good coffee. A Great Dane waiting outside for its owner. A woman on a green bicycle, her basket overfilled with flowers.

Roy scurries up beside him. If something in his face has soured, he quickly corrects it. 'There are things I need to talk to you about.'

'Can it wait?'

'You think I'm just some old loser, right?'

A fine spray of spittle arches through the air and Kit feels it land on his cheek. The guy is just too intense. He needs to cut him off. 'Look, Roy, I don't hang out with my customers. I apologize if I've led you to believe otherwise.' Roy's face falls, hangdog, and Kit feels bad, but he must be cruel to be kind. 'I want to do business, of course I do, but I met up in person because I thought you might lead me to Wolf. He was a bit of a boyhood hero of mine. Long story.'

'Oh, man. That must be hard. Looking back and suddenly realizing things weren't quite as they seemed.'

'That's not what I meant.' Or was it? This guy is messing with his head.

'Listen, Kit. I don't want to talk here.' Roy lowers his voice. There's an odd, hankering look in his eyes. 'But there's something else I need to talk to you about. I know you're busy now. But how about later? Your neck of the woods if it's easier. What do you say? It won't take long.'

'Not tonight.' Never. Just walk, Kit tells himself. He raises his hand in farewell.

'Ah. Almost forgot. I've brought you something.' Roy dips into his jacket pocket.

Kit might have to block him.

'After the other night, you mentioning that peg doll of yours, the one you lost as a lad? Well, it got me thinking, and I've since had a bit of a rummage through all my old London boxes – no good at throwing things away – and . . . happy days. I found it.'

Kit starts to wonder if the man is slightly unhinged.

'Must have caught my eye on a Portobello market knick-knack stall.' Roy folds Kit's fingers over the tiny object.

It's the weight Kit recognizes. The wooden hardness of the body under the crumple of the blue cloth. The sprout of hair. A bit of Kit lost and found. A peg of time in his unfurling palm. 'Little Me,' he stutters, his guard lowering, letting Roy slip right back in.

23

Maggie

Notting Hill, May 1998

Another midnight, rolling us into Monday. A few hours later, the discovery of another hole. Not in the garden, thankfully. A small hole, the size of a fifty-pence piece, in Kit's shorts pocket that hinted at Little Me's fate and reignited Kit's quest to find him. Crawling under his bed, Kit didn't care that he was late for school. I tried to yank him out by his feet, but he escaped, leaving me holding empty socks. His shirt lay crumpled and grubby in my lap. I hadn't done any washing. But it was Monday, the first since Mum had left, and Kit had to go to school.

'I want to stay at home with you and Nico,' Kit said tearfully, wriggling out from under the bed. 'I love it with you, Maggie.'

'Oh, Kit.' I realized I'd been obsessing about Mum, listening to her answer-machine message a dozen times. I'd replayed my aunt's message too. She had a surprisingly steady voice, no detectable drunken slurring. The agent's message was more worrying: not like Mum to slip up at work. And above all this, always circling, swooping and darting, like the swifts, Wolf's kiss.

'Please, please, please, Maggie. Can I stay at home?' Kit begged.

I pulled him to my knee, rested my chin on his head, and tried to think clearly. Even if I instructed Kit not to mention Mum's absence at school, he'd likely blurt it anyway. Mum would be called. But she wouldn't pick up. And this would corroborate Kit's version of events, and the school would have a duty of care to report things. When I thought about each domino toppling, the risk didn't seem worth it. Especially as we'd heard from Mum, who would surely be home soon. Did it matter if a six-year-old missed a couple more days of school? We could do some reading practice.

'I'm phoning to report my son's continued absence . . . Kit injured his leg skateboarding last week' – if you're going to lie, stick as close to the truth as possible – 'and it's still not better, and he also appears to be coming down with a rash-like thing,' I added, keeping our options open.

'Excuse me,' Miss Swinton said. 'One moment.'

I caught my breath, preparing defences, anxiously listening to the clicking of Swinton's computer mouse, the phlegmatic clearings of her throat. 'Mrs Parker,

just checking our system and it seems there are out-
standing payments. May I check that you received last
month's letter – one of four, I believe – requesting
settlement of the fees?' I squirmed on my mother's
behalf. *Four letters.*

'The cheque is in the post.' A line I'd heard on TV,
and all I had.

Possibly Miss Swinton had heard this line before
too. 'Excellent, Mrs Parker,' she said coolly. 'As
explained, we cannot accept Kit back into school until
last term's fees are paid.' She paused. 'We do have a
hardship fund if . . . No? In that case, we look forward
to receiving the cheque, Mrs Parker,' she said, her tone
terser. 'And to seeing Kit back at school soon.'

Kit and I celebrated freedom with a quick Dr Seuss
lesson – Kit, a surprisingly engaged pupil, mastering
new words quickly – then pick 'n' mix from Wool-
worths on Portobello Road, and a trip to Gav Out
Back's. Wolf's eyes lit up when he saw us. Gav grunted
irritably, not even saying hello. Wolf put his hand on
my waist, and whispered in my ear that Gav was like
that with his customers too. Not to take it personally.
We were fine to hang out.

Gav had A Presence. Occasionally a customer
would dare venture inside, navigating the assault
course of stock, and Gav would either ignore them or
eye them suspiciously over the top of a bit of furniture, as if to catch them shoplifting a chest of drawers.

Wolf would try to compensate, and the few sales of that day were his. I listened, secretly enthralled, as Wolf bantered on the phone with upmarket international dealers, enthusing about latest finds. It was hard to imagine anything from that dingy shop working its way into a fancy house in New York, but they did, Wolf said. If you know, you know.

Since Gav often didn't open the shop before midday or keep regular hours, he wasn't one to notice or care about things like Kit bunking off school. And he wasn't a fan of mainstream education. When Kit asked how to be 'an antiques-shop man', Gav snorted. 'You learn on the hoof. Take Wolf here. Left school at sixteen. Now look at him.'

'Not sure you're selling it, Gav,' said Wolf, drily.

I bit down on a laugh. Gav picked up on this, whipped around, glaring at me. 'What's funny?'

'Nothing.' A blush seared my cheeks.

'You're no better than my nephew, you know that?' he growled.

I was so mortified to be spoken to like that I had no idea what to say. My face burned hotter.

'Your issues, Gav. Not hers. Give it a rest,' said Wolf, in a low, warning voice.

He and Gav eyeballed each other and the atmosphere in the shop bristled. With no warning, Gav clapped the back of Wolf's head with some force, making me catch my breath, then roughly pulled Wolf towards him, half hug, half headlock. 'How much do I love this boy? Like the son I never had, Maggie. Go, take a break, you lazy reprobates. Grab me a sandwich. And some Rizla while you're at it.'

I wanted to run out of that shop, but Wolf sauntered, as if what had just happened was nothing out of the ordinary.

Further down Portobello Road, less ordinary still, a snowstorm. In a cordoned-off part of the street, the movie crew was back with their walkie-talkies, light reflectors, booms, cameras and a billowing blizzard of foamy white, a flurry of fake winter.

Kit took my hand, then Wolf's, and announced that he had 'a Christmassy feeling'. We swung him, laughing, his feet lifting. At one point Wolf leaned over Kit's head and kissed my mouth. I didn't care about the famous actors in the blacked-out vans, who they might be. I was with Wolf, and no Hollywood star could match him.

A few steps along, I spotted the unmistakable tiny leopard-print-clad figure of Suki, chatting to Clemence, wearing a floaty white dress. Unprepared, I felt cornered, not knowing what to say about Mum, wondering what it must look like, me, Kit and Wolf holding hands like cut-out paper dolls. They waved. We had to keep walking.

'Hello, you lot.' Clemence pointed down the street excitedly. 'Seen the snow, Kit?'

Kit dutifully broke the news, 'It's not real,' then lowered himself to the kerb, rummaging in his paper bag for sweets, Nico beside him. He held up a cola-bottle gummy and offered it to Clemence who smiled and said, 'A boy needs to keep his colas.' Kit folded it into his mouth. A pigeon pecked around his feet.

'How are you doing, Maggie?' Side-eyeing Wolf, Suki pushed her flume of hair out of her heavily made-up eyes, a gold charm bracelet jangling on her wrist, catching the sun.

Since Londoners seemed to ask how you were but not expect an answer, I let the question ride. 'This is Wolf,' I said instead, realizing they were waiting for an introduction.

Wolf nodded hello. Self-possessed, he wasn't the sort to ingratiate just because someone was older.

'Golborne?' Suki's eyes narrowed, trying to place him. 'Antiques? I think I recognize you.'

'I work in my uncle's shop. Gav Jones.' He spoke his irascible uncle's name with an air of proud defiance.

'Ah, yes,' Suki said, and shot a look at Clemence that I couldn't read.

'Gav has old toys that go . . .' Kit moved his arms stiffly like a puppet. 'Skeletons on strings!'

Clemence whispered to me, 'Beautiful soul.'

'Such a handsome boy,' said Suki, ruffling his hair.

Kit said nothing: adults came out with this sort of stuff all the time, just as they loved to pat his shoulders, ping his ringlets. Beauty – like Kit's, like my mother's – turned you into public property. I wasn't envious of that. 'Mum's still not back,' Kit said, the sweet a lump in his cheek.

I winced. He'd done it again.

'Oh.' Clemence looked disappointed. 'I was planning to pop over. What time is she home, Maggie?'

Wolf caught my eye. I opened my mouth to speak, and the pause stretched and stretched, until finally, nervously, ramblingly, I told them, starting with Mum's unslept-in bed last Friday morning, the fretting and hoping and the missed telephone call. My voice got quieter. Explaining the situation out loud was like stepping back and seeing how big this thing really was. You can't tell the size if you're right up close. When I finished there was a snap of stunned silence.

'Shit,' muttered Suki, glancing at Clemence, something unspoken writing itself in the space between them, like a speech bubble in a cartoon strip. 'But Dee Dee left a message on the answer-machine, you say?'

'Yeah.' Feelings rushed up my throat, and I had to stare at Suki's gold charm bracelet to control them: a heart, a pair of ballet shoes, a wishbone. I wanted that bracelet more than anything. That shiny wishbone good-luck charm.

'And she sounded all right? Are you sure, Maggie?' asked Clemence, her eyes too searching and kind to look at directly.

'It was a bit of a rubbish line. But she sounded, you know, totally okay.' For some reason, having dropped the bombshell, I felt it was my job to reassure them.

'You've been managing all alone?' Clemence put a hand on my shoulder.

'I'm honestly fine,' I said, feeling uncomfortable.

'Well, your mother obviously trusts you to hold the fort, Maggie,' said Suki, stealing another worried look at Wolf, as if his presence bothered her. 'I guess you're eighteen.'

'Almost,' I said, glancing back at the fake snowstorm, wishing Mum would appear out of it, snow in her hair.

Suki's brow knitted: I'd never seen her look so serious. 'Have you told anyone else? Apart from your friend here.'

I shook my head, realizing that they'd relay all this to Marco, and Marco would also know that I'd lied to him when he'd come over. Maybe it didn't matter. I had a funny feeling we were all saying what we thought the other should hear, concealing the boundaries of one another's ignorance.

'I was going to call the police. Then Mum left the message.' I was now worried I'd got it all terribly wrong.

'So, you didn't?' Suki persisted. 'You didn't call the police, Maggie?'

'No,' I admitted huskily, with a wave of shame. The risk hadn't been mine to take. 'I'm sorry.'

Wolf put his hand on my back. The rollercoaster of the last few days – the highs, and lows, the lack of proper sleep – hit hard, and I just wanted to lie in a cool dark room curled next to him.

'You did the right thing, Maggie,' said Suki, unexpectedly. This was even harder to take somehow. And I knew if I exhaled, I'd cry.

'But at some point, Maggie might have to call the police,' ventured Wolf. 'If her mum's not back. Or doesn't call again.'

'You really don't need to get involved,' Suki said, with a tight smile.

'I think that's up to Maggie,' Wolf flashed, so confidently, dangerously himself and more than a match for Suki.

'Obviously, if Dee Dee *hadn't* left a message, it'd be different,' said Clemence, quickly. 'But it's complicated, Wolf.' She nodded down at Kit.

I hadn't blown that bit out of proportion at least.

'Especially if you're in the public eye, I'm afraid,' Clemence added.

'The tabloids will get tipped off.' Suki shook her head. 'It'll be a feeding frenzy. Ugly, ugly.'

Wolf shot me a sceptical look, and I realized I'd underplayed my mother's fame to him because I didn't want it to be the most interesting thing about me.

'But where is she, Suki?' I whispered, so that Kit wouldn't hear.

'We'll do some discreet digging, won't we, Clem? Leave it with us. Don't worry, Maggie, your mother is going to be just fine,' she said firmly, as if she needed to believe this as much as I did. 'There will be an explanation.'

'In the meantime, my son's room is empty during uni term time,' Clemence offered, more concerned. 'Only a single bed, but I've got a sleeping bag and camp mat for the floor . . .'

'Honestly, we can manage.' I didn't want to swap one set of problems for another either. Or lose our freedom.

'Well, come to the café anytime for a feed. If I'm not there, I've got a load of catering gigs on this week, get them to call me.' Clemence reached into her bag. 'You must need money.'

'Oh, no, thanks. I found money in the house.' I couldn't bring myself to mention the size of the wad.

A moment passed. The sun seemed to grow hotter, the shadows longer. I sensed that Suki and Clemence were silently calibrating the situation, working out what to do. Like they might know something that explained Mum's behaviour, only they weren't telling me.

'Don't worry. I'll look after them.' Wolf took my hand brazenly, for all to see. Pleasure and embarrassment shot to my fingertips. Kit leaped up and grabbed Wolf's other hand, tugging on it, bored now, wanting to leave.

'We'd better go,' I said apologetically.

'Look after yourselves. Stay in contact. And . . . Maggie?' Suki's hand on my arm, that wishbone glinting. 'For now, hold off on the police, okay?'

'Well, that was a bit weird,' muttered Wolf, as we turned a corner onto a quieter street, the dappled shade of cherry trees, Nico pulling on the lead, keen to get home.

'Normal for my mother's friends,' I said, newly unsettled, unsure exactly why. 'But yeah.'

24

Maggie

The Old Rectory, May 2019

'I'm more of a cat person.' Suki warily eyes the dogs, the obedient minority in their baskets, the others patrolling and sniffing under the kitchen table. The light – greened by the ivy trailing over the window – lends the kitchen a pondlike tinge, the air a watery quiver.

Suki and Clemence have drunk tea from Cora's chipped, not entirely clean mugs, chatted about Kit, Clemence's location-shoot catering business and barrister son, Maggie's books, Paris, Suki's online vintage venture, a subsequent marriage and divorce. And all Maggie can really focus on is that it's Monday, almost midday, and what a bisection of west London might look like: the sediment stratified, the broken capillaries of old pipes, broken pottery, bricks, maybe a scrap of robust cloth. She thinks of other things too, pale in the sump of clay soil, and wonders if, by the end of the week, surely by next, she'll either be able to breathe easily and return to Paris, or if she'll barely be able to breathe at all.

She almost wants it to be next week already, whatever the outcome. Some certainty. Since she impulsively messaged Kit Wolf's real name, he'll be searching the internet. God, she wants him to succeed this time. She's itching to search for Wolf herself.

'Well, this fellow looks like he might breakfast on your neighbour's sheep,' says Suki, as Teabag, a gentle Staffie cross with an unfortunate brutish underbite, squats at her feet.

'Cora would be the first to shoot him if he did,' says Maggie, distractedly, reeling herself back.

'Cora has a *gun*?' Clemence is unsure if Maggie is joking, which she isn't. Both women glance at the door, half expecting the infamous sister to drunkenly stagger in, shotgun crooked over a tattooed shoulder.

'Well, we should go.' Suki picks up her handbag. 'Sorry to miss the chatelaine,' she fibs, 'but I have two utterly spoiled, hypersensitive cats, who protest-pee indoors if I stay away too long.'

Clemence leaps up. 'No, no. I insist on a quick garden tour first.'

Outside, the sky is ripped with copper, the sun fizzing at the clouds' edges. Herded by the sheepdog, they walk past the sundial on the lawn, the glossy dark tulips, the oniony whiff of alliums, the summer's first flush of roses, and the small orchard where Nico is buried. Suki's full skirt swishes as she moves, her heels crunching on the hoggin path. Clemence's white trainers are quieter and pause frequently. 'Does Cora really manage this vast garden on her own?'

'Even if she could afford help, which she can't, Cora would do it by herself.' Maggie is proud of the way her aunt has transformed the Old Rectory's gardens from the manicured sterility of her grandparents' years to this luxuriant mix, the wildflower meadow beyond. 'A labour of love. The harder the better. She likes that. The honesty of it.'

'Well, she's got her work cut out for her, then.' Suki's words catch on something.

'It's beautiful,' says Clemence, quickly. 'I love it.'

'Didn't know you were into gardens, Clemence,' says Maggie, wondering what Suki meant.

'Oh, hit with the menopause.'

'Not me, Maggie,' mutters Suki. 'I've just become . . . slightly cross.'

'*Slightly?*' teases Clemence.

Suki's laugh is crunchy and infectious.

At the back of the garden, they sit on the meadow bench, watching the wind shivering across the grasses, a red kite hovering, suspended. The hum of bees, the scent of the stables, carried on the wind. Maggie relaxes a bit, un-scrambles. 'I've been wondering about Mum a lot recently.'

'Marco told us,' Clemence says.

'There's some secret, isn't there?' Maggie lays it out straight.

Clemence and Suki stare straight ahead. They've been expecting this, Maggie's sure. She can sense their conspiratorial alliance.

Clemence takes a breath. 'We like to put terrible events down to one particular thing.' She folds back her white shirt cuffs then laces her hands neatly over one knee. 'It's easier to say it was *that*. But when you've lived a whole lot of life, you realize it rarely is one thing.' She pauses. 'And it wasn't one thing that led Dee Dee to walk out that day.'

Maggie's pulse quickens. She wonders what Clemence is trying to say.

'It was so different back then, Maggie.' Suki digs into her bag for sun cream and pats it onto her nose. 'We didn't discuss mental health or take it particularly seriously. It just wasn't A Thing. Instead, we met up with our girlfriends, sank a bottle of wine or two, or sat up all night talking to them on the phone. Maxed out our credit cards on things we couldn't afford and didn't need. I know, terrible! We took pride in just soldiering on.'

Maggie's pretty sure this isn't quite what Clemence was getting at. Or Marco. The wispy white clouds race across the sky, faster and faster.

'Your father's money was bundled into these complicated offshore schemes. Dee Dee couldn't get hold of it because he'd died without a will. Over a certain amount, I believe, money is held in trust for dependants, rather than the spouse. Something like that. Anyway, it wasn't easy.' Suki sighs. 'Incidentally, my heels are sinking into the grass, like tent pegs. Can we head back to the house? Also, my cats.'

Clemence stands, offering a hand to Suki. 'Your dad's death was a terrible shock, Maggie. I think she hid from you how much of a shock.'

They start walking again, Maggie ruminating.

'She wouldn't allow herself to grieve. It ambushed her later,' adds Clemence. 'Then your grandmother's stroke. One thing after another.'

'But when I look back, if I'm being honest with myself, I think Mum started to change earlier, Clemence. In Surrey. When Dad was still alive, and everything was . . . idyllic. Only it wasn't quite, was it?' Maggie says, articulating it properly for the first time, the moth-wing flutter of her childhood stilling for a moment.

Neither Suki nor Clemence reply. The roof of the house rises beyond the trees. Then the alliums, the tulips, the sundial, and finally the patio's stone setts, where they're greeted by Harold, carrying Cora's gnarled sheepskin slipper in his mouth.

'You told me Mum would be fine, Suki.' Maggie doesn't mean to sound so accusatory. 'That day, on

Portobello Road. The moviemakers' fake snowstorm. You remember?'

'God, I remember! The snow scene. *And* that first-love heat billowing off you and Will Derry.' Suki eagerly switches the subject.

'If you could bottle that,' says Clemence, with a low whistle. 'Oh, my goodness.'

So, it *was* real.

'Are you still in touch?' Suki strokes Harold's coat thoughtfully, as if assessing its potential as a stole.

'No.' Maggie tries to sound neutral.

'Oh, shame. Never saw him around again after that summer. Or the iffy uncle –' Suki stops abruptly, registering the slam of car brakes, the dogs sprinting to the side gate, barking excitedly.

'Oh, Cora's back early.' Maggie hopes this is a good sign, and Cora's breakfast meeting went well.

'We have to shoot,' says Suki, with a snap of alarm. 'Come on, Clem, London's calling.'

'And my phone. One sec.' Clemence digs in her capacious handbag, plucks out her mobile. 'Marco!' She smiles at Maggie. 'Can I call you back? I haven't got time to talk about the builders now, we were just about to . . .' Her voice trails off and her smile vanishes. 'Whoa. *What?* What did you just say?'

25

Maggie

Notting Hill, May 1998

'I said, Maggie Parker, you are beautiful.' Wolf tipped onto his side and traced a fingertip over the curve of my breast. 'Skull-blowing beautiful.'

'I'm really not.' Yet I lay in my bed, my milk-pale body exposed, and didn't feel a need to hide it. Seeing that one of my hairs had caught on the stubble of Wolf's chin I picked it off. 'But you can say it again if you like.'

Wolf whispered it in my ear, and we did it in our rumpled nest of sheets, as Kit watched TV downstairs. After days of watchfulness, I forgot myself, lost in his warm, smooth skin, his distinct smell – burned sugar, beeswax polish, fresh sweat – the way he held me in his arms, crushing me, his urgent hand sliding between my legs, my own need to press into it. The gathering and sparking and opening, stronger each time. It had never happened for me like that before – not once with my grateful teenage chess-champion ex-boyfriend in Surrey – and it made me cry. It felt like we'd invented sex. Afterwards we lay, panting, Wolf inside me, my face pressed into his neck, our breath rising and falling, the sheet tugged over us in case Kit burst in. My body felt bone-less, capable of unknown magic. Like I'd slipped back into my skin, having previously been living outside it.

Our second Saturday morning. My mother had been gone for more than a week. Eight midnights. Cooper had done more lingering and smoking, lean-ing against the lamp post opposite, waiting for her too. Aunt Cora had left another message – 'For Christ's sake, I'm still your sister, Dee Dee' – as had Mum's apoplectic agent. But having finally confided in Mum's friends, I felt as if I'd passed on some of my fear, like a baton.

Clemence kept popping over with tasty things from the café – smoky jollof rice, sticky ginger cake – as well as treats for Nico. The previous evening, Marco, looking frazzled and whiffing of salons, had arrived with news that Mum had left a short message on his home phone. A little cryptic. Unfortunately, he'd been doing a private client's hair at Claridge's when she'd called. But, no matter, one of Clemence's café customers might have a lead. And did I have a number for Mason, our old manny?

Mason. At his name, I'd blanched: last month, I'd

walked into the kitchen and he and my mother had leaped apart. But I tried to put aside any judgement – Mum being found the most important thing. Only Mason's number wasn't on the cork board: at some point, Mum had unpinned him. Marco told me not to worry, he'd track him down. And he'd find Mum too. Just give him a couple of days. The weekend. I'd nodded, relieved. If anyone could find Mum . . . I imagined London shrunk to a miniature model, Marco striding over it, bending down and plucking out Mum with his fingers, a benevolent King Kong.

Shamefully, that Saturday afternoon, sunshine falling across my bare shoulders, my forehead pressed into Wolf's armpit, a part of me no longer wanted Mum to return. Not at that moment anyway. I wanted to know she was safe, of course – more than anything – and when she'd get back, and I could have done with a break from Kit, but mostly I craved Wolf. His smell. His runaway laugh. The way his conversation could leap from the Spice Girls to head-spinning stories of fake antiques, the counterfeits so good they fooled the most experienced dealers, to the expansion rate of the universe. How he'd study me as I read my book: 'I'm reading it with you by just watching your eyebrows, Maggie.' Other times, he'd ask me to read aloud, and I'd lie with my head on his bare belly, holding a novel aloft, and Wolf would listen like he always listened, with absolute attention, his breathing slowing and quickening with the plot. When I finished, he'd say, 'Just one more page,' like Kit.

Wolf had been back to his rented room to get a change of clothes, and spare shirts to keep at mine. For the last two nights, we'd slept wrapped in each other's arms, our legs pretzeled together. I no longer dreaded midnight. In the mornings, Wolf cooked pancakes, teaching Kit how to flip them, Nico eating those that slapped to the floor. He'd had another word with Bucket about fixing That Godawful Hole. Like other locals, we hovered curiously at the security-controlled edges of the film shoot, where the air was always buzzy. We took Kit skating under the Westway: no injuries. When Wolf worked at the shop, Kit and I hung around, Kit munching Jammie Dodgers, charming Gav with his enthusiasm and random questions, while Wolf and I shot secret smiles, and I slotted my knee between his under the trestle table.

Already, I couldn't imagine life without him. An urge to declare my love – what else could it be? – loaded at the end of my tongue. But I didn't dare risk the disaster of those feelings not being requited.

'Better check on Kit,' I said, realizing we'd been a while, swinging my feet to the floor. Wolf kept hold of my hand as I walked backwards until only our fingertips touched. My gaze still fastened to his, eyes like ocean photographed from space, I tugged a jersey strappy dress over my T-shirt, then ran downstairs to check Kit wasn't sticking forks in the toaster.

Happily, he was watching *Tom and Jerry*, cross-legged, his arms draped over a football, Nico snoring in a discarded jumper beside him.

It took me a second to realize that the ball, black and white leather, wasn't one I'd seen before. 'Have Mum's friends dropped round?' Wondering why I hadn't heard the door, I twisted my hair into an elastic, catching the smell of Wolf in it.

'A man knocked on the window,' Kit muttered.

'What man?' The cold feeling was back. I peered out at the street. A mother with a pushchair. A flock of teenagers on BMX bikes. Two elderly women chatting.

'The man said boys should play with footballs. Not little dolls.'

My mind started to turn, slowly, grinding with guilt that I'd been upstairs with Wolf. I glanced back at Kit. 'You didn't let him in?'

Kit held the ball tighter, lest it, too, vanish. Tom and Jerry chased each other across the curve of the TV screen. 'A bit in.'

'What does that mean?'

'One shoe in.'

I could picture this all too well: one intruding shoe, a barrier to closing the door. My heart started beating high in my throat. 'And the man was wearing a hat?'

Kit nodded hesitantly, unsure if he was in trouble. 'Daddy isn't here. Mummy isn't here. Mason isn't here.' Worried, he reeled through the absences in his short, eventful life, counting them off on his fingers. 'But Wolf is upstairs?' he double-checked.

'Wolf is upstairs,' I reassured him. 'And I am here. I'll always be here for you, Kit. For ever and ever. Swear on Nico's life.'

'So, we don't have to be scared about anything?'

'Definitely not. Maybe just a bit brave.' I wasn't going to bullshit him.

'In cartoons scared is like this . . .' Kit widened his eyes as far as they'd go. 'And brave is this . . .' He puffed out his chest, and I laughed.

'Hey.' We turned to see Wolf in the doorway, fully dressed, raking his hand through his hair, where my fingers had just been, and I melted. 'Need to haul myself back to the shop, Maggie.'

'We're coming too!' Kit flicked off the TV. Like me, he'd have followed Wolf anywhere.

Using a man's holey sock – I tried not to dwell on its likely origins – as a duster, Kit bent over the trestle table, jumbled with newly acquired items, separated onto wooden trays: broken, dirty, clean. He had a smear of grease on his nose, like an initiation mark. As Kit polished, Gav sat beside him, peering at items through a magnifying loupe, his leather-apron-clad paunch pressed into the pocked table, his breathing loud and asthmatic. Kit had won him over. I hadn't. Still the girl from the terrace messing with his nephew's reliability and 'pickling his head with lofty ambitions'.

But Wolf shone like buffed gold in that dimly lit shop. With his expansive intelligence and rare goodness, he had a lucent quality. And Gav didn't like it. He wanted Wolf to stay working for him, not reaching further. 'You're trouble, Maggie,' he said grouchily, sticking an unlit rolled cigarette behind his large red ear. 'I can always tell.'

'Heard that, Gav,' warned Wolf, bristling. Their confrontational gazes locked like antlers. Gav glanced away first.

Later, when Wolf slipped his hands around my waist from behind, Gav teased, 'You do know you're not the first to fall for him, Maggie? Blame those Frank Sinatra eyes.'

I was too stung to speak. Wolf had become the antidote to my fear and loneliness. He'd saved Kit's life, and it felt like he'd somehow saved mine too. But the sex – so astounding and so early on in a relationship, no waiting, no games – had made me vulnerable. The thought of Wolf with someone else, in his past or his future, physically hurt.

'Anyway, Wolf, you're fired.' Gav lifted his chin

and scratched his thick stubbled neck – *rasp, rasp*. 'I'm hiring this lad. Although I've worked you long enough, Kit.' He reached over and whipped the sock from my brother's hands. 'Don't want to get done for child labour along with everything else.'

'We'd better head home,' I said, feeling flat and dislodged, staring at the dirty floor.

Gav cleared his throat, with a catarrhy crack. 'Maggie . . .'

I glanced up warily, bracing for further cruel details about Wolf's past love life.

'For what it's worth, Wolf's never been this useless before. Nico would be more use to me, frankly.'

I smiled at him shyly, hoping he knew it was a thank-you.

'Here, Wolf, you waste of space, take this.' Gav dug into the baggy depths of his trouser pockets, pulled out a car key and tossed it in Wolf's direction. 'Slow today. I'm heading off soon. Do something useful this weekend. Check out Alfie's Antiques Market, or a bit of competition. Report back.'

'You sure?' Wolf paused, waiting for the catch.

'Go! Before I stab you in the eye with my screwdriver.' We were turning away when Gav called, 'Oh, sorry. Forgot to tell you, Maggie. A bloke came nosing around as I was closing yesterday. Some twat in a hat, fancied himself as some sort of Joe Strummer. Looking for Kit. Pretty sure it was the same guy who worked this street a couple of years ago, trying to shift hot stock.' Gav picked up an automaton, flipped open its back, exposing its brass clockwork insides. 'So, I threw him out. Advise you to keep better company.'

I exchanged a look with Wolf. Not good. Cooper knew my little brother's name. And where Wolf worked.

'He's a creep,' said Wolf. 'Been hanging around Maggie's house. Turned up this morning, gave Kit a football. Out of the blue.'

'What?' Gav glanced up abruptly, his small eyes hard and bright. 'I don't like the sound of that. I don't like the sound of that at all. You don't mess with our boy.' He reached across and slapped a ham of a hand on Kit's shoulder. 'You need to step in, Wolf.'

Something unreadable passed between them.

Wolf rolled his eyes wearily. 'Gav, no one operates like that any more . . .'

'Bah,' Gav scoffed. 'Knock the old ways, if you like, but they get the message across efficiently. Less trouble in the end.' With a small grunt, he bent down to the automaton again, gently pushed a tiny brass cog with the tip of his finger. The clockwork click-clicked; the mechanics were set in motion. 'Don't come crying, asking me to fight your battles for you, that's all I'm saying.'

26

Kit

London, May 2019

On the corner of the Parkers' old Notting Hill terrace, a huddle of people straining to see a commotion further down the street. Kit follows the collective gaze to a flash of yellow tape. A row of bollards. Two police cars. One of those ominous unmarked vans. The small crowd is speculating about what has happened. Some sort of accident on a building site, a man says. No surprise, a matter of time, tuts an older lady.

Not wanting to be a ghoulish spectator to someone else's misfortune – Kit's been on the other side of that – he hopes no one is too hurt and scoots off, head down, in the direction of Notting Hill Gate tube. Unable to believe Little Me is in his possession once more, his fingers seek the lump of the peg doll in his jacket pocket, a part of his childhood, lost and found. God, life is strange. Roy stranger.

Occasionally Kit glances over his shoulder, half

expecting to spot Roy's face in the crowd again. But he seems finally to have gone home, placated by the prospect of meeting up later. Boldface in Kit's mind: for one *last* time. Maybe he agreed too easily. But he'd been overwhelmed by Little Me's return, touched that Roy had thought of him. It can't be a fluke, Roy finding it on a market stall. Kit likes to think objects, especially old ones, have a sort of consciousness and keep trying to find their way back to their owner. The places they belong. Roy was a conduit: maybe they were always destined to meet, just for this reason. Also, there's the 'something else' he wants to talk about. And Kit can't quite extinguish his curiosity, despite suspecting it'll be absolutely nothing, just Roy's excuse not to eat dinner in a soulless city apartment on his own.

At the entrance to the tube, Kit pauses. A memory flares, then another and another, as if by a lit fuse. His sister tugging him by the hand through Portobello Market, under the bridges, to a labyrinthine antiques shop. Dancing on a grimy roof terrace among the chimney pots. The aurora of light flickering off the Westway. A movie camera on a wheeled cart. A sweet little dog called Nico snuggled under a Spider-Man duvet. Fistfuls of happiness snatched from the sadness.

Feeling a surge of gratitude for all this, and Wolf's real name, Kit wrestles with whether to call Maggie and tell her about Little Me's return and Roy. The problem is, Roy will require rather a lot of explaining, and Kit hasn't time: he needs to get home to his fast Wi-Fi to search for Will Derry – and Maggie being Maggie will worry, he decides, descending the tube steps.

Back at his Bloomsbury flat, Kit fires open the laptop. *William Derry*, he googles, then narrows it down, *antiques, antique toys, flea markets, antique fairground collectibles, Tetbury dealers* . . . Nothing, nothing, nothing. Wait. He changes tack. Searches under Images. No, no, no . . . Whoa. Kit clicks on a photograph. A pap shot, some sort of gallery opening. A man – forties? – in a dark suit, black specs, white shirt, shouldering away from the camera, uncomfortable in its gaze. Kit expands the by-line: *Will Derry, private client adviser, Lordats Auctioneers*. He flicks to another shot, a different event, a different jacket, Will Derry looking similarly ill at ease at being photographed. But caught face-on this time. Is it? Could it be? Those eyes: surely the ones his sister described in boyhood bedtime Wolf stories. 'The palest, most unreal blue, like the first frost of winter, bluer than you've ever seen in eyes before, Kit,' she'd say. And there they are, staring back at him. Kit feels a circuit deep inside connect, light up. Even if the photo was black-and-white, he'd recognize him.

Kit throws back his head, lets out a small whoop

of joy. The search for Wolf is over. A search that had become a torch in his fatherless dark, leading him to unexpected places, in and out of the antiques world and back to himself, showing him who it was possible to be. Wolf has run beneath Kit's life all this time, hidden, invisible, like the river Fleet under London.

And so close: Lordats is only a mile and a half from Kit's flat. And Wolf *was* the real deal, just as talented as Kit remembers, soaring from his humble beginnings to work for one of the world's most prestigious auction houses. Elated, he whirrs the search engines again, trying to find contact details. But Will Derry's job as a private client adviser is one that involves the utmost discretion, an under-the-radar guiding hand to the sort of people who are so wealthy they make no noise, wear no obvious labels, leave no trace.

But Kit is a match for them. He is at home here too. He can navigate the alleys of the internet like Soho's backstreets. After typing out a message – honest, heartfelt, attaching a photo of Little Me – he tries a few likely name variations adapted to the company's general email address. Heart thudding, Kit presses send, pushing his messages in bottles into the fathomless data ocean and waits, breath held, to see if one doesn't bounce back.

27

Maggie

Notting Hill, May 1998

Up on the roof terrace, we were gods. Secret rulers of the city. Sunday afternoon, and summer had cracked open with a Coke-can hiss. The blue sky filled with music from an unseen party, little mountains of sound rising and falling. Kit danced, his bare feet kicking up grit and grime, his arms whirling. I grabbed him – too close to the edge, don't be a moron – and tugged him down again. A pigeon shuffled through the brick dust, greedily eyeing Kit's sticky bag of Iced Gems.

It'd been a blazing day. Kit's face glowed from the sunshine. Ours from sex that morning, the anticipation of it happening again.

Kit settled, squatting in front of Wolf with a huge grin, his elbows resting on Wolf's knees. 'What you staring at, kid?' Wolf asked, then lightly play-punched his arm with his fist. Kit punched back, hard, showing off, and Wolf groaned, 'My arm, my arm,' and we laughed, sank back on the sofa cushions we'd dragged across the broken slates. Wolf leaned back against the chimney stack, a king against his throne, and I wedged myself into the V of his legs, clamped there by his thighs, the thrilling cleave of him.

All down the terrace, in the broiling afternoon heat, windows were ajar. A woman sunbathed on the roof terrace opposite. Seagulls stalked the long pincushion of the street's TV aerials, waiting to dive-bomb for food.

Beyond the neighbourhood, London sprawled, hazy in the heat, alive, all soft tissue, no edges. I thought of the millions of people in this vast city, my mother only one. Marco had said he'd find her by the end of the weekend. He hadn't long. I tapped a tooth impatiently with my fingernail. There was still time – just – for Mum to do a star turn and be the surprise guest. So, I kept trying to beam, like some sort of human satellite dish, a desperate message: *Please come home, Mum. I love you, I'm sorry for whatever made you leave. Whatever is wrong, I'll fix it. And Kit has been such a good boy.*

I considered Kit, now inspecting a tiny spider in the palm of his hand. This funny little kid whom I'd previously considered barely more sentient than Nico and who was now a true brother for whom I'd lay down my life. I owed him, I realized. It had been Kit who'd forced me out of my solitude, my closed room of grief and self-loathing, and into the world. However hard I tried, I couldn't summon homesickness for Surrey any more. Finally, my heart had moved to London.

Kit had helped me, but had I helped Kit? I wasn't sure. He looked kind of feral. Dirty feet. Matted curls. Face tanned brown as biscuits, peppered with freckles. One of his wobbly upper milk teeth was loosening, dangling from a red string. He refused to pull it out since he didn't want to make it 'homeless'. If Mum were here, it'd be neatly excised and stored in the little tin box, where she sentimentally kept all our milk teeth. Kit would also have been at school all week. Instead, we'd practised reading and letters, using library books and fashion magazines. He'd been more interested in learning about convex and concave glass in old funhouse mirrors. How to unscrew a clock face. Always to keep his eyes peeled for 'sleepers', dusty under-priced pieces, hiding among the clutter of a junk stall, that turn out to be life-changingly valuable and rare. Utterly useless facts. But he looked free and ridiculously happy, in a way that felt kind of wrong, and disloyal to my mother.

I caught myself. One thing I'd learned when Dad had died, and I'd got this awful overwhelming urge to laugh at his funeral, was that people don't behave as you expect when the bad stuff rolls in.

Kit went to dart off, join Nico downstairs, and Wolf grabbed him by his T-shirt, aware of the drop two feet away. 'Whoa. I'll take you in, little man.' I could hear them chatting – football, the World Cup in June, how England would smash it, '66 all over again – as they picked their way across the roof.

The music grew louder. Sounds of voices, laughter, a party. A firework, prematurely let off, shot up, spiralling silver, like a giant egg whisk in the blue, then vanishing. When Wolf returned, we kissed each other's smiles. Pawed each other, urgently, fumblingly, undid the necessary zippers and buttons. Time went elastic, speeding up, slowing down, and we kept talking, laughing, moving in and out of each other's minds and bodies, until I felt the flash, a new space inside me opening, blowing everything else away. Afterwards, I traced my finger lightly up the back of his neck, enjoying the weft of his hair. The music from the street party grew louder.

'I should return Gav's van,' Wolf said slowly, lazily, not moving. 'It's a day late already.' We'd not been anywhere, just further into the place we made together. 'He'll be mightily pissed off.'

'Eek. Not sure I'd want to see that.'

Wolf smiled. 'All bark. Well, mostly. He's been good to me, Maggie. Took me under his wing.'

Not a place I'd have wanted to be. 'But you could work for someone else. You're smart, Wolf, and you get all the sales, and you know everything.'

'Ha, I don't. Gav knows his stuff, apart from the

customer-relations side, obviously. I want to learn the business. Pick his brain like a lock.' He surveyed the rooftops hungrily, as if the city would belong to him one day. 'When I'm done learning, I'm out of there. Bigger things. And we . . .' He paused uncertainly. 'We can make plans? You and me, we've got an energy, right? We could do anything, Maggie.'

Since Mum had left, I'd been living hour to hour, day to day, meal to meal. I hadn't been able to see past her return, or Kit. Suddenly I could. And it made my heart sing. 'Anything.'

'So?' He rested his chin on his hand, his gaze curious, like he wanted to eat me up. Nobody had ever looked at me like Wolf did. 'What's your dream, Maggie Parker?'

I'd dumped my dreams when Dad died. 'I don't know.'

'Yeah, you do.'

'I'm just not sure I'd be any good at it.'

'No! What is this?' He tapped his head. 'Think like a boxer, remember.'

So, I placed my dream on my palm and offered it to him, tentatively, hoping he wouldn't laugh. 'A writer, then. Like, one day. When I've lived a bit. Have something to say.'

He didn't laugh. He traced my upper lip with one finger, and I could smell me on his skin. 'You do know I'm holding you to that, don't you?'

I nodded, knowing he would.

'Right, I'm swivelling the clock hands something mental, round and round . . .' He made the motion with his fingers. 'And, whoa, we've arrived slap bang in the future. You're writing your books. From the heart. No boring bits. I'm, like, *the* main man in antiques. Where do we fancy living? Pick a place.' As he spoke, the world opened, and fell deliciously apart, like the segments of a chocolate orange. 'London? New York?'

'Paris,' I said, not realizing I knew the answer until I'd spoken it. A choice based on the novel *Bonjour Tristesse*, an unforgettable slice of *tarte Tatin*, and a formative memory of standing on tiptoe and peeking into a cluttered Paris bookshop window while I was with my grandmother, who hadn't let me go inside.

'Hmm, okay. We could make Paris work.' He glanced at me shyly, admitted, 'Actually, I've never been to Paris.'

'You'd love it.' Even though I'd only been once, I pictured myself showing him around the streets, as he had done for me here, making the city come alive.

He cocked his head on one side, perhaps imagining this too. 'You have family there or something, I think you said?'

'Aunt Cora.' I thought about the messages she'd left Mum, the estrangement I didn't fully understand.

'Well, I'd better learn me some French sharpish, then.' Wolf was quiet for a bit, and I could sense his mind turning.

'What?'

'Nothing.'

I squeezed his earlobe with my fingers. 'Tell me.'

'I think we were meant to meet, that's all. At that exact second. On Powis Square.'

'Me too.' I was struck that life seemed to pivot on fleeting moments that could so easily not have happened, and were only revealed as significant in hindsight.

'This thing between us, it's . . . vibrational. Is that even a word? Like the air between our bodies . . .' He starred his fingers and swiped at it, as if under water. 'It's different from the air elsewhere, right? It's not like I know you, but I recognize you, deep down. I did immediately.' He searched my face. 'Does that make sense?'

'Perfectly.' I could only define what we had in terms of what it wasn't. Not friendship or lust or a meeting of minds . . . all these things but something else too, a collective state that we created, entirely anew, from being in each other's company. We lay down again, and I turned my head so that the tips of our noses were touching, and we breathed each other's breath, then burst out laughing, stupidly belly-laughing, for no reason at all other than we'd found each other. The music grew louder; Lauryn Hill blew towards us on the breeze.

'Would you dance with me, Maggie Parker?'

I shook my head. 'I'm a terrible dancer.'

'But you haven't danced with me yet.'

I rolled my eyes, resistance slipping. Wolf pulled me up and he held my waist and, of course, he was a sinuous dancer, the music rippling through him, and somehow moving into my body too.

If I was still a crap dancer I no longer cared, and we carried on, pressed close until the song changed and we grabbed the cushions, bundling downstairs, high on ourselves, the music, our sugar-spun plans for Paris, the life that glistened beyond this one, grown-up, entirely free. On the first floor, Wolf drifted off to use the bathroom, and I ran downstairs to find Kit.

A cool draught swept over my feet as I reached the lower ground floor. Two steps from the bottom, I saw them.

Kit was outside on the terrace, knees lifted, doing keepy-uppies with the football. Pressed against one glass door was the imprint of a man. He turned, glanced over his shoulder.

I gasped. 'What – what are you doing here? Get out.'

'Kit let me in.' There was a reptilian look in Cooper's eye that would haunt me for years after. Worse, the way he smiled at Kit, who smiled back uncertainly, trying to be polite.

I grabbed my brother, swung him to my hip. His Kicker caught the edge of the soil heap, flicking dirt.

He shrank into me, and I held him tighter, wanting to scream for Wolf, nowhere to be seen.

'I came to collect what's mine,' Cooper said casually. I could smell alcohol on his sour breath.

'Take it.' I kicked the ball towards him. He ignored it. He hadn't come for that.

'So, your mum's not back. Left you all alone. Nice. What would the great British public think of that, eh? The model of motherhood, the beautiful widow, doing a runner.' Cooper's smile created clown-like sickles at the sides of his mouth but didn't reach his eyes. 'You look young. How young?'

Sensing it'd be a bad idea to confirm my age, I said nothing, glanced over my shoulder at the empty kitchen, willing Wolf to appear.

'Not an adult anyway.' Cooper's mannered mildness carried a cold undertow. 'Always easier for parents to walk out than walk back. Know what I'm saying?'

'Please leave.' My voice had a tremble to it now.

'Thing is, we had an arrangement, me and your mother.' Cooper sighed, drawn-out and stagey. 'And, being a decent sort of chap, I kept my part of the bargain.' He dug in his pocket, pulled out a cigarette, spun it like a baton between two fingers, then lit it with a green plastic lighter. 'Most wouldn't, to be fair.' He dragged on it hard. 'These tabloids.' He shook his head, raised an eyebrow. 'Grubsters.'

The cloying smell of honeysuckle, the bass of the

party down the road. Still, I didn't fully understand. It was more like something flickering at the edge of my vision, not yet fully seen.

'But those filthy old hacks pay for scandal. They pay good.' He pulled a sorrowful face. 'Much more than your mother.'

My brain was snatching at what he was saying and flew to the wedge of notes in the dresser drawers, my mother's jumpiness, the shadows under her eyes, and it all started to fit. Like the volume of the soil heap fitted with the size of That Godawful Hole.

Cooper frowned. 'Did she leave me any money?'

Like my mother, at that moment, I wanted to give him any amount of cash – the entire envelope – just to disappear. But something in me held firm. 'You're blackmailing my mum.'

'Oh, I wouldn't call it that. I'd say protecting.' He spread his gangly arms wide. 'I'm the dam holding back her dirty floodwater. Bargain at the price.'

'*Get out.*'

'Or what? You going to call the cops? Go on, then. I'd say that could backfire pretty messily.' Cooper looked amused. 'Hey, I've got a better idea. Call your mother.'

'I don't like this, Maggie,' Kit whimpered.

Everything felt brittle and precarious, as if we were standing on a thin crust that could crack open. Behind us, footsteps. Wolf. I'd never been so relieved to see anyone. He took one look at my expression and hissed at Cooper, 'What the fuck are you doing here?'

Cooper clearly hadn't been expecting Wolf. 'Calm down, junk-shop boy,' he said, brazening it out. 'No business of yours.'

Wolf stepped closer, his pupils dilated, the blue a thin Saturn ring. 'Get your skinny arse out of this house.'

Cooper laughed. 'Feeling at home? Got yourself an uptown girl?' He turned to me. 'You need to watch this one. I wouldn't trust him as far as I could throw him.'

Wolf grabbed his arm.

'Get off my jacket.' Cooper roughly flicked off Wolf's hand. 'Don't think you'll be accepted into this sort of family. They don't like us plebs. And your old man detained at Her Majesty's pleasure. Chip off the old block, eh?'

Wolf pushed him hard in the chest. Cooper stumbled then spat in Wolf's face. I held my breath, horrified, watched the thick foamy spittle drip from Wolf's brow.

'Take Kit upstairs, Maggie. I'll get him out.' Eyes blazing, Wolf wiped his face, a wild anger rising hard and fast.

Kit buried his head in my shoulder, his mouth damp against my neck. I knew he was scared but I didn't want to leave Wolf.

'Go, Maggie,' Wolf said, his voice dangerously low.

Kit clung tighter. Cooper's fist swung in Wolf's direction, and Wolf ducked, Cooper smashing thin air. 'You'll have to do better than that,' Wolf scoffed.

As I backed into the kitchen, Cooper shouted after us, 'You tell your mother that Kit is *my* blood, much more than hers – you hear me? So unless she wants her family secrets plastered –' Whatever Cooper was going to say next was extinguished by a thud, a growl, the sound of someone charging forward on scuffing feet, then the sickening crunch of flesh and bone.

28

Maggie

The Old Rectory, May 2019

The smell of damp dog and ripe vase water. Maggie shivers in a shadow that falls upon only her, bearing no relation to the sunlight splashing through the windows. The shock, amplified for having been long anticipated, reverberates, fizzes. She's in the Old Rectory's kitchen, a chair spindle pressing against her spine. Above her, the constellation of Suki's and Clemence's round, worried faces. Cora, wringing a red gingham tea towel in her hands, as if it were a turkey's neck.

Maggie replays the horror. Clemence on the phone to Marco. Her own legs weakening, as if someone had taken a croquet mallet to the back of her knees. Then, stretching towards her, Cora's strong horsewoman's hands and the words, 'What are you two doing here? What have you said to Maggie?'

The remains have been found. It's all over. She desperately needs to get hold of Wolf. Warn him. Her mind skitters, trying to get a foothold. How long will it take pathologists to date the skeleton, identify it – dental records? – and match it to missing-person reports? Days or weeks? She pictures a corpse laid out on a pathologist's stainless-steel slab, a wretched twist of rags and bones, gummed with mud. The worms will have done their worst. Maggie's stomach starts to heave again. She wants to teleport back to Paris, her little desk, her writing, its swooning star-crossed lovers. The world she's created to escape the terrible place in which she now finds herself.

'Human remains?' Cora is saying. 'Christ. I don't know what to think. It's too bizarre.' Her face pleats with worry. 'How long has Marco lived there, Clemence?' she asks more sharply.

'A year. That house has had many residents between Dee Dee and Marco,' Clemence says, answering an unspoken question.

'At the very least, a record producer. A banker. Oh, yes, and a family who upped sticks for Somerset,' muttered Suki, thumbing her glasses up her nose, her face pale.

'I bet those remains will turn out to be historic.' Clemence presses the back of her wrist to her forehead, as if trying to absorb the news. 'Old, old. Like something from one of your books, Maggie.'

Maggie nods but her stomach swoops with a cold liquid fear. Her heart beats a metronome in her ears.

'Or an animal,' says Cora, twisting the tea towel in her hands again. 'Animal skeletons can look eerily human sometimes.'

A moment passes. Just the sound of the wind in the trees outside. Dogs panting.

'I can't believe it. Of all the houses, you couldn't make it up,' mutters Suki.

'Poor Marco sounded in a right state,' says Clemence.

'You should get back to support him,' suggests Cora, not quite hiding her keenness for the women to leave.

Clemence hesitates. 'I'll wait to check Maggie's okay. I had no idea it would hit so hard. I'm sorry.' She winces. 'I . . . I should have thought.'

Beneath her breath, Cora agrees, then steps towards Maggie, placing a hand protectively on her arm.

As if staking a counterclaim, Suki lays a hand on Maggie's other shoulder. 'You sure you're all right, darlin'?'

'Come, Harold!' calls Cora. 'Sit. Be an emotional support dog. Do something useful for once. There. Good boy.'

Harold dutifully wedges himself like a hairy hillock against Maggie's legs. 'Honestly, I'm fine,' says Maggie, far from it, then glances around for her phone, scared of missing any call from Wolf, in case he's been tipped off too. 'My phone . . .'

'Here.' Cora retrieves it from the table. 'Yes, one of us should call Kit,' she says, assuming this is what Maggie is about to do.

Kit. Maggie cannot protect him from this any longer. He will soon discover everything that happened that day. Everything she's not told him. And she must face his judgement. And if he can't forgive . . . what then? Kit has always been the reason she's refused to sink. If her tragedy-walloped little brother could still find joy, then she must too. With Kit around, life never felt pointless. Because life *was* the point: that was the lesson they'd learned together. She couldn't undo what had happened, but Kit could still be the boy who rose golden above the darkness. And she tried to do everything in her power to keep him there.

Only now that big-sister power is draining away. As one of the many occupants of that house, Kit will be interviewed by the police. With great interest, if the forensic dating proves accurate. He'll have to mention his troubling memory of running up the stairs, a sense of something bad happening below. She'd never ask Kit to lie. As she has done.

'Are you sure she's okay, Cora?' Suki is whispering.

'What Maggie needs is sugar. A biscuit.' Cora rummages in the cupboard.

Maggie's mobile pings on her lap. Her heart misses a beat. Wolf? No, Kit.

Found him! Reads Kit's WhatsApp message. Maggie

freezes with white-hot panic. An attachment appears, blurred, waiting to be opened. Her finger hovers, shaking. Fearing it'll be a screenshot of a news headline, she forces herself to tap it.

The Old Rectory vanishes, Cora, Suki, Clemence, the dogs. Maggie is, at last, alone, with Wolf, or rather a grainy photo of Wolf, twenty-one years on. Reading the picture caption, she makes a small involuntary noise and covers her mouth with her hand: *Meet Will Derry of Lordats, Mayfair. x*

'What is it?' Cora slips a shortbread biscuit into Maggie's fingers.

Maggie stands up, gripping the back of the chair and dropping the shortbread, swiftly devoured by Harold. She turns to Suki and Clemence. 'Can I get a lift back into London with you two?'

Cora tries to steer her down again. 'Don't be daft. You're not going anywhere, Maggie. Sit.'

But Maggie must do this. And she must do it now. 'Please, Suki.'

'Sure,' says Suki, puzzled at first. 'If you really think you're up to it.'

'She's not,' Cora says.

Trying to reassure her aunt, Maggie takes her hands. 'Cora, there's someone I must see.'

'Kit? Then I must come! Kit needs me too.' Cora's voice catches. 'Don't push me out. Let me be there for Kit, Maggie.'

Those words sting. But Maggie's bond with Kit is not something she's engineered at the expense of his relationship with Cora. If anything, it's partly to compensate. 'Cora, it's not Kit I'm going to see. Not yet. Trust me?'

Since Maggie wouldn't put it past Cora to stand in the drive with her pack of dogs obstructing their way, she wastes no time in grabbing her overnight bag, running back down the stairs, and out to Suki's waiting car in the drive.

'Fast as possible, please,' says Maggie, as Cora breaks forth, rushing out of the porch, beckoning her back.

'Hold those pelvic floors, ladies!' shouts Suki, and they rev down the potholed lane and back to London, its buried layers of broken lost things, bones and secrets, to warn a man Maggie has always wildly, stupidly, loved, without ever knowing his true name. Perhaps without ever knowing him at all.

29

Maggie

Notting Hill, May 1998

No more fighting noises. Or voices. Just music from the party down the road. I wanted to go downstairs, and check Wolf was okay. But Kit looked terrified, and Nico was whinnying, both huddled in my bed, the duvet roofed over their heads. I'd wedged *Pride and Prejudice* under the door, making it harder to open, and a chair under the handle, trying to barricade us inside.

'I've forgotten how to feel brave, Maggie.'

I put a finger to my lips. 'Ssh.' Pulling up my bedroom window further, I leaned out, straining to see, but the parasol obscured the part of the patio where I'd left Wolf and Cooper fighting. I could make out the football, glowing white, and the shape of Cooper's hat, a silhouette against the paler paving stones. The glint of the builder's spade, leaning against the wall.

Cooper's words still wheeled, woozily, impossibly in the air: 'You tell your mother that Kit is *my* blood, much more than hers . . .'

So, Cooper was a biological relation of Kit? How close a relation? Although this was possible, it felt wrong, a law of the universe broken. Kit was ours. A Parker. *My* little brother. And yet I knew nothing of Kit's pre-history since my parents had never discussed it with me. The idea that his blood relatives might try to reclaim him was terrifying.

I chewed over Cooper's last words. 'So, unless she wants her family secrets plastered –' What secrets? And why hadn't Mum reported Cooper to the police? Unless the adoption was somehow illegitimate . . . My thoughts crawled to dark places.

Another five minutes passed. Hearing a tread on the stairs outside, then Wolf mumbling my name, I moved the book and the barricading chair, and cautiously inched open the door.

Wolf's face was waxy and grey, his jaw swelling, his eye starting to pulp and his nose a gory mess. I closed the bedroom door behind me, hiding the damage from Kit. Wolf covered his face with his hands, trying to stem the blood streaming from his nose onto the seagrass landing carpet. He started to sob noiselessly, his shoulders heaving up and down. Cradling his head in my hands, I asked what had happened.

'Cooper came at me with this broken lump of paving from the pile,' he mumbled, gasping. 'I . . . I twisted away . . . His hand drew back to . . . to smash down this thing on my head. If it hit me, I knew it'd kill me . . .' His voice cracked with a hard sob. 'So, I punched him with everything I had left, Maggie.'

I pulled Wolf's hands away from his eyes and they were terrified, and I think I knew, in some limbic bit of my brain. The boxer's punch. The muscles I could feel adrenalin-pumped under the sleeves of his shirt. A blurred horror spread inside me.

'He . . . he's . . .' Wolf was stammering, his mashed mouth muffling his words, breathing so fast, almost hyperventilating. I held his hands and made useless shushing noises in a vain attempt to calm him down. 'I've just called my . . . my uncle . . .'

Outside on the street, a police-car siren screamed. I tensed, braced. But the noise faded.

Bewilderment flashed across Wolf's face, and he started to shake with shock. 'I . . . I was going to phone 999 too. But Gav's like, no, no, don't be an idiot. He says he's going to deal with it . . .'

I nodded numbly, having no idea what this could mean.

'. . . and I need to get us out of here. You two can't see anything. You don't see Cooper, then . . . then you don't know. We can use Gav's van. Where can you go? Far. Far away. Paris! Can you go to Paris?'

I was watching myself at a distance, my speech dubbed, my mouth saying yes.

Every instinct was screaming, run, run, run, keep Kit safe, get him out of there, and somehow, in minutes that I'd never be able to talk about, or recall clearly, while Wolf wiped his face, changed into the spare shirt he kept in my room, I'd grabbed a small rucksack, stuffed it with a few clothes, the envelope of cash, our passports from the dresser drawer, a pair of Mum's sunglasses, before snatching the note with Aunt Cora's telephone number off the cork board, slamming the pink front door. Nico under my arm, Kit piggybacking on Wolf, we ran down the street, fleeing Notting Hill just as I'd fallen in love with it, until we arrived, breathless, at Gav's van. The light starting to fade. The sky pressing down, the entire weight of the universe – and our future – above it.

30

Kit

London, May 2019

Kit needs to get on. He's got work to do. Things to fix. Calls to make. But he still sits inert on his sofa, staring at his phone's email inbox, a blueberry vodka in one hand, Little Me in the other, reliving the last time he saw Wolf. The hole on the floor of Gav's van, the road surface whipping past underneath. The honks from other vehicles as they wove through the backstreets, across Waterloo Bridge. Wolf wearing big sunglasses, his nose misshapen from his nosebleed, poor Wolf. Maggie breathing like she was sucking through a straw. His six-year-old self not sure what had happened, only that it was bad. And quite possibly his fault. Then, Waterloo station. Wolf at the barricade, still in those sunglasses – his mother's sunglasses he realized, the word Chanel in gold on the arm – and cradling Nico, shouting to his sister that he loved her, making other passengers stare. Straining, twisting on Maggie's hand, Kit had tried to keep

Wolf and Nico in his sight for as long as possible. After that life started to move so fast, so unstoppably, like the road through the hole in the van floor. And Wolf was no longer in it.

Until now.

Kit knows it's been just a couple of hours. But . . . fuck. Why hasn't Wolf responded already? It's been twenty-one years since they last spoke! Kit has called Lordats, worked his charms on the rather frosty woman on the front desk, and now knows for sure that Wolf is at work today, and one of the email addresses he'd used correct, the others bouncing back. Never meet your heroes, they say. Never email them either.

Kit broods on possible reasons. Wolf doesn't remember him. Agony. He's become too successful, too establishment, and thinks Kit's trying to brown-nose his way into the grand auction house, a young man on the make, asking for favours. Excruciating. Wolf wants no reminder of who he was – the brutish young man Roy recalls – when he worked at Gav Out Back's shop. Disturbing. You need a splinter of ice in the heart to be truly successful. That's what every-one says.

Whatever the explanation, the disappointment is crushing. While Kit recognizes melodrama as a dis-tinct possibility, he still feels gutted – and a fool. All that wasted time and energy, the head-first skidding down internet wormholes. The chase of a childhood dream that, like a mirage, is lost as soon as it's found.

Wolf, as Kit knew him, has gone. Drawn into a luxury international life, selling history's exquisite treasures to the world's elite. Unaware that across the grinding, churning city, tinkering with collectibles in a little Bloomsbury flat above a vintage-map shop, there is Kit, forever measuring himself against a boyhood mentor, someone he's blown into extraordinary holographic proportions over the years. Neither will Wolf have any inkling that Kit has searched for him, as he would an irreplaceable antique stolen from under his roof, the quest gaining a life of its own, as addictive as any computer game. And as unreal. That now over, Kit feels flat, robbed of purpose. He sips his vodka, relishing the unpleasant burn down his throat, and starts to worry about how Maggie might have reacted to the photo of Will Derry he pinged across. He should have shown it to her in person. Ominously, she's not replied to the message. Needled by the thought that he's upset his sister, he texts *Are you OK?* As Kit tends to do when not feeling okay himself.

Maggie is typing. *Yes. In London right now.*
Wht?
Sorry. Really need to tlk to you. It's v v important. Best we meet in person. U in this evening?

Kit remembers his arrangement to meet Roy. *Out*

*for a bit – early supper at Giovanni's. Long story. PLEASE
come and rescue me early and give me an excuse to leave.*

K. Got to go. Love u.

Kit glances at his inbox again. If Wolf replies to
his email soon and offers to meet, Kit knows he'll
stand up Roy. His sister too. He'll drop everything –
and be in Mayfair so damn fast sparks will fly from
the leather soles of his shoes.

31

Maggie

Paris, May 1998

The Eurostar bored under the sea, the view from the train window a hypnotic blur of blacks cut with flashes of blinding light. Clutching his toy car, Kit slept, his head on my lap, his eyelids twitching, a smile flickering on his lips, like a puppy when it dreams. I'd covered him with my mother's pashmina, grabbed in the panic of our departure, hoping it might somehow protect us. It didn't look substantial enough for the task.

Given that the world had proved itself yet again to be a perilous place, I couldn't rely on the tunnel not to collapse, swell with salt water, and pipe us out to the sea. Noting the emergency-exit signs and the hammers behind glass, I planned escape routes but couldn't plot one out of our bigger situation.

It was like pulling at a knot, trying to loosen it, but only making the knot tighter. The cash I'd found in the envelope could buy us train tickets – and time – but no solution. Cooper remained dead on our patio.

A human being, Kit's blood relative, who a few hours ago had been strutting around Notting Hill in his trilby . . . gone. A life puffed out, like a candle. Any 'family secrets' Cooper had threatened to expose now dwarfed by mine.

Exhaustion, although not sleep, never sleep – I'd surely never sleep again – throbbed in my eye-sockets. The clack of the train's wheels measured our growing distance from all we'd left behind. Wolf, who didn't own a passport. Nico, left in Wolf's arms, since she wasn't allowed to travel either. My missing mother.

All hope – what a terrible sort of hope it was – relied upon Wolf's frenzied phone call to Gav, and Gav helping us at his own great risk. Which probably meant getting into the house and burying Cooper's body. To do this, Gav, wheezing, overweight Gav, would have to either break in or scale the garden wall since, in my panic, I'd left the back door unlocked but the house keys inside. Mistake after mistake. And where was Wolf now? Gav had instructed him to go straight from Waterloo station to his old school friend Tyrone's flat in east London and stay there until his mashed face had healed. But I wasn't at all sure Wolf would do this either. I feared he'd go back.

All of it was so far out of my frame of reference. I had nothing to draw on, no understanding of the sort of shadowy world Gav might inhabit – if indeed he did – or its rules. In books and movies baddies and heroes were mostly clear-cut, and justice meted out in the end. But the person I desperately loved, the kindest, best person I'd ever known, had turned into that baddie while trying to protect me and my little brother. It made my head spin.

'Maggie.' One of Kit's eyes opened. His breath was stale. He needed food and to brush his teeth. 'I didn't like that man.'

'Nor did I.'

'Nico didn't like him,' Kit said, as if this irrefutably proved something.

'Exactly. Forget about him, Kit.' I rearranged the pashmina, which was slipping off his legs, tucking him back in. 'Can you do that? Pick that man out of your mind and throw him out of the window?'

Kit's gaze flew to the glassy black, following his thought. 'Done,' he declared, and seemed to fall asleep. Kit never would mention Cooper again.

My imagination wasn't so biddable. Cooper danced in the corners of my mind, a nightmare showman: 'And now, ladies and gentlemen . . .'

'Maggie?' Kit muttered, not opening his eyes.

'Yes, Kit.' I steeled myself for the next question.

'I'm hungry.'

'Don't worry. We're almost there.' I stroked his hair off his face. 'We'll get something in Paris. Something delicious. Go back to sleep. You get places quicker if you sleep.'

Fearing other people could see the fear – and guilt – in my face, I was careful not to meet any other passengers' eyes, pulling up my sweatshirt hood, turning my body at an angle from the aisle. But there was one elderly French lady sitting opposite, immaculately dressed, red lipstick and a crocodile-skin handbag on her lap. I worried about her, the way she kept glancing over before she tottered purposefully away. Paranoid she was about to fetch the guard, I was considering shaking Kit awake to move carriages when she returned with a paper bag from the café car. Apologizing for the quality of the food, she insisted I take it, dismissing my mumbled gratitude with a flap of an arthritic hand. For a few minutes, our bellies filling, the world felt like a brighter place. And I loved that little old French lady with all my heart.

Emerging from the tunnel, signposts in French. Modern tower blocks at first, then the glisten of Paris, followed by the blare and glare of the Gare du Nord. As the other passengers bustled, chatted, I clutched Kit and our knapsack and fought against a feeling of smallness in that station – crowded, vast, ribbed with girders – and the unknown city beyond.

Our survival in Paris pivoted on Aunt Cora, the notoriously undependable person upon whom so much now depended. Also, Wolf having managed successfully to call her and tell her which train we were on, the last of the day, we'd made it by seconds.

A batshit-crazy plan. Wolf could easily have lost the number in our haste. Cora could be drunk. Not even in Paris. Given the frosty relations between her and my mother, she might not want to see us at all.

'Where are we, Maggie?' Kit mumbled, his head lolling on my shoulder, as I carried him to the platform.

'On holiday in Paris,' I replied, straining to see through the milling late-night crowds and scanning the concourse. Over a choppy sea of heads, I spotted a woman waving. Petite, dressed quietly in navy, over one shoulder she carried a large floppy bag, a tiny whiskery nose poking out of it. My aunt, and she was walking towards us. She bore little resemblance to the shouty drunken Cora of old, or even the hesitant woman I'd last seen at my grandmother's funeral. Her grey-blue eyes were clear. Very pretty. She wore her hair in a shiny bob, the colour of red setters. When she hugged me, there was a warmth that took me aback.

'Maggie! Kit. Oh, my goodness, Kit . . .' Aunt Cora squatted down to examine her nephew. 'You've no idea how much I've longed to hang out with you, Kit.' I couldn't think when she'd last seen him, possibly at my father's funeral, although there had been no interaction. Kit hadn't gone to Granny's. 'Would you like to stroke Pierre?'

Kit stared blankly at his aunt, a stranger to him,

then her miniature dog in the velvet bag. He shook his head.

'He's tired,' I explained apologetically.

'You must be too, *non*?' There was an unexpected nimble quickness to Aunt Cora, in the way she spoke and moved, a reminder of how little I'd seen her in the last few years. But there was a deeper familiarity too, hers a voice from my earlier childhood before she and Mum had fallen out. 'Right. You must tell me everything but wait until we get to the apartment.' She considered Kit. 'If you take Pierre, Maggie, maybe I can carry Kit to the taxi.'

I tried to hand Kit over, but he clung to me, the only thing left in his world that hadn't changed.

I rolled down the taxi window, breathed in Paris, its lights, its nocturnal bustle. None of us spoke. I was grateful my aunt wasn't one of those women who felt the need to fill silences or asked endless questions straight off.

'*Ici, merci,*' Aunt Cora said to the driver. The taxi braked hard. An apartment building loomed, grand and old. On each floor, tall windows, many lit up, opening onto delicately ornate metal balconies. A giant boxy grey hat of a roof.

We stepped into a dimly lit foyer, with walls of faded pale green and flaking gilt mouldings. A metal birdcage lift. A wall of postal boxes. Barely alive palms in pots sat at either side of a wide stairwell that swooped down, its mouth opening with a scrolled flourish.

'Our elderly diva of a lift is broken again and I'm on the sixth floor,' Cora apologized. 'Let me take that bag.'

'Can you walk it?' I asked Kit, who shook his head. Cora didn't offer to carry him this time.

Ascending the stone staircase, Kit doubled in weight, and lugging him took the last of my strength. Voices, some shouting, some laughing, swilled behind apartment doors on the different landings. Unfamiliar cooking smells seeped out. Even the cigarette smoke smelt different, stronger, as if it might be tinged brown, not grey. To think we'd only ever been a train journey from my aunt. This whole new world.

Finally, the apartment. The smell of dusty hot radiators, cigarettes and earthy herbal tea, camomile, something like that, the undrinkable stuff. Aunt Cora led us into a small spare room with a futon on the floor, a flowery duvet turned back expectantly. Fighting the urge to collapse into it, I laid Kit down and tugged off his shoes and sweaty socks, settled his head on a strange long tube of a pillow. After staring transfixed, as if she'd never seen a little boy before, my aunt said she'd better leave me to it. Within seconds, Kit had fallen asleep, mumbling Wolf's name, so I returned to the main room, the life of which I knew so little.

The apartment was fronted by two big windows; their shutters open to the Paris skyline, twinkling, like a net of fairy lights. I could have just stood there, sinking my eyes into it, but Cora pointed to her blue sofa: 'Treat it as your own, Maggie. Put your feet up.'

'Thank you, Aunt Cora.'

'Why don't you just call me Cora?'

I nodded, grateful for this – less awkward – and took in my surroundings. A high moulded ceiling and panelled walls, the parchment-pale paint peeling in places, and the only pictures line drawings of horses and dogs. Sparsely furnished. A small round café-style metal table. A green glass ashtray. A promising stack of paperbacks – English and French – on a scratched Perspex coffee-table, others on shelves. Bigger books stacked like pillars. A yoga mat rolled in one corner. A guitar leaning against the wall.

'*Chocolat chaud*? Personally, I like it at night.' Cora offered a steaming hot chocolate, muddy dark. Sitting next to me, cross-legged, she nodded down at the ashtray. 'My last vice, I'm afraid.' Pierre hopped onto her lap. 'But I'll smoke on the balcony, don't worry.'

I couldn't explain how far down on my list of worries her smoking might fall. Neither was I sure I could talk without bursting into tears. It was such an enormous relief to feel that an adult was in charge and not me. To sit and sip sweet cocoa and know that Kit was safe, warm in bed.

'So,' Cora prompted, when I still didn't speak, 'what's going on? Your friend, Wolf – is he more than a friend?'

I nodded, my throat starting to close.

'Well, he was very cryptic on the phone. Wouldn't be drawn.' Cora put her cup on the coffee-table, turned so she was facing me, and spoke firmly. 'Listen, Maggie, I am your aunt, not your mother. And anything you have done, I have done far, far worse, okay? Seriously. I won't judge you.'

I nodded but knew she would. Any person would. I'd fled the scene of a crime, left a man dead. If I told her, she could easily call the police on Wolf. I couldn't risk it.

'You're not pregnant?'

I shook my head.

Cora looked relieved. 'When I was a teenager, I ran away from home four times. Each time I was fetched back by my parents. The fourth time aged seventeen – your age – I ran away and no one came to fetch me back. It's best to resolve things if –'

'It's not that.' And I haltingly explained about my mother not coming home, the message on the answer-machine, Marco's promise to find her. Cora's expression darkened and she kept asking me to repeat things: 'Sorry, *how* long has your mother been gone?' Under the worry, a restrained anger. 'What the hell is she thinking?'

'No, no, it's my fault too.'

'How can it be your fault, Maggie?' Cora retorted, as if she'd already picked a side, and it was mine.

My resistance to London. Flunking college. Barely leaving my room. Cora dismissed all this with a flick of her small hand. 'Bah. Why should you, or any girl of seventeen, toe the line? In fact, I'd say it's your duty not to.'

Because my aunt was kind and I liked her and I felt like I'd had to be brave – and in denial – for so long, the sobs were volcanic, engulfing. The shoulder-shaking, snot-bubbling sort. Cora held me firmly, her chin resting on the top of my head. 'Maggie, you've done nothing wrong,' she said, over and over, until I almost believed it.

Eventually, my eyelids grew heavy, the shock of the day mingling with memories to form slow, swirling, cinematic half-dreams. The midnight-blue of my mother's vintage Madame Grès evening gown. The draped folds of the fabric, fluid as Mum walked, holding a glass of champagne, the sparkling liquid the same colour as her eyes. The wink of a diamond. My father wearing a black jacket, the velvety moleskin one he called his James Bond. Leaning down to Mum's ear, telling her she looked beautiful, too beautiful, and he was so goddamn proud she was his.

At some point, I was aware of Cora settling a

blanket over me, then moving around, unfamiliar light footsteps, the digestive gurgles of the apartment's pipes, the whiff of cigarette smoke, then the click of a telephone, and different calls, hushed and heated. Hearing my mother's name and trying to listen, I fought to surface. The dragnet of sleep pulled me back down, only for me to bob up again with Pierre licking my hand, Cora's voice rising, 'Well, you'd better retrieve her, Marco. A good mother wouldn't do this! . . . What? Why can't I say that?' Her voice shook. 'No, Marco. I trusted my sister to be the mother to Kit that I couldn't be. She took my precious little boy, and now she's abandoned him.'

32

Kit

London, May 2019

The sinking sun paints a copper line across Kit's living-room floor. Zilch from Wolf. Not even the briefest reply to the email. Kit shuts his laptop. His pride is hurt, his head jumbled. His stomach snarls with hunger and he's stupidly smoked in the flat, without opening a window. Screw it, he'll honour his dinner with Roy. His feet numbly prickling from sitting cross-legged on the sofa for so long, Kit stands up – and snaps out of a spell.

He glances at his phone: another missed call from Cora. Kit hesitates, knowing he should ring her back. A good son would. But he's not like other sons, Cora not like other mothers. With a stab of perception so sharp it hurts, it strikes Kit his search for Wolf, on a slow simmer over the years, intensifying these last few days, has been an elaborate psychological distraction. A displacement technique. By fixating on Wolf, he's been able to ignore real-life relationships. Especially the one with Cora.

Kit's index finger hovers over 'Call'. It shouldn't be this hard. He's still not sure why it is. And always has been, ever since Cora told him one winter's afternoon. He'd been sitting at a kitchen table next to Maggie, who clearly already knew. There was cake.

Cora has said sorry so many times since, explained the self-treachery of alcoholism, the quicksand of her life at the time, and how she'd not been able to care for him properly. It was like being in a thick blizzard, he remembers her saying once, and she couldn't see even a foot ahead. Deemed unfit to keep him, she hadn't wanted him fostered by strangers. He deserved a solid start, a safe home. And if she hadn't been involved in his early life, it was the decision of his legal adoptive parents, Dee Dee and Damian. Not hers.

Grown-up Kit hears Cora's devastated contrition. The regret. The pain. But he still has little-boy hands firmly cupped over his ears, just as he had that day. If Cora was someone else's mother, Kit would be much more understanding.

Having seen friends battle with addiction, Kit knows the way its jaws clamp and tear, trying to pull them down into a death roll. Addiction couldn't care less if you're a new mother, or you grew up in a nice house in the country, or if you're breaking your sweet sister's heart, it wants you lying alone under the surface so it can strip every bit of flesh until you're gone. Yeah, Kit gets all that. But it's much harder to be liberal and sympathetic when that shit-show is yours.

And if he feels guilty about their fractious relationship – and he does, persistently, but not as guilty as she – then he reminds himself of the vow he made as a boy. To keep Cora at a distance so as not to risk being rejected again since that would destroy him completely. This tactic has worked okay so far. Hasn't it?

Yet his mind often draws back to Cora. Galloping alongside him when he was a boy. He remembers the mud spray, the thunder of hoofs, the big country sky. How they were always most at ease together riding, not talking, not even looking at one another, just moving through a landscape. He misses it. That feeling. A rare, fleeting sense of completeness.

Kit leans back against the wall and stares at her number. Cora, for all her faults, tries to show up, again and again – unlike Wolf – while he often inflicts on her what Wolf has just done to him. The indifferent slight of non-response. Evasion. And if he'd let her, she'd be here to diss Wolf – 'Bah! His loss!' – and rescue him from Roy, with one of her absurd Cora-isms: 'Sorry to interrupt your dinner, but I need to reclaim Kit to deal with the dogs.'

Maggie has always insisted Cora is on his side,

even when he's not on hers. For the first time, tenderized by disillusion with Wolf, Kit feels this to be true. But when he slips on his corduroy jacket, he drops the phone into its pocket, and puts off the call for another day.

33

Maggie

London, May 2019

In the grand foyer of the Mayfair auction house, Lordats, Maggie discreetly picks dog hairs off her trousers. The building is both reverently hushed and busy, its gleaming marble floor criss-crossed by purposeful, impressive people. The men have the stubbled look of film directors, the women chic and clever in black, the older contingent resplendent in their expertise, with the satisfied air of having enjoyed a fine lunch. Few take any notice of Maggie, clearly not a high-net-worth client seeking a Lucian Freud sketch for her downstairs loo.

The Gina Lollobrigida lookalike on the front desk eyes Maggie coolly over the top of her red-framed glasses as she talks on the phone. Maggie's offered her old name, rather than Foale – 'Could you just say it's Maggie Parker, please?' – so that Wolf recognizes it.

Shifting from one foot to the other, her turbulent thoughts skiff back to the human remains. Who might remember seeing her, Wolf and Kit fleeing that day? Or Gav. What sort of forensics might damn them? Saving Maggie from freefalling further, Lollobrigida puts down the phone. 'I'm afraid Mr Derry has a meeting.'

Maggie doesn't hear the rest. Humiliated, rejected, she turns for the exit. Heaving back the weighty brass door, she feels a light tap on her arm.

'Ms Parker?' A glossy lock of dark hair has dislodged from Lollobrigida's up-do, as if she's just run across the atrium. 'Mr Derry was hoping you'd meet him by . . .' She pauses breathlessly, double-checks the Post-it note in her hand. '. . . Peter Pan in Kensington Gardens? In one hour. May I let him know if this is possible?'

For two decades, Maggie has yearned for this day. Rehearsing it, writing it, dozens of times, disguised as historical fiction, tucked between eighteenth-century bedsheets. And now it is here, in real life, in real time, she is . . . not ready.

In John Lewis, Maggie whirls around the make-up counters, spraying perfume, sweeping on too much bronzer then wiping it off in streaks. She buys a clothes brush, attacks the dog hairs. Outside, Oxford Street boils with crowds. Nervous sweat trickling down the back of her knees, she raises her arm, jumps into a black cab.

Hyde Park. Maggie leaps out. Quick march towards

the Serpentine, west of the Long Water. Finally, there's Peter Pan, the bronze boy lifting his bugle. But she cannot see Wolf. Of course he's not coming. He'll have had second thoughts. She shouldn't have turned up at his work, breaking all their rules, invading his world. What a fool she is.

Then it starts. The crackle of something tuning – like an old dial-up connection. Maggie's gaze shifts a few degrees to the left, sliding along the railings to the man standing by a wooden bench under a large lime tree. He is watching her, wearing black-rimmed glasses, his eyes the colour of sea from space. Maggie's breath catches. The rest of the park blurs to a swirl of green.

Shakily, Maggie walks closer until she's under the tree and fastened to that gaze once more. Wolf. Her Wolf. Not a mirage, or a man in a photo, but alive, real, his older face proof of a life lived. She's had to grieve him: he may as well have died. And here he is.

Under his breath he says, 'Maggie.' She can smell his cologne – leather, woodsmoky, expensive. He doesn't try to kiss or hug her, so she doesn't dare.

'Are . . . are you still known as Wolf?' she manages, a stupid question but a wonder she can speak at all. She feels over-filled, unstable.

'Only to you.' He smiles slowly, searching her face for something. He's had his chipped tooth fixed. She feels strangely sad about it.

The air rearranges itself around them. She doesn't

know how long they stand there, derailed, time sliding backwards, forwards again. Only that Wolf looks older than she'd expected, altered by what he carries. And she desperately wants to run her fingers over the lines around his eyes, the silver at his temples, feel the nub of his navy suit, worn with a white shirt, brown suede brogues. Kit will approve. And the same urge that blew up in her seventeen-year-old body returns, just as forcefully, a need to bury herself against him, zip herself under his skin. But she no longer has permission to do this. They cannot do this.

No wedding ring, Maggie notes. But he must belong to another woman. Someone taut-bodied, polished and not covered with dog hair. Even if what happened hadn't, Wolf has ascended beyond her reach. As an antiques man with a forensic eye, he will see her joins, the wear and tear, the patination on her thirty-eight-year-old writer's face from frowning at a computer screen, a body that ingests too much cheese and sits too long.

'I did try not to be found.' Wolf glances around him. 'But I'm glad you managed it.'

'Kit found you.'

'Ah. He sent me an email. This beautiful email, Maggie, I . . .' He palms his clean-shaven cheek. 'I haven't replied. I can't, obviously.' He looks pained. 'Does he know?'

Maggie shakes her head. 'Not yet. But I sometimes

wonder if, deep down, he does.' It's easier talking about Kit, rather than the two of them, the chasm of the years. 'And it's his brain protecting itself. Blocking things out.'

Leaf shadow plays over Wolf's troubled face. The earthy coolness of the Serpentine reaches towards them. He is waiting: he knows there's a reason she's come.

'So, the builders have found . . .' Maggie can't say 'remains'. Nor does she have to. She's never seen anyone drain of colour so fast.

'I am sorry, Maggie.'

'No, I . . . I'm sorry.' If Maggie could, she'd reach back into the past and scrub away the love that grew so rapidly, so intensely, leaving a good man with blood on his hands, another dead. 'So sorry.' Her voice breaks. She mustn't cry or make any sort of scene. Trying to sniff back the tears, she makes an ugly snort. 'I ruined your life.'

'No, no, Maggie. In a way you saved it,' he insists, as she shakes her head, disbelieving. 'You did. You gave me hope. You seemed to believe, against all evidence to the contrary, I could do anything.'

'You're where you deserve to be.'

'No. I should be in jail.' Agitated, Wolf rakes back his hair, just as he always did. It is still thick and boyish but for the grey, with that same sticky-uppy crown. 'Or in hiding like Gav.'

'Where is he?' She catches herself. 'Sorry. You don't need to answer that.'

'I can't anyway, Maggie. I've long given up waiting to hear from him. Never did forgive me for dragging him into it, I guess,' Wolf says heavily. 'Gav has a track history of cutting people out of his life. He's done it before. Step out of line, become a liability, that's it. Not a man to do things by halves.' He's staring grimly out at the water, the flotillas of ducks and geese, his heavy dark brows drawing together. 'But there have been sightings over the years. He's like bloody Lord Lucan.'

'That must be so hard. To know he's out there somewhere. Not to be in contact.' She's not sure what other family Wolf's got.

'Well, it's my fault. I should never have called him. Put him in that position.' Wolf's jaw grits. 'And I'm not surprised Gav went to ground. Shut up shop. Even if he wasn't spotted that night, he'd have got paranoid, I know he would. Claustrophobic. Terrified of prison. Any small space. The man couldn't even step into a lift.' He waits for a couple to pass before continuing. 'And, like me, he'd have known this day was coming. London moves. Clay soils, things subside. Someone renovates.'

A possibility slips darkly towards Maggie. If pressed, they could let the police think Gav had killed Cooper. Appalled at herself, she doesn't suggest it.

They are quiet for a moment. She wants to hold Wolf and tell him it'll be okay, but she cannot, and it won't.

'That summer, three times I walked into a police station to confess, then lost my nerve and slunk out again.'

Picturing it too clearly, something in Maggie scrunches tight. 'I wish you'd told me all this at the time. Talked to me. Let me *in*.' She blows out, trying not to cry. 'Remember when you called me that Christmas? Out of the blue.'

Christmas Eve, 2003. One of those stormy winter nights, Maggie peeling sprouts for the next day. Having not heard from him for years, the last thing she'd expected was the Old Rectory's landline to ring, Wolf at the end of it, setting her heart on fire again. Even though her own lovely boyfriend had been sitting nearby on the sofa. Even though Wolf was almost unintelligibly drunk, and she could hear a party thumping in the background. He'd just wanted to wish her a happy Christmas, he'd slurred. That was about as far as they'd got. The call lasted a few seconds. Afterwards, Maggie had pressed 1471, retrieved his number and texted him her own mobile number, asking him to call her back. But he never did. A few weeks later, when she inevitably broke and phoned him, that mobile number no longer existed.

'Drinking and calling, never a good look. You must have thought . . .'

'I *missed* you, you've no idea.' Her voice cracks.

'Maggie, I was a total mess afterwards. For a long time,' he mutters, in a way that suggests this is a great understatement.

'I'd have been there for you,' she whispers angrily.

'And I couldn't be there for you,' he says, voice slung low with sorrow. 'I'm deeply ashamed of that, Maggie. Among many other things.' He is quiet for a moment. 'People think trauma is a uniting force. But it's the loneliest, isn't it? Pushes you away. Apart from everyone else. Like being in a sealed cold dark room.'

Neither of them speaks. Too much to say. Too many things that came before. Wolf's hands knot and unknot restlessly. Hands Maggie once held and kissed. And she wonders. 'Do you still box?'

'No!' he says, with a small laugh that quickly fades. 'Obviously not.'

'You must miss it.'

He says nothing, his shoulders square beneath his jacket, as if he's holding his breath.

'Still,' she says, after a while, 'you did think like a boxer.'

Believe you can win. Especially if you're losing. Maggie has always clung to those words, spoken in a smoky Portobello pub decades before. She's often quoted them to Kit.

'You remember that?' Wolf says, with a surprised smile.

Maggie feels as if she's revealed too much. She's also sure that if they were to lie down on the grass, under a tree, staring up at the dimming London sky, the gap of the years would close, and they'd know everything about one another without a word being spoken.

'Well, it's true that after a few months I realized that if I wasn't man enough to hand myself in I had to get my act together in some way. Couldn't just stand on bridges, wishing I had the courage to throw myself off.'

'Jesus.'

'I didn't, did I?' Wolf pauses, daring to look at her, his gaze a flame of blue. 'I thought of you, Maggie. Those conversations on the roof terrace, remember?'

'Yes.' Always. They'd forged their dreams up there, nestled among the rooftops.

'Well, that's what walked me off the bridge, so to speak.'

This kills her. A brilliant green leaf whirls down, and lands on her sleeve. She picks it off, twirls its stem in her fingers, studies it, knowing if she looks at Wolf, she'll lose it.

'So, I finally took what was left of Gav's stock, the stuff I'd put in storage, safekeeping for him – I discovered he'd swiped the smaller valuables before he left, no doubt in a hurry – fixed it up, sold it on, and with that money I bought and sold more stock, planning to pay Gav back. Got myself on evening courses, then found work as an assistant at Christie's, proving myself over and over. But I could never relax. Never ease up, not for a second. Worked all hours. Living on coffee and cortisol. Never took a day for granted.' Wolf smiles with a shrug. 'Hence the grey hairs.'

'You've come so far.' And he'll lose it all.

'I know what it must look like. But I have tried to atone, Maggie, in my own small way. Mentor schemes. Bursaries . . . Barely scrapes the surface, I know.'

A perturbed silence thickens between them. Wolf clears his throat and stares down at his feet. Maggie wonders how it's possible to miss someone so much and have them standing right next to you.

'When your first novel came out, I opened a bottle of Dom Pérignon,' he says suddenly. 'Toasted you alone in my King's Cross flat.'

'Hang on.' She tries to get her head around this. 'You *knew*?'

The mischievous grin she remembers so well. 'After reading each book, I left a five-star Amazon review. Under another name, obviously. But I always hoped you'd know they were mine.'

'Oh, my God, no. I had no idea! I don't even read my reviews since I'm tortured by the bad ones.' Maggie wants to tip her head back and scream. 'What can we do? Tell me, I'll do it. There must be a way out of this.'

'Maggie, what happened wasn't your fault. There's no "we".'

The shadows of swollen dark clouds are moving across the expanse of water, like creatures beneath the surface.

'But it was self-defence! You didn't mean for the punch to kill Cooper,' she whispers hotly.

'Ssh, please.' Wolf lowers his voice. 'A jury won't believe that. Not after all this time. I'm going down, and I'm not taking you with me.'

Wolf's preparing for jail already, Maggie realizes, with a shudder. He will bow his head at the sentencing. Plead guilty. Apologize to the court, to everyone affected. Thank the judge. Be a model prisoner. She cannot let this happen.

'But what if no one links you to our house?' Desperation builds in Maggie. She pushes Clemence and Suki from her mind, knowing they remember him. 'What if you can get away with it? I mean, if I don't say anything when the police interview me . . .'

'Maggie, no, no. That's perjury. You'll get into all sorts of trouble.' Wolf swallows. 'More trouble. You'll need a good lawyer too. I'm so sorry.'

'But me naming you won't bring back Cooper, will it? And if no one is charged then . . . then . . . who loses?'

Wolf shakes his head. 'Maggie, please.'

'Okay. Well, leave the country, then. Like Gav. You still have time! You do! There must be places you can go. South America? Anywhere.'

'I'm not running. Not any more.'

She looks up at the tree, its hoop skirt of leaves. The thought of losing Wolf again. She can't bear it.

'Hey. I'm tougher than I look in this suit.' Wolf's eyes glint with some of his old defiance, a refusal to be cowed. 'I'll be all right.'

Maggie starts to feel dizzy. A cockapoo bolts past, trailing its lead. A mother, a startled baby bouncing on her hip, charges after it.

'So, you're going to walk away from here, nice and easy, okay? Back to your life. Your books. Paris. And when the police call, which they will, you will not lie for me, Maggie. Just tell the truth, please?' He steps forward – Maggie catches her breath – and places a light kiss on her cheek. 'You. Me. We had that, Maggie. Not for very long. But some people never ever have it.'

Maggie can no longer hide her devastation, or hold back the tears.

'You must go,' he says, with gentle insistence.

'I don't know where to go any more. I can't write. I – I don't know how *to be* now. Can we not . . . walk? Just for a bit? It's been so long. Please.'

Wolf looks torn, then resolute. 'CCTV everywhere. It won't play well, us meeting like this, conspiring. It'll look really bad for you.'

Late-afternoon sunshine pricks through the leaves. And with it a spike of clarity, a crushing certainty: she still loves this man, body and soul. After all these years. Despite everything that happened. Whether or not he loves her back.

'Goodbye, Maggie Parker,' Wolf says softly.

Too choked to speak – she hates goodbyes and hates this goodbye more than any other – Maggie watches Wolf shape-shift into Will, a successful London antiques adviser once again, strolling away from the statue of Peter Pan, with its tantalizing, terrifying promise of never-ending childhood.

Bereft, filleted, Maggie stares until Wolf vanishes into the leafy parakeet-green, then she sinks to the bench, takes out her phone and scrolls down and down until she finds a suspiciously rapturous review to her last novel, posted by 'skateboard98' and reads it, shaking all over, her heart leaping at the last line.

34

Kit

London, May 2019

A sudden downpour, rain falling like glass drops, shattering on the pavement. Holding his jacket over his head, Kit dashes five minutes down the street to Giovanni's, his home from home. And, yes, there's Roy at a table by the rain-greased window, baggy-faced and reading the newspaper, nursing a beer, almost finished, suggesting he's been there a while. The sight makes Kit's heart sink, even though Roy messaged earlier to reserve some bigger-ticket items, including a post-war Scandinavian painting and a French automaton that Kit's been struggling to shift. He'll make a tidy profit on both.

'I got waylaid. Sorry, Roy.' Kit shakes off his jacket, hangs it on the bentwood coat stand. The familiar tomato-basil smell is comforting. It's not his usual table, though, and is next to the draughty door.

Roy has spruced himself up. A pale blue shirt, a navy blazer. 'Kit, you don't look too clever. You all right?'

Kit nods, chewing his lip, still smarting about Wolf.

Roy cocks his head, eyes him curiously. 'Come on, tell me.' He presses harder. 'What is it?'

'I found Wolf,' Kit admits quietly, unable to hold it inside.

Roy sucks in a wheezy gasp. 'You didn't. Where?'

'Lordats.'

'The auctioneers? Oh, my days.'

'He works there, yeah. Will Derry.'

'Will Derry?' Quietly marvelling, Roy pulls a stubby pencil from his jacket pocket, scrawls these details on the corner of the *Evening Standard*. 'Done well for himself, hasn't he? This Mr Derry.'

Kit nods, still glad about this. But he's aware of a bad feeling building inside too. Something a bit off about Roy tonight. A hecticness. And it dawns on him that he actually doesn't much like this man. He's not sure why. A dissonance between what Roy says, that light affability, and the colder, intense look in his eyes as he says it. Maybe that. Or the chemistry is just wrong. Kit should never have got involved.

The old waiter walks over and smiles. 'Usual?'

'Same,' says Roy. 'Whatever he's having. And your finest house white.'

Kit pecks at his phone again, checking no email from Wolf has landed.

'Lordats.' Roy whistles under his breath. His foot taps nervily under the table.

With a sinking heart, Kit realizes he's blurted Wolf's workplace far too hastily, like an over-sharing spurned friend.

'You won't be the only one glad to have found him,' Roy mutters, compounding Kit's regret.

'You mean the people who say Wolf owes them money?' Shit.

Roy looks at him blankly, seeming to have forgotten this earlier claim.

'I don't want to cause trouble.' Kit starts to panic, imagining an ugly chain of events, caused by his indiscretion. 'Do you mind not saying anything to these people?'

'Oh, right, yes, yes,' says Roy, edgy and preoccupied. Fingering the newspaper's ruffled edge, he clears his throat. 'I've got something to show you, Kit. It's big. Bigger than Wolf.' Shaking out the *Evening Standard*, he flops it open in the centre of the table. 'Grate your eyeballs on *that*.'

'*Suspected human remains found in Notting Hill house.*' Kit reads on, slack-mouthed, the restaurant shrinking to the black letters on the page.

'Not exactly the movie ending, is it?'

'Jesus. I saw police vans there earlier today. A part of the street roped off. Our old street,' he murmurs, his hand over his mouth.

'Your old house.'

'*What?*' The past leaps into his lap, knocking Kit

back in his chair. 'Oh, my God. That's – that's mad.' He can't take it in. 'They must be historic. Dig anywhere in London and there are old burial sites.'

'They'll find out quickly, I imagine.' Roy broods. 'The police will be crawling all over the place.' A muscle twitches in his jaw. 'Unless those bones still have meat on them, they'll be wanting to talk to all the past residents, Kit.'

'Shit. You're right.' Maggie will hate this. She's the sort of person who sweats when innocently walking through Customs. He readies to stand up. 'Sorry, Roy. I should go and call my sister.'

'But we've ordered. And you look like you could do with a feed.' The wine arrives. Roy tastes it, with an unnecessary mouth swill, and nods at the waiter. 'Kit, no one wants to hear news like that over the phone.'

Kit hesitates. Roy might be right. And he's seeing Maggie later. Yes, better tell her in person. He attempts to ease a sudden queasiness with a gulp of wine. It doesn't help.

'To think we were so recently yakking about Wolf and that temper of his.' Roy speaks mildly but sharply eyes Kit over the rim of his wine glass. 'The funny atmosphere in his uncle's antiques shop. Didn't you say he was your sister's boyfriend back then? Hanging out at that house.'

Kit can't remember what he told Roy now. Only wishes he hadn't.

Roy's face grows grave. 'It'll be your duty to tell the police about that. You know, do the right thing.'

Kit stares back at him blankly, something inside twisting uneasily.

'I mean if a chap is going to threaten to kill his uncle, what else is he . . .' Roy hangs a line of unthinkables in the ellipsis.

'That's quite some leap! Jesus, Roy. The remains could be three hundred years old.'

Roy holds up his large, spidery hands. 'Yes, yes, of course. Sorry. Imagination drifting a bit, that's all.'

Kit's disquiet grows. The restaurant door opens and shuts, breathing cold air down his neck. New diners settle in, glad to be out of the damp evening and inside the neighbourhood Italian, where it always feels a bit like Sicily. Just not for Kit. Not today.

'Forget I said anything.' Roy raises his glass. 'Anyway, here's hoping they nab the bugger who did it.'

Kit reads the article again, upside down, and frowns. 'Er, the house isn't identified in this.'

'Just came from a pub on Portobello Road. Everyone's talking about it. And knows exactly which house. Now owned by some hair-teaser tycoon.' He smiles through a grimace. 'Had a couple of cub reporters trotting into the bar – everyone looks so flaming young – sniffing around, asking dumb questions, establishing it was Dee Dee's old place.' The foot is tapping under the table more ferociously now, his thigh shaking the edge of the tablecloth. 'It's a starry neighbourhood, and glamour sells newspapers.' He drops his voice. 'But you'd know that, right?'

Kit doesn't answer. He hates that the Parkers' family story was ever consumed as light entertainment. The waiter shuffles over and slides two bowls of *fusilli al tonno* to the table.

'So,' says Roy, spearing pasta with his fork. 'The other thing I wanted to talk to you about?'

Kit had forgotten about that. It doesn't feel important now. He fidgets with his phone, wanting to scroll and see what the online sleuths are saying – he's as bad as anyone.

Human remains. It rams at Kit again. 'You know, Roy, no offence, but can we leave it tonight? I'm not sure I can eat right now. This is turning into an exceptionally weird day.' He slides twenty quid out of his wallet and tucks it under his water glass. 'I've put those items on hold for you and sent over my bank details.'

'Wait, please.' A fleck of tuna quivers on Roy's lower lip. He looks vulnerable again in the way older people can, like they need saving. 'Hear me out. It won't take long.'

Kit stifles a sigh. 'Go on.'

'It's about you being adopted,' Roy says, in a measured voice.

Kit stands up, reaching for his jacket. Blood rushes to his head. 'Not the time, mate.'

'There's never going to be a good time, Kit, that's the thing. And it's been long enough.' Roy's face tautens, gearing up. 'So, I'm just going to come out with it.'

'With what?' Adrenalin starts to pump. Oh, God. A nut job. A Dee Dee obsessive. He's fallen for it. The checks in the red gingham tablecloth start to jump.

'I have reason to believe that I am your biological father, Kit.'

It's like the silence after a huge explosion. 'No,' Kit breathes, stepping backwards. 'No, you're fucking not.'

'Yes, Kit, yes! Me and Cora. We were in the same bad scene. Wild times. You can ask her about me,' Roy says, in a fast, low voice.

The restaurant starts to swim. Kit feels trapped, duped by this man. Some dirtbag from Cora's dissolute days, not an antiques customer at all. He suddenly wants his sister. 'Bullshit.'

'Hear me out,' Roy begs. Other diners peer over curiously. 'Sit down. Please?'

Although Kit wants to run, something grips him, makes him sink to his chair.

Roy grips the stem of his wine glass, his expression intent. 'I'd totally lost touch with my old crowd, you see. Been travelling, touring in a band, dabbling with antiques and the rest. So, it was five years *after* you were born that I bumped into a one-time buddy from that era who asked me about rumours Cora had had a baby and given it up for adoption. He assumed I knew! So, I did the maths, worked out the dates. But I couldn't find Cora to ask. She'd left the country, in a bad way apparently, and then one day I turned on the TV . . .'

Kit wants to squeeze his eyes shut. He wants to un-see Roy. Un-hear what's coming next.

'And there's Cora's supermodel sister! And she has her kid in the studio, modelling children's clothes and the camera panned to your face . . . and there you were. And I thought . . . *Whoa*. Strong Foale genes in that one.' Roy drains his wine. His hand is shaking. 'I had no idea she'd adopted you until I picked up a mag in the doctor's waiting room a few months later, and there's this big interview, Dee Dee talking about how she and her late husband had completed their family with adoption because she'd not been able to have another child and how grateful she was to this kid's unknown birth-parents. And, you know, back of my head, these bells started ringing. I worked out the dates again and they fitted, and I thought, Surely, surely, *surely* she hasn't adopted Cora's baby . . . Nah.'

Kit shakes his head, unable to metabolize any of it.

'So, I hunt down Dee Dee, easy enough now she's in Notting Hill – a pap photographer points me to her house – and I test the waters. I say, "That's Cora's baby . . ." and I tell her I think the kid is mine. And you know what? She doesn't deny it.' Roy clicks his tongue. 'The woman just stares at me, like I'm a piece of dirt, and tells me to leave her alone. After that, I'd watch you, Kit. Skateboarding. Walking to school with some young Kiwi bloke. Kicking a ball about.'

A black-and-white football shoots across Kit's mind's eye. It stills, sharpens into focus, and he can suddenly picture it in their little Notting Hill garden. And there's something disarranged, sinister about that football. With a jolt, he remembers the sickly sweet smell of the heaped honeysuckle that hung over the brick wall.

'I – I wanted to hug you, Kit. Like I want to hug you now.' Roy's eyes glisten with tears. The tip of his nose has pinked. 'I've thought of this day a long time.'

But it's a day Kit has always dreaded, never sought. He stares down at the tablecloth, numbly shaking his head.

'Not long after you lot moved away,' Roy continues, settling back into his story, oblivious to Kit's mute horror. 'Clean vanished from London. Who knows where you were? It was before Facebook, all that. People just left back then. You couldn't easily trace them. Not if they weren't in your neighbourhood.' Kit can almost see Roy's mind turning as he speaks, stopping and starting, a pathway of words, one put down then another. He knows he's being led somewhere but is too stunned to ask the right questions. 'So, you know what I thought? This gives me time to step up. Make myself worthy. Get my shit together.' Roy shrinks back in the chair slightly. 'It's taken a fair while, I give you that.' He drains his glass of wine. 'I'm not pretending to be a saint, Kit. I've done some bad things in my time but show me a man who hasn't.'

Kit's shock is numbing, lobotomizing. All he knows is that, on some instinctive primal level, Roy makes his skin crawl. He cannot bear the idea of him as his father.

'Why do you think I kept that little doll, eh? I found it on your doorstep, Kit, knew it was yours.'

'No,' Kit mumbles, his stomach roiling, his mouth dry. Finally, he finds the words. 'You're manipulative and you've tricked me. And I don't believe . . .'

'Oh, Kit. When I was young, I was a looker, just like you. Our cheekbones are the same.'

Kit's fingers touch his own. He wants to claw them out from under his skin.

'We can do the DNA thingamajig,' Roy says more desperately. 'Think about it, Kit. You won't be alone any longer. And nor will I. You'll have my back, won't you, your own flesh and blood? Then we can pool our resources. Open a business! Father and son, right?'

'Stop. Just stop,' Kit shouts. Other diners are staring, a concerned Giovanni striding over. On the skin at the back of his neck, he feels the damp backdraught of air from the opening restaurant door. Hears his name uttered and, like a miracle, Maggie. But she stops in her tracks, staring at Roy, her confusion chased by an ashen dawning, a look of appalled recognition. She covers her mouth with a hand, and Kit thinks she's about to vomit.

35

Maggie

Paris, May 1998

Apart from the seam of light at the edge of the shutters, the room was as dark as a box. Footsteps echoed on distant stairs. I lay on the futon, Kit curled against me, his little-boy heart ticking against my forearm, his sweaty foot stuck to my calf. When he stirred, I stroked the curls off his forehead, settling him back again.

As my eyes adjusted to the gloom, the room took shape. The space was mostly taken up by our futon. Within reach of my outstretched arm, a desk, a dangling lamp cable. I pressed its switch, puddling light across the desk's neatly arranged surface: a big beige computer, some notebooks, and a wedge of papers – my aunt's work as a translator, I guessed. And a silver-framed photograph of two girls. Extricating myself from Kit, I reached up and grabbed it.

I recognized them both immediately, even though, growing up, there'd been no photographs displayed of my mother and Cora as girls. In this one, they looked around nine or ten, standing in the meadow near the Old Rectory's stables. Mum is smiling, at ease with the camera, wearing a red polka-dot dress with frills. Cora is in shorts and a T-shirt, boyish, elfin, staring down the camera lens as if challenging it to a fight. Then I noticed their hands. Their little fingers not just touching but curled, hooked into the other's.

'*Bonjour*,' whispered Cora, cracking open the bedroom door. A black button nose pushed through, quickly followed by a bolt of silky autumnal fur and a wagging tail. Cora padded in wearing blue and white striped pyjama bottoms and a vest top, the dense map of tattoos on her upper arms a jerking reminder of the time I'd seen her at the family wedding, rambling, swaying and barefoot in a skimpy party dress. Her gaze dropped to the photo, and I coloured, feeling caught out.

Cora smiled, scooped up Pierre and sat lightly on the edge of the futon. 'We were dear friends once, your mother and I.'

Not knowing what to say, I fumbled the picture back onto the desk.

'As you and Kit clearly are too. He's lucky to have you, Maggie.' Her arms crossed on her knees, Cora gazed at Kit with a look of wonder. I took the opportunity to cross-reference the determined line of their chins, their aquiline noses, then glanced back at the photo. And it took a moment to see it. For that shiver of understanding to travel through me. Kit resembled the girl in the photograph.

So, I'd not dreamed Cora's telephone call the previous night. *This* was surely the family secret Cooper had been threatening to expose if my mother didn't cough up. Given she'd not told me or Kit, I guessed she'd have done anything to avoid it being splashed over the papers.

'What is it, Maggie?' Cora laid a hand on my back. It felt light and strong, inquisitive, gathering information by touch.

Part of me wanted to stay silent, let the secret live on rather than force it into the light.

'Maggie?' she asked again.

'I overheard you on the phone. Last night. Talking about Kit.'

We sat on the sofa, facing the half-closed shutters and the laddered sunlight, Cora curled into one corner, me the other, hugging a cushion to my belly.

'He was yours?' I whispered, willing her to deny it.

Cora swallowed hard, nodded, her eyes filling. 'I stopped the drinking, and everything else, when I was pregnant,' she burst out, as if this was always at the forefront of her mind. 'But – but then I didn't.' She tries to steady her voice. 'I couldn't cope. Social services were going to take him off me. Your grand-mother stepped in with a plan. Part of it was this apartment in Paris. An extremely generous method of excision. A way of getting me out of Kit's life so he could settle with his new family, my sister's.'

A plan. My grandmother always had one. My heart sinking, I raked back, remembering how, after my new brother arrived, the house filled with well-wishers' flowers, cards and presents – knitted blue hats, teddies, floppy fabric books – but never my aunt. Not once had she visited.

There was no big Old Rectory family Christmas after Kit joined us either, I remembered. As I thought about all this, queasily, the story of our family rewrote itself, distorting our past and reaching into our future, twisting that out of shape too. Everything I'd believed was no longer true.

'It must have been very hard for you, Cora.' I couldn't think of anything else to say, and reckoned she must have loved Kit even if she couldn't mother him.

Cora swallowed. It took her a while to speak. 'Yes,' she said, her voice racked. 'Yes, it was. You are very sweet. Thank you, Maggie.'

I fiddled with a cushion zip, flicking it back and forth. 'So, is that why you and Mum don't get on?' This was harder to understand now that I was in Cora's company. Kind, smart, a bit unusual, Cora struck me as exactly the sort of woman Mum normally liked.

'It's complicated.' She stood up. 'Now what would you like for –'

'So, who is Kit's dad?' I blurted, queasily picturing Cooper doffing his hat.

Cora slowly sat down again. 'Okay.' She took a moment to compose herself, staring at her hands, bare of rings, or nail polish, with biro marks on her fingers. 'I'm not entirely sure who the father is and, yes, I'm fully aware of how appalling that sounds, Maggie.' She took a shaky breath. 'This is very painful. Would you mind if we left it there? For today. There's a lot going on.'

Agitated, I twirled a hank of my hair. 'A guy called Cooper turned up at the house, and he said . . .'

'*What?* Cooper?' Cora's face flushed. Her mood changed. 'Hang on, Maggie. Tell me everything.'

I realized I'd walked right into it, placing Cooper at our house, which Wolf had told me not to do. I didn't mention the fight, only Cooper blackmailing Mum, his claim that Kit was of his blood. I took a breath, voiced the question I dreaded being answered. 'Could . . . could Cooper be Kit's dad?'

Cora's hesitation stretched uncomfortably. Finally, with obvious reluctance, she nodded, muttered, 'Possibly.' I squeezed my eyes shut. Wolf having killed Kit's biological father put a sick dark spin on the already catastrophic events. What if Kit wanted to find the man when he was older? Or started asking questions? What if, what if . . .

I stared down at Pierre, the fine hairs on the top of his ears, and I felt crushed, unable to conceive of any sort of future. How would I possibly have a normal life, carrying such a secret? Like something huge and lumpen, badly hidden under a jumper.

'Maggie, lovely. It's okay,' Cora tried to assure me. 'I'd heard that Cooper had convinced himself he was the father of my baby. But he has no proof – and nor do I – and no claim on Kit,' she said firmly. 'He's an opportunist, only seeking money. And I'll somehow make sure he never hassles your mother again, I promise,' she added, not knowing Wolf had already done that. 'Listen.' She held both my arms and spoke softly, intently, her face very close to mine. 'Kit was adopted by your family, the Parkers, and that is that, okay? Legal. Final.' Her expression was grim. 'Believe me, I know.'

I nodded, bit the inside of my cheek.

'Maggie,' Cora said urgently, as if some terrible possibility had struck her. Her hands released my arms. 'Does Kit know?'

'No.' Oh, poor Kit.

'You won't say anything? About me. Or Cooper. Your mother didn't want to tell him until he was older, and now is not the time.'

'I won't say anything.' This was a grown-up mess. I didn't want to be the one to break the news. Or mention a dead man's name to Kit or anyone else. Not anytime soon. Ever again, if I could help it.

'I'm so sorry you had to find out like this, Maggie. I really am.' Unexpectedly, she leaned over and gave me a hug, kissing the top of my hair. 'You're an amazing girl, Maggie.'

I closed my eyes, relieved to be held, but also feeling unwashed, and in need of some time alone. 'Can I use your shower?'

'Oh, Maggie, of course. Anything. Let me get you a towel.'

The water pumped out in spurts, fogging the tiny bathroom with steam. Closing my eyes, I tried to rinse myself clean of everything I'd done, seen, heard, while contradictorily not wanting to wash away Wolf, the last places our skin had met. I couldn't see how life would ever be okay again, yet I found pleasure in the hot soapy water, the slippery memories of Wolf, his fingertips tracing down my spine. These opposing feelings swirled, twisting around one another, joy and horror, desire and fear, a surreal suspension and one I'd somehow sustain for years afterwards.

Head on one side, drying my hair with the towel, I returned to the living room, my bare feet on the parquet floor, and stopped. The shutters were now folded back, framing Paris beyond. The rooftops went on for ever. Cream and grey and brown. Spires. Clocks. Pigeons. I stepped onto a narrow metal balcony that felt as precarious as I did, and Paris flew into my heart. A hand around my calf startled me, and I looked down to see Kit. 'The world feels too big,' he mumbled sleepily.

'Only because you're small.' I ruffled his hair and tried not to think of Cooper.

In Kit's presence, Cora and I couldn't discuss anything further, and Cora's attention shifted. Wherever Kit moved in the apartment – and he wanted to inspect everything, plucking the guitar strings, playing with the shutters – her pale grey gaze followed, Kit her magnetic north.

Everything in me pointed at a pinned dot on the earth, a tiny terraced garden in Notting Hill. Desperate to pull away from it, and calm my leaping, spiralling thoughts, I flicked through Cora's bookshelves, discovering authors I'd never come across before, many French. I felt a kinship to my aunt, a fellow reader, a sense of having been robbed of it for years too.

'Lunch,' Cora called. The everyday normality of such an announcement was another surprise. I'd previously never imagined my unruly alcoholic aunt would eat lunch. Or have folded white towels. Or have given birth to my brother, a prism that changed everything, sending pitch-dark shadows and sparks of light into unexpected places.

On the round metal table, salads and quiches, which Kit gobbled up, watched by Cora, who then produced profiteroles and small snakes of jellied orange, coated in chocolate.

Around teatime, I could see Kit's eyelids growing heavy, starting to close. Full, sated, he looked wiped out, so I put him back to bed, then returned to the table. Taking a cue from my aunt, I drank bitter black coffee from a tiny porcelain cup, even though I didn't normally drink coffee. We didn't discuss Cora's relation to Kit any further – its magnitude too large, too dizzying – but it sat there beside us. As did Mum's absence.

Cora kept checking the big man's watch on her slim wrist, then glancing at the door, her attention dropping out of our conversation, then returning. We talked about the bookshops I must visit – could she take me? She'd love to – and the best walks in Paris, her favourite, a circuit taking in the city's finest grand clocks. Was I a walker? What about Kit? What did Kit love to do most? Eat? Read? Finally, my cup was empty, and the caffeine beat wings in my chest. Pierre curled up on my lap. I stroked his hair, long and plush, like the human hair on Gav's antique fashion dolls.

When the intercom buzzed, my aunt put down her

cup with a smart clink, walked to the door with slow deliberation, pressed the intercom with the heel of her hand and waited for the visitor to walk up six flights of stairs. They took for ever. Eventually, a knock. The front door opened, and my aunt took a sharp breath. 'Where the hell have you been?'

36

Maggie

London, May 2019

'Better let you guys catch up on things,' Cooper says, tearing off a scribbled-on corner of newspaper, stuffing it into his pocket, before slipping out of Giovanni's, shooting one last triumphant smirk at Maggie.

The restaurant has fallen silent, the other diners staring, wondering if the odd scene is over. Distraught and confused, Kit clutches his jacket. Maggie needles with shock, unable to accept Cooper's aliveness. The rangy street swagger replaced by a slight stoop and shuffle, a hipster trilby by wispy grey hair. The chiselled face hollowed and sagged with age.

As Cooper disappears outside, greased back into the city itself, Maggie sinks to the chair, her head in her hands. In her blunt shock, she can make no sense of any of it. Cooper. The *Evening Standard*, spread open on the table: *Suspected human remains found in Notting Hill house*. Kit, who appears almost concussed. She dreads what Cooper has just said to him. 'Can we get out of here?'

Outside, Maggie half expects Cooper to be lurking by a lamp post, just as he always did. But the street is emptying fast, people rushing along with umbrellas, the city engorged with rain, fizzing in the gutters, boiling up from the drains. Rain drips into her eyes. 'Do you want to talk, Kit?' she asks shakily.

Impossible to know where the story even starts now. *Cooper. Is. Not. Dead.*

'I want to walk. Or my head will explode.'

'If you don't mind getting wet.'

'I couldn't give any fucks.'

'I need to make a very quick call first. Really, really sorry. But I must.' Maggie urgently dials Lordats but drops straight to voicemail. She needs to find Wolf.

If Wolf had got it wrong, and Cooper was not killed by his knockout punch to the head – in their blind panic, it'd not occurred to them to check for a pulse – but came round and walked away, Wolf needs to know this. If Cooper is not dead, isn't Wolf free? They are free. And Gav has some explaining to do.

Dulled by shock, Maggie's mind snags on the newspaper headline, unable to make sense of it. Their old house, surely. But how can there *still* be human remains? She scrapes weakly at possible explanations. Perhaps they are connected to their old landlord, who wanted to rent out in haste then vanished off to India. Or they could be historic, part of London's grisly archaeology. A potter. A pig farmer. Yes, yes, that.

All Maggie knows is that Cooper is alive. And for twenty-one years she and Wolf have kept apart, sure they'd incriminate one another, roped to that house, that day, that man. Believing something unspeakably ugly had sprung from something so beautiful: death from love. Maggie tries to calculate the stolen time: at least seven thousand midnights. Wolf's review of her last novel swells her heart again: *Life-affirming. Reread over and over, just to share time with this author on the page. 5 stars.* skateboard98

'Could you walk to Mayfair, Kit?' Wolf had said he worked late. There's a small chance. 'Lordats.'

'No,' Kit bites back. 'Wolf blanked me. Not that it matters now. Nothing fucking matters now.' He stares down the street, eyes blazing like lamps. 'Roy . . .'

'Roy? No, no, Kit. That was Cooper. He . . . he . . .' He's meant to be dead? She has no idea how to begin.

'Well, he told me he was Roy fucking Smith.'

The penny drops: Kit's notebook, Roy's name circled. 'He used to call himself Cooper,' she manages.

'Roy. Cooper. Again, doesn't matter now, does it?' Kit spits furiously. 'I know who I am.'

'He told you,' Maggie mutters numbly.

'So, you knew.' Kit shakes his head.

'Kit, I didn't know for sure,' she stammers, clinging

to that shred of doubt. 'If Cooper is your biological father, it's got nothing to do with who *you* are. You are my wonderful Kit.'

'I'm not yours, Maggie,' Kit flashes, rummaging in a pocket for cigarettes. 'I'm not Cora's. And I'm sure as hell not that conniving . . . I belong to no one. I never did.'

The hiss of a lighter. The dirty smell of cigarette smoke mixing with rain. Kit starts striding away.

'Cora and I love you, Kit.' Maggie runs to keep up. 'We love you so much.'

'So much you hid the truth from me?' Kit splashes across a deep puddle, skimmed with oil, no longer caring about his cherished shoes. 'Like all my life? Don't deny it!'

Every line Maggie has rehearsed falls away.

'I mean, Cora, yes, I get it. She has form in that area. But you? *You*, Maggie? I've always known you've had your secrets, not told me stuff . . . but this? This wasn't your fucking secret to keep.'

'But you never wanted to know, Kit,' she gabbles, flailing. All the little white lies, omissions and decisions, the kicking of cans down the road, everything she'd thought was right is revealed as glaringly, seismically wrong. Irreparably, given the expression on Kit's face.

'But it's different if *you* knew, can't you see that?' Kit says, with a hollow laugh. He angrily wipes tears out of his eyes. 'But you always think big sister knows best, don't you, Maggie? Control the narrative! It's no wonder you've got writer's block. You want to know why?'

Maggie nods. Her heart twists on the knife. She deserves it.

'Because you cannot *tell* the truth so you cannot *write* the truth. And a real artist is all about truth. And you – you're all surface. You are constitutionally incapable of going deeper.'

Maggie wants to gouge Kit's words into her skin so she never forgets them because he's right. And a bit of her wants to die.

'But this is not a book. It's my life. Only in the freak-show clusterfuck of my life, where no one is who they say they are, I am, always, *always* the last muggle to know anything. Any other secrets we can bleed out, right here on the pavement? Because if there are, and you don't tell me, I will never speak to you again, Maggie. Or Cora. I swear, that's it. I divorce the pair of you.'

Something deep inside Maggie is crumbling, re-forming, shifting. But she's still standing there, her hair dripping into her eyes, the rain trickling down her neck.

'Say something!' Kit shouts furiously. But he can't look at her.

'I'm here to explain, Kit.' She tries not to sob. 'I came back from Paris to be here for this . . . to do this. I knew I'd have to tell you. Everything.'

'Everything?' he repeats, his ferocity tempered by apprehension. 'There are human remains in the back-yard of our old house, Maggie.'

'What I know,' Maggie promises, with an involuntary shiver. 'Which is rapidly turning out not . . . to be enough. Incomplete, I mean.' The facts dissolve as her mind reaches for them.

The rain softens to a dandelion-fuzz glow around the streetlamp. Kit seethes and smokes. Maggie's salty tears mix with the drizzle. 'So, shall we walk and talk? Please, Kit. You pick the route. I'll walk to Glasgow and back if you like. Anywhere.'

Kit storms away. A few paces on he stops. 'Fine!' he shouts, not turning around. 'Oh, screw you, Maggie. Mayfair is this way.' She runs to join him.

Thirty-three minutes later, they've covered Soho, Liberty's, Berkeley Square, the fateful fight between Cooper and Wolf, the desperate call to Gav, and Wolf's insistence they stay out of each other's lives. And how Cooper inveigled his way into Kit's years later. Throwing loose theories about his motivations, the newspaper article, their heads are too scrambled to push together the last loose bits of the puzzle. All Maggie knows, and can reassure Kit, is that those remains have nothing to do with her and Wolf.

'Maggie.' Looking stricken, Kit stops on the pavement. 'I didn't mean that about your writing.'

'No, no, what you said was true.' Maggie's voice

catches. 'And I need to find that again, Kit. Truth. In my life. In my writing. I need to be braver.'

Kit rolls his eyes.

'And I really am sorry, Kit.'

Kit says nothing. But when Maggie slips her arm into his, he doesn't pull away and Maggie feels like the luckiest sister alive. Walking on, Kit still cannot resist peering into a luxury antiques shop, its window displaying vintage Asprey, neo-classical French gilt furniture, and a German porcelain parrot worth more than a studio flat. They agree it's not much like Gav Out Back's shop, and not nearly as good.

Then they turn into the Mayfair square, Lordats' grand classical headquarters lit up and glowing. Maggie quickens her pace, but Kit stiffens and places a warning hand on her arm. 'Hold your horses.'

Two plain-clothes policemen, or detectives, Kit says. Maggie would never have realized. But now she can see it. The way they're walking smartly down Lordats' illuminated shallow stone steps, closely flanked either side of Wolf, who is carrying neither a bag nor a jacket, his rain-damp shirt flattened to his shoulders. Silhouetted in the building's windows, late-night-working colleagues watch the humiliating scene. Jolted by the injustice, Maggie leaps forward, pulling away from Kit, rushing towards the men.

Wolf doesn't look happy to see her. He shakes his head, grimacing, his face drawn.

'Out of the way, please,' says one of the men.

In their terrifyingly neutral expressions, their efficacy, Maggie senses the might of the state, legal forces gathering. She wants to flee – she's avoided the police all her life – but stands her ground. 'He hasn't done anything,' she explains, her voice shaking, trying to be polite and reasonable. 'Wolf, I've just met Cooper. In a restaurant. He's alive! He survived.'

Wolf double-takes. For some reason, the policemen take no notice.

Maggie realizes where they're headed. A black BMW parked on yellow lines by the entrance. Matching their swift pace, she walks in an absurd crablike sidestep, not understanding why Wolf isn't fiercely protesting, and the police still not listening.

Kit sprints across the road and stands beside the car, his hands spread on the bonnet, staring at Wolf, transfixed, as he approaches. One of the policemen opens the rear passenger door and instructs Wolf to get inside, with a cool civility that could turn on a hairpin.

'Wolf,' Kit calls.

Recognition dawns and Wolf's distraught face floods with surprise and softens. 'Kit?'

Maggie is panicking. Clearly Wolf hasn't heard her properly. 'You've done nothing wrong,' she shouts, trying to get him to grasp this.

The policeman is telling her firmly to step away. The passenger door is shutting, and Wolf is trying to force out the words, 'They've had a tip-off that the remains are . . .' his voice shatters '. . . Gav's.' The door clunks shut, and the BMW accelerates down the street, spraying up an arc of water with such force it looks like arterial blood spilled from the city itself.

37

Maggie

Paris, May 1998

And there she was. Like a startled fawn drawn out of a
forest, my mother stood trembling in Cora's apartment
doorway, her arms linked with Suki's and Clemence's,
Marco rising behind, his baseball glove-sized hands on
her shoulders. Mum and I flew together, and she pulled
me to her chest. 'Maggie,' she whispered, running her
fingers over my face. I wanted to shout at her, and hug
and hit her, all those things, but I just tipped my face
into her hair, searching for her smell, instead finding a
lanolin-tang, an unwashed mustiness.

The physical change was a shock. In her absence,
I'd pictured Mum as I'd last seen her, black dress, ballet
flats, lips glossed, mascara-eyed, with her model's scis-
soring strut. No longer. She was fragile and bony
under her woolly cardigan, a frumpy cream thing.
Beneath it, a baggy floral dress, hitched in at the waist
with an old leather belt, her bare legs – unshaven, short
dark hairs like iron filings – poking over the top of

mud-spattered wellingtons. Mum looked vulnerable. Bizarre. By her standards, a bag lady. She looked ill. 'What happened to you?'

'Oh, Maggie.' My mother's eyes glassed with tears. She didn't seem able to answer this question. 'I cannot tell you how sorry I am.' Her voice was wobbly and hoarse. She held my hands tightly, desperately. 'Thank you for looking after Kit. Thank you, thank you.'

'That is *not* enough, Dee Dee,' said Cora, barely able to restrain her anger. 'What on earth . . .'

'Cora, leave it, she's completely exhausted,' pleaded Clemence. 'Give her a minute.'

'A minute? She's had days!' Cora retorted.

His face stern, Marco turned to Cora. 'She needs to rest, eat, and not be pushed too hard or . . .' He pulled back. 'You're going to have to give her time, Cora.' He paused, lifted an eyebrow. 'Really.'

'Damn it,' Cora muttered, under her breath, covering her mouth with a hand.

I wasn't sure I'd ever forgive my mother either. Part of me didn't even want to look at her. I also couldn't look anywhere else, wanting her never again out of my sight.

Mum glanced around in panic. 'Where's Kit?'

'Asleep. Come.' I led her away from her friends' nervy vigilance and my aunt's burning gaze and into the guest bedroom, warm and salty with the fug of sleeping boy.

Kit was star-fished on the futon. Mum knelt and bowed her head, like a penitent figure in an old religious painting. Outside the room, I could hear the others talking in low, charged voices.

Kit sensed Mum before he saw her. His eyes opened slowly, unblinking, funnelling her in, then he reached up and silently circled his arms around her neck, drawing her close. Overwhelmed, I edged out of the room and sank against the wall outside, drew up my knees. Marco walked over, squatted beside me with a huff. 'I told you I'd find her, Maggie.'

I looked up, wiping my wet eyes on my knees. 'Where *was* she, Marco?'

'Your grandmother's house.'

My arms goose-bumped. The floral dress, the cardigan, the muddy boots, all Granny's.

'We picked her up early this morning. Swung past your house, grabbed your mother's passport from the dresser, before we all jumped on the Eurostar. I can see you're confused and hurt, understandably, but I promise you that she was desperate to see you two, Maggie. Didn't want to hang about or get changed, nothing.'

I tried to absorb this. Presumably using Mum's keys, Marco had been *inside* the house. Only to the dresser in the living room, not downstairs. Still. Clearly nothing had seemed amiss. This was some comfort. 'But Granny's? Did you just guess?'

'No, no. Someone at Clem's Café said they'd spotted her with Mason, the kiwi nanny guy.' Marco paused, any judgement silenced. 'Getting on the back of his motorbike,' he added, in an apologetic whisper.

Mason. I said nothing and felt everything: fury, relief, and a sense of betrayal on Dad's behalf. Although I'd suspected something had once gone on, I'd had no idea it was more than a clinch, or that it'd continued after he'd left the job.

'Late last night, I tracked down Mason to some dive in Acton,' Marco continues. 'He'd last seen her at the Old Rectory and was surprised that she still wasn't home.' He palmed his shaven head. 'I'm so sorry we didn't find her earlier, Maggie. It seems kind of obvious now.'

'I should have found her,' I muttered. Instead, I'd been free-floating with Wolf, wrapped up in our little world, which had now imploded.

Before Marco could respond, Suki walked over, her cowboy boots clip-clopping on the parquet floor, quickly followed by Clemence and Cora.

'Hey.' Clemence sat down beside me, wrapped an arm around my shoulders. I leaned into the tickle of her hair because Clemence smelt perfumed and together, unlike my mother, and was wearing the softest dove-grey sweater. 'She'll be okay, she will, Maggie.'

'I – I don't understand, Clemence.'

'I'm not sure your ma does yet either.' The afternoon sunshine caught in Clemence's eyelashes and made her brown skin gleam. 'It seems like everything got too much, Maggie. But she's back now.'

'This is ridiculous,' muttered Cora, her arms crossed. 'Dee Dee went AWOL for days! And we're meant to applaud this – this reappearing act? Not ask questions? No. We need an explanation.'

'The full story will come out, Cora. It always does, doesn't it? In the end,' Suki said spikily, clearly on a short fuse. 'And I hardly think you're one to talk.'

'Hey.' Clemence held up a warning finger to Suki.

The air drew tight and close. No one spoke. For a few drawn-out moments, Clemence held all the power in that room, that one steady finger suppressing something too big to say out loud. I thought of Wolf's favourite word, *craquelure*, but these hairline fractures and cracks were loyalties and secrets. So intricate, it was impossible to tell who knew what.

The stand-off was broken by a bedroom door opening, Mum carrying Kit, his head against her shoulder, regressively babyish. We all stared at her, seeing different people – mother, sister, friend. But she didn't look strong enough to be all these things, perhaps any of them. I feared it was only the weight of Kit that rooted her in the room, and that if anyone opened the doors to the balcony, she'd blow away, light as a leaf, across the rooftops.

'I didn't mean to stay away so long,' my mother said quietly.

I wanted to shake her.

'Sit down and eat something, for God's sake, Dee Dee,' said Cora, her anger crumpling into concern. 'Look at you. Jesus.' She pulled out a chair, and my mother sat, cuddling Kit on her lap. My aunt pressed a piece of bread into her hand and Mum shared it with my little brother, tousled and still dozy. Seeing them together again, it felt almost as if Mum had never gone, the period of time she'd been missing circular rather than linear. Yet my own life had shot off on a completely new trajectory – and only Wolf and I knew the extent of it.

'I lost track of the days.' Mum looked more perplexed by this than anyone.

'Maybe yourself too,' suggested Clemence, standing up, walking to the window and gazing out at Paris, unrolled like wallpaper. 'You've been unwell, Dee Dee.'

My mother closed her eyes, and the lids flickered very fast, until she pressed them with her fingertips. 'Yes, yes, I suppose I have.' She looked at me again and lowered her chin into Kit's hair. 'So much better for seeing you two.'

'For Christ's sake,' Cora said.

And Clemence shook her head, and mouthed at Cora, 'Not now.'

'But how did you know we were here?' I asked Marco, then remembered hearing Cora on the phone to him the previous night.

'Wolf!' interjected Clemence, his name flying into the air like a hot spark. 'Well, his friend. Late yesterday afternoon, closing up the café, a young guy appeared at the door, carrying Nico.' She shot me a puzzled look. 'Um, Tyrone, I think he said his name was.'

I nodded. The best friend Gav had instructed Wolf to stay with in east London until his mashed face had healed.

'Explained you'd gone to visit your aunt in Paris, Maggie, but hadn't been able to take Nico on the Eurostar, so left her with Wolf. But dogs weren't allowed at Tyrone's place, and would I take her? So, of course, I said yes.'

I could feel the others watching me carefully. But if anyone thought there was something peculiar about my sudden flight to Paris, or Tyrone's appearance at the café, rather than Wolf himself, they said nothing.

'Where's Nico now?' Kit's bottom lip quivered.

'At the café with my mum,' Clemence assured. 'Who is a total softie and let her sleep in her bed last night – against my house rules!'

I was relieved to hear this – Nico hadn't slept alone in her basket since Mum had left.

'So, honey, do not worry,' Clemence continued. 'You will soon be reunited.'

'How kind of Wolf and his friend to make sure Nico had somewhere to go.' My mother accepted all this without query. She eyed me more curiously. 'Kit has just been telling me all about your chap, Maggie.'

'Extraordinary eyes!' Suki said. 'Unmissable.'

My face burned as my blood ran cold. Wolf was too distinctive for anyone to forget.

Clemence turned from the view. 'I hate to say this, but I do need to get back to work and relieve my mother, who is quite possibly offering free cake to half the neighbourhood.'

With a heave, Marco stood up, his knees cracking.

'It's a flying visit for me too, sadly,' said Suki.

'What a massive pain I've been for everyone. God, I'm so sorry,' said Mum, looking tearful. 'You didn't all need to come.'

'We wanted to.' Clemence walked over and rested an arm around Mum's shoulders. 'You'd have done the same for us.'

'But are you up for another train journey, Dee Dee?' Suki asked doubtfully. 'Back to London.'

My mother looked thrown, unable to make any decision.

'Oh, one other thing!' Clemence pulls a face. 'Sorry, with all this going on, I forgot to mention the builder.'

'The builder?' Mum repeated. I caught my breath.

'Pippa popped into the café, looking for me to get a message to you, since no one was in at yours,' explained Clemence. 'Anyway, all a bit last minute, but Bucket has found a small window between jobs, so he's going in to fix the mess in your garden. Lay down a new patio. Starts this afternoon. Pippa's given him a key.'

This afternoon. That hit hard. And I remembered that Wolf had hassled Bucket to finish the job. I dropped my forehead to my knees. Having had no confirmation on what Gav had or hadn't done, it was impossible to know what Bucket might find in the garden. Sweat prickled at the nape of my neck.

'I could try to call Pippa and reschedule it, Dee Dee?' Clemence suggested.

'Yes,' I said, too insistently. 'You've got to put him off, Mum.'

My mother shook her head. 'No, no. I've been waiting weeks.'

'But you're clearly not right,' I argued.

A silence spread, filled with worry and questions, and Mum's friends exchanged charged glances.

Marco cleared his throat. 'I'm afraid there's something else that might have a bearing on heading straight back to London, darling,' he said cautiously. 'We didn't want to mention it earlier, Dee Dee. And I'm sorry to load this on you right now, I really am. But someone seems to have tipped off the press. Your agent called the salon, a bit frantic, asking if I knew where you were, saying she hadn't been able to get hold of you for days.' He coughed, looking uncomfortable. 'Some sort of tabloid story brewing.'

My mother paled.

'Model mother does a runner. Leaves kids home alone,' Marco said hesitantly. 'Not . . .' He glanced in Cora's direction, away again, but not quickly enough. 'It'll just be a silly tabloid splash, Dee Dee.'

But a true story. Had Cooper sold it before he came over to our house? Perhaps a way of showing he was serious. He'd been hinting at it.

'Tomorrow's fish-and-chips paper,' said Clemence, not entirely convincingly. We all knew how damaging it could be.

'But I'm guessing you *may* get a welcoming committee of toerags with cameras,' Marco said. 'And it's not what you should be dealing with right now, Dee Dee. You really do need to call your agent. And you need to rest, babe. Out of the limelight. Let it blow over.'

Mum lowered her face to Kit's hair, her eyes closed.

'Stay in Paris, Dee Dee,' implored Cora.

'You could get your agent to pump the line that you're on holiday with your kids?' suggested Marco. 'That might help.'

'Dee Dee, Marco's right. Wait it out. I'll look after you here. All three of you,' Cora insisted, her gaze pinned to Kit. 'Please. Let me. You can explain everything in your own time then. We'll take it easy, I promise, Dee Dee. No rush.'

Awkwardly waiting for my mother's response, unsure which way it would go, no one spoke. Like one of those scenes in a play that make the audience fidget and clear their throats. Suki flicked her pendant necklace on its long chain back and forth, sending a coin of reflected light against the wall.

'Okay, Cora,' Mum said, with a sigh, almost as if she'd lost the energy to fight with my aunt, their estrangement limping towards surrender. I knew my mother really was unwell then. 'I'll stay. Just for a day or two.'

'You sure, Dee Dee?' asked Suki, glancing apprehensively at my aunt.

'I promise I'll take good care of her,' Cora said. 'She is my sister.'

Although it was unclear if Suki scoffed or coughed, she did open her mouth to say something – and a hard look from Clemence shut it again.

'Well, if that's settled, and everyone's happy, a quick coffee at Café de Flore, then London bound?' Marco asked Clemence and Suki. They hugged Mum, making her promise to look after herself, eat and sleep.

Clemence turned to me. 'Your mother hasn't got much with her, Maggie. You'll need to sort out some clothes.'

'Love the current outfit. Very Englishwoman goes

rogue in the country.' Suki's remark was a little too close to the bone. 'But you can't be in Paris and not go shopping, Dee Dee.'

'She can borrow my clothes,' Cora said matter-of-factly.

'I'll shop,' said my mother, quickly, with a smile, a glint of humour that proved she was in there somewhere. Everyone laughed a bit too loudly.

'You see, Suki? We will find a way through. The clothes issue . . .' Cora hesitated, and again her hungry gaze swung pointedly to Kit, sitting on Mum's knee, like she wanted to yank him off it and pull him to her own lap. '. . . and everything else. Won't we, Dee Dee?' This time, Mum didn't answer and her arms tightened around my little brother.

38

Kit

London, May 2019

Gav Out Back – four feet under. In his pocket, a plastic business-card holder. Still sealed and preserved within it, Gav's cards: a helpful steer to whom the femurs and gold fillings belonged. A tannin-heavy leather workshop apron, still largely intact, with a magnifying loupe in the pocket. Composting under a Notting Hill patio all this time. Gav didn't deserve that, Kit thinks, dropping two slices of bread into his toaster.

Already, rumours that the remains have been identified are running hot on social media and, no doubt, in the Bulthaup kitchens of Notting Hill's grand villas and in the chattering length of Portobello Market. A paper has run a story on 'the Notting Hill house mystery' and its celebrity past residents, featuring Dee Dee but also Marco, along with gratuitous headshots of his starry salon clientele. Julia Roberts and Hugh Grant don't escape either since a *Notting Hill* scene was filmed on the road.

Online armchair detectives can't decide who might have done it. But, without any evidence, they've decided Gav was a ducker and diver, entangled with underworld criminals, tarnishing his trade with fakes. Other dealers, even those who disliked him, have leaped to his defence, one of their own, and insisted Gav was the genuine article, an eccentric misanthrope, who preferred antiques to people, his passion for unusual collectibles barely scraping a profit. No one was surprised when he bailed from the shop: he was far behind on the rent but wouldn't have touched a fake in a million years. Kit's sure this is true.

That morning, in his Bloomsbury kitchen, four miles east of Gav's grisly grave, Kit also feels . . . grief. Raw and unexpected, the grief he fails to inhabit when standing by the graves of Dee Dee and Damian Parker. Like it's found a route out. He can't stop thinking about the bearish man with the beanbag belly who'd set him to work, dusting with a sock. And he feels a reverberating deep sadness about Wolf too. The sight of him ducking into the unmarked police car. His pitiful wet shirt. His compliance. In the rain that night, Kit's cartoon fantasy had finally dissolved. Wolf was just a normal bloke – well, wasn't he? Kit cannot believe Wolf killed Gav . . . and yet the police must have grounds to believe he was involved. It niggles.

Hearing a waking rustle coming from the living room, Kit snaps out of his stupor and tries to focus on making breakfast. Three tightly wrought days have passed since Wolf's arrest. Maggie has barely left Kit's flat. Refusing the bedroom, she's taken residence on the sofa, googling legal processes and miscarriages of justice into the early hours, the laptop on her knee. Can't sleep anyway, she says. If Kit mutters about the blue light – 'Are you giving me a screen ban, Kit?' – she'll switch to Kit's vintage-magazine collection and manically flick the pages, poring over images of Dee Dee. Still, she doesn't sleep. Her eyes scarlet-veined. Hair like an alpaca's.

Kit isn't faring much better. His galloping heart only slows when he checks his phone and sees there's still no message from Roy/Cooper. For now, the great survivor has gone quiet, cockroach-slipping between the cracks. But he won't have disappeared. Kit knows a message is coming. Something else too. A sense of stirring, electricity in the unsettled London air and inside him, like weather in the blood.

The pathology report, expected to confirm Gav's identity, will take some time, but the police have already brought in Maggie and Kit for questioning, having linked the Parker tenancy to the month Gav was last seen alive. Faced with the iron-hard eye of Detective Simpson at Paddington police station – and the frightening precision of her dark lip liner – reticence didn't feel like such a good idea. Kit was pushed hard on his memories of the antiques shop, the confrontational relationship between nephew and uncle. Maggie's interviews took longer and aren't over. She's told them everything, she says. The fight. The phone call to Gav. All of it. But the truth hasn't set Wolf free. The police have successfully applied to hold him for another forty-eight hours without charge. Until Wolf's out, Kit worries for his sister. He's never seen her so low.

Unable to leave her menagerie, Cora can only call, thankfully. Kit has been avoiding these calls. So they have been having triangular disjointed conversations, variations on Cora saying, 'Bring Kit to the Old Rectory. We all need to talk.' Aware he's punishing Cora by staving off her back-up troop of apologies and explanations, he also feels she deserves it. He has told Cora – via Maggie – that he will need time, a very, very long time, not to be revolted by Cora and Cooper's coupling, the subterfuge, the generative secrets, even if Cora protests that he mustn't leap to conclusions, that there are complexities – oh, please – they must talk through, face to face. But he does not want to see Cora's face. Or discuss anything. He's not ready.

But when Kit does sleep – self-medicated with red wine and weed – he dreams of horses. Cora riding alongside him, just as they used to do. The drum of hoofs. Big sky. He and Cora not talking, not even looking at one another, just moving, moving, moving.

With a ping, the toast flies up. Kit spreads it with the thick-cut English marmalade Maggie misses when she's in Paris. He's already been out to the deli and bought Earl Grey tea and a bag of peaches, soft, just as she likes them. A bunch of peonies from the florist. He arranges them on the rattan tray. There. Perfect. Whatever happens with Wolf or Cora, Kit will be there for Maggie as she's always been there for him. Lies or no lies. What else is there in the end? Apart from human kindness. Some marmalade toast. Without her, he's a ruin.

'Breakfast, Mags.' Kit knocks back the living-room door with his knee.

The sofa is a tangle of blankets. Sitting up against the pillows, Maggie wears a borrowed pair of his pyjamas, far too big. She looks like a hyper-exhausted child on a sleepover. 'You do still believe Wolf is innocent?' she asks abruptly: zero to eighty in seconds.

He rests the tray on the side table. 'Do you?'

'Without any doubt!' Maggie shakes her head. 'Oh, my God. Seriously. I was *there*, Kit,' she says, not for the first time, unwavering in her version of events. 'And, unlike you, old enough to remember it properly.'

The day he's always asked her about, that feeling. Kit had always known something had happened. Never imagining it'd be as bad as this. 'Budge up.' He sits on the sofa, near her feet. 'You should eat something, Maggie.'

'Can't eat. Can't write. I can't effing *breathe*.' Maggie doesn't even look at the tray, doesn't notice the effort he's made. Anything. Her Parisian friends have been messaging, her agent calling, but she ignores them all. Maggie is not okay.

The alarm she's probably felt about him over the years, Kit feels now. He's awed and horrified she's managed to live normally – relatively, for a Parker/Foale – all this time, believing Wolf killed Cooper. Would he have kept Wolf's secret? Perhaps. If the death wasn't intentional. If it was in self-defence. If Cooper had started the fight. But it does stretch even Kit's elastic libertine ethics. On the other hand, Cooper isn't dead – Kit almost wishes he was. It must have been Cooper who sent the police to Will Derry of Lordats, phoning them straight after their hideous dinner at Giovanni's. Kit catches himself. He's trying extremely hard not to think about that dinner.

'Maggie, calm down. You've got to calm down. It's not all over. Wolf has a rapacious lawyer, the best in the business.' Better than yours, he thinks, terrified she'll be prosecuted for aiding and abetting. Maggie has already been instructed to stay in London, not to travel back to Paris. 'He'll sort it.'

'Why are the police still holding him, then?' Maggie tilts back her head and stares at the ceiling, her mouth forming a Munch-like silent scream. 'What the hell has Cooper told the police, Kit? What sort of lies – Wait, no, you've already given me a taster,' she rambles furiously. 'Wolf's fictitious debts. The punch-up Cooper supposedly witnessed. Wolf threatening to kill his uncle. Total stitch-up.'

'Maggie, stop.' Kit hands her a cup of tea. 'Drink.'

Maggie sips, and disinterestedly puts it down on the tray. A moment passes, punctuated by the Boucheret clock's pretty tick. The top of the number fourteen bus trundles past the window.

'Do I think there was tension between Gav and Wolf? Yes,' she says. 'But there was love too. And why on earth would Wolf have gone back to our house after dropping us at Waterloo, then got into a murderous skirmish with his uncle?'

Out of the corner of Kit's eye, a peony sheds a petal, then another.

'Deep down, you know who did it, Kit. However disturbing that is for you to process.'

Kit closes his eyes. He cannot bear to think of him.

'Cooper has been feeding you lies, Kit, trying to prepare the ground to make Wolf look guilty. For you to back up his version of events, knowing you could be a key witness. You've been manipulated, you do know that?'

Kit swallows hard. His own gullibility is humiliating.

'Let's go over this again, then. No, no, we must. You say Cooper first got in contact in mid-January?' She sits up straighter, pulling her legs towards her, wrapping her arms around her knees. 'Exactly when the basement planning application went in. See? If Cooper killed Gav, he'd have kept an eye on any house renovations, as Wolf always did. Signed up for Kensington and Chelsea's online planning alerts or – or just walked past and seen a planning notice stuck to a lamp post! Wait.'

Maggie scrambles up and starts exhaustingly to pace the sitting room, the turned-up pyjama bottoms dragging on the floor, her hands clasped behind her back. 'This month he sends a message, dangling a carrot about knowing Wolf or some such? By then he'd have seen the basement boarding. Known the net was closing in.' She whips around, a finger raised. 'But if he could only find Wolf, he had a chance to blame it on him. And before you say anything, yes, yes, it's a long shot, I realize that, but an egotist like Cooper, who'd got away with things all his life, would have believed he could pull it off.' She laughs hollowly. 'No wonder he needed to reach out to you, exploiting a little boy's uncertain memories, your need for a –' She stops.

'Say it,' Kit says darkly.

Maggie walks over, sits beside him, the energy whistling out of her. 'Sorry.'

'No, let's go there, Maggie.' Kit doesn't mean to sound bitter. 'So, you're saying Cooper emerges from the woodwork to find his long-lost son only to groom him to help cover up his hideous crime? Nice psychopath.'

'Maybe Cooper did want to find you too. For other reasons. More human reasons. He truly believes he's your father, you think?'

'I do.' Kit recalls the tears in Cooper's eyes at Giovanni's, the small flashes of vulnerability, and neediness.

'Okay, that actually makes sense.' Maggie frowns, quiet for a moment, working it out. 'He's been ill. He's getting older. He's not got much money, or a means of earning it, and he sees you've got a good business going on, something he's interested in, and he feels a connection with that too. Why does one motivation preclude the others? It's possible to hold many contradictory urges in our heads and hearts at the same time.' She breathes out loudly. 'Believe me.'

Kit looks away, pins his gaze to his shelves of antiques because they reassure him, block bad things out. He understands their construction, their mechanics, their flaws, and the skill of their makers. Each one a tiny, beautiful world in which he can shelter, like a bee in a golden hive. Whereas the idea of Cooper being his father makes him feel skinned, exposed, hurled into cold black space.

'I've an idea!' Maggie grabs his arm.

'What?' he asks warily.

'You can visit Cooper. You can get him to confess!'

'Don't be mental.'

'But he wants you in his life. You're his weakness.'

Kit shakes his head, something in him seizing tight. 'No, no way. You're grabbing at straws, Maggie. And my arm.'

Maggie releases him. 'But you could try? Wolf is in a perilous position. This is a chance to shunt things along. Please, Kit.'

Kit's resistance gathers. 'So, Cooper is a psychotic killer, and you want me to drop round for *a cup of tea*?'

Maggie steeples her hands over her nose. 'Shit. You're right. I'm not thinking straight. Appalling idea. Forget I ever said it.' She stares at the breakfast tray, noticing it at last. 'Oh, Kit. The peonies. The peaches. I don't deserve any of it. But thank you.'

39

Maggie

Paris, May 1998

Finally, just the four of us. After Mum's friends had gone, the Paris apartment shrank, and we were left facing one another. Busying, retreating into practicals, I ran Mum a bath. Cora cooked an omelette, leaving Mum resting, Kit brushing her hair. Cora and I bolted to Galeries Lafayette and returned with a froth of lingerie – no plain knickers in Paris – and T-shirts, too-short jeans and PJs, which Mum declared '*parfait*', signalling a ceasefire of sorts.

Knowing the builder was fixing That Godawful Hole, I was jittery. Still no word from London. Would new paving slabs be slamming down like coffin lids? A shameful thing to hope, but I did.

When the phone finally rang, I gasped so hard it burst the popper on my jeans. But it was Lucinda, my mother's agent, dialling in a storm of radio and TV offers to talk about 'the urge every busy, exhausted working mother feels, to walk out of the house, leaving her kids behind'. We all agreed it'd be a terrible idea to say anything, and when Lucinda tried to persuade her – 'No such thing as bad press!' – Cora plucked the phone out of Mum's hand and coolly, firmly told the agent to turn down *all* offers and tell the hacks to respect Dee Dee's privacy. After that call, I wasn't the only one on edge.

By supper, Kit – always a conduit for tension – had had enough. Pushing Mum away, clinging to me, he sobbed and raged that he missed Wolf. He missed Gav's shop. London. Why were we in this strange flat in Paris? With this Cora person? Nico would be lonely! I assured Kit that Nico would be spoiled rotten, and apologized to my mother, saying Kit just needed time, having no idea that loyalties forged in days could last decades.

I cuddled Kit, my comfort, my continuum. I'd gone from missing my mother to missing Wolf. It was also hard to accept Mum was back. Partly, she wasn't. Not completely. Even after she'd rested and eaten and bathed, Cora keeping her promise to go easy, there was something unsettlingly ... not right. Subdued. She seemed to react to every question with a slight lag, like an old person. Or she'd start talking and her sentences would snap in half before she'd finished. I found myself endlessly pressing her presence to memory – the way she stowed her hair behind her ears before sipping coffee, the tiny hardening bubbles on the bar of soap after she'd used it – in case she disappeared again, or there was a blow-up with my aunt and she suddenly left, which, given the circumstances and their history, didn't seem unlikely.

Something wiry and difficult was constantly, silently thrashing between them. I didn't care. What I wanted, desperately, was a begin-again button, a freeze-frame enabling my mother, after hesitating in the porch that first evening, to have turned and come back through the pink door. Wolf wouldn't have found a way into my life, I realized. But the rest wouldn't have happened either. You couldn't rewrite one bit of a story without rewriting it all.

Where *was* Wolf? While the others were occupied – Kit finally soothed by tiresome games of Clock Patience – I repeatedly called the number on Gav's business card that I'd kept safe. No one answered. I needed to tell Wolf that Bucket the builder was back, filling in the hole. Ask him what Gav had done.

A teal-blue night drew over the Paris rooftops. Cora was cooking a ham and pea risotto, stirring the pan, adding stock from a jug, when my mother stepped onto the balcony. Gripping the rail, Mum leaned over, looking down, the breeze ragging her hair. When she finally walked back inside, declaring Paris 'too beautiful to take in', we exhaled, and my aunt's stilled hand started to stir again.

Given Mum's mental state, Cora and I still trod

carefully, not pushing too hard, tucking bigger questions inside little ones. Finally, with Kit in his bath and out of earshot, we could wait no longer, and Mum's story emerged in stops and starts.

That first evening, after leaving the house, Mum met 'a man' at a café on Notting Hill Gate. A man who'd been hassling her for money: 'Long story,' she muttered, sipping her peppermint tea, her gaze snagging on Cora's.

At this point, saving her unnecessary white lies, I announced that I knew Cora was Kit's biological mother – Mum sucked in her breath hard, her eyes darting with panic – and that Cooper, Cora's ex-lover and Kit's possible biological father, had weaponized this secret. 'Right?' I asked, when Mum didn't speak.

For a second, I could have sworn she was going to deny it. She glanced at Cora, and I caught a puzzling tiny shake of Cora's head, as if answering a question both understood, and I didn't. 'Yes,' Mum said eventually, hoarsely. 'Thereabouts, Maggie.'

'Why did you not just tell me when Kit joined our family?' I said indignantly.

'Because to tell you, not Kit, wouldn't have been fair. I was planning to tell him when he was much, much older.' Mum's expression darkened. She stared at the table. 'We – me and your dad – agreed it was in Kit's best interests not to say anything. And in the family's,' she added, barely audibly.

'Well, I didn't!' Cora burst out, making me flinch. 'I didn't agree with that, Dee Dee. But it wasn't up to me, was it?'

'No.' My mother pressed her fingertips to her closed eyelids. 'By then, it wasn't, Cora.'

Everything felt jagged, ugly, and I didn't want to be there, caught between the two warring sisters, a history too enormous for a seventeen-year-old to begin to understand. Kit started to sing in the bath, his voice silly and pure.

'If we'd not adopted Kit, he'd have gone to another family.' Mum paused. 'And it still took you four more years and two rehabs to get sober.'

My aunt's face seemed to twist with silent agony. You had to keep paying for really bad mistakes, over and over, I realized. Cora had lost her baby. There was no begin-again button.

To my surprise, Mum reached across and touched Cora's arm. And it was such a little thing, light, brief, but it felt so intimate I had to look away. Cora stood up quickly, hiding her watering eyes, and stalked off to the kitchen. I heard the strike of a match, smelt sulphur. Returning with a candle, a chunky white one in a saucer, she took a cigarette from her handbag, lit it over the flame, and went outside on the balcony to smoke. Possibly to cry. My mother and I sat quietly, and she held my hand, and whispered, 'I'm so sorry, Maggie,' and I hated her for being weak, vulnerable, and apologizing. Her trembly hand. I wanted her unrepenting, defiant and glamorous, shouting, 'Why can't I go away for a few days? You were just fine, Maggie!' Because I wouldn't have had to forgive her then. Anger was easier than forgiveness.

Cora returned, recovered, smelling of cigarette smoke. She sank to her chair. 'Shall we go back to that evening you left, Dee Dee?'

So, Mum picked up the story, trying to explain – to us, to herself.

No more money, she'd told Cooper that last night. She'd given him hundreds and wasn't giving him a penny more. He didn't chase after her, and she'd thought that was it. Never did she imagine he'd turn up at the house or hassle me. Let alone Kit.

'Why did you give that nasty piece of work *any-thing*? Ever?' Cora was incredulous.

My mother had to think about this, frowning, reaching for an answer. 'The first time, back in February, I – I thought it'd be just the once.' She twisted her wedding ring on her finger. 'God knows what I was thinking. He had this big sob story. Couldn't pay his rent. Oh, and how crazy hurt he'd been to hear from someone else that you'd had a baby . . .' Mum's voice trailed off. 'He couldn't find you, Cora. You'd deliberately cut ties and were harder to trace. I refused to give him your number.'

'Thank you.' Cora refilled their glasses with fizzy

mineral water. 'But I think he just followed the money. You should have told me.'

Something unreadable flew across my mother's face, perhaps the reason she hadn't confided in my aunt. Candlelight pooled in the angles of her face, under her cheekbones, the dips of her eye-sockets. In that moment, Mum seemed both older, a version of herself waiting down the line, and younger, the fresh-faced model she'd been.

'Stupidly, I thought I could deal with it. Cooper swore if I told anyone, the police, even my friends, if he got any hassle, he'd "light the fuse".' Mum pulled quote marks with her fingers. 'Just one more pay-ment, and he'd vanish out of our lives for ever. He kept promising that. And I kept believing him, com-pounding my shame that I'd got suckered in in the first place. And I'd started to feel so unwell, so tired, and I just wanted to pay him off, Cora – the price seemed worth paying.' Her eyes grew bigger, darker. 'You see, it was all spiralling, paying rent while strug-gling to sell our Surrey house. Racking up debt. Cash felt like – like Monopoly money.'

A moment passed. 'Mum, at this point, you should have just told us about Cora. That would have shut Cooper up.'

Mum nodded, acknowledging this. 'Maybe. But you and Kit have been through so much, Maggie. I didn't want to rock your lives any more.' She stared down at the table, her hand covering her mouth. 'Yet here we are.'

Slowly, I began to see how everything was held together, like a spine of tiny fastening hooks and eyes down the back of one of Mum's cocktail dresses, each bad decision securing the fallout, tighter and tighter. How I wanted to unhook each one.

'Keep going, Dee Dee,' said Cora. 'So, you've left Cooper, and you went . . . ?'

To her second date of the evening with Mason, Mum admitting to the on-off-mostly-off fling, shot me an apologetic, sheepish look. Mason had taken one look at her, shaky from the encounter with Cooper, and said she needed a break, a weekend away. Maggie could Kit-sit and, hey, wasn't her old family house empty, the one with the meadow and the glow-worms and the vault of starry sky? She could show him where she grew up. 'An impulsive absurd idea,' Mum acknowledged. The sort of thing a seventeen-year-old might do, only to get grounded for eternity. But they'd roared out of London on Mason's motorbike into the countryside dark.

Mason left unhappily the next morning. 'I didn't want to give another man anything of myself.' Alone in the house, Mum ambulated around the dusty rooms, carrying Granny's ashes in their pot, before deciding to scatter them on the rose garden – 'A good fertilizer, she'd approve,' said Cora. Then Mum fell asleep. 'It was an exhaustion I'd never experienced before.' She slept for sixteen hours.

The next morning, trying to call home, she discovered the Old Rectory's landline had been cut off. The phone box in the village had been vandalized. The day passed in a blur. To leave that message on our answer-machine, she'd had to get a bus to another village with a semi-working phone, if she shook the handset, but then ran out of the coins with which to feed it.

'The tiredness got worse. Like anaesthetic,' Mum said, as if it was enveloping her again. She pressed her cheeks with her palms. 'And I'd . . . lie there, feeling like I was slowly disappearing, listening to the barn owls in the roof, knowing something was wrong with me, but not what.'

'You're depressed, Dee Dee,' Cora said quietly, after a shocked pause.

Mum rolled a blob of warm candle wax between her fingers. They were still a bit dirty under the nails, dry and cracked. Not the model's hands she maintained with sunblock and cream – sometimes with silk gloves overnight – and the sight of them, perhaps more than anything else, upset me. 'But what did you *do* for all those days, Mum?'

'I pottered. Slept. Lay in the dark. And I remembered, Maggie.' Mum smiled distantly. 'Little things. Your grandfather mowing the lawn, like he was going into battle. My mother sewing at that clackety Singer machine – you know the one, Cora, with the pedal – where she made those frilly dresses that I secretly hated.'

'What?' squealed Cora, and the candle flame shuddered. 'But you loved those frocks!'

Mum shook her head. 'Cora, I *loathed* them.'

Cora cursed and marvelled under her breath, as if this small detail rejigged her childhood in some fundamental way.

It struck me that secrets were sewn into the very fabric of the Foales. Deception to avoid conflict – and so as not to ruin lunch – a family tradition. Anything but the truth.

Cora laced her hands behind her head and leaned back on her chair, appraising my mother. 'Houses don't like not being lived in. How bad a state is it?'

'Better than me.' Mum covered her face with her hands. 'God, my life. I need a stiff drink. Have you got a –' She stopped, too late.

I could feel some sort of molecular collision. The air grew thin.

Cora's voice was low, sparking. 'No, I cannot offer you a drink. Because, as I have been continually trying to tell you, Dee Dee, I am sober. Clean. Every morning, I wake up and newly commit to being sober. And I will have to do that for the rest of my life, and I will do that, I swear I will. Just as I told Damian that fateful night.'

'What night?' I asked, confused. The next instant, of course, I knew.

Mum's face darkened. 'Cora demanded to meet your father for a drink after work.'

'A lime soda in my case,' Cora said steadily.

'You accosted him at his office.' Mum's eyes filled with tears.

'How else was I meant to –' Cora abruptly stopped talking, as if she'd slammed into something immovable.

So, Cora was the reason Dad had been driving home late. My mother had never admitted this to me before. It sank in slowly. The candle flame stretched blue. A moment passed. I could hear footsteps on the communal staircase. The clank of plumbing.

'I was desperate. And I was trying to convince Damian to allow me some access to Kit. That was all. It really was.' Cora took a breath. 'Look, Dee Dee. You can see now. I have a home. A career. Friends . . . a sweet little dog.' Her voice husked. 'I just don't have family.'

These words, the sort you can't unhear, rippled out into the room. Pierre sat up on Cora's lap, sensing the disquiet, his brown eyes moving between us.

'There's a reason for that, Cora,' my mother said eventually.

'But I want – I *long* to have my family back in my life, Dee Dee. You, Maggie . . .'

Uncomfortable, my loyalties torn, I fidgeted with the pepper grinder and felt like one of the pepper-corns trapped in the column of glass.

'. . . and Kit,' said my aunt, in a steelier voice. 'I want Kit back in my life, Dee Dee.'

No one spoke. Paris hummed outside the window. I wanted to grab Kit and run back to Wolf, our little made-up family, the Notting Hill streets.

'You can't just walk back in, pick up where you left off, Cora,' breathed my mother.

Cora's eyes flashed dangerously in the candlelight. 'Right. But you can?'

40

Maggie

London, May 2019

'Cora?' Pale straw stuck to a black fleece sleeve. Cora's tigerish face. Kit's jungle-green living-room walls. 'What on earth are you doing here?' Maggie mumbles, realizing she's fallen asleep on the job, and in an armchair, with the cool ridge of her laptop wedged against her thigh.

'Kit called me.' Cora puts down a cup of tea. 'I figured you had to be pretty bad for Kit to pick up the phone and actually call me.'

'But the animals . . .'

'Turns out that the awful new neighbour in red trousers is quite sweet in a crisis. The dogs seem to like him.'

Maggie rubs her gritty eyes. 'Where's Kit?'

'Dashed out. Meeting someone. Or, more likely, escaping me. You look a state.'

'Thanks.' It is late afternoon, Maggie realizes. The

London sky dimming outside the window, the building shimmying as a lorry roars past.

'Well, I know an unravelling when I see one.' Cora sits on the sofa, tilts her head on one side, thoughtfully. 'You still love this Wolf guy, don't you?'

'Complicated.' Maggie blows on the hot tea.

'Well, the rest of it is complicated. The love bit isn't. We always know deep down.' She reaches for the antiques guide on the side table and starts casually flicking through it. 'And what if Wolf did it?' she asks, not looking up.

'He didn't.' There is no doubt in Maggie's mind. Her belief in Wolf's innocence is clear, pure and unshakeable. Even when she forces herself to consider alternative scenarios, nothing sticks. She knew him. She could look into his eyes and see exactly who was inside. 'If he's charged, I will fight to clear his name.'

Cora nods resignedly, as if she was expecting this. 'No better person to have fighting one's corner than you, Maggie.'

Dust dances in the afternoon sunlight, the theatre of curiosities that is Kit's flat. His whereabouts start to nag. Where is her brother?

'Let me get hold of Kit.' She grabs her phone, stupidly low on charge. Straight to voicemail, then the screen turns black. Damn it. 'Are you sure Kit didn't say where he was going?'

'Kit hardly invites me to nose around his social life. Why?' Cora grows more alert, catching Maggie's unease.

'One sec.' She's reluctant to voice her suspicions and freak out Cora too. But Kit can be impetuous, reckless. And driven by an oversized sense of loyalty. A parachute of panic starting to open, she stands up, drawn to his laptop on the dining table.

'Tell me what's going on.'

Wishing she didn't have to do it, Maggie opens the laptop and furrows through Kit's Instagram shop's posts and comments. No Roy. No Cooper. Oh, hello. Who is this? @treazurehunter has been messaging Kit. Intensely in fact. For some time. Since January . . . The last one sent today: *Sure, having a quiet one, come over* . . . A west London address. Maggie turns to Cora, waiting impatiently. 'I've got a horrible feeling Kit has gone to Cooper's flat.'

The colour drains from her aunt's face. 'But you said Kit doesn't want anything to do with him. Why the hell would he do that?' She dips into her bag for her ancient mobile – shattered screen, held in place by cling film – puts on her reading glasses and calls Kit. 'Not picking up.'

'Let's just go.' Maggie scrawls the address on a bit of paper. 'It's my fault. I'll tell you en route. Where are you parked?'

*

Stuck in traffic – an accident: fire engines, ambulances, gridlock – Maggie considers leaping out of the rattling Land Rover and sprinting to the nearest tube. She bites the inside of her cheek. Should she call the police? What would she say? But she can think of some west Londoners who might get to Cooper's flat far quicker. 'Cora, this is a long shot, but you don't have any of Mum's friends' numbers on your phone?'

Cora's fingers drum on the steering wheel. 'Why would I?'

Maggie curses under her breath. 'How dangerous is Cooper, Cora? I mean, on a scale . . .'

Cora slides her hand into a car pocket, retrieves her mobile and throws it on Maggie's lap. 'Call Marco. Number in my Contacts.'

41

Kit

London, May 2019

On a rundown main road, snarled with traffic, Kit picks his way along the litter-strewn pavement to an offal-red door. Hesitating at the plastic intercom, unsure which button to push – the numbers are faded and indecipherable – he glances up at the narrow brick building rising above the kebab shop's awning. Four floors of grimy windows, hung with defeated net curtains. One of these is the 'fancy-man pad' belonging to Roy Smith. No, Cooper, Kit mentally corrects. He must remember who he was, what he did.

Stalling, Kit lights a cigarette with unsteady hands. He'd always feared any search for his biological father might drag him to a place he didn't want to go. This feels like that place.

Grinding his cigarette half smoked into a bin, Kit checks his phone, switched to 'do not disturb' in anticipation of calls from Maggie. He gets the flat button wrong – not a great start – and an elderly woman answers, asks if he's the boiler man, then buzzes him in anyway, telling him the Roy fella is on the top floor.

'*Mi casa, tu casa.*' Cooper throws open his arms. Kit grimaces through the gauche hug, trying not to recoil.

The front door opens directly onto the flat's sitting room, where meaty cooking smells and Cooper's soaking of cologne don't quite mask the mustiness of an older man living alone. He takes in the shiny leather sofa, a stained brown nylon carpet, and greige walls. A battered Stratocaster guitar on a stand. The 1930s circus sign Kit sold him, not yet hung, leaning against the skirting board. And – oh, no! – a small table, set with wine glasses and folded napkins, anticipating dinner. Kit tries to smile but his mouth is so tense it barely moves.

'You can see why I want a few more antiques, eh?' Cooper snaps off a loose thread from his shirt sleeve. There's a different energy to him today, edgier, sharper.

'I can.' Cooper still hasn't paid for his reserved items.

'Well, don't just stand there. Come in, come in.' Cooper shuts the door with a hard clunk.

Kit feels a flare of panic. Trapped in a flat far from home. Nobody knowing where he is. The idea he'll be able to extract any sort of confession seems laughable.

'I'm touched you came over, Kit.' Cooper stares at

Kit for longer than is comfortable. 'It must have taken some guts.' A small smile. 'I'm guessing your sister isn't my biggest fan.'

'Afraid not.'

'I wasn't lying about my name, Kit. Nothing like that. Went by my middle name Cooper back then. Bit more rock 'n' roll than Roy. Orbison excepted.'

'Ah.'

'Call me what you like, eh? And don't worry about your sister. She'll come round.' Cooper speaks quickly, nervously. Smiles too hard. 'Let me get you a beer, son.'

Kit's molars grind. He notes the display on the mantelpiece, above the electric fire, the few personal items in the otherwise forlornly bland flat. An arrangement with an antique-y bent, suggesting Cooper's interest isn't entirely fabricated: the little crystal animal figurines Kit sold him, a fine small brass clock – Italian, Kit's guessing, nineteenth century – a rather lovely lump of antique coral on a stand, a white item he can't quite make out slid behind it. An old Leica camera, pointing directly at him, without a lens cap, triggering unpleasant associations.

Kit will never forget the explosion of flashbulbs outside the Notting Hill house the day they returned from Paris. The long hungry snouts of the lenses. The clicking, the jostle, the shouting . . .

'Over here, love!'

'Why did you leave your kids home alone, Dee Dee?'

'Would you call yourself a good mother, Dee Dee?'

The reporters' knuckles were rat-a-tatting at the car window, trying to get a reaction from his mother, who was scared to get out of the car and begging Marco to reverse, drive away. They would never spend another night behind that pink door.

'Have a seat.' Cooper's palm lands on Kit's back, steering him away, a gesture that feels both convivial and slightly controlling. 'Beer first.' Cooper presses a bottle into his hand. 'Wine later. That's the proper order of things, isn't it?'

They sit side by side on the squeaky sofa, facing into the room, the view from the window – a derelict building, boarded up – and the threat of the set dining table.

Cooper stretches out his legs, clad in tight blue jeans. A flash of pink sock above a black suede desert boot. The dandy-ish sock tugs at Kit. He pictures Cooper carefully selecting them.

Cooper clinks his bottle against Kit's. 'To us.'

'To us.' Kit forces out the words. He daren't meet Cooper's eye.

'I can see you're dead nervous, Kit.'

Something in Kit seizes. He hides his inability to smile with another swig of beer.

'But it'll not always feel this strange. Me and you.

Not once we get to know each other properly. We need a bit of time to air, like a good bottle of wine, eh?'

'Can I use your bathroom?' The words fly out too quickly.

'Sure. Just out there, on your left.'

Locking the door behind him, his heart racketing, Kit fumbles with his phone, turns on Voice Notes. *Record*. 'This is for you, Gav,' he mutters, under his breath. It just might be the bravest – and most foolish – thing he's ever done.

As Kit emerges, flustered, realizing too late that he's not flushed the toilet, Cooper eyes him sidelong, more carefully. 'So, what's the latest, my man? Back at the Parker HQ.'

'Wolf is still being held at Paddington police station.' Trying to sound conversational, Kit's voice comes out too high. 'Not charged, though.'

'He will be,' Cooper says determinedly. 'You been interviewed yet?'

'Yeah.' Kit is unable to meet Cooper's hardening gaze, scared he will instantly know what he's up to.

'You did the right thing? Told them what you remember?'

'I did.' Kit's sweating fingers are now leaving marks on the cold beer bottle. He tries to think of a leading question, but his brain is dulled by panic, the proximity of Cooper on the sofa – he can feel the icky warmth of his leg next to his own – and all Kit wants to do is leap up and run away screaming with his hands in the air.

'Good man, Kit. Good man.' Cooper turns on some music — a jangly guitar band Kit fears will muddy his secret recording — and taps his foot, his fingers thrumming on his knee. 'That bad blood between Wolf and Gav. Warning signs. Everything so clear in retrospect.'

Kit takes a breath. Now or never. 'I'm not sure Wolf did it, actually.'

Cooper's musical jigging stops. 'I beg your pardon?'

'I can't see how he'd have done it, that's all.' Kit prays his phone is recording. 'I mean, can you?'

A growling silence. Kit's sure Cooper has seen right through the clunky question until he murmurs quietly, 'I can see it *all*, Kit.'

Kit frowns: he doesn't have to feign not understanding.

Cooper purses his mouth. 'Okay, let's take a tempestuous uncle. A nasty temper on him, right? An upstart nephew who's had it with being pushed around! An amateur boxer with itchy fists . . . A humdinger row kicks off.'

Kit tries to banish any sign of scepticism from his face, and lets Cooper talk, manically, like a man unable to stop.

'One punch leads to another. A brick wielded in a fist maybe. I mean, you're a bloke, Kit, you know how that red mist comes down.'

'Yeah, course.'

'Then, oh, wait, what's this?' Cooper leaps up and mimes peering into the ground, hands on his hips. 'A hole waiting in the garden? Handy! A spade? Handier still!' His gaze fixes on the middle distance, and he seems to be talking to himself now, as if Kit weren't in the room. 'Couldn't have had an easier burial. Didn't even need to dig.'

His heart hammering, Kit sticks his hand into his pocket, creating a bit of space around his phone, trying to give it a better chance of picking up Cooper's voice. 'No man should be buried like an old dog in a garden.'

Cooper looks at Kit in surprise. 'No? I guess not,' he says, as if it'd never occurred to him before. 'Anyway, you know what Wolf would do next?' He tips back his head and takes a loud gulp of beer. 'He'd nick what he could from Gav's shop, that's what. And you know what he'd say?' He puts on a camped-up Cockney accent. '"My uncle! He's only gone and disappeared!" And then . . .' he whispers, and the hairs on Kit's neck spike '. . . he'd spread rumours of sightings. So everyone thinks Gav is alive somewhere. Probably living his best life in Marbella.' Cooper shakes his head admiringly. 'I have to grudgingly admit that Wolf is one clever little bastard.'

Kit stares at Cooper in astonishment. If he is guilty and describing his own actions, not Wolf's, the brazen deceit is as dizzying as the detail, and the arrogant certitude he's got away with it.

'Of course, no one expects remains to be dug up after twenty-one years.' Cooper raises his beer bottle to Kit. 'But every man's luck runs out in the end, eh?'

Kit nods and wonders at what point his will.

'You don't look convinced. Come on, shoot me your own true-crime theories then.' Cooper's mood seems to slump. 'Before I baste our spuds.'

Kit inhales to speak. 'I remember a man coming over that day.' Don't say it, Kit thinks, as he's saying it. 'My sister says it was you. That they left you in the house with Gav due to come over.'

The agonizing pause – Kit holds his breath – is broken by Cooper's gunshot laugh. 'Well, she would say that, wouldn't she? There ain't no liar like a liar in love, Kit.' He leans closer, too close, his beer breath warm on Kit's cheek. 'Haven't they lied to you before? Every single one of them.'

That hits the target. Yes, Parker family history has endlessly shifted, straining to contain its secrets. No, his sister hasn't always told him the truth, far from it.

'You need to ask yourself who you can *really* believe, Kit.'

Kit mentally falters then rights himself. 'But you blackmailed Dee Dee, threatening to expose that I was her sister's child.' He cannot keep the contempt from his voice. 'You wanted money.'

The song ends with a screech of guitar and a thunderous crash of drums. Silence.

'Money? Oh, no, Kit. I wanted *you*, my boy. Did no one ever tell you that?' Cooper drops this at Kit's feet, like a sweet bloody kill. And even though Kit knows – he *knows* – that Cooper extorted money from Dee Dee, a little part of him can't kick away that kill. 'It wasn't right, Dee Dee hogging you to herself when there I was, your own likely flesh and blood, not even told by Cora that you *existed*. Treated like pond life by both those spoiled women. That whole family. Dee Dee was trying to *pay me off*, Kit. Don't you see? Flapping cash in my direction. All so she could keep up that wholesome image. Hide her family's tawdry secrets.' His lips curl with disgust. 'What sort of mother gives her baby to her sister? Rehomes it like an unwanted puppy.'

Ouch. Not wanting Cooper to see his hurt, Kit stumbles up, drawn to the mantelpiece, as if by the power of the objects displayed. Staring at them, trying to master a tumult of emotions, he feels a funny sort of vibration. A sense of things falling into place, slotting together. He slips his hand behind the lump of coral and plucks out a puppet – a whole skeleton, in all its delicate Gothic glory – and instinctively his fingers are drawn to the string at the back. He pulls. The skeleton's limbs fly apart, dismembering, dispersing mid-air, then re-forming. Kit's memory does the same.

'A genuine Tiller-Clowes,' Cooper puffs, pride clouding his judgement. 'A miniature of the larger ones that toured Victorian music halls. Worth something, that is . . .' As he realizes his mistake, his voice trails off.

'Funnily enough, I'm sure Gav had one just like it,' Kit says, as mildly as possible, not very mildly at all. His voice is unstable. Pulling the string again, he thinks of Gav, Wolf, and reaches for courage he didn't know he had. 'The antiques you sold in Spain. Gav's old stock?'

The hush is unbearable. Cooper's face seems to glaze, all warmth and animation sucked out of it.

'Be careful, very careful what you say next.' Cooper walks over, takes the skeleton puppet from Kit's hand, then whispers in his ear, 'And remember who you are. You're not one of them, Kit. You're like me.'

The words crawl over his skin. 'I'll never be like you.'

'You *are* me, Kit! A younger version. Strip away your Bloomsbury flat, your poncy clothes, those curls, and, yes, Kit, you're cut from the same dirty cloth. Both of us trying to find our place in the world. Wanting our slice of fancy things. The rattle of gold. That dope kick of extravagance, eh? Cut us and we bleed schemes and dreams.' Cooper clenches his fist, slowly draws it towards Kit's face. Loose skin over lumpy knuckles. 'See this?'

Kit nods, his mouth dry, his heart pounding.

Kneeing Cooper in the balls is a distinct possibility. But Kit has never won a physical fight in his life. Or kneed anyone in the balls.

'This fist will have your back. Always. Not like that lying sister of yours. Or Cora. Jeez.' Cooper snorts derisively. 'She always was a hot mess. And, you may as well know, off her head, Cora went with anyone. I mean . . .' He chuckles, his throat crackling. 'Hey, she went with me.'

Instinctively, Kit swipes away the fist, a furious knight-like loyalty to Cora – whom he is allowed to criticize, no one else – overriding any fear.

It happens so quickly, Cooper's knuckles meeting Kit's lower abdominals, then diving into Kit's jacket pocket and pulling out his phone. Gasping, winded, bent over, Kit peers up to see Cooper shaking his head. 'You think I'm stupid? A poor stunt to pull on your old man, Kit. Recording me.' He switches it off. 'Disloyal, you know?'

'You killed Gav.' Kit's hatred burns.

'Should have stayed tinkering in his dusty little junk shop, shouldn't he?' Cooper's eyes are blank and mean now – affable Roy has left the building – and his mouth sloppy, free-talking. 'Instead, I come round from Wolf's beating to see this walrus of a man hauling himself over the garden wall. You know what he said to me, Kit? "You're meant to be dead." That wasn't very nice, was it? Not very nice at all. I put two and two together.' He taps the side of his temple. 'Wolf had left me out cold in a muddy hole. Good punch, I give him that. Panicked and thought he'd killed me, the fool. Done a runner. And along comes that fat old uncle, ready to help dispose of me. How I laughed.' A smile twists out of his mouth. 'Gav didn't like being laughed at. Accused me of all sorts of nasty stuff. Such disrespect. Didn't know when to shut it either.'

'Give me my phone.' Kit tries to grab it back. But Cooper is already swinging down the top half of the window and teasingly holding the phone outside the dirty glass. Then he opens his fingers, and it's gone.

Kit charges. Cooper steps neatly aside, like a matador. A second later, a fist slams into Kit's face, so fast, so hard, Kit cannot believe it, even as he registers the soft fruit splitting of his skin, the spray of blood down his shirt and the wall. The white-blue ring-light flash of pain along his jaw. The horror of one of his own teeth rolling across the nylon carpet. Stunned, disbelieving, Kit's touching his bloody mouth with his fingers, when another punch flies in, harder, higher, clipping his eyebrow, smashing a sunset into his eyes.

A bovine lowing sound comes from Kit's throat. Gathering himself, he lunges towards the door, but is felled by a vicious kick to the back of his knee. For a moment he just lies there, the room spinning, the pain completely astonishing, mesmeric, and it dawns on Kit that he may not get out of the flat alive. And he almost begs for mercy, resigning to his fate, but he hears Maggie's voice in his head, Maggie whispering, *'Get up, Kit, get up, think like a boxer . . .'*

Kit twists and kicks, clipping the underside of Cooper's chin hard with his foot. And now Cooper is writhing on the floor. Kit reaches again for the front door. But hands clamp to his ankle, refusing to let go. And there's a noise, a knocking, and he's not sure if it's coming from within his pounding head, or from outside, but he's inches from the dull glint of the door's catch, and, with one last jerk of energy, everything he's got, he reaches up, up, up, stretching from the manacle of Cooper's grip, and he flicks that catch. The door flies open. Another violent yank from Cooper and Kit's face is rushing towards the carpet but landing on . . . a huge silver trainer.

A man is helping him up. Big warm hands. A thick gold ring worn on a thumb, coiled like a snake. Through the dripping blood, Kit sees a face he recognizes. Marco? He twists to check Cooper, now curled up on the carpet, softly groaning.

'I've got you, Kit.' Marco is cradling Kit's head against his chest, and Kit's tongue is working its way into the gory gap where his tooth once lived, and the butchery smell is making him gag, the pain sharp and clean, coming in waves, looping over one another, a

Slinky tumbling down the stairs, and he's wheezing, sobbing. 'I cannot bear that he's my father, I cannot bear it.' And he sees some sort of struggle in Marco's green-hazel eyes and hears the words, 'Darling, that man is *not* your father.'

42

Maggie

The Old Rectory, August 1998

An exploding sun of yellow feathers. Sequins. Floats. Steel pan bands. Dancers. My mother sat cross-legged on the floral sofa, glued to the TV screen: 'Look out for Clemence and Suki!' But I was searching for Wolf in the Notting Hill Carnival crowds. The picture kept fuzzing – a pair of particularly amorous doves on the roof were apparently to blame – and I leaped up to wiggle the aerial. If I could have stepped into the screen I would have done. But I was stuck at the Old Rectory, torpid and drowsy in the bank-holiday heat.

Nico and Pierre dozed on the cool stone flags: like their respective owners, they'd formed an unexpected alliance, one that occasionally flared into confrontation, then settled again. The windows were ajar, and the breeze blew in hairdryer-warm, full of insects. Outside, grass crisped into hay and the floating fine dust lent the air a metallic shimmer.

The sweet scent of freshly baked cake wound its

way from the kitchen. Earlier, Cora's hand had whipped the mixture around the bowl with the force of an industrial metal whisk while I cut tiny carrots out of fondant icing, pressing in little ridges with a fruit fork, thinking of Wolf's dextrous fingers, miniaturist's tools.

I felt his presence in the dovetail joints of Granny's furniture that I'd once thought boring and fusty. As I waded into the river, the water's ice-lolly tingle breeching my thighs, on still summer evenings when Kit and I watched glow-worms swaying on the meadow grasses, I'd connect those tiny greenish wavering lights to spell Wolf's name. Whenever Cora played her guitar, humming along quietly, I'd hear the chords of his favourite songs. Wolf's face was the last thing I saw at night before tipping asleep, the first on waking. I ached for him. I relived his rumbling laugh, the smooth warmth of his skin – and the last times we'd spoken.

On the evening of my eighteenth birthday, Wolf had phoned my aunt's flat in Paris, just when I'd given up hope of ever hearing from him again. Calling from a phone box, his voice was guarded. He was living in east London, lying low and waiting to hear from Gav. No, he still didn't know the details of that night. Only that we'd got lucky that Bucket, a spliff head, was presumably too stoned to notice that the hole was half the depth it'd been before. I had so many questions, but Wolf didn't want to talk about 'it', just my birthday, the café lunch of *steak frites*, the boat trip down the Seine, then to Ladurée for *macarons*. Then the beep-beep-beeps started, and Wolf said he had to go and hung up, without leaving a telephone number or details of where I could find him.

Mid-June. My mother had decided we'd stay at the Old Rectory; our landlord wanted to sell. So, Cora and I returned to Notting Hill to clean the house and extract the rest of our belongings. I left a message on Gav's shop phone, saying I'd be there that day, just in case Wolf picked it up. But like many things, it felt hopeless.

Having scrubbed the 'nosebleed' from the seagrass carpet, making it substantially worse, I went downstairs to retrieve toys from behind the sofa, where I found a lumberjack shirt, still smelling of Wolf, and bundled it into my bag. A few minutes later, as if summoned by that shirt, Wolf appeared furtively at the lower-ground window.

Rushing outside, I threw myself at him. But he pulled away, snapping off a chunk of my heart. His face had healed but his eyes were dull. He looked diminished, torn up inside, and wouldn't set foot in the house. He wanted to tell me, face to face, that it was too risky for us to be together. Given what had happened. It was over. We'd only get in contact if something important changed, and it was essential the other knew that, okay?

No, no, it wasn't okay. I sobbed shamelessly. I told him it wasn't over. I wouldn't let it be over. Grabbing a biro from his denim jacket pocket, I scrawled the Old Rectory's telephone number on his forearm. Wolf made me promise to write my books and do all the things we'd planned on the rooftop that night, only without him. Then he slipped away, and I sank to the front step, where we'd once eaten cinnamon rolls, with sugared lips, and I cried.

Cora came looking for me. Seeing my tear-wrecked face, she pulled me into her arms, 'I know, Maggie, I know,' she muttered into my hair. Almost like she knew everything.

At the Old Rectory, I hid Wolf's shirt at the back of my drawer, inhaled it frequently and waited for him to call. We tipped into September. Kit started at the local village primary school. I was mopped up by a further-education college, the sort that offered second and third chances, a place for losers, I snottily thought at first.

Leaves gingered. Conkers rained down. The morning air grew damp as a dog's lick. Gloves were purchased and lost. Wellies, in ever-growing boy sizes. More milk teeth lost. Mud. So much mud. It'd shoot up the inside of your trouser leg. Flick into your scalp. The smell of bonfires. Then the first frost arrived, and the ground became glassy and brittle, the tall thistles royal spectres. Galvanized by the cold, the country-side, the family returned to her, Cora started chopping logs, swinging down her axe, all splinters and sap and sweat, building a vast pile in the woodshed, anticipating a long cold winter. Still Wolf didn't call.

Then there was the afternoon we told Kit.

All of us assembled in the kitchen. Mum thin and pale in a wooden armchair, a blanket over her lap. Low sunlight falling across a yellow jug of fern leaves and thistles on the farmhouse table. Something sputtering on the stove. Cora and my mother watched Kit nervously, clearing their throats. Cora had baked a windfall apple cake because it was Kit's favourite and cut him an ominously big slice. I sat beside him, worried, ready.

'Kit,' Mum said softly, 'there's something about our family we feel you should know now ... about me, your aunt Cora, and you.' Kit listened, without emotion, and ate his cake. Later, Mum asked me if he'd even understood. I assured her he had. He'd rested his bare foot on top of mine under the table. That night he'd crept into my bedroom under the eaves, and we'd hunkered under my duvet, listening to the barn owls fussing in the roof. He'd wanted to know if I was still his big sister, and I said always, and whether he had to call Cora 'Mum' now, and I said not if he didn't want to and he said, 'I don't. I never will.' And he never did.

After that, Kit begged to return to London, to a life that no longer existed. Trying to help him settle in the countryside, Cora arranged riding lessons, then a pony. She'd take Kit riding, hacking across fields and they'd come back with shining eyes and cheeks, the atmosphere between them temporarily smoother. But he still misbehaved badly at school, with just enough charm and mitigating circumstances not to be expelled.

At my college, I slowly got to know the raggle-taggle mix of students. And I found irreplaceable friends.

During those long winter evenings, I wrote love poems – all about Wolf, all terrible – which I typed into Cora's computer and stored on a floppy disk that would later corrupt. In my short stories, Notting Hill kept leaking onto the page, each word a damning footstep leading back to Cooper, so I didn't save those. If I had any chance of one day becoming A Proper Writer then I had to bury Maggie Parker, I realized, and tell stories about worlds and eras different from my own. Hide in the dimness of gas light, or wartime smog.

But the only story I truly cared about was my mother's. I couldn't really think beyond that. I didn't want to. However stubbornly hopeful I tried to be, I knew, deep down, it was the dark side of the moon.

When the doctors found it, the brain tumour was

the size of a peach stone and tucked deep inside Mum's beautiful brain, where it couldn't be excised without damaging the precious matter around it. Having grown undetected over the course of months, the aggressive cancer didn't explain everything – nagging questions remained. I shoved them away – little point in asking now. It explained enough: Mum's headaches, the disorganization, the mood swings, her inability to cope with the demands of a small boy, and her capitulation to blackmail. The time she'd gone missing, without knowing it, she was already trying to outrun what was inside her.

One foggy winter evening, my aunt charged upstairs to my room, and said breathlessly, 'Your friend is on the phone, Maggie!' She didn't need to say his name.

'I miss you,' I said, instead of hello. Wolf didn't say it back. His voice was flat, faint and far, far away. He asked after Kit. 'Mum's dying,' I said, since this was the only answer to his question, and I could feel his shock, then anguish in the silence, the way it'd brought back his own mother's death.

Suspecting he'd called to tell me something important, I asked what was up. 'Nothing,' he replied, not being drawn, the trials of his own life and Gav's disappearance left unspoken. He didn't want to take me away from my mum – 'Just be with her while you can, Maggie' – and he should go. Angrily, I told Wolf he didn't have to go, that it was a choice not to be with me, and he listened to me rant and sob until I ran out of steam and finally let him say goodbye.

Later, Cora knocked on my bedroom door. 'Let him go, Maggie. You are so, so young. I know it's hard to believe now but one day you'll meet someone you connect with and love even more than Wolf.'

She was wrong.

Mum refused the hospital treatment that might have extended her life but also made it intolerable. Her decision to stop fighting and live out her last weeks on her own terms, in her own bed, was shattering. I wasn't ready – I'd never be ready. It felt like the days Mum had been missing in London had been a rehearsal for this. So, the anniversary of her walking out that evening – the Notting Hill sunset tangled in her hair – would always be the reminder of the point at which her light started to fade. My mother's last journey, in many ways, it was the beginning of mine.

All I could do was be with her, as Wolf had said. But knowing she'd leave again for good pressed down physically, a weight on my chest. On some days I secretly wished she was already dead so that I wouldn't have to see her deteriorate and suffer.

Needing to escape the cancer, the house, all of it, Kit and I would sit on the meadow bench, watching the hawks hunting as dusk stole across the trees and the grasses, the sky pinks and inks, the colour of heaven. An all-white heaven would be too clinical, like being stuck in a giant bathroom. I wanted it to be soft and silky, folded and undulating, like Mum's beloved Madame Grès blue evening gown.

Some days were beautiful, though. Electrifyingly so. The closeness of death made everything richer, details magnified, like squashed flowers dried in a press: the hairbrush splay of a pine cone, the bumblebee-gold of Mum's eyes, which seemed to intensify as the end drew near.

I would have done anything to have one more year with her, another month, week, day, hour, minute. Please give us more time, I'd pray every night on the off-chance that God did exist, which, given everything that had happened, seemed rather unlikely. But worth a shot.

In the end, the only gods who bothered showing up were human. Kind palliative-care nurses in clumpy shoes. Villagers with roast chickens and apple crumbles, bubbling from their Agas. Strangers' get-well cards and letters, bagged and forwarded by Mum's agent, the dodgy ones removed. They ranged from 'As a teenager, I had a poster of you on my wall,' to candid chronicles of their own cancer battles. Or sympathy with the 'model mother does a runner' story that had unexpectedly blown out of all proportion, catching the public imagination, migrating from the tabloids to the broadsheets, sparking think pieces about society's unhealthy idealization of motherhood, then confessionals on TV chat shows: 'I walked out too – and didn't return!'

Mum read every single stranger's letter. She said people were kinder than she'd ever imagined.

Cora proved this too. Her arms stretched around us. If giving up her literary life and recovery network in Paris, nursing her dying sister, trying to help parent a boy who resisted her at every turn, and running a disintegrating country house with crows in its chimneys was a big ask, Cora didn't show it. Not once did she complain. Instead, she rolled up her shirt sleeves. She bathed my mother, spooned her soup, took her to the loo, checked the meds, and changed the drip: the bodily things I couldn't bear to do. If Mum was having a bad night, Cora would sleep on a camp mat on the bedroom floor. Or, at Mum's request, play guitar until she settled, finger-picking folk tunes.

Armed with an old drill and toolbox, she transformed the formal dining room into a bedroom, so Mum needn't struggle up the stairs. We painted the walls pale pink and hung family photographs and fashion shots. Her childhood doll's house became our project. Cora fixed the façade then bought a doll family from a local antiques dealer to replace the one she'd hurled into the river decades before. Kit trailed fairy lights behind the windows and the three of us carried it, wobbling, into the new bedroom. Mum said she loved it even more than she had as a girl, and that the new doll family were far less uptight and bossy-looking.

Every evening, Kit and I would squeeze up in Mum's bed, turn off the main light so just the little house was lit, glowing, fairy lights flickering, and it felt oddly like Christmas, anything possible.

In the study, late into the night, Cora sat at Grandpa's old leather-topped desk, notebooks towered, working through the administration of all our chaotic, entwined lives, and the financial mess my father had left. She fiercely guarded my mother from any press – the two reporters who showed up on the doorstep left very quickly, cowed, never to return.

Suki, Marco and Clemence visited whenever they could, falling out of Suki's yellow Mini, a jumble of leopard print and armfuls of blowsy flowers, Portuguese *nata* tarts, stacks of fashion magazines, and a seasoning of gossip, direct from the café, the saltier the better. Marco claimed to have an 'in' on the *Notting Hill* movie – he'd wangle premiere tickets when the time came. They'd dress up like the old days, and have a riot, wouldn't they?

Cora sighed and called them, with a slight archness, 'The Fab Three'. In the kitchen, peeling potatoes, she'd roll her eyes when the shrieks of laughter in Mum's bedroom started, then music – De La Soul,

Woody Guthrie, Fleetwood Mac, no ballads allowed – and later she'd knock on the door, saying Mum needed to rest. She couldn't show them out quickly enough.

Those three never left Mum as they found her. Marco would wash and style what little duckling wisps remained of Mum's hair, and Suki and Clemence would wrap her in cashmere and shearling, which my mother, bone-thin and always cold, adored.

To Cora's bewilderment, dying only heightened Mum's love of fashion: a perfectly stitched bias seam or cuff, handmade Italian velvet slippers, the colour of garnets, a vintage Hermès scarf worn as a head wrap. Life's joys. 'We're all fireflies, Maggie. Never keep anything for best,' she advised one afternoon. Afterwards, I went upstairs, shook Wolf's lumberjack shirt from my drawer, put it on, and lay on my bed, letting the suppressed hurricane of sadness blow through me.

If Marco, Clemence and Suki arrived at the Old Rectory like a party, they left like a funeral. As soon as Mum's bedroom door was shut, the grief contained while in her company would slide down their faces, wreaking havoc on Suki's mascara. A soupy hush would descend, the familiar clearing-of-throat awkwardness that surrounded dying. The clipped relaying of medical information: their sharp inhalations; their disbelief that, no, nothing more could be done, really. Mum was near the end.

The mood of forgiveness that had bridged Cora

to Mum hadn't quite reached Suki, Clemence and Marco, who were courteous but cool with my aunt, which I didn't understand. Knowing how hard Cora was trying and everything she did, I was annoyed, so I kept Mum's friends at an aloof distance, making it clear I was on Cora's side, partly out of a sense of self-preservation: my mother was dying and my aunt was all we'd got left.

My mother knew this too, I guess. She wanted us to love Cora, who was to look after us when she was gone. And she needed to believe that some sort of wholesome happy family movie would keep rolling without her, that we'd be loved and safe.

The night Mum died, holding my hand, hoar frost laced the windows. The sky was a bolt of midnight silk, stitched with stars, as if it knew. Nico and Pierre kept vigil at the foot of her bed, and after Mum took her last breath, the fairy lights in the doll's-house windows glittered and glowed.

43

Kit

London, December 2019

A low winter sun jumps between the bare branches. Without its deciduous leafy cocoon, Highgate Cemetery is starker, stripped back to its original function, the digestion of London's dead. Kit's breath is a white coronet. He's wearing his new nut-brown brogue boots, shearling lined, bought at a generous discount from a friend who works at a fancy boutique. Boots Dee Dee would surely have loved, and Cora thinks are an unjustifiable extravagance. Kit could simply wear thermal socks and wellies, as she does, and his feet would be better off. As with many things now, they agree to disagree.

Cora can't help but clomp slightly ahead, used to rougher, more uneven ground. Soon, the Parker graves, finally softened with paw-pads of moss: it's been a long wet winter only now starting to icily chill. Kit arranges Dee Dee's peonies in the confit pot, next to a jam jar filled with fat red berries and fern leaves, a sign they're not the only people to have recently visited. Maggie, Kit suspects.

With the tip of his tongue, Kit checks his ruinously expensive porcelain tooth, a replacement for the one Cooper knocked out. It still doesn't feel real. The tooth. The fight. The bizarre rescue by Marco and, a few minutes later, Maggie and Cora. The discovery of Kit's undamaged phone, caught in the kebab shop's saggy awning. Along with the puppet skeleton – unfortunately for Cooper, a particularly rare example, its provenance well documented and damning – the phone's recording was enough to excite a tangled denial then confession from Cooper, who, as he was led down, shouted at Kit across the courtroom, 'Wait for me on the other side, Kit!' A murderous fantasist to the end, yet a man who also pitifully, genuinely seemed to yearn for a son, if only as a wishful extension of himself. Cooper didn't appear to have one friend or family member to support him in that courtroom. No one who'd visit him in prison. He was a beast, yet Kit felt sorry for him.

'Maggie should be with us,' Cora says suddenly, interrupting Kit's thoughts. 'That's what Dee Dee would want.'

Kit can't think of anything adequate or useful to say. Cora needs Maggie's forgiveness even more than his. It turns out he's not the sun around which she orbits, a realization that had felt like a demotion then an enormous relief. He no longer feels responsible for Cora's happiness, or guilty that he doesn't call her 'Mum'. They've agreed 'Cora' suits her much better. The moment for 'Mum' has long passed, like many others. They must look forward, not out of obligation but a hard-won love between two people who are perhaps a little too alike.

'It's been months now, Kit, and I feel . . .' Cora's voice breaks. Kit stiffens, knowing he also hurt her like this before they reconciled. Maggie had to comfort Cora then, no doubt better at it. He never knows what to say.

'. . . like I've lost a daughter. I can't see a way back.' In the flat winter light, with her sylvan-silver hair and pewter eyes, Cora has an elder-of-the-winter-woods air. The strain of the last few months has aged her. There's a hole in her acrylic knitted gloves and her thumb pokes out red and rough. Something about this upsets Kit, who makes a mental note to buy her a more luxurious pair.

'I'm sorry, Cora.' It doesn't bear thinking about, being ghosted by Maggie. He tentatively reaches for Cora's hand – his mother's hand, the hand that first held his, with near identical thumbprints. Cora glances down in surprise at this clumsy attempt to act like a supportive son, awkward for them both. But she squeezes it with a brisk thank-you, not unlike how she might squeeze a dog's paw, which is more than enough. Kit's hand gladly retreats to his coat pocket.

They are still learning how to be, he and Cora, carving out a relationship from a hunk of misunderstandings and screw-ups and bad behaviour on both sides, although mostly hers. Kit has come to accept he will always find Maggie's company easier than Cora's, and that their little family is different from others. Like a three-legged stool, it requires a deft distribution of weight not to tip over – and it is currently lying on its side.

'Maggie feels betrayed.' Cora tidies a skeletal leaf from Dee Dee's gravestone. 'Rightly.'

There's no point in pretending otherwise. Kit nods.

She fusses unnecessarily with his carefully arranged posy of flowers. 'On her deathbed, Dee Dee said it was my secret to tell, Kit. And only to reveal it when I thought the time right and the hurt justifiable. But that time never came.' Cora is unable to stop circling this. 'I always planned to tell you and Maggie, I really did. I knew I had to be fully accountable. But each time I tried, I pulled back. I couldn't do it, Kit. And Cooper seemed to have just vanished. So, it became easy to rationalize: the damage couldn't be justified. You'd never tried to find out your biological father's identity. Didn't want to know. And you and Maggie had already had to deal with so much. And, yes, of course I was petrified of poisoning our relationship too.' She pauses, unsure, checking again. 'But it hasn't, has it?'

'For some reason, no, Cora.'

Ironic that the one vast thing, this total rearrangement of his history, the scene shuffle of his life, that Cora so dreaded revealing has settled him. Maybe it just boils down to this: Kit Parker makes sense. The gaps are filled. The discordant noise has quietened and tuned. His sense of being somehow provisional, makeshift, has gone. No one is more surprised than he that, in forgiving Cora, he has somehow forgiven himself, without ever knowing he needed to do so. Protecting himself against any possibility of future rejection cannot ensure it doesn't happen, he has come to realize; it just means he's not able to feel its opposite.

'I hid the past to seize our future, Kit.' Cora sticks her hands into her pockets and arches back, staring up at the marbled London sky. 'I guess there are different breeds of secrets,' she says to herself.

'Like dogs?' He hopes Cora's humour is intact.

She smiles, nods. 'Very much. That was a protective secret, Kit. A guard dog.'

Morally iffy. But so much is. Even Dee Dee leaving his father's identity to Cora's discretion. Kit will never know if she stayed silent to shield herself from public humiliation or whether, as he suspects, she'd been trying to protect her sister. By the end, she needed her children to love Cora if they were to have any chance of stability. And Dee Dee would also have known that women are always the first to be condemned, tarred and feathered. Even when the conjugal act takes two.

Kit still can't believe Cora did it. Jealousy? The ultimate act of self-destruction? There are reasons perhaps. No excuses.

'I was appalling.' Cora reads his mind. 'I will regret that encounter to the end of my days – and it was just once, Kit, a joyless drunken mistake that left us both wretched with self-loathing – but I'd never undo it. Because then you wouldn't exist.'

Although Kit now accepts you don't need to be born out of love to be loved, he doesn't want to dwell here. 'So, Marco's do in Notting Hill next week?' he asks, swiftly changing the subject.

'The afternoon drinks thingy? Oh, I don't think anyone wants *me* there! I'll be *persona non grata*.'

'You were sent an invitation.' Kit was bemused too.

'Surely a mistake.'

'It's to remember Gav.'

'I never even met him. Anyway, I can't leave the animals,' she says quickly. 'Not in this cold.'

'That neighbour, you know, Mr Red Trousers, he seems very keen to help out. Isn't he at the Old Rectory today?'

'Oh, sure, he loves the dogs.' Cora, rarely embarrassed, colours slightly.

Kit wonders if Cora, single for as long as anyone can remember, might have met her match. Good luck to the guy: he's going to need it. As for Maggie . . . oh, Maggie, insisting that any future with Wolf is impossible. Too much guilt and grief and hurt: 'scar tissue', she calls it.

'Anyway, we're not the same people we were back then, Kit,' Maggie said on the phone last week.

'Bullshit,' he replied, pointing out it's surely no co-incidence that Wolf lives literally *above* St Pancras station in one of those extraordinary historic apartments; that he must hear the rumbling of Maggie's Eurostar train through his goosedown pillow. But Maggie won't let herself believe it.

Kit glances at Cora, stamping her cold feet, and decides to pull one last lever. 'Maggie is popping into the party en route back to Paris.' He shrugs, smiles. 'Just saying.'

Cora is silent, musing on this. 'You know what? I'll give you a minute alone. Meet you back at the gate,' she says, over her shoulder, striding away into the thicket of her own thoughts.

Left alone by the gravesides, Kit fights a desire to light a cigarette. He doesn't know how to do this next bit. What to say. Only that he must say something. So, he straightens his navy pea coat. If style is character, he wants to look grown-up, decent – the sort of man his father spectacularly failed to be for one night, the fallen hero who gave Kit life – and he edges closer to Damian Parker's grave. The years peel away, until he's just a little boy again, riding on his father's shoulders. 'Hey, Dad.'

44

Maggie

One week later, Notting Hill

Marco's house was hard for Maggie to enter but it's proving even harder to leave. There's the retrieving of her new coat, buried under others in the crammed cloakroom, then the prospect of wheeling her wonky suitcase along the hallway, which is heaving with guests, as if the Portobello crowds have simply switched course. Still they keep coming, flushed from the hard snap of December cold, their swishing scarves brushing the scented candle flames: bespectacled antiques dealers, neighbours, a woman wearing a holly-leaf-garland tiara, a sozzled old guy in antlers, anyone, it seems, with the slightest tenuous thread of connection to either Marco or Gav – selectively recalled as 'a rough diamond' and 'a legend' – and whose fate is discussed in low, thrilled voices: 'I couldn't roast chestnuts out there myself, could you?' Well, no.

Finally, Maggie spots her coat and teases out her mother's old pashmina, stuffed into its sleeve for safe-keeping. She catches the whiff of other women's perfumes and, through the window, which is ajar, cigarettes from the smokers in the garden. Trying to leave without fuss, she dips her gaze to avoid being sucked into another conversation – 'Maggie? Maggie! *Ohmy-God*, it's Dee Dee's girl!' – and edges towards the front door, passing the new glass staircase leading down to the kitchen, still the lowest floor, Marco having decided to ditch the basement plans. The scruffy boho nineties have been scrubbed from this house, now airy and slick, with an excess of bathrooms. But Maggie likes to think the butterflies Kit felt-tipped on rag-rolled cobalt walls still flutter under the grass cloth covering, and long-lost Lego lurks under the floorboards.

'Maggie! Are you attempting a French exit?'

Maggie turns, guilty as charged. The sight of Wolf instantly floats something inside her, as it always has. 'You know I'm hopeless at goodbyes.'

'Paris?'

Maggie nods, smiles bravely, dreading the chaste kiss on the cheek that now accompanies their farewells. 'Just called an Uber for the station.'

A pause stretches. Wolf looks dishevelled. Despite being back in his old manor, he also looks completely lost.

If Maggie finds this party difficult, it must be so much harder for Wolf. She fears he'll never forgive himself for calling Gav that day and, as a punishment, will always deny himself happiness. Maggie also knows, first-hand, that grief doesn't disappear. Like a spill of glitter, you keep finding little bits everywhere, for ever, and in the oddest places. 'Sorry,' she says, feeling bad. 'I don't mean to maroon you.'

'You've never done that, Maggie.' Wolf bites down his lower lip, wrestling with something. 'You've been a true friend, always, all these long years, when anyone else would have just –' He's interrupted by an arm clad in a velvet jacket sleeve, slung around his neck from behind, holding it in a playful head lock. Wolf rolls his eyes, smiles, knows exactly who it is. 'Kit, my man.'

Maggie glances away. It's bittersweet seeing Wolf and Kit together, their bantering easy brotherliness. The way they can disappear down a rabbit hole of antiques, as surely as if they were back in Gav's shop.

Kit's dinner jacket, though. Not unlike the black moleskin one – 'the James Bond' – her father used to wear. How could she not have seen him in Kit before? That movie-star smile. The appetite for life. The way he bends down to tie shoelaces.

Since that news broke – and nearly broke her – Kit has grown up quickly, changing from one day to the next. She puts it down to the peace he's finally made with Cora, something Maggie had given up hope of ever happening. The secrets, Cora's and her own, wrought more damage hidden than revealed, she realizes now.

No longer the little boy with red Kickers, Maggie sees a young man with a rare gift for life, who can find delight in the most surprising things, some of which can fit into the palm of his hand. Wolf says she should take some credit. But Maggie firmly refuses it. Kit is Kit.

'Make Maggie stay, Wolf.' Kit never does want her to leave. But he doesn't need her here. For the first time, Maggie doesn't worry – well, not so much. He carries his own light now.

'I've got to work, Kit. Finish my book,' she explains, keen to get back to it.

'But you filed your book!' Kit protests.

Two months late. But done, thank goodness, its corset laces tied. 'This is a different novel.' She hesitates, won't say any more.

'Ah, but Paris is an hour ahead!' Kit declares, with champagne-fuelled enthusiasm. 'Which means you have an extra . . .'

Maggie smiles wearily. 'No, Kit, I lose time, rather than gain it.'

'But there'll be dancing later, I can feel it, and with this lot it'll be worth a ringside . . .' Kit's voice fades, and his gaze fixes on someone past Maggie's shoulder.

Maggie freezes. Although Kit had warned her that

Cora might attend, she doubted she'd have the nerve. And so nearly to have missed one another, their exits and entries perfectly timed.

She turns slowly. It's a physical shock, seeing her aunt, the first time since May. Cora looks startlingly out of context, despite the palm-green dress that Kit has surely made her buy, very Dee Dee – and not very Cora. Maggie knows her aunt, looking strained, would far rather be sitting at the Old Rectory's fireside with the rescue dogs, but clips any sympathy.

This is a woman who betrayed Maggie's mother in the most unforgivable way. Who let Kit believe Cooper could have been his father, who wrote 'unknown' on Kit's birth certificate to hide her own shameful secret – one that it took Marco to expose, and a DNA test to confirm, matching herself and Kit as half-siblings. And yet . . . Cora has been like a mother to Maggie, her port in many storms. She loathes her. She loves her. It is unresolvable.

'Hello.' Her aunt sticks out a hand, and pumps Wolf's too fast and hard. 'I'm Cora. I've heard *so* much about you.'

A minute flinch, but Wolf has no reason to hide now. Like Maggie, he's still getting used to this.

'Good to meet you at last, Cora,' he says diplomatically, with a warm smile.

'I'm very sorry about your uncle. He was a bit of

an old sod, I hear,' Cora says, making Maggie wince. 'But your old sod, right?'

'Exactly,' says Wolf. Disarmed, Maggie can tell. 'Yes, that's exactly it.'

Maggie shifts uneasily, wishing someone would whisk Cora away.

'How do you plan on surviving this party, Cora?' Kit teases, trying to break the tension.

'Oh, my villagers would eat this lot for breakfast.' Cora eyes Maggie's coat, then her suitcase, her face falling. 'Leaving already?'

'Heading back to Paris. Work, you know.' Maggie sounds almost rudely polite. Too weird making small-talk with Cora, neither of them any good at it.

'I'm so, so glad you're writing again.'

'Thanks.' Desperately hoping Cora doesn't ask what the novel is about, Maggie's gaze skates away. 'Well . . . enjoy the party,' she adds, sounding stilted, and rather as if she means the opposite.

Wolf clears his throat. 'I'll see you to your taxi, Maggie.'

Maggie hugs Kit and doesn't hug Cora and starts to pull her unwieldy suitcase through the clog of guests towards the front door.

'Wait!' Cora elbows her way through the crowds, Kit following. 'Any thoughts on Christmas?'

Christmas. Cora doesn't seriously think . . .

'Only it's less than three weeks away and, obviously,

I don't expect you to come to the Old Rectory. I mean I understand perfectly if you don't, or can't, but I thought I'd better check. In case . . .' Cora's voice fades hopelessly. 'Well, you know. The dogs would like it.'

Kit, standing behind Cora, mouths, '*Please* come, Maggie,' and holds his hands in prayer. She replies with a small shake of the head.

'You're very welcome too,' Cora says to Wolf, glancing back at Maggie, unsure of the nature of their relationship. 'I always cook for five thousand.'

'I've already got plans,' Maggie says quickly. To be alone in Paris – but far less alone than she was in her marriage. Eating her body weight in delicious food, working her way through her book pile, watching movies in bed – even *that* one, finally – meeting up with friends, and Kit staying for new year. She's had worse.

'Of course, don't worry,' Cora says, failing to maintain her composure.

Maggie turns, walks on. Wolf reaches down and squeezes her hand, a rather powerful squeeze: he's started boxing training again. She glances up curiously, and he widens his ridiculous blue eyes, flinging them back in Cora's direction. Maggie stops, a still point among the swilling guests.

Death and betrayal have been the shaping forces in her and Kit's lives . . . or love. Love the reparatory force that has squeezed into the cracks, and tried to fix and heal, haphazardly, imperfectly. She can view it either way. That's what Wolf says. She can choose.

Maggie's thoughts fly to her mother, as they do daily, the big-hearted woman who knowingly gave a home to her sister's and her own cheating husband's baby. Who carried the secret of that treachery until her last breath. If she never was fully at ease with the arrangement – and what sort of saint would be? – she forgave her sister in the end. Even Marco, Clemence and Suki, the only other people who knew the sordid truth, have now offered Cora an olive branch. Or at least a party invitation. Perhaps Maggie could do the same. Perhaps a begin-again is possible.

'Cora!' Maggie calls, over the heads of the throng.

Cora turns slowly, her eyes glassy, impossibly sad.

'*Maybe* I'll come for Christmas,' Maggie hears herself say, against her better judgement.

'Yes!' mutters Kit, and in his excitement, jolts Cora's cocktail glass of cranberry juice, spattering it down her dress.

Cora is clearly far too thrilled to notice or care. 'Maybe is wonderful,' she stammers.

Wolf shoots Maggie a look that knocks her sideways. She doesn't understand it.

What has she done? Maggie is not sure. But she's aware of a lifting sensation, an unexpected lightness. She's felt mauled these last seven months, questioning everything, hating Cora, hating her late father. What can you do with that hate? That fury? In which little dank psychological cupboard can it live?

A shout interrupts such thoughts: 'You're forbidden to leave, darlin'!'

Oh. Oh, no. Suki, Clemence and Marco are approaching in a colourful galleon fleet.

'Brace,' Maggie mutters to Wolf. She steals a glance at her stiffening aunt. 'I need to . . . No, really, I have to go . . . Paris, yes. Any time, Clemence, come, come. I'd love a visit.' Maggie stands on tiptoes and kisses Marco's cheek. 'Thank you. For remembering Gav like this. For everything, Marco.'

'And the new front door?' Marco tilts his head to one side, with a circumspect smile. 'Too much? Too soon? Please put me out of my misery here, darling.'

'Marco, the front door is perfect,' Maggie assures him.

'My sister's favourite shade of pink,' Cora dares add.

Marco slams his palm to his heart. 'That's enough. I'll take it. Thank you, ladies.'

'Your button . . . Excuse me.' Suki reaches across and adjusts Maggie's coat. 'Wrong hole. There. Better. Good coat.' She stands back, admires it. 'Love that astrakhan Peter Pan collar.'

'Paris,' Maggie admits. She'd never known she could have such strong feelings for a coat, or ever justify spending so much on herself. But her mother was whispering in her ear, encouraging her. 'In the sale.'

'Oh, you'll never regret an expensive coat,' says Suki. 'But . . . wait, I see Dee Dee in you. Don't you, Clemence?' She gestures under the chin, lifting it, and exaggeratedly stands straighter. 'You're holding yourself differently, Maggie.'

'Queen,' Clemence says, with a nod.

'My Uber . . .' says Maggie, apologetically. Wolf puts his hand gently on her back and guides her to the door.

'*Bon voyage!*'

'*Oh, my God, Marco!* It's snowing, like the movie! How the hell did you make that happen?'

Finally, they escape. Snow – real snow – is falling in flurries, settling on the pavement, sleeving the bare branches of the crab-apple tree. Maggie turns and takes one last look at the house. Through the misted windows, the shapes of people talking, laughing, starting to dance, their movements blurred, sequin-shot. Maggie's glad she dared step inside it – the house, the party, her mother's late-nineties world – but she's gladder to have left, and is craving her own bed, which suddenly feels very far away indeed.

'Our taxi.' Wolf points across the street.

Maggie looks at him quizzically. Of course, he lives in King's Cross. But part of her would rather say goodbye here, not draw it out any longer.

'I'll see you off at St Pancras.'

'You don't have to.'

'I want to.' Wolf holds open the taxi door, then slides in too. He is warm, and solid, and everything Maggie's ever wanted, and she doesn't think she can bear it.

Billowing in from the Arctic, the snow blows into Paris fashionably late. Eleven fifteen, she's in another taxi, whizzing past the Louvre, and the night sky is sweeping an ermine cloak across the city.

Wolf is still beside her, having dashed off to grab his passport from his St Pancras apartment, spent a small fortune on a Eurostar ticket, and bumped them both up to first class. 'Did you plan this?' she whispers, because everything feels delicate, like it could shatter still.

'Maggie, I only have the clothes I stand up in. So, no.'

Joy darts under her skin. 'Why did . . . ?'

'Something about that ridiculous suitcase, with its dodgy right wheel that I'm itching to fix. You know me.'

She smiles. Because she does.

'And Gav,' he says more solemnly. 'A realization at the party that he'd clip me around the ear if I wasted . . . He liked you, Maggie.'

'Funny way of showing it.'

Wolf laughs, the laugh that rumbles around his chest afterwards. Maggie feels a shudder of desire, and confusion, unsure why he's in the taxi, who they are, what they are now.

'Let's walk,' she says. She needs air.

They get out at Pont Neuf. Light, stone, onyx-black water. Maggie wraps her mother's pashmina over her head, and Wolf tucks it under her chin, his fingertips brushing her skin. Snowflakes salt their dark coats. Over the huge river, the old bridge stretches away, its stone arches bathed in umber light, linking the city's right bank to the left, other things too.

They stop halfway across the right arm of the bridge, where the wind cuts, and the air is so cold and sharp it's like breathing in tiny fragments of glass. Holding up her phone, careful not to include Wolf – old habits – Maggie snaps a bad blurred author selfie to post later.

'One more.' Wolf folds his big coat around her like wings.

Maggie, who'd happily live inside that coat with him for ever, holds up her phone. 'You sure?'

'Do it.'

Maggie and Wolf. There they are. Beaming. Glowing from the cold, each other. Spangled in light. The first photo of them together. The only one in existence. Too precious to post.

Wolf pulls her closer. She wants to kiss him. She

wants to kiss him badly. But she doesn't want to ruin things – 'a true friend', he called her at the party – or lose him again, so she points, as he once did on a London roof terrace years ago, and she says, 'See? Over there? The Conciergerie clock that's been telling the time since 1371 – 1371!' A stop on her favourite Sunday walk. Across the river, yes, yes, the bank where she loves to cycle. A block away, the café where she's been writing her new book, fuelled by *tarte Tatin*. But Maggie really wants to say, 'Look, Wolf, look at us.'

'So, when will you read me this new opus?' he murmurs into her hair. 'Out loud. Just to me.'

'No pressure, then.'

'None.'

'I need to write the last chapter first.' Maggie smiles and the cold taps at her teeth. 'Maybe I'll end the story here. Pont Neuf. Snow. Screw it, go all in.'

'You sure I'm not wearing breeches?'

'A lumberjack shirt for most of it.'

Typing that first page – a thirty-something divorcee on a lipstick-red bicycle in Paris, a phone ringing in her straw bag – had drawn electricity into Maggie's fingertips, a hunger to excavate the story she'd forbidden herself ever to write. One she'd believed had started with her mother walking out of a pink door – but turned out to have started somewhere else, far earlier. It's the truest story she's ever told. And the fastest she's ever worked, scenes, characters, her bloodied, bruised heart slipping onto the page. Changing the names, cutting out the stuff that sounds way too far-fetched for fiction, she's left her mother as a beautiful contradiction, a mystery, as perhaps all mothers are to their daughters. (And, in Cora's case, to her son.) Unexpectedly, in searching for Dee Dee Parker, she has somehow mapped Maggie Foale, the spaces between the typed letters the narrow alleys leading her exactly here. This precise moment, in a lifetime of them. A snowflake, starting to melt on her eyelash. Her back pressed against the whump of Wolf's heart.

'So, if you've sorted your ending . . .' Wolf draws her closer, his nose skimming her cheek '. . . can we begin?'

'Yes,' she breathes, with a shiver that is the chill but also not.

'Shall we, then?' Wolf asks. At last, Maggie hears happiness in his voice. They start walking again, faster now, heads down, laughing at how wildly cold it is, how indecently beautiful, rushing through Saint-Germain's snow-globe streets. Climbing the apartment building stairs because the birdcage lift has broken, Maggie says breathlessly, 'Wait for the view. You'll love the view.'

Wolf says, 'You, Maggie, it's always been you,' and she tugs him out to the balcony, the snowflakes falling through indigo dark, the clocks of Paris striking midnight, their two hands one.

Acknowledgements

Writing this story, time speeded up, my deadline ticked down, and the moving parts had to be delicately clicked into place, which was only possible with the feedback and support of those around me. So, heartfelt thanks to my editor, Maxine Hitchcock, Madeleine Woodfield, Clare Bowron, Hazel Orme, Beatrix McIntyre and the brilliant team at Michael Joseph. My agent, Lizzy Kremer, and, also at David Higham Associates, Orli Vogt-Vincent and Maddalena Cavaciuti. Designer Lee Motley for the gorgeous book jacket. Jane Edwards for reminiscing about nineties Notting Hill with me. Sophie Somborn for reading my Paris chapters. Jessica Bendell for reading the north London bits. Ali Knight and Edward Porter for those nostalgic Portobello wanders. Christopher Howe for the inspiring chat about antiques one afternoon in his Pimlico Road shop. *Notting Hill*, the movie. (In all cases, any mistakes are my own.) Thank you, Claire Douglas, Sarah Vaughan and the other amazing authors who generously read early proofs. How lucky I am to have shared the same wink of time on this 4.5-billion-year-old planet with you, Ben. Thank you for holding the fort – and my wobblier antique purchases – while I wrote, and for a million other things. Together, we've clocked up almost seven thousand midnights. Oscar, Jago and Alice – and the world's hairiest time-eater, Harry – I love you all dearly.

Read more by Eve Chase

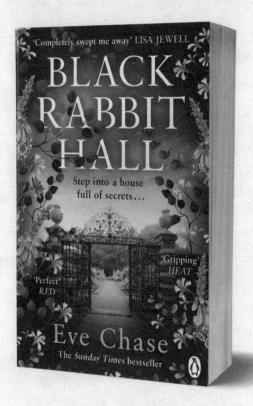

Available to buy now

NURTURING WRITERS SINCE 1935

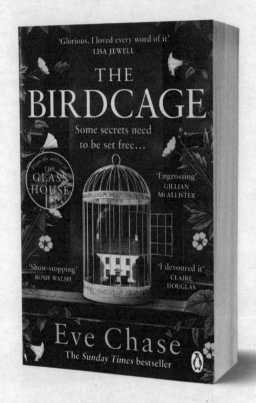

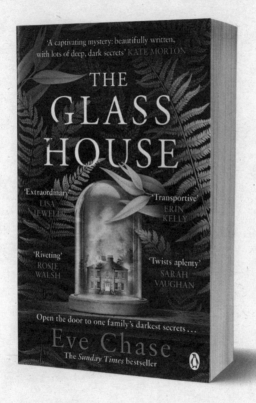

Read more by Eve Chase

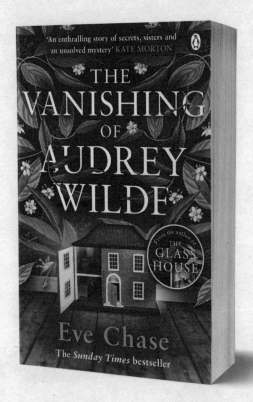

Available to buy now

He just wanted a decent book to read ...

Not too much to ask, is it? It was in 1935 when Allen Lane, Managing Director of Bodley Head Publishers, stood on a platform at Exeter railway station looking for something good to read on his journey back to London. His choice was limited to popular magazines and poor-quality paperbacks – the same choice faced every day by the vast majority of readers, few of whom could afford hardbacks. Lane's disappointment and subsequent anger at the range of books generally available led him to found a company – and change the world.

'We believed in the existence in this country of a vast reading public for intelligent books at a low price, and staked everything on it'
Sir Allen Lane, 1902–1970, founder of Penguin Books

The quality paperback had arrived – and not just in bookshops. Lane was adamant that his Penguins should appear in chain stores and tobacconists, and should cost no more than a packet of cigarettes.

Reading habits (and cigarette prices) have changed since 1935, but Penguin still believes in publishing the best books for everybody to enjoy. We still believe that good design costs no more than bad design, and we still believe that quality books published passionately and responsibly make the world a better place.

So wherever you see the little bird – whether it's on a piece of prize-winning literary fiction or a celebrity autobiography, political tour de force or historical masterpiece, a serial-killer thriller, reference book, world classic or a piece of pure escapism – you can bet that it represents the very best that the genre has to offer.

Whatever you like to read – trust Penguin.